Novels by Sarah MacLean

These Summer Storms

HELL'S BELLES
Bombshell
Heartbreaker
Knockout

THE BAREKNUCKLE BASTARDS
Wicked and the Wallflower
Brazen and the Beast
Daring and the Duke

SCANDAL & SCOUNDREL
The Rogue Not Taken
A Scot in the Dark
The Day of the Duchess

RULES OF SCOUNDRELS
A Rogue by Any Other Name
One Good Earl Deserves a Lover
No Good Duke Goes Unpunished
Never Judge a Lady by Her Cover

LOVE BY NUMBERS
Nine Rules to Break When Romancing a Rake
Ten Ways to Be Adored When Landing a Lord
Eleven Scandals to Start to Win a Duke's Heart

THESE
SUMMER
STORMS

THESE SUMMER STORMS

A NOVEL

SARAH MacLEAN

BALLANTINE BOOKS

NEW YORK

Ballantine Books
An imprint of Random House
A division of Penguin Random House LLC
1745 Broadway, New York, NY 10019

BALLANTINE BOOKS & colophon are registered trademarks of
Penguin Random House LLC.

HardcoverISBN 978-0-593-97225-0

Printed in the United States of America

BOOK TEAM: Production editor: Jennifer Rodriguez
Managing editor: Pamela Alders • Production manager: Erin Korenko
Copy editor: Briony Everroad • Proofreaders: Deborah Bader,
Claire Maby, Cameron Schoettle

Book design by Elizabeth A. D. Eno

For Mark & Chiara

THESE
SUMMER
STORMS

CHAPTER

1

THERE WAS SOMETHING ABOUT TRAINS.

If she marked the minutes of her life, Alice Storm would not be surprised to discover that she'd spent nearly a third of them in transit:

- The shiny crimson bicycle that had been her seventh-birthday present and most prized possession, until her brother had sent it flying into Narragansett Bay, never to be recovered.

- The white rowboat her father had captained into that same salty sea every Saturday in July for her entire childhood, because he insisted on *facing nature as God intended.*

- The endless line of nondescript black town cars with silent drivers that ferried her from private school to private art classes to the Storm family's Park Avenue penthouse, New York City muffled and dim beyond the window.

- The skateboard she'd ridden into a tree one Sunday morning during her first year at Amherst—determined to prove herself a completely ordinary eighteen-year-old—resulting in an arm broken in three places.

- The helicopter that airlifted her to Boston to be pinned back together and returned her to school in time for a nine A.M. Art History midterm, before her classmates could discover there was nothing ordinary about her.

- The private jets that took her around the globe whenever her father issued an international summons on a whim.

- The commercial jet that had taken her to Prague eighteen months earlier, diamond ring tucked into her boyfriend's carry-on bag.

- The subway car she'd been on that afternoon when her phone had rung and stolen her breath—Incoming call . . . *Elisabeth Storm* (never *Mom*)—all beige walls and harsh lights and advertisements for clear skin and uncluttered apartments and that one William Carlos Williams poem about plums and iceboxes and forgiveness and the parts of us that will never change.

And still, there was something about trains.

Probably because she'd discovered those herself. All the other ways she'd traveled through the world had belonged to someone else. Were shared with someone else. But trains . . . they were her secret.

They did not come with flight plans, no siblings jockeying for position inside, no mothers calling for champagne, no fathers playing silent judge. They did not come unmoored. Instead they remained locked into their path, weighty and competent, unchanging. Unable to be sent over a cliff and into the sea. A marvel of modernity that ran counter to all the technology that came after them. Solid. Even. Stable. Constant.

Alice dropped her suitcase onto the luggage rack inside the door of the train car and found the first empty row, tossing her worn olive green canvas satchel onto the aisle seat and sliding over to the window, hoping that a Wednesday night on the 9:32 P.M. Northeast Regional would reward her with a row to herself in the last few hours of peace before what was to come.

Before she faced the barrage of family—with one glaring, irreversible absence.

Through the window, on the train platform beyond, a group of twenty-somethings tumbled down the escalator, laughing and shouting, a collection of duffels and weekender bags, bright smiles, sundresses, shorts and sunglasses, as though night hadn't fallen outside. And maybe it hadn't for them. Maybe they were in that gorgeous moment in life when there was no such thing as the dark. Instead, it was all daytime, full of promise and empty of fear.

Behind them, a freckle-faced, redheaded family of five, a teenager in hoodie and headphones, twin girls no older than ten, and their parents, loaded down with suitcases and backpacks and a *Paris Review* tote that might have once been for literary cachet, but was now for stainless steel water bottles and organic snacks.

A middle-aged Black woman in flowing linen, her tiny silver roller bag the only evidence that she was traveling. A tall, stern-faced white man in his thirties, leather duffel in hand, backpack slung over his shoulder. An elderly, ruddy-cheeked man in a cream-colored windbreaker, pushed in a wheelchair by an Amtrak employee in a trademark red cap.

One by one, they piled onto the train.

Alice had been wrong; the train wouldn't be empty. Instead, it would be packed full—laden with a few hundred New Yorkers headed north for a weekend of cobalt skies and gray-green ocean during the most magical time of year in New England, when the rest of the world was back to school and work and Northeasterners were spoiled with one last week of sun-soaked seclusion, clinging to the promise of endless summer.

She'd forgotten it was Labor Day weekend.

The lapse in memory seemed impossible, considering she'd left her freshly painted, newly organized classroom in Brooklyn six hours ear-lier, planning her own final long summer weekend as she waited for the subway. Pilates that afternoon. The Grand Army Plaza farmers' market for the last of the heirloom tomatoes. Governors Island on Saturday with Gabi and Roxanne, who insisted she leave her empty apartment. A long Sunday, painting in the last of the summer glow, before school made the days too short for sunlight.

Then her phone rang, and she'd forgotten.

Leaning back against the rough fabric of her seat, Alice focused on the train schedule, announced over a staticky loudspeaker, the conduc-tor's voice thick with New England—*Old Saybrook, New London, Wickford*—loud enough to keep people from the wrong train, Amtrak hoped—*Providence, Back Bay, South Station*—loud enough to keep her from remembering.

The train lurched into motion, the awkward first step before it gained speed and momentum, heavy and smooth. Familiar comfort.

Next stop, New Rochelle.

She exhaled. Four hours to what came next.

"Is someone with you?"

It shouldn't have surprised her but she startled anyway, straightening to meet the serious, gray gaze of the man she'd seen on the platform earlier—tall and stern. Taller now that he was close. Sterner, too.

Dark brows rose, punctuating the question as he tilted his chin in the direction of the seat next to her, where her ancient canvas satchel sat, forgotten.

No one was with her.

"No." She grabbed the bag and shoved it to her feet. "Sorry."

The noise he made in reply was almost impossible to hear above the sound of the train on the track, the white noise of the air-conditioning, the slide of his overnight bag onto the rack above. He folded himself into the space she'd cleared, knees pressed to the back of the seat in front of him.

On another day, she might have paid closer attention, but she did not have time for noticing him. In fact, she vaguely resented his presence for reminding her that she was single again, for filling up the seat with his long legs and the kind of judgment that came from strangers who had no idea that you'd had *a day*.

That you were preparing to have *multiple days*.

Five days. And then she was out. She could survive five days.

She cleared her throat and adjusted her position in the seat, closing her eyes, trying to lose herself in the rhythmic thud of the wheels as the train shot out of the tunnel in Queens and they left New York City behind.

An hour into the ride, they pressed east along the southern coast of New England, and Alice, unable to sleep, phone dead, and lacking capacity to focus on the book she'd shoved into her bag as she'd rushed from her apartment that afternoon, peered into the inky darkness outside the window, where Long Island Sound lay still and flat and invisible in the distance, beyond the saltwater marshland of the Connecticut coast.

It would have been impossible to see anyway, thanks to the late hour and the dark sky, but the view had competition—the fluorescent lights reflecting the inside of the train car against the glass, casting a pale glow over the cluttered shelf across the aisle, full of sleeping bags and suitcases and a large tote bag with electric pink piping, pickleball paddle jammed into the side pocket. Beneath the collection of travel detritus, two teenage girls laughed at a curly-haired boy hanging over the seat in front of them, a goofy smile on his face. On another night, Alice might have smiled at the picture they made—late-summer perfection. But tonight, it was a different part of the reflection that distracted her. The bright, shining rectangle glowing in her neighbor's lap.

His phone was open to some social app, one with endless scroll.

He should turn that off. Endless scroll rotted a person's brain. It had been rotting hers before she boarded the train, searching for the dopamine hit of makeup tutorials and cat videos . . . antidotes to her mother's call—the first she'd made to Alice in five years.

Her seatmate paused, a headline impossibly large against the darkness outside. She had no trouble reading the text in the mirrored reflection.

TRAILBLAZING GENIUS FRANKLIN STORM, DEAD AT 70

His thumb hovered over the link.

Don't, she willed, not sure she would be able to look away, even though she knew the story within. Had known it since she was born. Franklin Storm had stepped into his parents' garage in North Boston at the age of seventeen and changed computing and the world with $1,107 and a dream. He'd made computers large and small, brought them into homes and schools, and placed them in pockets and on wrists the world over.

That was the first paragraph. The ones that followed would be about his company, his vast collection of art, his philanthropy, his charm, his daredevil tendencies (no one should be too surprised by a gliding accident, really). And then, his family.

There'd be photos, probably from his seventieth birthday, taken that past April—the ones Alice had pored over in the Style section of the *Times.* Captions. A footnote about the child not pictured (not invited). A reminder of why.

Don't open it.

He didn't. Alice breathed again.

Swallowing the urge to tell him to read a book or something, she reached down and pulled a newspaper out of her bag. She hadn't held a print newspaper since she was a kid, when a stack of them would be delivered to the apartment every morning.

Still, she smoothed her hand over the front page of that morning's *New York Times,* printed twenty hours earlier, rendered instantly obsolete in this world where (allegedly) BREAKING NEWS came all day, all hours, directly to a person's preferred rectangle, there, then gone. Turned instantly into the past to make room for the future—a shift so quick that the present simply disappeared.

Why had she bought it? Alice rubbed a thumb across the words, tattooing herself with the ink of yesterday's news—the Before. Tomorrow's paper would be the After.

The top of the fold on the front page would be devoted to her father's death—the biggest story of the week. Of the year.

Longer for Alice (and her therapist).

She traced a headline about inflation. Another about unhoused New Yorkers. A third about the solar power revolution. Stories that were more important than anything the paper would say the next day.

Stories she couldn't read because there, in her peripheral vision, her seatmate had turned over his phone, and the back of it gleamed smooth, black obsidian, without any reflection, its only mark a swirling silver S, like the eye of a hurricane.

Years ago, when she was young, that insignia had words that came with it—repeated over and over on television commercials. Radio plays. Print advertisements. The whole world knew them.

Storm Inside™

The world didn't know the half of it.

CHAPTER

2

BEFORE THE ROBBER BARONS of the Gilded Age changed the face of American business with steel and banks and oil, Commodore Cornelius Vanderbilt changed the face of American travel, snapping up and consolidating more than a dozen small railway lines and amassing a fortune that few had ever seen outside of royalty. (Who needs titles when you can have trains?)

In 1870, Cornelius Vanderbilt II—nepo-grandbaby to Cornelius Vanderbilt, Original Flavor—did what rich young men have done for as long as they have been rich young men: He used his grandfather's money and power and influence to make it easier for him to have friends over for parties.

With his brother, young Cornelius established the Newport and Wickford Railroad and Steamboat Company, overseeing a mere three and a half miles of train track from the main rail line connecting New York and Boston to the port of Wickford, RI, a sleepy town with wildly desirable geography. Wickford was located on the western edge of Narragansett Bay, the 147-square-mile estuary that divided the western, mainland half of Rhode Island from the eastern side of the state, an archipelago where New York City's wealthiest nineteenth-century families built the over-the-top mansions that would remain a hallmark of Rhode Island tourism and American film for more than a century.

It was the Vanderbilts who put Wickford on the map, quite literally, plucking valuable farmland and ocean views from unsuspecting Rhode Islanders (eminent domain isn't just for present-day billionaires) and laying the track that would become the safest, easiest journey to Newport for New York's elite, along with their dogs, servants, and secrets. It also opened up access to a collection of small private islands peppering the Bay.

On that particular Wednesday before Labor Day, as Amtrak Northeast Regional train 1603 crossed the Rhode Island border, it occurred to Alice that if the Vanderbilts got one look at the train's worn maroon carpet and polyester-blend upholstery, they would have bemoaned the ceding of rail travel to the common man and paid someone to set the whole thing on fire.

Robber barons would robber baron. Of that, Alice was certain.

She'd been raised by one, after all.

With a soft "Excuse me," to the long legs in the aisle seat, Alice gathered her bags and headed for one of the three doors that would open to the elevated platform of the once-again-sleepy town—no longer a hub of travel for the wealthy and famous.

Staring at her newly charged phone, she ignored the red bubbles at the corner of every app she used regularly. Fourteen new voicemails. Sixty-three new emails. One-hundred-and-twenty-one new text messages.

She swiped to a rideshare app, her thumb hovering over the green square as she waited for the SOS at the top of the screen to turn to bars indicating service. And tried not to impart double meaning into that SOS.

"This is my stop, too."

She whirled to face the words, and the man standing there. Tall, stern, long legs, rotted brain. Nice voice, quiet and deep. The kind of voice that made someone want to listen. Alice hadn't noticed that before.

"Sorry?"

"I'm only saying it so you don't think that I'm following you."

It was a perfectly nice thing to say. But Alice Storm, third child of TRAILBLAZING GENIUS FRANKLIN STORM, DEAD AT 70, had spent a lifetime being followed.

The train began to slow.

"That sounds like something someone following me would say."

The corner of his straight, serious mouth tilted up. Barely. "Scout's honor."

Before she could respond, the conductor came through the automatic doors. "Wickford?"

It came out like *Wickfahd,* and Alice couldn't help her smile at the sound of her childhood. "Yes."

"Nice place for Labor Day weekend," the conductor noted.

Her smile faded.

"Sure is," the man who wasn't following her replied.

"Gonna get some lobster?" *Lobstah.*

The train stopped and the doors opened with a heavy slide, a modern-day portcullis. "Sure are."

Surprised by his use of the plural, Alice looked back. He wasn't looking at her.

The conductor tipped his chin toward the train platform. "Lucky. Have a good weekend."

"Thank you," Alice said, stepping down onto the platform as her neighbor replied, "You too."

The words were lost in the rhythm of the wheels, steady and reliable, already headed north. Alice hesitated, watching the train go and, for a wild moment, wondered what would happen if she ran after it, like in a movie, leaping from the end of the platform, catching the end of the last car. Riding it all the way to Boston. *Hero shit,* Gabi would say.

Alice sighed. The likelihood of her catching the back end of an accelerating train aside (zero likelihood, for the record), doing so would change nothing. The news would still be the same.

That, and her family was already expecting her not to show up, and she refused to give them the satisfaction of being right.

Alice's phone showed two bars, thankfully, and she made quick work of summoning a ride. It was too far of a walk to the docks, and too late to wait inside anywhere—nothing in the quiet town was open past ten, even on the last week of summer.

She set her bags down in the cone of a bright yellow streetlamp—staying outside the light to avoid the potato bugs that danced around an enormous NO LITTERING sign—and settled in for the twenty-minute wait for the driver she'd been assigned, watching as the handful of other passengers piled into cars lined up along the street. A few happy hugs and excited hellos and slammed trunks later, the street was empty except for two cars and an SUV parked on the far side, dark and quiet.

Leaving Alice alone.

Or, alone-ish. Thirty feet away, her neighbor stood under a streetlamp of his own—braving the potato bugs—phone in hand.

Looking her way, he lifted the rectangle as though it meant something. "My ride . . . isn't here."

"It's okay."

"I don't want you to think—"

"That you're following me."

He nodded once. Firm. "Right."

"You're doing a good job of throwing me off the scent."

"Good."

A few minutes passed. Her driver, Benny, would arrive in seventeen minutes in a gray Honda. Which meant she'd be at the wharf in twenty-five minutes. On the island in an hour.

If she was lucky, everyone would be asleep. It would be almost two in the morning. Everyone should be asleep.

Please let them all be asleep.

A rumble sounded in the distance, far away and almost unnoticeable, the heavy promise of a nearby storm, the kind that came on summer nights by the water, streaks of lightning and roaring thunder and rain that soaked you through the moment it started, before it blew past, leaving clear skies and bright stars in its wake.

Dad loved a summer storm.

The thought whispered through her, and she sucked in a breath at the sting of it—an ordinary thought that had no place in her extraordinary relationship (such as it was) with her father. Eager for distraction, Alice checked on her unlikely companion, still staring at his phone.

He was in gray slacks, which was weird. Normal people didn't wear business attire in South County in the middle of the night. Especially in the first week of September, seventy-five degrees and full of the humidity that came with being five minutes from the ocean.

Nevertheless, gray slacks and a white button-down it was, the only nod to the time or season or location the way he'd rolled up his sleeves to reveal forearms Alice noticed—as a student of the artistic form, not for any other reason.

One of those arms boasted a spill of black ink that she couldn't identify at a distance. She wondered if the people he dressed for knew about that tattoo. Hiding pieces of yourself was something Alice recognized.

Her gaze tracked up to his face, along the sharp line of his jaw, unyielding. *Distracting.*

She called across the wide expanse separating them. "You were a Boy Scout?"

He looked over immediately, as though he'd been waiting for her to speak. He didn't miss the reference to his words on the train. With a dip of his head, something a lesser observer might call chagrin, he replied, "I wasn't."

"Impersonating a uniformed officer is a pretty serious infraction, you know."

He put a hand to his chest. "I'm sorry."

"I'm not mad, just disappointed."

White teeth flashed and he looked away, down the quiet one-way street, as though willing a car to come around the corner and stop him from making a bad decision. When it didn't come, he said, "What if I told you I'm good at building fires anyway?"

"An arsonist, then."

"Nah." He shook his head. "I'm even better at putting them out."

Considering Alice was about to walk into fire, it was the exact right thing to say. "In that case, you can wait over here with me . . . if you'd like."

On a different day, at a different time, she never would have made the offer. Twelve years riding the New York City subway gave a girl a very real sense of self-preservation around even the handsomest of men. And if the subway hadn't, up until two months ago, the existence of the handsome man she'd been intending to marry would have made her tread very carefully around this one.

But there was something reckless about that moment, in the dark, in the dead of night, in that place somehow uncomfortably close to her real life and wildly far from it, with a man who might have been the last person she met for a while who didn't know exactly who she was, exactly why she was there.

What was the harm?

The invitation hung between them in air heavy with salt water and the coming storm. Long Legs stayed perfectly still, time stretching until Alice thought he was going to decline, and she would have no choice but to walk directly into the sea from embarrassment.

"Are you going to set a fire?"

I already did. "You never know."

When he moved, it was all at once, with no hesitation. Nothing but a long stride claiming the space between them with even, steady grace, and then he lowered himself to the bench next to her with a level of control that few people had so late at night.

Like a train. Like she was a scheduled stop.

She smiled and he looked at her, curious. "Is that for me?"

Another day, another time.

"I was just thinking about trains."

His gaze flickered to the tracks behind her. "Wish you'd stayed on it?"

"How'd you guess?"

"I might feel the same way."

For a heartbeat, she wondered why, but she knew better than to ask, knowing that her questions would summon his own. Instead, she spilled a new conversation into the silence hanging between them. "Trains make me think of Duke Ellington. He was a—"

"I know who Duke Ellington was."

"Are you a musician?"

"Are you?"

"No. But my father—" She cut herself off. She didn't want her father there.

The handsome stranger didn't notice. "Why do trains make you think of Duke Ellington?"

"He toured the whole country, with a full orchestra, in a private rail car."

"Hmm," he said, the sound low and thoughtful. Alice liked it. "Sousaphones don't really fit in the overhead on the Amtrak regional."

"I don't think there was a sousaphone."

"If you say so," he said, and she couldn't help her little surprised laugh. There was something easy about this man, smooth and competent. The kind of guy who made you want to mess him up a little, make him have some fun.

Except, there wasn't time for fun.

She looked at her phone. Benny was ten minutes away. She pushed away the messy thoughts and was left with jazz. "Most people don't know that Duke Ellington's orchestra went stratospheric here. In Rhode Island."

"Do you think that private rail car stopped here? In Wickford?" He exaggerated it like the conductor on the train. Long and flat, missing the *r*.

"It did, in fact. A few times."

"And all we got were lukewarm hot dogs and day-old coffee."

"The fall of civilization," she said, softly, thinking of the many ways she'd traveled to this place in her life. Expensive cars. Helicopters, sailboats. She resisted the memories, turning, instead, to the excellent distraction before her. Solid and tall and with those forearms that—

The tattoo was a compass. Geometric and beautiful, arrows extending in long, fine lines to his wrist and elbow. She spoke to it. "You're not local."

He didn't have to reply. She was right. Anyone would see it. He was pure stranger comes to town—nothing about him even close to homegrown by seaweed and salt and clam shacks on the beach. He was too serious. Too smooth.

He lifted a hand. Hesitated. "You have . . . paint in your hair."

She brushed the hair and his hand away, self-conscious and unsettled by how easily he had identified the paint, as though he knew where she'd been that morning, before she'd gone to her classroom, before her mother had called and everything had changed, back when it had been a perfectly normal day, distant now. The past.

Before.

He cleared his throat. "I should introduce myself," he said, extending that hand that hadn't touched her, like they were normal people doing a normal thing. "I'm—"

"Don't."

He didn't. "Why not?"

"Because then—" Then she would have to introduce herself. And then he'd know. And then it would get weird. And this wasn't weird. Well, it was weird, but it wasn't weird in the way that every other interaction in her lifetime had ended up weird.

Storm like *Franklin Storm?*

Storm like *Storm Technology?*

Storm like *Storm Inside™?*

Yes, she'd answer, and always with a laugh—like it was the cleverest, most original thing anyone had ever said—when what she'd really meant was *No. Not like that. That's my father.* When what she'd really meant was *Don't think about it. Don't remember. Just let me be commonplace. Common name.*

And then she'd pretend to be someone else. Because someone else was always more interesting than the truth, which was this: No matter how hard she tried, the most interesting thing about Alice Storm had always been her last name. She had been an outline of a person, shaded by the stories of her father—madcap genius, daredevil billionaire, visionary world-changer. And then she'd been shaded by the story of what she'd done to him—how she'd betrayed him, how he'd exiled her. How she'd either deserved it or was better for it.

Another rumble in the distance, louder. Closer. *Of course.*

"Names make things complicated," she said, finally, meeting his gaze, intent beneath a furrowed brow, like he was trying to understand. "I know it sounds dramatic, but my life is complicated enough this week. Any chance we could just . . . skip them?"

He understood. "Sure." He nodded and looked down at his phone. "My car is almost here."

She mirrored his actions. "Mine, too," she lied. Benny hadn't moved since the last time she'd checked.

"It's late," he said. "Are you going to a hotel?"

"No." A hesitation, leagues long. "Are you?"

"I'm staying at the Quahog Quay."

Her brows rose at the mention of the motel that had been a Wickford landmark since electricity had come to South County, with its blinking neon VACANCY sign. No one ever stayed at the Quahog Quay. "Why?"

"Why the Quahog Quay? Or why, in a more existential sense?"

"I assume you chose the Quahog Quay for its clever name."

He didn't hesitate. "I can't resist alliteration."

Alice smiled and tilted her head, warm from something other than the summer evening. "Do you even know what a quahog is?"

"I assume it's not something to be discussed in polite company."

She laughed. "And the existential sense? Why are you here?"

A pause. "Work."

"Superior business center at the Quahog Quay, I hear."

"I prioritize a quality fax machine." When his smile flashed in the darkness, something coiled inside her: desire. And then, with a heavy thud, something else: suspicion.

She met his eyes. "Are you a journalist?"

"No."

She had absolutely no reason to believe him, and still— "Scout's honor?"

"Should I build you a fire to prove it?"

A rumble in the distance, and she looked to the sky. "Think you can do it before the storm gets here?"

"I'll have to owe you one."

"I'll hold you to it."

When she returned her attention to him, there was something in his eyes that she hadn't seen in a while. That she hadn't realize she missed. "Good."

She liked that word, clipped and certain, as though this was a man who made promises and kept them. Who'd be around long enough to keep them. Then he was closer, and something had changed, making her wonder what would happen if she took a night for herself before facing . . . the inevitable.

Another rumble, a reminder that any wild thoughts about a one-night stand with a perfect stranger were just that—wild thoughts. And Alice Storm was simply not the kind of person who made good on wild thoughts.

She had a father who did that, and look where it got him.

DEAD AT 70.

The words crashed over her, discordant and unwelcome and she hated them for it. Grief shouldn't feel like this, should it? It should feel like screaming and crying and rending of clothes. Not like this—empty. Like she wanted to fill it up with anything but sadness.

Like she wanted to fill it up with this man. With one night.

A car door slammed in the distance.

She cleared her throat and looked back to her phone. "Dammit."

"What happened?"

She shook her head. "The universe. My ride canceled."

A gray SUV turned the corner from Main Street. Long Legs said, "That's mine."

"Thanks for keeping me company." There was no reason for her to feel like this, like his departure was a loss. Like he was a port in the storm.

"Are you okay?" No reason for him to notice that she wasn't and still, it felt— "Do you . . . need a ride?"

"That *definitely* sounds like you were following me."

"Okay, but what if I don't want anyone *else* following you?"

It was a really decent thing to say. The kind of thing she'd remember fondly in an hour or so, when she recounted this bad day (understatement) to her best friend. A sort of, *And then a really handsome, very decent guy asked me if I would be okay by myself,* kind of memory. *And I wondered what he would say if I said, "Definitely not, you should stay and protect me. And also let me climb you like a tree."*

And Gabi would laugh, and Alice would talk about the rest of the day—her ride bailing and the train being loud and packed with people and the missed calls requesting comments and interviews she was never going to give. And the calls that never came from the people who should have called. And somehow, everything would seem better when she hung up the phone.

Except this wasn't the kind of bad day that was made better by a phone call. This was the kind of bad day that came along once in a lifetime. Because the bad luck—the ride and the train and the texts and the missed calls—it was all layered on top of something worse.

My father died.

The words were a knot in her throat.

My father died, and we hadn't spoken in five years, and I don't know how I feel.

She couldn't say them to the stranger. Instead, she stepped toward him, tilted her head to the side, and tried for a different kind of feeling. "If I let you give me a ride . . . what happens next?"

Something flashed in his eyes. *Heat.*

That felt good.

The heat wasn't alone, though. It came with regret. Or some cousin to it, like that decent guy didn't want to be so decent, but would be, nonetheless.

The car pulled up beside them.

She tilted her chin toward it. "I'll be fine. It was nice meeting you."

"We didn't meet," he said. "No names, remember?"

"Maybe we will," she replied. "Someday." They wouldn't, but Alice stored the idea away like a memory anyway.

Lightning flashed.

She counted. *One . . . two . . . three . . . four.*

A heavy rumble of thunder.

"Five miles," he said.

She didn't look at the car this time. "You should go before . . ." *Before I make a bad decision.*

"You're right." He didn't move.

They were so still, hanging like the salty humidity around them. Was he going to kiss her? Was she going to kiss him? Surely not. That wasn't the kind of thing Alice Storm did, right in public, in Wickford, Rhode Island, in full view of a thousand insects and the driver of a Kia Sedona, rideshare timer counting down on the dash.

And still . . . she was tempted. One kiss. One out-of-character decision. One stolen moment. One last reprieve, a mad scramble to avoid the unavoidable.

Another rumble, this one in his chest, lost in a much louder one above, a wicked crack, breaking everything apart: the sky, rain suddenly everywhere, all around them, in heavy sheets; the darkness, a flash of lightning so bright and close that they should have felt the heat of it; and then, her name shouted from what seemed like inches away.

"Alice!"

She turned.

The bright light hadn't been lightning. It had been a camera flash. "Alice!" the photographer shouted again, compact, wrinkled, unshaven, as though he'd been waiting for the train for hours. And maybe he had?

Another shout. Another man running from the far side of the street, where the three cars had been sitting, dark. Watching. Waiting for something worth photographing.

How had they known she would be there?

How had *she* not known *they* would be there? There were two stories this week, after all. One Storm gone, the other returned.

"Alice! Were you and your father still estranged? Why didn't you come with your brother and sisters? Are they speaking to you? Are you welcome at home?"

Years of training kicked in. *Head down. Stay on course.* But there was no course. Benny and his Honda had bailed on her, and she was alone under this streetlight in the rain, outside a closed train station, surrounded by the enemy.

Unmoored.

"Please." She held up a hand, knowing it was futile. "Don't—"

Before she could finish—*what had she been going to say, even?*—she was in motion, pushed behind the not-a-Boy-Scout (but-honestly-kind-of-a-Boy-Scout?), her view blocked by his wide shoulders, plastered with rain-soaked white cotton.

"Get back," he said, his tone unyielding.

They didn't get back. Of course they didn't. Pictures of Franklin Storm's daughter today were worth this decent man's annual salary, and the paparazzi knew it.

More flashes as the rain poured, and Alice felt just slightly like she was drowning. "Who's your boyfriend?"

"Is it serious?"

"Goddammit." The man who was decidedly *not* her boyfriend sure sounded serious. "Get in the car."

A lifeboat.

She turned to get her bags, and he grabbed her hand, strong and sure. "No." The word stopped her in her tracks. "*Get in the car, Alice.*"

He said her name like he'd been saying it for a lifetime, and she obeyed him instantly, unsurprised to find the driver already opening the rear door. Behind her, she heard Long Legs growl, "I said, get *back.*"

Another rumble of thunder, covering up whatever happened to cause a sharp shout and a high-pitched "What the fuck?!" as she climbed inside the car, the driver looking past her as he said, "Those assholes deserved that."

Once inside, Alice ducked her head and waited as her unexpected rescuers shoved bags into the trunk and joined her. The driver turned around, excitement in his eyes. "Guessin' you don't wanna head where the app is sending me."

"Not yet," came the terse reply from her companion, whose name she still didn't know. She should ask him. But maybe if she didn't, he wouldn't ask her, either. Or anything else. Anything like *Why are paparazzi waiting for you in this sleepy Rhode Island town in the middle of the night? Why aren't you speaking to your family? Come to think of it, who is your family?* "Think you can lose them?"

A big smile—this driver was going to get free beers forever on this story. "Dumbasses are from New York City. They know nothin' about Rhode Island."

"Let's lose them, then."

"Yessir." The car peeled out of the drive, barely missing the man who leaped out of its path, the engine straining to live up to the full require-ments of a getaway car. "Then to the motel?"

"We'll drop her first."

It was a prompt, which she'd answer, eventually. Just as soon as she looked away from his hand, balled into a fist, attached to that forearm that boasted the compass, wet with rain and, in the flash of the street-lights beyond, red-knuckled.

Like he'd hit something.

Later, she would chalk it up to a wild combination of grief and lone-liness that she liked those knuckles, scraped and raw. But in the mo-ment? When he turned his fist over and opened his hand with a ragged, "Here," she liked it for other reasons.

Especially when she recognized the small rectangles on his palm. A pair of external SD cards.

Her eyes flew to his, and he said, "From the cameras." That was it. Nothing more, no pressing her for information he was, frankly, owed, considering he'd committed some light assault for her.

There was something powerfully appealing about a man who still didn't seem to care who she was, or why she'd brought chaos into his life.

"Are you okay?" he asked, the second time since they'd left the train. *No. But this helps.*

"Where to, sweethaht?" The driver, this time.

Where *was* she going? She'd been so sure of her path—so certain she'd been on the right one. And now . . . nothing made sense. Nothing but this moment. She'd been in danger, and now she wasn't. And to-morrow, everything would return, but tonight, this made sense.

He made sense.

She reached out—not for the SD cards. Instead, she put her hand in his, capturing the rectangles between their palms, reveling in the heat of his touch, rough and firm. Steady. Like the train.

Unlike everything else.

"The Quahog Quay."

CHAPTER

3

IT WAS NOT A walk of shame.

Yes, Alice had slipped from beneath the heavy arm hooked over her hip and remained perfectly still, clinging to the edge of the too-small bed in Quahog Quay Room 3, staring at the door through which they'd crashed a handful of hours earlier in a breathless tangle of rain-soaked bodies and baggage (literal and metaphorical).

Yes, once she'd been certain he wasn't going to wake up, she'd collected her discarded clothes like they were unexploded munitions and crept to the bathroom, closing the door like she was cracking a safe.

And yes, when she'd exited the bathroom after washing her face and combing the salt and sea through her hair, she'd studiously ignored him, handsome and half-naked and asleep as she snuck out into the six o'clock sun peeking over the Bay, golden and gorgeous, promising to burn away the remnants of the night before.

She walked the quarter mile from the clapboard motel to the docks, eager to get there before the harbormaster or anyone else in that small town full of big mouths would see her—but not because she was ashamed.

At least, not because she was ashamed of her one-night stand, which, while deeply out of character for Alice, had proven really pretty great—in more ways than the obvious.

Growing up Alice Storm, she'd learned to be suspicious of people who appeared from nowhere. The threats were myriad, from the obvious (photos and gossip about spoiled rich girls were the hottest of modern commodities, the messier the better) to the insidious—charming, clever parasites who would do anything, say anything, for proximity to wealth and power.

Franklin had trained all his children to be wary of any kindness that appeared freely given, resulting in something of a skills gap when it came to interpersonal relationships. The first blush of attraction that made fast friends and breathless romance for the rest of the world was not to be trusted for Storm children, and Alice had built her shields early—especially when it came to sex.

Over the years, she'd selected partners like other people selected cars, with careful consideration: miles per gallon (a career outside of tech), safety ratings (interest in Alice, but not Storm), resale value (willingness for a long-term commitment).

Sure, she'd made some mistakes (one colossal one), but the truth was, one-night stands were not well rated by *Car and Driver*.

But Alice hadn't been herself the night before, and her world wouldn't be itself again for a while, and she'd *liked* that big, steady man with his strong hands and sure touch and his willingness to step into the fray to keep her out of it.

She'd liked how different he was, not like the refined, polished boys of her youth or the frivolous, boisterous man she'd been planning to marry. Long Legs had been full of quiet steel when he'd punched a photographer and taken her hand in the darkness. And then he'd been deliciously rough—his palms stroking over her skin, the way he kicked the motel-room door closed behind them with a massive *thud,* his gruff words as he'd pressed his heavy weight to her, asking what she liked. Telling her what he liked. Praising her body, her touch, her kiss.

No hesitation. No apologies. Just . . . *truth.*

Truth was rare and precious in Alice's life, so, yes. She'd basked in the truth of that man and his desire and his ability to anchor her to her own body for a few hours.

A calm before the Storms.

Alice tossed her bags into one of the three skiffs moored at the far end of the salt-weathered dock, loosened the lines and fired up the outboard motor, tucking the night away, a secret to keep with all the others as she sailed out of Wickford Harbor for the first time in five years. Since the day her father exiled her, finally, after she'd disappointed him for the last time.

The storm from the night before had blown east toward Cape Cod and out to sea, but the scars of it remained, Narragansett Bay churning beneath the small boat, choppy enough to make the six and a half nautical miles to Storm Island a challenge.

Alice had sailed since before she'd walked, however—learned at Franklin Storm's feet how to adjust and accommodate, how to work with a mercurial sea, how to respect it. It might have been years since she'd been at the helm of a boat, but she fell back into it with ease, heading into bright sun, reveling in the sting of the salt water on her skin.

She navigated the small boat northeast into the Bay, unthinkingly taking her father's favorite approach—via the southern tip of Storm Island, where a small, ancient building housed a fog bell atop the steep, rocky slope.

For many, this was the least interesting angle of Storm Island, but her father loved an entrance, and this route, around the cliff's edge on the western side of the island, gave visitors and gawkers a breathtaking surprise, the rock sliding away to reveal a patchwork of trees and fields marked by centuries-old stone walls, leading to an enormous nineteenth-century manor house on the highest point of the island, like a character in a gothic novel, but without the woman in the nightgown running away from the ghosts within.

To be honest, though, the day was young.

Alice slowed the skiff as she came around the cliffside, taking in the view. The house, tall and imposing, all gables and stained glass, surrounded by a few acres of lush wild thyme in deep greens and bright whites and purples. The boathouse, with its weathered cedar shingles, large enough to house her father's prized sailboat, *The Lizzie,* in the off-season. Rugged slate steps from the dock up the rocky hillside to the house. Ancient trees—her father's favorite red oak, enormous and strong. Still there.

Five years, and nothing had changed. Except everything.

She pushed the thought away, shoving it past the knot that rose in her throat as she docked the skiff and climbed the hill to Storm Manor, letting herself in through the unlocked front door (the benefit of a private island—difficult to burgle), hoping she was the only person awake.

Hoping she'd have some time to armor up.

The door closed behind her, shutting out the bright morning sun, returning the foyer to quiet darkness. Alice's eyes adjusted, and a tall, lithe, perfectly pressed, artfully graying woman came into view, descending the wide central staircase.

There would be no time for armor. Her mother had arrived ready for battle.

"Alice!" Elisabeth Winslow Storm gave her third child a long inspection. "You came."

There was no excitement in the observation, only a slight edge of surprise.

"Nice to see you, Mom," Alice said, ignoring the bait, dropping her bags inside the door, and running a hand through her hair, wild from the wind on the Bay.

"I didn't hear the helicopter."

Alice hadn't ridden in a Storm helicopter in years, and Elisabeth knew it. "I took the train."

"Did you." A beat as Elisabeth hovered on the final step, one long, graceful hand barely touching the elaborately carved newel post. "How resourceful."

Resourceful was one of Elisabeth's words. The ones all mothers have, designed to push all the buttons they've installed. The ones that serve as placeholders for other, more pointed words. In Alice's mother's case, *resourceful* was joined by *interesting, creative, modern,* and *charming,* and required a tonal reading that often flummoxed the recipient (it should be said that the only thing Elisabeth had ever in her life found authentically charming was Franklin Storm, and even that hadn't lasted).

Alice's first language had been her mother's, however, and she knew the meaning of *How resourceful*. It translated to, *That was awfully stupid*.

"That must explain why it's taken you a full day to get here. Though, I wasn't sure we'd see you at all."

Irritation flared, and Alice couldn't help her reply. "Mom. Really?"

Elisabeth lifted a slim shoulder. "You haven't been here in years, why would I expect you now?"

Because my father died. Because your husband died. Because this is what families do—even ones like this.

Too much for six in the morning. "I'm here now," Alice said.

"Mmm." That single sound held an entire State of the Union address. "No Griffin?"

No Griffin, ever again. Alice swallowed back the truth and lied. "He couldn't get away from work."

"Work," Elisabeth repeated, in a tone that underscored the whole family's feelings about Alice's (now secretly ex) fiancé. "Busking keeps him busy?"

"He's an actor, Mom," Alice said, loathing the knee-jerk defense of a man she was no longer emotionally required to defend and somehow couldn't stop defending.

"Is he." Elisabeth stepped onto the gleaming hardwood floor of the foyer. "I thought he worked in a café." There was no thinking about it. Griffin was a largely out-of-work actor in New York City who, when he needed cash (which was all the time), picked up shifts at the coffee shop his best friend managed. Elisabeth knew it. Everyone knew it. Had known it. But Alice hadn't cared, because he'd been *hers*. "No matter. As you say, you're here now and it's nice to see you after so long away."

Alice leaned in to her mother's brief embrace, releasing her clenched teeth as Elisabeth delivered a kiss somewhere in the vicinity of her left ear. She wondered how many offhand (pointed) references to the last five years she'd have to endure before she'd done the proper penance.

She did not wonder when her mother would assume some responsibility for what had happened five years ago. For what had happened since (or not happened, as it was). *Responsibility* was not one of Elisabeth's words.

Leaning back, Alice caught one of her mother's hands and studied the older woman's face, impossibly smooth skin interrupted by a barely visible handful of fine lines the envy of women thirty years younger—the combined product of excellent genes, a militant commitment to sun protection, a facialist who made house calls, and a dermatologist with a client list whose net worth was equivalent to the GDP of a small European country.

Not even widowhood could keep Elisabeth from her skincare regimen. To the untrained eye, she looked smooth and dewy and unpuffy and fabulous, but daughters are trained from birth to read their mother's emotions, and Alice noticed the tiny cracks: the tightness at the corners of SPFed lips; the red wash peeking above the tidy neck of the white long sleeve cotton tee that was a staple of her summer wardrobe—one of a dozen or so identical tops that cost more than most people's weekly salary; the barely there swell beneath the stunning blue eyes Alice had not inherited as the only Storm child who favored their father. Eyes that, just then, were a touch bloodshot.

Not that Elisabeth Winslow Storm would ever admit to having lost sleep or shed tears for her husband of more than forty years. Emotions were not a commodity in which Alice's mother invested. "You know we're having an event on Monday. Greta is helping with arrangements, but I'm sure we can find something for you to do."

Not a funeral. Not a service. An *event*.

Alice swallowed around the knot that ached in her throat. "You told me on the phone." It was one of the few things Elisabeth had said to Alice when they'd spoken the day before.

Your father died.

He was in one of his idiotic toys.

We're having people to the island on Monday. People to the island. Like it was a garden party. *I suppose it's a good thing it's a long weekend.*

When Elisabeth remained silent, Alice took a deep breath and asked, "How are you doing, Mom?"

"Me?" Tidy blond brows rose and Elisabeth extracted her hand from Alice's grip. "I'm fine."

So much for the possibility of her homecoming looking like it did in the movies. There was nothing close to the grief of central casting here, not even twenty-four hours after Franklin's death. No shared tears. No long embrace. Not a hint of her mother's emotions.

Elisabeth must be feeling *something*, no?

The fact that she was disinclined to inspect it notwithstanding, Alice was feeling something.

Alice tilted her head. "Really?"

"We all die eventually, Alice. Have you had coffee?"

Years of speaking fluent Elisabeth Storm ensured Alice knew better than to say anything more. She lowered her satchel to the floor. "No." She followed Elisabeth to the rear of the house, where the narrow, dark hallway opened into a massive, bright farmhouse kitchen complete with an entire wall of greenhouse windows, and tried for light conversation. "Who else is here?"

Elisabeth waved a hand in the air, toward the ceiling and two additional floors of studios and offices and bedrooms and nooks and crannies. "Everyone. *They* all came as soon as they heard."

Alice gritted her teeth at the impossible-to-miss comparison to her siblings, her mother docking points for the seven hours Alice should have been sleeping under the same roof. She pulled a large French press down from an open shelf and set it on the counter. "I came as soon as I heard, too, Mom."

"Of course you did. By train."

Apparently, the train was going to be the thing, not the bit where the woman's husband had died, and without warning.

"Right." Alice crossed to the pantry, flicking on the exterior light switch before entering to get coffee, sadness welling as she reached for the enormous orange bag. Franklin Storm might have died a billionaire, but he'd been born a kid in Quincy, Massachusetts, and spent a lifetime loyal to Dunkin' Donuts.

Her fingertips stroked over the logo as she lingered on the rest of the pantry, the first of her father's ghosts. If she were going to paint his essence, she'd start here. A still life with old-fashioned hard pretzels, black licorice candy, kettle-cooked potato chips, tinned sardines. Three jars of spicy pickles. Heirloom tomato sauce he insisted on buying from a farm on the other side of the Bay, in Tiverton.

It's not worth eating tomato sauce if it's not from these tomatoes, he would say, his voice booming with excitement, matched only by the delight from the lady who ran the market, who fell a little more in love with the eccentric billionaire every time he wandered into her farm-stand.

That was the problem, wasn't it? Her father was incredibly easy to fall in love with, and absolutely impossible to love.

And easy to please if you weren't his daughter.

Alice had been a teenager the last time she'd been at Skipping Stone Farm, barely more than a barn in a field, rolling her eyes while the whole place fawned over Franklin as he loaded a case of the sauce, stickered with a mailing label and identified with a Sharpie, into the back of the ancient truck he drove around as though he were a normal person.

She pulled the jar down, running her fingers over its new, proper label. An artist's rendering of the barn. A website. Ingredients. It had come a long way, just like all the rest of them.

It was strange that the nutrition label was the thing that got her. There, in that pantry that smelled like her childhood summers, full of heavy salt air circulated by the ancient ceiling fan, surrounded by a million things that would never have made her think of her father and now would never make her think of anyone else, a fat tear spilled over and down her cheek.

"Don't let that door slam," her mother called from the kitchen, where she was setting a teakettle to boil. Alice swiped all evidence of emotion away. "It sticks, and we'll have to call Charlie to get you out."

Charlie, the carpenter/handyman/gardener/whatever else her parents needed at any given moment (married to Lorraine, cook/house-keeper/whatever else her parents needed at any given moment), lived in one of three small staff cottages on the north end of the island, waiting to be summoned to the main house, her mother's own personal errand boy at the ripe age of sixty-something.

"How are Charlie and Lorraine?" Alice called out, clearing her throat and straightening her spine, weirdly grateful for the question— something to ask when she didn't want to ask about anything important.

"They're Charlie and Lorraine." A classically Elisabeth reply, as if to say, *Why would there be anything interesting to say about that?*

Alice grabbed the coffee and returned to the kitchen, where her mother was no longer alone. Next to her, rummaging in the ancient metal-lined bread drawer that had been saved from the earliest iteration of the kitchen, wearing only pajama bottoms, was Alice's older brother. "Sam."

He shot up, a package of English muffins in his hand. "Hey! The prodigal returns! And Dad not here to slay the fatted calf."

Alice offered a tight smile, the only defense against Sam's trademark snark. "Funny."

"It wasn't meant to be," he said, his false warmth sliding into something that might have been unpleasant if he weren't so good at it. "Whadja do, walk?"

"She took the *train*," Elisabeth said.

He smirked, the annoying expression that older brothers learned early and used often. "You could have hitched a ride. There's a helicopter."

"It might surprise you to hear that the last thing I wanted to do yesterday was share a ride with Dad's PR team while they decided how best to protect the stock price."

"Look at you, woman of the people," Sam retorted. "I bet you get so much love at the monthly meeting of the 99%, what with how you're not allowed within a city block of Storm headquarters."

And there it was. The reference to the past. Alice headed for the coffeepot on the counter. "How is Storm headquarters, Sam? How's that job down the hall from Dad going?"

"Well, he's dead now, so not great," Sam said, lacking any sensitivity, as if he were made of Teflon—nonstick, but toxic.

It occurred to Alice that somewhere in her brother's emotions (such as they were) was a thread of . . . anticipation? Here was Sam's chance to make a play for the title he'd believed was his birthright from the moment he'd learned the word *nepotism*—CEO of Storm Incorporated. As far as Alice was concerned, Sam could have it. But they all knew the truth—that if Franklin were already in a grave, he'd be turning over in it at the idea.

"Dammit!" Elisabeth cried, turning in a circle at the butcher block island.

Alice and Sam looked to her. "What?"

"I left my damn tablet upstairs!"

And then to each other, the animosity between them disappearing in a way only siblings experienced. Sam quirked a brow at Alice. Elisabeth's irritation felt outsized for the inconvenience of leaving a tablet on a different floor of the house. "Okay . . ." he said slowly, as though he was speaking to a moody toddler. "We'll get it for you."

"I don't need anyone to get it! I am perfectly able to get it myself," their mother shot back, slamming the coffeepot down on the counter before storming from the room.

Alice slid a look at her brother. "She seems to be taking everything well."

Sam nodded. "Couldn't agree more."

The grandfather clock in the foyer chimed, marking seven in the morning. Sam leaned against the counter, sandy blond and tan with summer, the kind of attractive men approaching their forties often were, effortlessly taking up space. On closer inspection, however, Sam didn't look so effortless. He looked tired. "You're up early," she said. The observation was a question. *What are you up to?*

The toaster sprang, producing his English muffin. He didn't move, returning Alice's inspection. It was only fair, she supposed, telling herself her cracks were better hidden. Lying to herself.

"So are you," he replied. *You first.*

Well. She wasn't about to tell him what she'd been up to. Sam would sink his teeth into Alice's night at the Quahog Quay—the *Who?* and *What?* and *Why wasn't it your fiancé?* and *Come to think of it where is your fiancé?*—and wield it like a weapon for the next five days.

So they tucked their truths away and retreated to their respective appliances.

"She's pissed," Sam said. *Truce.*

"Mom?" Alice scooped coffee into the pot. "That's normal, no? Stages of grief stuff?"

"Please. Like we didn't all know he'd die in some kind of hot-air-balloon-sky-diving-submersible-travel-to-space shit."

"Jesus, Sam."

"Like it's not true?"

Franklin Storm had died in a gliding accident, which the Internet was surely already calling not only the most billionaire death to ever billionaire, but also the most Franklin Storm death to ever Franklin Storm. Her father had never found a way to defy death he didn't immediately attempt, and usually for cameras.

"Yeah, but it's not like we expected it to be *yesterday.*"

He took a bite of his English muffin. "Fine."

"Try to have some . . ."

"Some what?"

Humanity? Empathy? Alice shook her head. Empathy wasn't a family trait for the Storms. It had never been rewarded. "I don't know. He's *dead.*"

"And it's a big fucking deal, big enough to bring *you* home," he said before crunching into his muffin again, loud and extravagant, making one of those points that brothers loved to make, as though they meant something.

The teakettle screamed.

"Yeah. I know. Big enough to make you talk to me," she said, knowing it was futile to point out that her siblings had watched her leave and never said a word. Franklin might have been the catalyst for her leaving home, but it was the rest of the family that kept her away, too afraid of how he might punish them if they did anything else.

"That reminds me . . . I have an NDA somewhere for you to sign." He meant it to be funny. It wasn't.

Alice poured boiling water into the coffeepot, saved from filling the silence that fell between them when the kitchen door opened, letting in a wash of early morning sunlight and Greta, the eldest of the Storm siblings. "Oh my gosh! *You're* here!" Greta said, sounding more shocked than Alice would have liked.

She swallowed her irritation and opened her arms, playing unflappable. "Surprise," she said.

"I mean, of course you're here."

Silence fell, just long enough to be awkward before Greta crossed to Alice and hugged her, so fast it almost didn't happen.

When they pulled apart, Alice filled the weird silence with, "How are you . . . doing?"

"I'm fine," Greta said, unsurprisingly parroting their mother as she ran a hand through her long sandy-blond hair, a perfect match to Sam's, and down the billowing fabric of the tank she wore over black yoga pants. "I was"—she waved to the door—"taking a walk."

It was a broad lie, one Greta had told a thousand times over the years. Everyone knew exactly where the eldest Storm sibling went in the evenings after she thought the whole house was asleep, but now wasn't the time, so Alice elected not to comment.

Sam had no such tact. "You know, Greta, now that he's dead, you don't have to hide it."

"Hide what?" Greta said, her voice rising an octave as she fiddled with her diamond tennis bracelet.

Alice pulled a mug down off a large open shelf. "I think he means you and Tony."

"What about me and Tony?" Greta asked before she realized she'd broken the cardinal rule of the Storms—never accept the premise of a question. She struggled to recover, spine going impossibly straighter. "Tony, Dad's Tony?"

"Not *Dad's* Tony anymore. I think it's fair to say you get him in the will."

Alice looked up. "Sam!"

"Come on! It was a joke!" He spread his arms wide. "Like we aren't all thinking about it."

"We're not all thinking about what we get in the will, Sam," Greta snapped. "Just you, angling for that promotion you couldn't score when he was alive."

"You're very touchy for someone who got laid all night, Greta," he replied.

"Sam . . ." Alice said, as though she could stop him. Which she couldn't. She'd never been able to before, and now—she no longer fooled herself into thinking she had any control.

"Point is, it's stupid for her to keep it a secret now."

"Stupid or not, it's none of your business," Alice said. The affair between her sister and her father's chauffeur/body man over the years was the worst-kept secret in the family. Everyone knew about it, even as Greta refused to make the relationship public for fear of Franklin's censure—a fear that Alice knew firsthand wasn't unfounded—not because Tony was an employee, but because he belonged to Franklin.

Franklin Storm was a man who liked to amass. Land, art, companies, experiences, money. Power above all, but also attention. And people. And he didn't share well.

Alice extended the steaming mug to Greta, an offer of sisterly solidarity. The eldest Storm accepted the mug, but not the support, her attention already on the kitchen door. "Is Mom up?"

"Is she ever," Sam said.

Greta looked from one to the other, her tone going sharp. "What's that mean? What happened? Is she upset?" Of all of them, Greta was the most tuned in to Elisabeth's moods, always looking for ways to make her happy, one of the myriad reasons she kept her relationship with Tony secret.

"In a sense?" Alice said.

"She nearly threw a coffeepot at Alice."

Greta's eyes went wide.

"I *know*," Alice retorted. "And Sam was *right there*."

Everyone laughed, and for a moment it all felt okay.

"When did you get in?" Greta asked, heading for the fridge.

"A half hour ago?"

Greta lifted a yogurt in Alice's direction. "This morning?"

She nodded at the question and the yogurt.

"Yes, let's probe that," Sam said, sounding like he was fifteen and not a grown man. "We all know where Greta was last night, but where were *you*?"

Alice focused on peeling the foil top off the little terra-cotta pot. "There was a storm. I didn't want to risk sailing in it."

It was Greta's and Sam's turn to share a look.

"Yeah. You're going to need a better one than that if you want Mom to believe it," Sam said. "There's always a storm."

No kidding. "Exactly. And we shouldn't sail in them." She paused. "Plus, there were photographers."

That stopped them. Sam spoke first. "Where?"

"At the station."

"How'd they know you would be there?" Greta asked.

Sam cursed under his breath. "They knew because Alice prides herself on being Not Like Other Storms. Public school teacher, hero of the proletariat, having forsaken the rest of us. But whether or not she was going to turn up was one of the truly interesting questions of the day, and by *interesting*, I mean *worth decent money*."

"It wasn't a question. Of course I came." Alice swallowed her irritation, shoving it down alongside the shame she already felt for not expecting the photographers. Her father would have expected them. She ignored the tightness in her chest. "I'm impressed you can use the word *proletariat* in a sentence, though, Samuel."

Sam ignored the insult; he wasn't the kind of person who got insulted.

"Did they get photos?" Greta asked.

Alice shook her head. "No." There was no need to share how close they'd gotten to photos.

A long moment passed while her siblings watched her, searching for the truth, which was thin on the ground when the Storms were together, told in halves and quarters, too valuable to give away for free and so tucked away and converted to secrets—a much better investment.

But Alice had told the truth (about the photos, at least), and they believed her (about the photos, at least).

"There's nothing going on with me and Tony," Greta interjected in that casual way people interjected when it was not at all casual. Which it wasn't. Greta and Tony hadn't been casual for seventeen years. When neither Sam nor Alice replied, she changed the subject, asking Alice, "You spent the night in town?"

"Mm-hmm. At the Quahog Quay."

A beat. *Dammit.* Alice was out of practice, having forgotten that conversations with her family were best treated like depositions. Answer the question asked and nothing more. Greta pounced. "With Griffin?"

So much for solidarity.

"No." Alice ignored the way her siblings stilled, immediately full of silent anticipation. Played it cool. "He had to work."

Greta sipped her coffee.

"Oh yeah? Does he have a real job yet?" Sam asked.

"Do you?" Alice hated how defensive she was of someone who'd packed up his stuff and left without any explanation, as though they hadn't been together for years. As though they hadn't been planning to be together for the rest of them.

Well. *Alice* had been planning that; Griffin, evidently, had been planning an exit . . . and she'd never seen it coming.

Sam smirked, knowing he'd touched a nerve.

Annoyed, Alice didn't hold back her pointed reply. "Where's Sila?"

She might have narrowly escaped her marital mistake, but Sam had run directly into his. His wife, Sila, had no doubt crowed to her mother, frenemies, and anyone else in earshot the moment she'd caught Sam Storm like a prize trout.

Sam shut up, and Alice resisted gloating once she found her own nerve. "You could have just said you were happy to see me, Sam."

"Why would I be happy to see you?" he retorted, and in the mouth of another brother, in another family, it might have been a joke.

But these were the Storms.

She looked to Greta, who stared into her coffee mug and said nothing. Of course. Alice set her coffee on the counter. "I'm going to un-pack."

Neither of her siblings replied. What was there to say? Not even thirty minutes, and they were all sliding into their old roles.

Family.

CHAPTER

4

THERE WERE SOME LOVELY things about Gilded Age manor houses.

An endless supply of rooms of all different sizes. High ceilings. Crown molding. Original hardwood floors laid out in meticulous patterns. Enormous sinks. Claw-foot tubs. Closets (one of America's greatest inventions) with enough space to have once carried bustles, corsets, and yards of silk and velvet.

Unflinchingly over-the-top in their design, full of nooks and crannies and any number of locations designed for secrets and gossip and yes, trysts, as older sisters throughout history could attest.

Storm Manor was designed to compete with the best of the nineteenth-century mansions in Newport—boasting all their extravagance, and with a private island, to boot. Sixty-three acres of rolling grounds and magnificent vistas of the Atlantic to the south, Narragansett Bay to the north, and some of the most beautiful landscape in Rhode Island to east and west.

Purchased from the Narragansett Indians in the 1660s by John Peckham, an Englishman looking to build himself a fiefdom on a new continent, the island came with a name in one of the Algonquian languages, Uhquŏhquot. It was not clear from the records at the Wickford historical society whether Mr. Peckham had asked for a translation of the island's name at the time of sale, but it was generally accepted that he hadn't, or he might have thought twice about buying a place called Tempest.

John died in a brutal storm during his first winter on the island, and his family immediately left, guided by the good sense of his wife, Mary, who was surely unsurprised by her husband's fate, considering his folly in purchasing the island to begin with. Mary didn't marry again (see aforementioned good sense), and lived to be ninety-three, if the gravestone in the Little Compton town cemetery was to be believed. Maybe it was Mary who finally asked someone to translate the name of the place: Uhquŏhquot became Storm Island, and was uninhabited for another two centuries, when it was claimed by the state and sold for five thousand dollars to a steel magnate who wasn't considered decent enough to be welcome in Newport—and who, considering the caliber of men who *were* welcome in Newport, must have been a real prince.

Storm Manor was built, big and brooding, on the hill—an enormous middle finger to the magnates to the south—and inhabited by that indecorous man and his odd, indecorous descendants until the 1980s, when it fell into disrepair, along with its owners' trust funds.

Enter the solution to their financial problems: Franklin Storm, full of youth, arrogance, and the certainty that the tens of millions burning a hole in his pocket were only the beginning. Storm Island was his destiny, he told Elisabeth as they stepped off the skiff onto the rickety dock for the first time. After all, it was already named for him.

Elisabeth wasn't so sure, but Franklin was born with a unique skill—the ability to convince anyone in the vicinity that his desires were theirs as well. Over the years that skill had seen him labeled a genius, a charmer, a charlatan, and a mystic, depending upon who was doing the labeling . . . but to Elisabeth, he was Frank, the man she'd fallen in love with, for better or worse (in those days, it was still better).

Together, they'd made the house a project, rebuilding the island as a private sanctuary. While the Park Avenue penthouse and the London rowhouse and the ranch in Wyoming had all hosted politicians and power brokers, Storm Island was reserved for family and extremely close friends, exclusively. Franklin knew better than anyone that the way to keep things valuable was to keep them secret. Everyone loved the promise of a secret, after all.

Everyone loved to lie about knowing those secrets, too. In tech and New York society alike, there was always someone ready to regale dinner party guests with wild tales of the private playground of an eccentric billionaire. And because everyone lied, no one knew who was telling the truth, making the house the stuff of legend. In stories, it was full of excess and oddity, and Franklin delighted in confirming the outrageous descriptions that inevitably came back to him, printed in society pages and asked about in interviews.

Not one of them was accurate: not the expansive topiary garden (nor, sadly, the life-sized elephant within); not the outdoor swimming pool to rival Hearst Castle's (impractical for New England winters and easily debunked by Google Earth); not the secret, underground lair, full of technological inventions in the vein of the Bat Cave (the place didn't even have reliable Wi-Fi, by Franklin's design).

What did exist was a house that smelled like history and Murphy's oil soap and the hint of the YSL Opium perfume that Elisabeth had worn for as long as anyone had thought to notice, and teemed with memories that stung as much as they soothed as Alice climbed the stairs to her childhood bedroom—the best thing about Storm Manor.

By the time Alice was born, Franklin and Elisabeth had already assigned large bedrooms on the second floor to Greta, then seven, and Sam, a five-year-old boy king. With their parents having commandeered a large portion of the third floor for their primary suite, Alice was left to the tower—a small, circular turret that rose from the southwest corner of the house, accessible by a narrow staircase tucked behind a door at the far end of the third-floor hallway.

There was something to be said for the fact that the Storms assigned the child who'd been . . . not a *mistake* exactly, but absolutely a *surprise*, to the tower room like a lost princess in a fairy tale, but that was be-tween Alice and her therapist every other Friday at 10:15 A.M. (therapy was another mark against her, if anyone was counting).

She made a mental note to move this week's session as she tossed her bags onto the bed, still covered in the tufted turquoise bedspread that had been there for as long as she could remember. The room was a time capsule of faded photographs on the fireplace mantel, shells and stones from childhood beachcombing excursions, second-place ribbons from riding camp hanging on gilded mirrors harvested from wherever par-ents found furnishings for their third child's second bedroom.

Elisabeth Storm had been born into New England money so old that it no longer existed, which meant a Puritanical loathing for trap-pings of overt wealth (private island aside), so it had not mattered that Franklin had been a self-made billionaire several times over when Alice arrived. There were very few things in the house that matched the chrome and steel and sapphire glass that had built the Storm name. Instead, it was filled with antiques collected from the Winslow branch of the family tree.

Alice made her way to the large windows inlaid in the curved wall and the breathtaking view she'd taken for granted before. Windows on three sides of the round space provided stunning views of the island: ancient trees, dominated by the enormous oak to the east; the small building that housed the fog bell on the southern tip, open ocean be-yond; and to the west, the dock and boathouse that greeted those who came in by boat from Wickford, in the distance.

Morning flooded the room with golden light and something like magic, because the years were suddenly gone and she was a kid again, watching the water, her music loud enough to annoy the whole house, wondering if she could hitch a ride with Charlie back to the mainland so she could linger outside the ice-cream shop with the cute boy behind the counter.

The budding romance she'd dreamed of had never materialized. Once she'd lied to him about having a summer job at the diner where his aunt worked (terrible coincidence, that), everything went south.

But Alice had her first taste of pretending to be someone else—someone who hadn't been sculpted by her parents—and that had been the beginning of the end.

Of course, the end had been a long time coming.

She lifted her fingers and set them to the glass, her gaze shifting to the water she'd crossed that morning, salty and crisp, already full of would-be captains sailing the last, lingering week of summer. In the distance, a handful of fishing boats were returning to Wickford Harbor, full of lobster and crab. A memory flashed, her father eating oysters on the docks at eight in the morning, bright-eyed and laughing with a group of fishermen as Alice stood at a distance.

This is the life.

Her throat grew tight. With sorrow, of course. But frustration, too, at the way it evoked *what might have been* rather than *what actually was*.

"Nope," she whispered the answer. She was postponing therapy that week. In a healthy way.

Alice spun away from her window and made for her bags to retrieve the only distraction a thirty-three-year-old woman could find in her childhood bedroom while hiding from her family.

Her phone.

Connecting to Wi-Fi, she watched as the red bubbles she'd ignored on the train the night before became angrier: twenty-three voicemails, one hundred and forty new emails. Two hundred and thirteen new text messages. She started there, opening the app and scrolling, already exhausted.

Her boss. Eventually.

The neighbor across the hall. Later.

A reporter from the *Times*. Absolutely not.

A few friends from high school she still kept in touch with. Unavoidable.

Griffin. She sucked in a breath at the bold name—one she'd worked hard to avoid since July Fourth, when he'd broken her heart and left her alone, with no good reason except . . . *It doesn't feel right anymore, babe.* She hovered over his name, unable to avoid the text preview. *Alleycat.*

She winced at the pet name. He'd been her partner for five years and played the role so well even she'd been fooled (he certainly wasn't such a good actor on stage). *I just saw the news and I don't even know what to sa . . .*

"Then don't," she whispered, exercising incredible strength (superhuman, really), swiping to delete the thread without opening it. Before she could change her mind.

Gabi.

Alice opened that thread, a string of unanswered texts populating the left side of the screen, increasingly urgent. Before she could read them all, the phone vibrated in her hand, her best friend's face flashing beneath the incoming Wi-Fi call.

Alice put the phone to her ear and opened her suitcase. "I regret setting you up with read receipts."

"So do I! You know all those songs about being left on read? Try being left on *unread*!" Gabi had been Alice's closest friend since halfway through their first year at Amherst, where they'd been reluctant roommates from wildly different worlds (was any world the same as Alice's?). After a few months, their mutual love of bell hooks and *Gossip Girl* (feminist cognitive dissonance be damned) forged their friendship, and by the end of their first year, Gabi was the only person on campus (outside of the Board of Trustees) who knew the truth about Alice's family. She'd been sworn to secrecy during the helicopter ride to Boston when Alice had broken her arm. Her only response to the revelation? *I guess that explains why you're so fucking precious.*

They'd been inseparable ever since.

"It's been eighteen hours since you texted me last. What the hell, Alice?" A pause, Gabi moving on her end, getting out of bed. "And every call going straight to voicemail? I thought you were dead."

Alice looked down at the contents of the suitcase, a bizarre mix of toiletries, shoes, and clothes that might or might not be useful in the next few days (pack in haste, repent at leisure). She pulled out a pair of white slip-on sneakers and tossed them into the corner of the room. "I'm not dead. Cell service on this island is nonexistent."

It was a reality Franklin could have changed if he'd wanted to, but there was nothing her father loved more than imposing control on his visitors like a benevolent dictator—all those William Randolph Hearst biographies he'd read had left a powerful mark. So it was spotty Internet beamed in from the mainland or nothing.

Another voice murmured in the background. "She knows what I mean," Gabi said before returning to Alice. "Was that insensitive? Referencing death? Roxanne says it's insensitive."

"You're a lawyer; I expect a level of insensitivity." Alice carried her toiletry bag to a low table beneath one of the windows. She watched the boats come in across the water.

"Exactly. It's part of my charm." Gabi didn't hesitate. "And Roxanne only cares because she's desperate to know the family gossip."

An outraged squawk sounded in the background, and Alice laughed at the familiar back-and-forth. Roxanne Wolf was the society editor for *Bonfire Magazine,* one of the few print magazines that had both the respect of New York's literati and enough money to keep itself afloat. Years earlier, it was Roxanne who'd helped Alice tell the story that had changed everything—the one that had demolished public goodwill for Storm, decimated the company's C-suite, and destroyed her relationship with her father.

And though the story could have sent Roxanne's career into the stratosphere, instead she'd passed it to a colleague she trusted, refusing to be the instrument of whatever unavoidable repercussions would visit Alice. When push came to shove, Roxanne would always choose their long-standing friendship over column inches, and all three of them knew it.

Gabi was still talking. "Where've you been? Are you okay?"

"My phone was off."

A pause. "Yeah, well, that sounds like something that should be for other people. Not me."

Alice smiled as, despite the questionable connection, she heard the quiet slide of the pocket door that separated the bedroom and living room in Gabi and Roxanne's Boerum Hill garden co-op. She closed her eyes and wished she was there, in that room, full of thrifted rugs and comfortable furniture and enough books to cut the usable square footage in half.

"Tell me," Gabi prompted.

Alice stared down at the glittering sea, one of the most beautiful views in the world, surely. "It's weird."

"That makes sense."

"No, I mean, it's . . ." She paused, searching for the right way to describe her feelings. A futile effort. Instead, she said, "The paparazzi met me at the train station."

"Oh shit. Really? Do you want Roxanne to get into it? I mean, I guess your dad's people could also—"

Her dad's people. Even dead, he had people. How was that not weird?

"No," Alice said. "I took— It's taken care of. And I'm on the island now, anyway."

"Ah. The island." In all the years of their friendship, Gabi had only been to Storm Island a handful of times. A spring break during college. A few weekends over the summers after college, until Alice stopped coming back. "And?"

"And . . ." She hesitated. On the other end of the call, Gabi waited until, finally, Alice finished. "Five more days."

"That bad, huh?"

"Well, please remember that my family isn't exactly good at . . . feelings."

"And you, so great at them," Gabi said, dryly.

"Hey! I'm . . . getting better."

"You are," Gabi replied instantly, in that way best friends did, knowing when to recognize flaws and when to absolutely ignore them. "How are you doing?"

"I'm . . . okay?" What else was she supposed to say?

"Bullshit. Do you want me to come?"

Yes.

But the Storms together like this, in whatever feeling this was—was it grief yet? It still felt like something else. Like Franklin was about to walk in the back door with his boots full of mud and throw them all into competition with one another—the first one to reach the north end of the island, the one who climbed to the highest branch of the red oak, the one who could name the painters on the walls of the library, the one who knew the Storm Inc. stock price at the opening bell. So maybe it was denial. But whatever it was—calling in reinforcements this soon would be admitting she couldn't hack it. Embarrassing.

A small white skiff cut across the Bay in the distance, nearly identical to the one she'd taken that morning. Alice raised a hand, her fingers dancing over the trail of white waves in its wake. "My mom invited people here for Monday. I don't know what it is. A memorial of some kind, ostensibly, but knowing my mom it will be an open bar and a string quartet or something. My dad wasn't religious, so I'm not even sure what we're doing with . . ." She didn't want to say *the body.* "Anyway. You don't have to—"

"I'll be there," Gabi said, unequivocal. Like their friendship. "Text me the details."

"You should bring Roxanne. It's a nice time of year."

"Oh, cool, because I was planning to bookend my best friend's father's funeral with some casual leaf peeping."

Alice couldn't hold back her laugh, returning to her suitcase and sorting through the contents. A black hoodie. A pair of ripped jeans. Two black tank tops. "Okay. Well bring her anyway."

Why so many bras? Why so few socks?

Why paintbrushes, but no paint?

"I will. How's your mom?"

A black dress, at least. A pair of heels.

"The same, but with additional unresolved anxiety."

"Fun! And everyone else is there?"

"Oh yes. The whole gang. Sam's being an asshole, Greta is fretting about my mom. I haven't seen the kids. Or Sam's wife, but I'm sure she's still terrible." The product of a billionaire father who'd spoiled her rotten before landing in prison for a few decades, Sila lacked capacity for change.

"Emily?" Alice's younger sister, the baby of the family. Ran a crystal shop in Wickford, burned sage like it meant something, and despite being the flake of the family, was everyone's favorite Storm . . . even Alice's.

The feeling was no longer mutual. "I haven't seen her yet."

"I thought everyone was there?"

"She's here, but I only got here this morning." Alice opened a dresser drawer and shoved everything inside.

"Didn't you leave last night?"

"I"—the words stuck in her throat as she realized where the line of questioning was going, and she closed the drawer with a smooth *thud*— "did."

"Where'd you stay last night?"

"At a motel near the train station."

"How come?" A pause. Then, sharply, "Holy shit, is Griffin there?" Gabi said *Griffin* like other people say *cockroach*. "That fucking guy. We all do things in the throes of grief, Alice, but surely we could avoid doing those things with that bridge troll."

Alice laughed. The problem was, Griffin wasn't a bridge troll. He was handsome and warm and funny and disarmingly honest (at least, he'd seemed to be)—exactly the opposite of everything Alice had been raised to want, which was enough for her to ignore all the reasons he was wrong for her, especially once her father had made his disapproval clear.

And then he'd dumped her with no explanation (so, maybe he was a little bit of a bridge troll).

"Do I have to remind you that you liked him?"

"Exactly why I loathe him now—I had to fully recalibrate my asshole meter after he—" A beat while Gabi collected herself. "God. Is he *back*?"

"You could have more faith in me, you know."

"I have endless faith in you in all things but this. My god, you're growing out *bangs* because of him. *I* practically got bangs because of him."

"Okay, first, that is a low blow; I was in a place. And second, I wasn't with Griffin last night." The words were barely out of her mouth when she realized what she'd given away.

"But you were with . . . someone else?" Gabriela Romero-Jiménez, the best attorney in the Brooklyn public defender's office, entered the chat.

"I have to go," Alice said.

"You absolutely do not have to go, you liar."

"Objection. Combative," Alice retorted.

"Overruled!"

Gabi's shout was punctuated by a knock at Alice's door. "Oh, shit. I really do have to go."

"No! Who is there? Literally no one is more important than me in this moment."

Alice laughed as the door opened and her younger sister's head poked through the gap, a perfect replica of their mother's face, albeit with a few more freckles (freckles wouldn't dream of taking up residence on Elisabeth's cheeks). "I have to go!"

"Is it someone famous? The president? The head of the World Bank?" Gabi asked in her ear.

"I don't even know who the head of the World Bank is," Alice said, before adding, "It's Emily."

"Ah," Gabi said, understanding more than Alice let on. "You should go, then. Tell her I said hi."

"Gabi says hi," she said to her sister, who offered a little wave and stepped into the room. She looked as she always did, ready for yoga or meditation or an emergency Reiki session—barefoot, in a tight black tank top and printed, wide-leg, gray samurai pants. "She says hi back."

"Text me about Monday."

"I will." Dropping her phone onto her bed, Alice crossed to Emily, stopping before she could hug her, not knowing if they did that anymore. "Hi."

They had hugged, though. Before. They'd been the pair, Emily so much closer in age to Alice than to the others. But now, Alice hesitated, and finally, Emily reached for her. "Hi."

Where Greta was cool rigidity and Sam was brash arrogance, Emily was the least guarded of the siblings. At least, she had been. Open and authentic in a way none of the rest of them were, which was ironic as her business—a holistic healing shop on the mainland—relied entirely on tourists with fat wallets and slim sense to stay afloat.

Or, rather, it *would be* entirely reliant on those things, if their father hadn't bankrolled the whole thing mere weeks after Emily graduated from college—a fact that set off Sam and Greta at every turn, despite Franklin having bankrolled Greta's entire life as an unfinished novelist and lunch date for their mom, and given Sam an office down the hall, where he got to play grown-up while their father paid for Sam's kids' private school and Sila's . . . whatever Sila was into at any given moment.

Maybe it was Emily's age—five years younger than Alice, with all the privilege of the baby of the family. Maybe the mistrust that had been coded into the rest of them had run out before Emily's DNA twisted into a double helix, but where the rest of the family hid their truths, fearing discovery and manipulation, Emily lived out in the open. She talked about feelings. Told people she loved them. It was equal parts refreshing and exhausting, and no one could explain quite how she'd turned out like she did.

Not even Alice, which was why she'd avoided her sister's early attempts to keep in contact, when she wasn't ready for feelings. Emily's honesty demanded honesty in return, and Alice hadn't been ready for that. And once she was ready, it had been Emily who'd disappeared. Tired of waiting.

It had been too late to apologize. At least, it had felt that way.

Alice stepped into Emily's hug, almost tight, almost cleansing, and then . . . over. There and gone—guarded—before the youngest Storm stepped back, out of Alice's grasp.

Oh. Alice let her go, disappointment hitting her like a wave, threatening to take out her sea legs.

"You came," Emily said, lowering her arms, a dozen beaded bracelets (labradorite, malachite, moonstone, peridot—you get it) clattering together.

"Of course I came."

Emily nodded. "I see that. I'm happy for it."

Words that felt like accusation or manipulation from everyone else in the family were full of something else here—truth. And somehow, that filled Alice with something closer to grief than anything she'd felt yet. Not even Emily had been sure she'd come.

Not even Emily could see the truth of why she'd left in the first place.

Alice swallowed her angry defense. *Practice radical acceptance,* her therapist would say. *Be open.* "How have you been?"

She barely avoided an outward cringe. Emily didn't seem to notice the pedestrian question, responding with a small delicate shrug. "Okay. You know. Until yesterday. But this part is nice; I wasn't sure you would . . ."

"Yeah. No one was," Alice said, trying to take the words at face value. Ignoring the words that filled her throat. *He was my father, too. Even though he would have preferred that weren't the case.*

"I was hoping you'd come for the Fourth." July Fourth, the long weekend that had been claimed by Franklin and Elisabeth forever—a holiday held for the family, in the tradition of all old New England money. If your ancestors fought in the Revolution, you were called to celebrate them with seersucker and boat shoes at the family compound on Independence Day.

Alice had missed the last five of them, but in June, for the first time in years, Emily had called her. Asked her to come. And though Alice had said she'd try, they'd both known she wouldn't. And she hadn't. "I—" She stopped, thinking about all the reasons she hadn't been on the island for five years. "I couldn't make it."

"Right," Emily said. "You're a busy person."

"What's that supposed to mean?"

"Nothing," Emily lied. "You're busy. You couldn't come to July Fourth. I wasn't surprised. It wasn't the first invitation you declined."

And there it was. The reminder that even as the baby of the family, all joy and silliness and delight, Emily was still a Storm, still able to seat a sharp point. Alice didn't misunderstand. "Dad couldn't have been clearer that I wasn't welcome here, Em. Mom, too."

"Yeah, but it wasn't their wedding," Emily replied. "It was mine."

A small family affair, the gossip sites had reported three years earlier, alongside blurry photos shot from a drone high above the island. Emily and Claudia in white boho dresses beneath a bower of flowers against one of the island's ancient stone walls. Barely twenty people in attendance. None of them Alice.

"I'm sorry," she said. And she meant it, despite it coming out sharp and jagged and heavy with resentment, because no one had ever thought to apologize to her for the way she'd been exiled. "Is Claudia here?"

"She will be. She's cooking tonight, so she went to get stuff from the farm."

Alice's brows rose. "Mom's letting her cook?"

Emily half smiled, the most she was willing to share. "Mom likes her more than the rest of us."

"Can't really blame her," Alice said, a peace offering.

"Right?" A glimpse of old Emily, her childhood companion. With Greta and Sam so close in age, they'd ganged up on their annoying younger sisters and then left, making their way in the world (ish), and leaving Alice and Emily behind to become a team—until everything had changed.

"Em—" Alice began, not really knowing what she was going to say.

"Maybe you'd like to meditate later?" Emily said at the same time, her own peace offering. "I could guide your practice if you like."

"Maybe," Alice demurred, resisting the urge to laugh at the idea that she had a meditation practice. Alice had anxiety practice. Irritation practice. And these days, what-the-fuck-is-happening practice. "How are you doing?"

A hesitation. "Pretty bad. You?"

Me, too. "It feels . . . strange."

"That's Dad's energy. It's not vibrating at the same frequency."

It isn't vibrating at any frequency, Alice wanted to say. *Dad is dead.* But she was unwilling to upset the truce they'd reached. Such as it was.

Just as the silence started to feel uncomfortable, Elisabeth called up the stairs. "Emily! Alice! You'd better come down here." Their mother's shout might have been described as sharp if it didn't sound so resigned. "We have a guest."

one hand fiddling with the base of the Rodin study on the lacquered end table beside her.

Sam somehow took up two squares of the enormous couch, leaving the third for Alice. Surrendering to the inevitable, she headed for the spot that had been hers for decades, tucking one leg beneath her as she settled into the soft leather, turning her back to the Eames chair nearby. The one that sat empty. The one everyone else was studiously avoiding.

Instead, they focused on Jack.

Jack, who had sat next to her on the train, and hadn't said a word. Who had followed her out into the night. Who'd kissed her in the dark and stepped up to protect her and then taken her to bed . . . pretending to be a good guy, all the while having been sent by her dead father for whatever this was about to become.

A game, no doubt. Franklin loved a game.

"Where is Arthur?" Elisabeth interrupted, before Jack could say more. Arthur Settlesworth, Franklin's forever lawyer, who came from a long line of estate lawyers if his name was any indication.

Jack paused, letting the question hang in the thick summer air, as though he knew more than he was willing to say. Which of course he did. "He's in New York."

"And Lauren?" Greta asked, tightly. Lauren Peabody, the head of Storm Inc. communications, no doubt somewhere close, figuring out the best way to spin Franklin's death into a higher stock price.

"Also at headquarters." Jack crouched and unzipped the backpack at his feet. The one he'd slung over his shoulder the night before, when he'd punched a photographer and stolen some SD cards for her.

Not for her, though. For her father.

"Evelyn?" Emily plaintively requested Franklin's longtime assistant— the woman they'd all called to temperature-check their father when they needed money, or a lifeline, or both.

"At headquarters," he said, sounding a touch kinder when speaking to Emily.

"The Men?" Sam said, his usually unbothered tone now clipped.

Mark Houseman, Larry Manford, and Adam Grossman, a trio of

board members her father had known since what seemed like birth, and whom he collectively referred to as The Men.

Jack produced a stack of plain white envelopes from the bag. She could hear a thread of irritation in his voice as he said, "It's just me. Franklin sent *me*."

"Who *are* you?"

Everyone in the room turned to Alice, their surprise palpable.

"What?" Now Elisabeth sounded irritated.

"I've never seen this man before," Alice said, hesitating for a heartbeat—less—instantly aware of the lie in the words. Except it wasn't a lie, really. She hadn't ever seen this version of the man—shirtsleeves rolled down, carrying some kind of final message from her father. The man she'd seen the night before had been a different one altogether.

Hadn't he?

She didn't have time to think on that. Not when Elisabeth said, in that way mothers do, "Alice. You know Jack."

"I swear to you I don't," Alice retorted, looking to him again, finding his gaze calm and unwavering, as though everything were completely normal. As though her thoughts weren't at sea, desperate for something to cling to. As though she hadn't clung to him the night before. *When he'd clearly known exactly who she was.*

She let her frustration slide into anger and repeated herself. "Who *are* you?"

Another man might have cleared his throat. Or shifted his weight from one long leg to the other. Not him. "I'm Jack Dean. I work"— a pause—"worked for your father."

Sam huffed a derisive laugh. "That's putting it mildly."

Alice looked to him. "Mildly how?"

"You know how they say every parent has a favorite child?" Her brother pointed to Jack. "There's Dad's. Jack Dean, the golden boy. Managing director."

While Sam spoke, Jack studiously avoided her, sorting through his envelopes.

Coward.

"Managing director of what?" Alice asked.

Sam replied. "Of Dad's right hand. The son he wished he had."

"Oh, for God's sake," Elisabeth muttered, shifting in her chair as Emily made a comforting sound in Sam's direction.

Emily had more patience than Greta, who'd clearly heard this particular song before, and said, "Do we have to do this now, Sam?"

"No. By all means, let Jack say his piece." Sam raised his hands. "He hates me, by the way."

Jack returned his attention to the matter at hand, as though Sam hadn't spoken, which Alice would have appreciated for the way it must have infuriated her brother—if she hadn't decided there was nothing about this man worthy of appreciation. "As I was saying—"

The door to the room opened, revealing Sam's wife, an impossibly slim white woman dressed head to toe in polo chic from Ralph Lauren circa 2004, white button-down, tan jodhpurs, and knee-high riding boots, her golden-blond hair pulled up in a high, tight ponytail. The only thing missing was a crop, which was too bad, as Alice was certain someone in the room was bound to require correction soon.

"Lovely. Here's Sila," Elisabeth said in a tone that to the untrained ear might have sounded warm but was absolutely not. "Why do you look as though you've been riding, dear? Have we imported horses?"

"Oh, Elisabeth!" Sila's high-pitched laugh was wildly out of place in the room. "You're such a card!"

The sisters shared a look at the words. Sila Evans had been raised in a gleaming penthouse apartment in midtown with all the trappings of new money made on the stock market. Her father, Mitchell, started in investments when five thousand dollars was enough to become hundreds of millions, after which he'd married Sila's mother (thirty years his junior) and made sure his only daughter didn't ever have to pretend at being a princess because she believed she was one already.

Mitchell's connections in New York and Silicon Valley had thrown Sila into the Storm children's orbit, where she'd aimed for Sam (more than once) and eventually hit her mark. A surprise pregnancy arrived with perfect timing, and the pair married in a quick summer wedding splashed across the society pages, mere months before the Evans family found itself splashed across very different newsprint; it turned out

Mitchell Evans had been the architect of one of the largest Ponzi schemes in history and was now serving 190 years in federal prison.

Sila had dropped the Evans from her name as quickly as possible, blithely expecting the Storms to clasp her to their bosom. If Elisabeth's baleful gaze was any indication, there hadn't been any movement on that front in the last five years.

"I hope I'm not interrupting," Sila said, absolutely hoping she was interrupting. She squeezed onto the center cushion between Sam's sprawl and Alice, fashioned a sympathetic look, and set a hand to Alice's thigh. "Hi," she mouthed, "we didn't think we'd see you!"

Alice offered a tight smile before her sister-in-law, ever undeterred, delivered one of her trademark whispers to Sam—too quiet to hear without studious attention and simultaneously too loud to ignore. "What's Jack doing here?"

Great. Even *Sila* knew who Jack was.

Alice looked to Jack. "So, you worked for our father, and he sent you to meet with us the day after his death?"

He nodded, the words spurring him into action. "It goes without saying that I wish I were here under different circumstances. I'm sorry for your loss."

The whole room ignored him—Storms rarely made time for platitudes. Sam pointed to the envelopes in Jack's hand. "What are those?"

He lifted them. "Letters."

The whole room froze. Alice could hear her breath, reed thin.

"From Dad?" Greta clarified.

"For you, yes," Jack replied.

Her father had left them letters. Of course he had. If anyone in the world liked a dramatic entrance, it was Franklin Storm. Why not a dramatic exit? But how? And why? And why did this *stranger* have them?

God, she'd slept in the same room as her father's final words the night before, and she hadn't known.

"That bastard," Sam said softly, extending a hand. "Let's see them."

Jack shook his head. "Not yet."

Everyone's eyes went wide.

"Why not?" Sila asked.

Jack didn't look at her. "I should explain why I'm here."

"Yeah, why *are* you here, Jack?" Emily asked, finally speaking up, her thumb stroking over the foot of the small Rodin.

A brief pause. Barely there. Just enough for Alice to notice the slight straightening of Jack's spine, like he was about to take a punch. Except he wasn't. He was about to deliver one. "I'm here to articulate the terms of your inheritance."

A collective breath filled the room, the house, the island. And then . . . Alice laughed. Everyone looked at her, a spectrum of shock and censure, but she didn't care. Instead, she said, "Oh, come on. Of *course* there are terms for the inheritance. Dad probably spent years deciding the whos and hows and whats of it all." She looked to Jack, still not moving. "Let me guess. A Storm Olympics redux."

A tiny furrow marked the space between his dark brows. Confusion loud enough for Alice to hear.

She explained. "Who could swim the fastest, run the farthest, jump the highest, spell the most complicated word, do the most difficult long division, name the most presidents. Who went to the best college, brought home the best partner, did his bidding with the least resistance. Everything was a competition for that man's praise. And now, we're expected to compete for his money."

Jack cleared his throat.

"Go on, then," she urged, feeling strangely triumphant—she'd spent every hour since she'd learned of Franklin's death wondering when the next shoe would drop, and finally, here it was, something she understood. "Do your worst."

"If this is about the trust, then why isn't Arthur here?" Sam asked.

"Arthur isn't here because I was tasked with delivering the terms." If he wasn't careful, he was going to take out the Modigliani in the corner with one of his bombs.

"What the fuck?" This, from Sam.

"Language, Sam," Elisabeth said instantly, before, "That's not possible, I would have known about it. Our wills clearly state that Arthur is the executor."

"Arthur is the executor of your wills, Elisabeth," Jack said with infinite patience. "This trust is a separate entity, consisting of Franklin's extensive wealth and holdings, including his stake in Storm Inc."

Stake was a small, insignificant word—wildly unassuming for what they were discussing, which was 35 percent of the largest publicly traded company in the world. An amount of money so large that it produced more interest in a year than a person (or five, in this case) could reasonably spend. It was generational wealth beyond anyone's wildest dreams—and if Jack was to be believed, it wasn't guaranteed to trickle down to the second generation.

"Holy shit," Sam said.

"Language, Samuel."

"It doesn't just pass to us?" Greta asked, leaning forward. "We're his heirs. Isn't it ours? What happens to it?"

"Your father left clear instructions for what comes next," Jack said, perfectly calm, and Alice had a wild moment of remembering the night before, when he'd cursed and ordered her into the car to hide her from paparazzi in a tone far less calm. She swallowed a manic laugh at the thought that a photograph was more unsettling to this man than tens of billions of dollars.

"Which is?" Emily asked.

Jack hesitated. His gaze slid to Alice, briefly, and she ignored the way her breath quickened and her body went warm. Her body was a traitor. So was Jack. "A game, of sorts."

She nodded. "There it is. So what is it? Survive a week without food or shelter? Dive off Moonstone Cliff and swim around the island? Eat a dozen serrano peppers in one sitting?" It could be anything. Franklin loved a challenge, the wilder the better—hence his glider crashing into a South County horse pasture the previous morning.

Jack lifted the envelopes. "These will explain."

He delivered them, each falling into hands eager for whatever nonsense competition they were in for. Hands willing to do whatever it took to ensure their cut. Because wasn't that why they'd been putting up with their father's bullshit for all these years?

But Alice hadn't put up with it, and so her hands remained empty. She closed them into fists in her lap while envelopes were torn open around the room—the sound of her final punishment.

He'd never forgiven her.

Greta read hers first. "*Why?*"

Emily stared down at her letter, brow furrowed.

"Fuck this," Sam said, Sila's eyes wide as she read over his shoulder. "Fuck this, and fuck him." He looked up at Jack. "And fuck you too, while we're at it."

Jack didn't flinch. Later, Alice would marvel at his disinterest in her brother's ire, considering the weight of the moment. As though Sam hadn't spoken, Jack said, "You've each been assigned a task—or series of them—which, upon completion, will activate the distribution of the trust."

"*Why?*" It seemed to be all Greta could say.

"It's the Storm Olympics," Alice answered. "Dad's favorite time of year, when he pits his kids against one another and waits for the last one standing."

"Fuck you, Jack," Sam repeated. "You've had a hand in my future for way too long. I know you've been whispering in his ear for months about me. *Years.* I'm calling a goddamn lawyer." Whatever was in Sam's letter—he *really* didn't like it.

"What do you have to do, Sam?"

"Descale boats. Clean the fog bell. Stain the dock." He crushed the letter in his hand. "Manual labor." He cleared his throat. "*Reshingling?*"

Greta's lips curved in dry amusement. "That's really going to mess up your manicure, Samuel."

"What Sam is trying to say," Sila said, as though Sam hadn't been extremely clear about what he was trying to say, "is that these really aren't the kind of things the *future CEO of Storm* should be doing."

His sisters' brows rose in unison, as Alice said, "Pardon?"

Sila continued, speaking for Sam. "Well, who else? He's the Storm."

"We're all Storms," Greta scoffed.

"Of course. But not like *Sam* is a Storm." Sila set a hand to her husband's thigh. "*Sam* is the future of Storm Inc. And with the kids"—she paused for effect, a smug smile settling on her face as she looked pointedly at Elisabeth—"we're the future of the Storm *family*, as well."

"Oh, *please*," Greta snapped. A bear, poked.

"The point is," Sam said, "he can't make us play a game to inherit."

It was almost impossible to believe that her father would turn the whole thing over to the empirically least serious of the children, but Alice was absolutely the wrong one to point that out, considering her past with her father, and the company.

Jack had clearly had enough of the children's sniping. "You're welcome to consult a lawyer, but I assure you it is a legal silent trust. And it was your father's wish that you not know his plan for the estate."

"Even now," Alice said, drawing everyone's attention.

"I don't . . ." For the first time, Jack seemed confused.

"Oh, come on. There's more to this game than a few final words." She waved at her siblings, all clinging to their white envelopes. "This is *Dad*. There's always a second shoe to drop." She returned her attention to Jack. "He *still* doesn't want us to know his plan."

He didn't reply; he didn't have to.

Her father must have loved him.

"We shouldn't be surprised," Elisabeth said, something unpleasant in her voice. "There was nothing Franklin liked more than control. And here we are." She lifted her letter and looked to Jack. "There, I've said something nice. Now what?"

"I'm not sure that was what he meant, Elisabeth."

"I'm not sure I care, *Jack*."

Alice looked to her mother. "What's that mean? 'Said something nice'?"

For a moment, it seemed as though Elisabeth might not answer. Finally, she said, "All right. I'll go first. Your father requests that I *tell the truth*. Though I can't for the life of me think of what that might mean. I'm perfectly truthful."

Alice bit her tongue. No one in the world elided truth like Elisabeth Storm.

"And on top of that, I'm to—" Elisabeth lifted the letter and read aloud. "'Say one nice thing about Franklin every day. Aloud. To another person.'" She looked to Jack. "For the rest of my *life?*"

Alice might have laughed at the horror in her mother's voice if she weren't so impressed by her father's incisive request. Saying something nice about Franklin would be nearly impossible for Elisabeth, and she'd once had to make conversation with Silvio Berlusconi for the duration of a state dinner.

"No," Jack said. "For one week."

Of course. A ticking clock. Even from the grave, her father loved a mess.

"What does that mean?" Greta snapped, revealing an edge that she almost always kept dulled. Whatever her task, it wasn't an easy one.

Jack explained. "If the requests are not honored within one week of Franklin's death, you are no longer eligible for the inheritance."

Alice had to hand it to her father, he'd always known how to motivate the family into action.

"Who is no longer eligible? Just the person who fails? Or all of us?" Greta clarified.

"All of you."

The family stiffened, the stakes growing higher—they not only had to worry about themselves, but also about one another. Sila sat forward. "What's everyone else have to do?"

Greta's letter collapsed in her tight fist. "We have to do whatever Dad wants. Again. Because it will always be what he wants. Forever."

The group went quiet. Alice looked to Jack, who did not have the grace to look uncomfortable, even when he met her narrow gaze.

Sam was furious. "This is insane. If one of us fails, we all lose? That's *millions.*"

"*Billions,*" Sila clarified, as though she checked NASDAQ:STOM every morning. Which she no doubt did.

Sam looked like he wanted to do crime. "And you? What do you get?"

Alice's gaze narrowed on the newcomer. What *did* he get for playing messenger? "That's not relevant," Jack said.

It seemed incredibly relevant, but no one spoke as Sam waved a hand in Jack's direction, looking to Alice. "You see? Dad's favorite."

Alice was beginning to believe it.

"This isn't a game, Jack," Emily said. "This is our *life*."

"What if we don't play?" Greta asked.

"We're fucking playing," Sam said. "Whatever is in your fucking letter—you're doing it, Greta."

She turned cold eyes on him. "Careful, Sam, you losing out on your share of the inheritance might be worth me losing mine."

And there it was—the game, afoot. Franklin would have delighted in watching the entire family struggle between winning together and sticking it to each other. Although the Storms had been raised to believe in Storms above all, no one had ever suggested that exiling family members wasn't fair play.

Look at Alice.

"What's he want you to do?" Sam was needling Greta. "Take the stick out of your ass?"

Greta folded her letter and placed it back in her envelope. "It's not your business."

Silence fell as she realized her misstep. If Greta didn't want everyone to know what her assigned task was, she shouldn't have made it a thing. Sam smirked in her direction, tucking his power away for future use, and directed his attention to Emily and Alice. "And what about you?"

Emily clutched her envelope tighter. "You're being an asshole."

He leaned back in his chair and flashed his irritating white teeth. "Tell us or don't. It's all going to come out anyway. Someone has to judge the damn game." He looked to Jack. "Speaking of which, who *is* going to judge the game?"

"I am." Jack spoke with unbelievable calm, like the whole morning was a perfectly ordinary, everyday occurrence. Like ordering lunch. Pastrami on rye with a side of emotional spectacle.

"You'll be here all week?" Alice couldn't keep from blurting out the question. Couldn't keep it from sounding panicked, couldn't keep herself from feeling fully betrayed by his long legs and strong hands and his compass tattoo.

Ironic, that, considering how he had thrown them all so far off course.

No one noticed her chaos (unsurprisingly). Instead, Greta met Jack's gaze. "I'll ask again. If we don't play, what happens to the money?"

"It will be divested."

Brows rose around the room. Elisabeth spoke. "To where?"

"I'm not at liberty to say."

The entire room went still; no one quite able to believe that he'd refused to answer Elisabeth Storm's question. She turned to steel. "I stood by his side while he made every one of those goddamn billions, and you're not at liberty to say where it goes if I can't summon one nice thing about him every day?"

The words were sharp. Accusatory. As though Jack had something to do with the rules. And maybe he did. But he didn't rise to Elisabeth's challenge.

Apparently, to Jack, doing Franklin's bidding, no matter how bizarre, *was* perfectly ordinary. Not that he seemed that interested in Storm family chaos, which was really delivering—frustration and anger and no small amount of entitlement setting them all off. "And if you fail to tell the truth, yes."

"And I'm to assume you know the truth, Jack?" The Storm children watched, eyes wide, familiar with the dangerous edge in their mother's tone.

"I would assume it, if I were you," he replied.

Holy shit. He was so composed, it was almost magnificent to watch. Except Alice refused to find anything about this man magnificent ever again.

"This is bananas." Emily broke the silence.

"Exactly!" Sam said, a son on the verge. "We don't *divest* wealth. Dad was a goddamn billionaire and we're just supposed to give up everything because he fucking wills it? That's not how billionaires work!"

"Rules of generational wealth aside, Sam," Alice replied, "I don't think that's what Emily meant."

She didn't like the surprise in Emily's eyes at the words, as though the youngest Storm hadn't expected Alice to understand her, even though Alice had always been the one closest to understanding her. "Um . . . right," Emily said. "I meant, how are we supposed to play one of Dad's stupid games this week? While we *grieve*?"

Sweet Emily. Ever optimistic. The idea that Greta, Sam, or Elisabeth had entertained a single emotional thought about the family or their father's death since Jack had set foot in the house would be laughable if it weren't so clearly impossible.

And then they proved it.

"We're going to call the lawyers," Sila vowed again, in an attempt to comfort a blustering Sam—and herself, no doubt. "This absolutely is not legal. Jack's not even *family*."

It was legal. Franklin Storm would have bribed Congress to make sure it was legal. And Alice wasn't the only one in the room who knew it. They'd seen him bribe Congress before.

Elisabeth was headed for the drink cart in the corner.

"Mom, it's nine in the morning," Alice said.

"Your father would approve," Elisabeth tossed over her shoulder, following with, "That's the truth. Isn't it, Jack?"

Jack let the rhetorical question lie. Apparently he didn't have a death wish.

Too bad.

"I don't understand," Emily said. "Why would Dad do this?"

"Why did Dad do anything?" Alice asked. "Manipulation. Control. His favorite weapons."

Emily shook her head. "What's the point, though?"

Elisabeth lifted a bottle of gin. "You've always had your head in the clouds, Emily. He's dead now. It's time to see him for what he was."

Jesus.

The whole family was ready to take swings wherever they could land them. Whatever it took to win.

Except Alice. Because Alice hadn't received a letter.

She tried to feel relief as her mother peeled a twist off a lemon and dropped it in her cocktail, and Emily wrung her hands, and Greta peppered Jack with questions, and Sila whined, and Sam went on about his attorney, who was also *Franklin's* attorney, so good luck to him.

It was relief she should feel, after all the years of battling her father for her own future. For her own identity. Relief, because he hadn't pulled her into this last, sordid game.

She didn't feel relief, though. She felt—*left out.*

Which was the point.

It didn't matter what she felt, she told herself as she stood and made for the door. For the hallway beyond. For her room. Or maybe outside. Maybe she'd go for a run, though running around and around the island wasn't the most freeing experience.

"Where are you going, Alice?" Elisabeth called after her from where she stood now, by the enormous fireplace, a yawning black marble hearth that must have threatened to sink the boat it came in on a century earlier. "You haven't told us what you're supposed to do."

"Nothing." She met her mother's gaze. "I didn't get a letter."

Everyone looking at her, a Last Supper of self-absorption. That her father had forgotten to include her in his game elicited complex emotions, but the fact that her family hadn't realized it . . . well there wasn't much to do but laugh.

Sam unfroze first, all his attention directed at Jack. "Does that mean she gets her cut free and clear? Or is she not in it?"

"She can't be in it," Sila said, and it was impossible not to hear a thread of glee in her words. "Oh my god. She's out. It's split *four* ways."

It shouldn't be a surprise. It shouldn't hurt so much, when she didn't care about the money at all.

Something flashed in Jack's gaze as he watched her siblings, barely there and impossible to miss. Disgust. And then it was gone, replaced with that unruffled calm that she was coming to realize was his zero state. He looked to his watch, slow and methodical, all the time in the world collected and stored in steel and Swiss movement.

Ignoring Sila, he said, "You'll find, Sam, that it's the nine o'clock hour. If you're planning to vie for your own cut, you're not allowed to speak for another"—he paused—"forty-three minutes."

Around the room, eyes went wide and jaws went slack. Except for Sam's, which narrowed and tightened. But he didn't speak.

Alice looked to her brother, another laugh rising. "You can't speak?" A pause. "I thought he sentenced you to a week's hard labor."

"He did. But that wasn't his only task." Jack answered for him. "During odd-numbered hours, Sam cannot speak."

It would not be too much to describe the response in the room as something close to delight. "At all?" Emily asked.

"At all," Jack confirmed.

"For a whole week!" Greta chortled. "Looks like Dad left us a gift after all."

Rude gestures remained available to Sam, and he was not above using them.

"This isn't fair," Sila whined, making Alice reconsider whether Franklin really had given them a gift—as Sam's silence would only serve to make Sila doubly present. "It's not just the not speaking. We have a whole list! Isn't this what *Charlie* is for?"

"It is strange that *Sam* has to do all this." It was impossible to miss Elisabeth's obvious lack of faith in her only son's abilities to accomplish any of the tasks on the list. Or to keep his mouth shut.

"The jobs are presented to the entire family," Jack interjected, "the kids, too."

"I know we said we didn't need Avery this week," Sila whisper-whined at Sam, "but I think we should bring her out. She can handle all this."

"I'm afraid not," Jack said. "No assistants or outside help are invited."

Sila turned an icy stare on him. "*Invited* suggests we have a choice, Jack."

"Oh please, Sila," Greta snapped. "You'd be here even if you were able to choose. Whatever it takes to secure the bag, right?"

"Greta," Emily said softly. A caution. "Try a centering breath."

Greta was not a centering breath kind of person. Especially not when Sila replied, lifting her chin and leveling her sister-in-law with a cool gaze, "I'm *here,* because *I* carried the *heir.*"

It was a clear dig at Greta, unmarried and without children, and it struck a chord, as it always did. Greta went rigid, knitting her fingers together in her lap to avoid the quieting touch Emily attempted.

Alice was not so subtle. While she didn't always understand Greta, she certainly wasn't about to let Sila take swipes at her. "Unfortunately, Sila, despite our father clearly believing he would rule from on high forever, there's no divine right of kings at play here." She turned to Jack. "Or maybe I'm wrong. Does Sila get anything for *carrying the heir*?"

She didn't miss the response that flashed across his face, fleeting, but clear. *Admiration.* Not that Alice was interested in being admired by him, a deeply unadmirable person. "Not to my knowledge, no."

"Looks like the boats need descaling after all," Alice said with a cool glance at the couple on the couch. Too bad they didn't have to dredge the septic field—if ever there were two people who needed to spend some time knee-deep in shit, it was Sam and Sila. "Anyway, I guess I'll see you all after you're done . . . wringing hands or whatever."

She turned and made to open the door, coming up against immediate resistance. Looking through the crack, she caught the surprised gazes of Sam and Sila's children, Saoirse and Oliver, who had no doubt recently had their ears pressed to the door. Her brows went up and the kids looked terrified, leaving a pang of guilt thrumming through her.

Of course they were nervous, knowing that they shouldn't be there, and not realizing she'd keep their secret. She hadn't seen them since they were nine and four. Alice had been so excited to be Aunt Alice back then, and she'd done the job, taking Saoirse to the circus and finger painting with Oliver. They'd been wild about her—the benefit of being a teacher. But she'd lost them when she'd lost everyone else five years earlier.

And now, it felt too late to win them back.

Before she could prove she wasn't a narc, Jack called out, "Alice."

The sound of her name curled through her, deep and full of something approximating . . . she didn't know what. Kindness? Pity? Probably pity, she decided as she turned to face Jack, who hadn't moved from his spot. Those serious gray eyes held her there, in the room, even as she told herself to turn and leave this chaos to those who'd inherited it. Who wanted it. "What?"

"You're not out."

He'd left her a letter, after all. She hated that she was grateful for it.

A bark from Sam (he must have thought it didn't count as speaking) was followed by a translation from Sila. "What? She doesn't get a task, but she does get the money in the end? That is *so* unfair!"

The protest did not garner sympathy.

"That's the point," Emily said.

"None of it is fair," Greta said, her voice heavy with something Alice couldn't name. "It's never been fair."

"Franklin never cared about fairness," Elisabeth said, lifting the lemon rind from her glass and taking a bite of it, sweet to her bitter. "So. Alice doesn't have to play and wins nonetheless."

It wasn't a win. It all felt awful. She shook her head and told the truth (a mistake). "I don't want to play."

"Oh, please. None of us do, Alice," Greta snapped. "Suck it up."

She looked to Jack. "Where's my letter, then?"

"You didn't get a letter," Jack said. It was definitely pity. "But your father left you a task, nonetheless."

"And what, you're assigned to deliver the blow directly?"

He nodded, the movement stilted. Almost like he regretted it. Which of course he didn't. If her father trusted Jack with playing judge, jury, and executioner for this ridiculous game, then Jack had known exactly what he was walking into. What he'd be doing that morning.

And what about last night? Had that been part of it?

She pushed the thought out of her mind, locking it away, along with all the memories she might have treasured before he'd turned up that morning and made her loathe him for knowing more than she did about her own future.

"You have to stay," he said. "For the entire week."

She laughed in disbelief. "No. I really don't."

It had been five years since she'd been there, and she owed them nothing. She didn't have to do her father's bidding. And she didn't have to stay with her family as they sniped at each other and vied for their lot instead of grieving. And she certainly didn't have to listen to this man who'd made her like him before he lied to her and embarrassed her.

"That's the requirement." He reached down into his bottomless backpack and pulled out a document. The details of the trust, no doubt. "Your father was very clear; your only task is to stay on Storm Island for the week."

Of course it was. Franklin had probably loved making that plan—bringing her back to the island for one final moment of control. A reminder that he remained the most powerful man in the room even now, even dead.

"But that's such an easy task," Sila protested. "It's bullshit!"

"Language," Elisabeth murmured.

"Sila's not wrong, though," Alice pointed out. "And you all know it. This is all bullshit. No way is Dad going to relinquish control when some boats get descaled and a few nice things get said about him and whatever Greta and Emily have to do. There's a second round to this game. And a third, at *least*."

A flood of emotion came, but Alice was quick enough to select the most powerful. Determination. "I, for one, choose not to play it. I'm out. You can have my cut. I'll be one less billionaire for the world to contend with. Let me know when you're ready to get back to planning a funeral."

"Not a funeral," Elisabeth corrected her. "A *celebration*."

"Right. Can't wait." God forbid they get anything like closure out of this. Alice turned on her heel and made for the door, feeling pretty proud of herself—so proud, in fact, that she was considering calling her therapist, after all.

"Alice." Now why did Jack say her name like that? Sure and smooth and commanding, like he could stop her.

Worse, why did she stop?

At least she didn't look back. Later, she'd be glad of that. Especially because of the shock that came when he said, "You can't forfeit. Everyone plays, or no one does."

CHAPTER

6

SOMEONE HAD TAKEN HER clothes.

It seemed impossible—and very strange—but when Alice stepped out of the shower in the small bathroom at the bottom of the steps to the tower, it was to discover that the clean pajamas she'd packed (the only outfit she'd actually nailed) were gone from where she'd hung them on the back of the door.

They were gone along with the dirty clothes she'd shucked to the floor before stepping into the almost unbearably hot spray, hoping she could incinerate the events of the day. The week. The summer, while she was at it.

It had almost worked, until she'd turned off the water, pushed back the curtain, and climbed out of the claw-foot tub to discover someone had been inside the bathroom while she was showering, and they'd stolen her clothes.

And her towel.

As far as an instrument of familial warfare, it was as juvenile as it went, so she had no doubt Sam had something to do with it. Aside from literally anyone with eyeballs being able to identify him as an ass from a distance, it was nine P.M., so he couldn't come and tell her what-ever he was thinking to her face—because he wasn't allowed to speak.

The memory of Jack hard-lining that particular rule that morning had buoyed her spirits a half dozen times that day, as she'd done her best to avoid the family after the morning's revelations—a feat, honestly, as her father's insane estate planning meant her family wanted eyes on her at all times. She'd escaped for a run around the perimeter of the island while Jack, she assumed, was kept busy assuring the rest of the family a fourth, fifth, and thirty-first time that yes, Franklin's trust was legal, and no, there wasn't some easy way out of it.

Her father had probably cackled his way through those letters he'd written, absolutely delighted to orchestrate one final week of chaos. He'd probably had the last, loudest laugh when he'd decided not to write to Alice. Her final punishment. The ultimate proof of her forever exile.

Except Alice wasn't interested in being played from the hereafter. She had friends she loved and a job she liked that paid rent on a one-bedroom in Park Slope (barely, now that she was just one person in there, but she'd make it work) and the glimmer of a future as an honest-to-God artist that was hers alone, in spite of her father's long-standing disdain for the dream. She'd earned it. Without him.

That was why he'd never liked her, wasn't it? Because he couldn't lord it over her with half a dozen things he'd done to give her the life she desired like he had with the rest of the family—subsidizing Greta's for-ever unpublished novel and Sam's career and Sila's myriad club mem-berships and Emily's crystal shop and his grandchildren's schools and camps and ever-changing interests—keeping them all close to home, where he could rule over them.

When people wanted something, Franklin put a hand in his pocket and smiled with a warmth that felt like the sun. But his attention came with a price—control.

And when Alice had stopped paying that price—albeit rather spectacularly—her father had no difficulty turning down the thermo-stat and leaving her in the cold. She'd spent five years discovering the world beyond the Storms, knowing that choosing to be outside their circle meant there was no space for her inside. Franklin and Elisabeth built a family like they were royals: in or out . . . no half measures.

Alice had chosen (or been chosen for): out.

If there'd been any question of her place either in the family or in Franklin's heart, the meeting over which his lieutenant—a man Alice did not know (except biblically, really embarrassing, that)—had presided would clarify it. Her father hadn't even cared enough to leave her any final words.

Instead, he'd left her something far worse: the family. The whole crew came looking for her after Jack had dropped his bombs—presumably to tackle the most urgent issue of the inheritance: keeping Alice on the island, as though she might bolt at any moment.

As though she wouldn't stay for her father's funeral.

Celebration.

Apparently, they'd taken her on as a joint project. And so, for the rest of the afternoon, she'd been visited by her sisters, mother, and brother in a procession reminiscent of Dickens.

Emily and Claudia arrived first, the Ghosts of Labor Day Vibes waylaying her as she returned from her run. For what it was worth, Claudia seemed authentically concerned about Alice's mental state (not great), and Alice could only run the perimeter of the island for so long, so she accepted the session her sister-in-law, a trained massage therapist, offered. Yes, Emily decided to drag out the singing bowl during the process, its ring offering a less-than-relaxing soundtrack, but it was better than what was to come when she returned to the house.

The Ghost of Mothers Present, Elisabeth, was in a flat spin. Greta had disappeared, which Alice chalked up to her finally being able to spend all the time she had with Tony in his staff cottage on the northern edge of the island, where her father's body man was surely lost without his lodestar—no longer waiting to be summoned by Franklin for guarding, driving, or piloting.

Good for Greta; at least someone was getting something nice out of this absolute nightmare.

Her refusal to acknowledge the Greta-and-Tony-of-it-all notwithstanding, Elisabeth did not feel the same way about the loss of her eldest and most trusted child. She was in dire need of an assistant—someone to whom she could delegate (her favorite pastime). And in the absence of Greta, Alice would have to do.

A series of chores began there, the business of death's aftermath. Searches for addresses and phone numbers, for forms and certificates. A video chat with Franklin's personal staff and the PR team at Storm Inc. An overview of the island's security with the corporate security detail—a precursor to a larger meeting that would involve the Secret Service (when Elisabeth said everyone was coming to pay their respects, she meant *everyone*). A call to a funeral director, summoning him to the island the next morning (celebration or not, remains had to be dealt with), calls to florists and caterers from the mainland vying for the opportunity to make a name for themselves—brushing elbows with the VIPs of the 1 percent on mysterious Storm Island.

For a woman who regularly commandeered staff on the corporate payroll for her own use, Elisabeth was strangely committed to keeping these particular arrangements in the family. Or, she might have just been committed to keeping Alice too busy to leave the island.

Then there was Sam, the Ghost of Arrogant Siblings, who spent his even-numbered hours turning on the charm for his sister, cracking jokes as though they hadn't been at each other's throats that morning. It might have worked if Sila hadn't been at his elbow all day, offering to help in her classic way—replete with weaponized helplessness. Saoirse and Oliver even dropped by the office where Elisabeth had trapped Alice, offering to share some whoopie pies purchased from a farmstand on the east side of the Bay (Alice's favorite—what a coincidence).

Everyone wanted time with Alice. Space with Alice. Because Alice held their future in her hands. No longer the black sheep, now the golden goose.

Everyone wanted time with Alice, that was, except Jack, who'd disappeared into Franklin's home office to get some real work done, handily avoiding the family in the process.

If only Alice could have done the same. Instead, through all of it—

the sound bath, the endless rounds of *So sorry for your loss* from caterers and florists, Sila's high-pitched insertions—Alice dwelled. And in the dwelling, she became more and more angry.

Jack had known who she was from the start. On the train. On the platform. When he'd punched a photographer. When he'd made her laugh in the dark. When he'd made her sigh in it.

And he hadn't said a word.

Not when they met, not when they were in the car together, not as they made out against the door of the hotel room . . . She resisted the urge to linger on the thoughts that crept in, unwelcome, as she'd closed her eyes and stood under the pounding shower . . . the feel of his fingers on the skin at her waist, his lips at the column of her throat, his eyes tracking over her face, the sound of his pleasure in her ear, the heat of him.

And then she remembered that Jack had followed her that morning and ruined everything . . . including any lingering memories of the night before.

He was a sociopath, obviously. At least her taste in men was consistent.

She'd spent a few more minutes in the shower, planning all the things she was going to say to him the next time she saw him alone, and then turned off the shower, rejuvenated with plans to be a brilliant, articulate woman-viper, laying Jack low with her erudite venom . . . only to discover her clothes were missing.

Sam.

Glamorous femme fatale became cranky sister. Annoyance flared, and she cracked open the door to the bathroom, poking her head into the hallway, fully prepared to hurl a full tube of Colgate into her brother's smug, gloating face.

The hall was empty. Too bad for a younger sister wanting to exact revenge, but a boon for a grown woman still dripping from the shower, needing to reach the safety of her bedroom while fully nude.

It wasn't the first time she'd had to do it—her childhood had been peppered with sandy post-beach showers and forgotten towels—so she made the familiar run for the tower steps, vowing to return to clean up the wet footprints as she flew across the hallway and up the stairs, bursting through the closed door to her bedroom, headed for the dresser, where a spare towel should have been in view.

The view was blocked, however, by the long-legged instrument of her family's upheaval. Her own, too, if she were being honest. Which she absolutely was not.

Jack turned to face her, his surprise at her arrival and her nudity only evident in the infinitesimal raise of his eyebrows.

"Shit!" Alice said, the sharp word matched by her instant movements, covering as much as she could—not nearly enough—with her bare arms. "What are you doing here?"

Unbothered, he reached into the worn leather overnight bag on the bed and removed a perfectly rolled bath towel. Extended it to her. "Do you need a towel?"

There was no way she was going to say yes. Had she not just vowed to be a viper? Were not vipers cool? Self-possessed? "You brought your own towels?"

"Good thing, too, as there seems to be a shortage of them." His gaze flickered down her body and back.

She ignored the lick of fire that came from the perusal. "A gentleman would turn around."

He didn't even pretend to think about turning around. "I'm offering you a towel. Isn't that better? Solving the problem?"

He wasn't solving the problem. He *was* the problem.

Surely the only thing more mortifying than being wet and cold and naked in one's childhood bedroom in front of a man who was responsible for both your most recent orgasm and your most recent existential crisis, was accepting that man's help to mitigate the mortification.

Alice scowled and headed for the bed, yanking the comforter hard enough to topple his overnight bag from the end. He caught the bag before it crashed to the floor (of course), and she studiously ignored him as she wrapped the bulky fabric around her, ensuring not an inch of skin showed below the neck.

"What are you doing in here?" she demanded.

"I could ask you the same thing."

"This is *my* room," she said, sounding like the petulant teen who'd holed herself up here for days.

"Well, this is awkward," he said, his lips twitching, as though it were all funny. As though he weren't under serious threat of her pushing him out the window. "This is my room, too." A pause, and then, "I sleep here when I'm on the island."

Her head snapped back in surprise. And something like betrayal. "Why?"

He looked around the room. "It's a question I've asked many times, too, I'll be honest. It's not every day a grown man is asked to sleep in a time capsule from 2005."

"There are three guest rooms, not to mention the staff cottages. And there's a bed in the boathouse."

He gave a little shrug, like it was all perfectly reasonable. Which it *wasn't.* "I think your dad thought I'd enjoy the view from up here," he said, his gaze sliding over her again, like a memory. His voice was deeper when he added, "You don't have paint in your hair anymore."

She resisted the instinct to run her hand through her hair. Resisted the way she drew tight at his notice. "I wondered how you knew it was paint."

"Your father was very proud of your work."

It was laughably untrue, considering the past, and Alice hated him for saying it. Hated him, too, for the knowledge that her family had so easily reassigned her bedroom. It shouldn't matter. She was thirty-three for God's sake. It was just a room.

But it did matter. It burned. "Why—" she started, then shook her head. "No. You know what? I don't care. This is *my* room, and I am *here.* Get out."

"I'm—" It was his turn to rethink. "I didn't know you were up here, Alice."

"You didn't notice my stuff was—" She stopped. Took in the room: the open closet, minus the empty suitcase she'd stashed inside and the black dress she'd hung within; the unadorned corner where she'd kicked off her white sneakers; the small vanity on the far end of the room, where her makeup bag had once been, and was no longer.

She pushed past him, opening the top drawer of the dresser, behind him. Empty. The second and third, barren matches to the first.

"Where's my stuff?" She turned in a slow circle, confirming what they both saw. Realization dawning. "Fucking Sam."

Surprise edged into Jack's tone. "Sam?"

"He took it."

"Your things?"

She nodded. "And my clothes and towel in the bathroom."

A pause. Then, "*Why?*"

She looked to him. "Do you have siblings?"

"No."

"Lucky."

"Is this . . . normal behavior? For . . . adults?"

"I wouldn't go so far as to call Sam an adult." She went to the closet, flipping through the remaining clothes hanging there—part of the time capsule of the rest of the room. A handful of sundresses from her teenage years, a bridesmaid dress from Sam and Sila's wedding, a wet suit.

"He's a *parent,*" Jack said, as though it meant something.

"Cute how you think having children makes you a grown-up," she said, flicking past a dress from her senior prom. "Didn't you work for my father?"

"I did," he said. "And he was a grown-up, Alice. And a decent one, in the end."

In the end. The qualification held years of weight. Of accusation. She hadn't been there to see him at the end, had she?

And whose fault was that?

Alice looked over her shoulder, past the overstuffed comforter at her shoulder, to meet his resolute gaze. "Well, he was a billionaire who thought it would be fun to make his grieving family play an inheritance game in the days immediately following his death by glorified toy, so the jury is still out on both his maturity and his decency. As it is on yours."

"My maturity?"

"Your decency."

After a hesitation, during which he clearly considered saying something and decided against it, Jack lifted his chin in the direction of the clothes in the closet. "I'm not sure any of those are going to make for comfortable sleepwear. Do you want me to go talk to Sam?"

Her brows rose. "What are you going to do, rough him up until he returns my pajamas?"

The words were out before she thought them through, and they came with a memory of the night before, of photographers and SD cards and raw knuckles and rain and this man's half smile as she slid her hand into his. And how she'd felt when he'd done it, like someone had finally, finally put her first.

But he hadn't been putting her first. He'd been putting Franklin first.

Clinging to the reminder, she said, "Thanks, but I've been dealing with my brother for thirty-three years. I can handle it."

"Feels like you need some . . . clothes?"

"I won't once you leave this room. Are you planning on doing that any time soon, or . . . ?"

He reached into his bag and pulled out a T-shirt and shorts. "You may not need clothes now, but you will for tomorrow." When she didn't move, he added, "Or were you counting on staying locked in your tower for the week?"

He was the first person to suggest she didn't already have a foot out the door, probably because he thought she wasn't leaving without her cut. Nevertheless, it was a refreshing change of pace. Alice waddled toward him and extended an arm through the bedspread to take the clothes with a disgruntled, "Fine. There's no need for you to keep pretending you're a good guy. I know the truth."

He nodded. "Me, too."

The words were low and deep, like a confession, and the sound of them fired something deep in her gut. She ignored it, because she'd been betrayed enough that day and she didn't need her body in the mix. Instead, she said, "Turn around, please."

Silently, he faced the dresser, and she made quick work of pulling on the clothes—a University of Delaware T-shirt, and a pair of running shorts that hugged her ample ass. Better than nothing.

Tugging the T-shirt down to avoid revealing every curve she had—it didn't matter that he'd seen them all the night before, he was the enemy now—she straightened and looked over to where he stood, back to her.

Only then did she realize that in turning around, he'd faced the mirror atop the dresser, which reflected the entire room.

His eyes were closed.

Alice stilled, watching him for a moment, taking in his face—all thick, dark brows and perfect bone structure and a strong jaw shadowed with a day's growth of beard. His lashes were dark against his cheek, which was tan from the summer sun.

Staring at him in the mirror, she said, "Delaware, huh?"

"Home of the fighting Blue Hen." He didn't look.

"Sounds terrifying," she said, knowing she should stop flirting with him. What was wrong with her?

"Are you done?" Did she imagine the roughness in the question?

"Yes." The word was barely out when his eyes opened and found hers, instantly, in the mirror.

"You didn't look," she said.

He was looking now, though, his gaze sliding over the clothes—*his* clothes—against her skin. He spoke to her bare legs. "A gentleman wouldn't." She didn't imagine *that* roughness, or the way it made her feel—off-balance.

Grasping for the upper hand, she said, "But seducing your dead boss's daughter . . . that's fine?" He stilled. He didn't like that. Good. He shouldn't. She lifted her chin.

"You're angry with me."

"Why would I be angry with you, Jack? You only misrepresented yourself before luring me into bed. What's there to be angry about?"

"I don't remember having to lure you."

He hadn't, but she absolutely wasn't going to admit it.

When she didn't speak, he added, "It was a miscalculation."

"I bet that stings. You don't seem like a person who makes miscalculations."

"I'm not." The words were like ice, and it occurred to her that another man might apologize, but Jack didn't seem to have that in him.

Good, as Alice wasn't feeling that forgiving. She leveled him with a cool look. "I wish I could say the same."

"I didn't lie to you," he said, the words clipping in his throat like he'd bent them to his will.

"No? All your *I'll build you a fire, You can't fit a sousaphone in the overhead, I'm staying at the Quahog Quay* jokes? Just a regular person in Wickford for *work*."

"I *was* staying at the Quahog Quay. I *am* here for work."

"Yeah, but you're not a regular person. You work for my father! Why were you even on the train? Don't you have access to the company helicopter?"

"Why were *you* on the train? Don't *you* have access to the helicopter?"

"I haven't had access to the helicopter in years, Jack. Which I'm sure you know."

A muscle clenched in his jaw. "Right. Because you're your own person."

She narrowed her gaze. "Because I'm not my father's person. Not like you. Managing Director of Franklin Storm's whims."

Gray eyes flashed. "I take my job seriously."

"Oh yeah, very seriously considering what happened last night at the Quahog Quay." She was poking the bear, but she didn't care. She held up a hand before he could reply. "I know. A miscalculation. So what did you do for him when you were calculating properly?"

A hesitation. "Whatever he needed."

"You put out fires."

He nodded. "Among other things."

Always so cryptic. "And you knew who I was."

He took a deep breath, as though she were the one who was annoying. "Of course I did. Your father paid me to know everything, without being told. But even if that hadn't been my job, I'd have known who you were because I've seen your picture on his desk every day for as long as I worked for him. I've listened to him talk about you. And I've been sleeping in your bedroom."

She blinked at the words. At the unexpected power in them. How dare he make her feel something other than anger? She didn't want it.

"If you recall," he added, "I tried to tell you who I was."

I should introduce myself, he'd said on the train platform. Before she'd stopped him.

"No names, right? They make things complicated."

"Is this the part where I'm supposed to feel like it's my fault that you knew who I was and didn't tell me? Are you seriously suggesting that I don't have the right to be angry that you knew I was your boss's daughter, and you fucked me anyway? Hours after his death and knowing you would be showing up the next day to drop a bomb on my family?"

He didn't reply, and his silence only further infuriated her. *Why?* She wanted to scream it. *Was it to stick it to me? To punish Franklin? To score some kind of point?*

"Turns out I was right," she said. "Names did make it complicated."

He ran a hand through his hair and looked out the window, where the darkness turned three sides of the room into mirrors, reflecting everything in the room . . . and somehow nothing important. "Yeah." He grabbed his bag and slung it over his shoulder. "Turns out you were."

He headed for the door, brushing past her, and she resisted the way her body reacted to his nearness, as though it hadn't forgotten the feel of him the night before. Instead, she watched as he opened the door, hesitating at the top of the stairs before he looked back and said, "For what it's worth, I'm sorry. I should have told you."

The apology surprised her. "Careful. My dad didn't believe in apologizing." When he didn't reply, she said, more to herself than to him, "I guess it was a walk of shame, after all."

"What else could it have been when you snuck out of the room at dawn?"

If she weren't so raw, she might have heard something compelling in the question. Something like disappointment. But she wasn't about to care for this man who had so clearly manipulated her. "Believe it or not, I didn't think of it that way until right now."

"Sleeping with the help," he said.

"Sleeping with a *liar*," she corrected.

He nodded, taking the blow like a champ. She shouldn't feel bad about it. He had lied to her. He'd known who she was, why she was here, why *he* was here—and he'd still slept with her.

"While we're talking about lies . . ." He looked over his shoulder. "Aren't you engaged?"

The question was pointed. A reminder that she, too, might have lied the night before. That she, too, had a secret.

"The house is for family. You can sleep in the boathouse."

He didn't hesitate that time. He left, closing the door behind him, shutting her in. She listened as he descended the creaky wooden staircase, away from the tower.

Alice should have turned off the lights and gone to bed. Instead, she turned off the lights and went to the window to watch him moving like a shadow as he crossed the field of wild thyme that stretched down to the water, his long legs eating up ground as he made for the boathouse in the distance.

He paused inside the cone of yellow light on the dock, moths dancing around him, and turned back to look up at the house, his gaze tracking over the hulking mass of it, dark and gothic.

For a moment, she thought he lingered on the tower. Then he was gone, and Alice was alone again.

CHAPTER

7

GRETA WAS SITTING ON the porch steps off the kitchen, staring at the ocean, when Alice stepped outside the next morning, mug in hand, wearing the T-shirt and shorts she'd borrowed under duress the night before.

Realizing the steps were occupied, she caught the ancient screen door with her shoulder. "Is it okay if I—"

Her sister nodded, not looking away from the sea, where the sun glinted off the white waves in the distance. Alice sat next to her, and the morning silence settled around them, heavy with the promise of heat to come and the barely there scent of Greta's Féminité du Bois.

Greta spoke first. "This sucks."

"It absolutely does," Alice agreed. Her sister looked over at the words, and Alice finally saw her face in the full sun. Bloodshot, swollen eyes, puffy cheeks, a red nose. "Whoa. You look like shit."

"*Thanks,*" Greta replied, offended.

"No . . . no." Alice reframed. "I mean . . . Did you even sleep last night?"

Greta looked down into her coffee cup. "No."

Casting about for something that might make her sister feel better, Alice said, "Where's Tony?"

It was the wrong thing to say. Greta closed her eyes and pressed her lips together for a moment and then whispered, "I can't talk to Tony. Not about this."

"Why not?" Alice's brow furrowed at the tacit admission that her sister might talk to their father's pilot about something other than a flight plan—the first time Greta had come close to openly admitting their relationship. "God, Greta. What was in your letter? Did he set you up with an arranged marriage or something?"

"No." Greta laughed through her sadness. "That would be crazy."

"And he'd never come up with something crazy. Not like prohibiting Sam from speaking for twelve hours a day."

Greta turned, smile on her face. "That one is pretty great, isn't it?"

"Diabolically great. Peak Dad." Alice waited for a bit, staring out at the gleaming ocean—blue turned gold in the sun. "But it sounds like whatever he gave you is just plain diabolical. What do you have to do?"

Greta sighed and looked back at the ocean. "I'm supposed to end it. With Tony."

Not diabolical. Cruel. "Oh *no*."

"Exactly." A long pause. "What an asshole."

There was no disagreeing with that. "You know, he can't control us from beyond the grave."

"Of course he can," Greta said in the way she said most things—as though there was truth and there was fiction and there was nothing more stupid than thinking one was the other. A beat, and then, "Tony wanted to tell him about us, you know. Ten years ago. Wanted to find another job and marry me. God, imagine what Dad would have done."

Alice sighed and thought for a moment. Then, "Maybe he would have let you live your life." The sisters side-eyed each other, and Alice laughed. "Okay. Maybe not."

"Maybe not." Greta shrugged a shoulder, as though the argument wasn't worth it. "The point is, he's left me with the worst task. I'd rather not talk for a week. Or . . . say *something nice* about Dad for a few days."

The disparity between the tasks was startlingly unfair, but Franklin wouldn't have cared about that. All he cared about was his ability to force them into action.

"So, don't do it."

Greta looked at her. "What do you mean?"

"Exactly what I said. Don't do it. Go public with your relationship, live your life." Alice paused. "What's the worst that can happen? Mom has to actually hire a secretary?"

"I'm more to Mom than just a secretary. She needs me."

Before Alice could find an apology (the kind that came with difficulty because it required an evasion of the truth), Greta waved the words away.

"If I don't do it . . ." Greta trailed off and shook her head, the rest of the sentence unspoken but heard nonetheless. *If I don't do it—I don't get the money. And it's always been the money.* "I have no discernible skills."

Alice didn't miss the deeper meaning. What would happen when Greta needed an identity? Who was she if not the money? The name? The power that came with it? Who was she beyond Elisabeth, and Storm Island, and the enormous, too-small world it afforded her?

Who were any of them?

Alice didn't know, and she'd spent five years trying to figure it out. "That's not true. You have an MFA."

An MFA and a book she'd been writing for a decade. Longer. Something she used to convince herself that she was more than her DNA. More than a statue, cast in her mother's mold.

Greta cut her a look. "Like I said."

"Well, worst comes to worst, you can go work for Sam. He's going to be CEO."

It was too horrifying to be considered a decent joke. "God, can you imagine how insufferable he'll be?"

"Learned from the best of them." Alice couldn't help her laugh at that, letting it free her for a moment, before she went serious again. "It's not so bad, you know. Paying rent. Grocery shopping. Buying furniture at IKEA."

"You have furniture from IKEA?"

Ignoring the horror in her sister's voice, Alice repeated, "It's not so bad, Great."

Maybe it was the words themselves—too hopeful. Maybe it was the nickname Alice had used for her when they were kids, bestowed the same day their father had brought autocorrect (at once deeply fallible and cosmically perfect) to the world—too heavy.

Whatever it was, Greta shook her head. "I can't."

"I'm sorry," Alice replied, meaning it. "You should have something for yourself. You deserve it, after all of this time." A long stretch of silence passed, full of things Greta wouldn't say, until Alice added, "Is there—something else? That Dad said?"

That Dad knew?

After an eternity, Greta shook her head and repeated herself, "Even if I were willing to lose out on the inheritance . . . the family comes first."

"What does that even mean?"

"You haven't been gone that long," Greta said, an edge of the robotic in her voice. "We're all we have."

"Cool impression of Mom," Alice retorted. "Tell me. If that's true, then where were you when Dad told me to leave and not come back?"

Greta went silent. What could she say?

"Don't worry about it," Alice said. "You weren't the only one."

"Alice," Greta said, finally. "You know how it is . . . It's not . . . easy."

Alice studied her sister, the way a smattering of her blond hair, turning gray at her temples, had escaped the topknot she wore. The tiny creases barely born at the corners of her eyes and lips, dancing around the truth of her age. Forty.

Forty years, and still consumed by the rules of her youth, determined to be the good child, the best behaved, the one who stayed close and gave all she had to the family. Raised from birth to be Elisabeth's shadow, her only concession to her own desires the gap year she'd spent at nineteen in Geneva between her freshman and sophomore years at Brown, from which she'd returned rail thin, obsessed with Kierkegaard, and with a habit for Parisienne Jaune cigarettes that she'd never confess.

Now, Greta lived in a 1920s bungalow on the East Side of Providence, where she hosted fundraisers for uncontroversial nonprofits and milquetoast political candidates, and scheduled biweekly lunches with her mother, all while keeping the most important part of her life the kind of private reserved for airtight NDAs and offshore accounts.

And even now, with their father gone, Greta couldn't see that she might finally make a break for it—that she could escape the heavy weight of his control. Instead, she grieved, cloaked in secrets that were barely visible, like the new freckles on the backs of her hands. Impossible to see, unless someone was looking.

Someone like Alice, whose chest went tight with anger and sadness at the realization that none of them would be able to easily escape their father's ghost—new to the job and already exceptionally good at haunting.

But maybe they could lighten each other's loads. "If I left," Alice offered to her sister's profile. "If I didn't stay the week—you wouldn't have to do it."

It was the wrong thing to say. Greta whipped around to face Alice, gaze sharp and dangerous. "You can't leave."

"Why not?"

"Because we all have skin in this game."

Alice shook her head. "I don't."

"Yes, you do. We all do. We're all Storms. Even you. Whatever happened between you and Dad, or you and Mom, or you and *us*. And all that other stuff you console yourself with—the real job and the real partner and the real life and real friends . . . what about us?" Alice didn't misunderstand that *us*. Greta. Sam. Emily. "You owe us, Alice."

Alice's eyes went wide, any lingering sympathy she might have had overcome with indignation. "I *owe* you?"

"Yes. You owe *me*." Greta's voice rose. "Everything is always about you. *Where's Alice? How's Alice? Has anyone heard from Alice?* For once in your life, maybe you could think about the rest of us."

"Maybe *I* could think of *you*? What were you thinking about when he *exiled me*?"

"Alice." The word was clipped and full of that firstborn arrogance that had always made them more rivals than friends.

Alice looked to the ocean, anger coming in hot. "Not one of you ever came to my defense, because all you cared about was this. Being here. The warmth of his approval." The words whipped between them, surprisingly sharp. "And let's not forget—the promise of an inheritance that suddenly isn't a guarantee."

"You love that, don't you? Literal billions, and we could lose it all, at your whim."

"Fuck the billions," Alice said. "I wouldn't pay the price for them then, and I cannot believe you're even considering it now."

Greta didn't reply, and Alice spoke to the ocean. "But of course you are. You were raised to."

"We're not all as perfect as you are," Greta said. "Standing in your convictions."

Alice whirled on her sister. "That's rich, coming from Mom's carbon copy. If you got any more perfect, you'd be up for sainthood. Someday, you'll climb out of Mom's purse and let yourself make some choices on your own."

"You're such a bitch when you want to be," Greta snapped, her mask slipping. Silence fell between them. What was there to say? After a long stretch, she asked, "Why do you hate it so much? Being here? What's so hard about being with us?"

An impossible question with an impossible answer, full of words like *betrayal* and *fairness* and *love*—and all the other things Alice wanted to say and prove and resist, and far more complex than what she was willing to share. "I didn't say I wouldn't stay." She sighed and turned away. "But if I didn't . . . maybe it wouldn't be the worst thing."

"For you."

For us, Alice thought.

Wanting the last word—a prized possession in their family—Greta changed the subject. "I thought Griffin went to NYU."

What did Griffin have to do with anything? "He did."

Greta lifted her chin in the direction of the T-shirt Alice wore. The one she'd forgotten about for the last few minutes. She tugged on the hem. "Sam stole my clothes, the asshole."

"Sam went to Harvard," Greta said, the observation carrying a clear question.

One Alice ignored. "And how proud they must be to have him on the alumni roster. Are you done?"

Greta wasn't done. "You know who went to the University of Delaware?"

Alice sighed. "I do, as a matter of fact. I confess, detective. He was in my room last night when I discovered that Sam stole my clothes. Mr. Dean . . . In the tower . . . With the running shorts."

Greta's brows rose. "By invitation?"

"Dad's invitation, as I understand it."

Greta didn't misunderstand. She grimaced. "We should have told him you were up there." *Should* was the realm of the Storms, especially when it came to their responsibilities to each other. "Or told you that's his room."

"It's *my* room," Alice said.

"Right. I didn't mean that," Greta rushed to correct herself. "But he always sleeps there. Because you never . . ."

She trailed off, but Alice heard it all anyway. "Well, he didn't sleep there last night."

"Impressive. Anyone else would have been begging for it."

"Well, his irritatingly good looks aside, I did not beg." Nor did she even think about begging. At least, not while he was *in* the room.

Greta's brows slid into her hairline. "I wasn't referring to you begging for it, actually. I was saying he should have been begging for it . . . considering how those shorts make your ass look."

It was an olive branch. The kind of non-apology only sisters were allowed to get away with even after all this time. After a beat, Alice accepted it, and the truce it came with. "Well, me in these shorts is the closest Jack Dean will ever get to my ass," Alice lied.

"Are you sure of that? Irritatingly good looks?" When Alice rolled her eyes, Greta added, "You know, Sila's been after him for years."

Alice blinked. "After Jack?"

Greta shrugged. "I could be wrong."

Maybe. But she probably wasn't. Greta was the most observant member of the family—a quality borne of having to be constantly on guard, lest someone discover the truth about her relationship. "What does Sam think?"

"Does Sam think?" They shared a smile and Greta added, "Honestly, I think that's part of why Sam can't stand him. That, and the fact that he's always gotten the promotion Sam was expecting."

It wasn't a surprise. Jack Dean didn't seem like the kind of man who coasted. "Sam ought to try working sometime." Alice looked to the ocean. "And you? What do you think of him?" *Why did she care?*

Greta was silent for a stretch. "I think there's a reason Dad loved him so much." It was a warning, and Alice didn't miss it. "Anyway. Sila's going to lose her mind when she sees you in his T-shirt. And those shorts. A real combo."

Alice made a show of looking at her behind. "Here I was thinking I should go find my clothes and change."

"And miss all the fun?"

For a moment, everything felt light again. Like they were just sisters and this was just an ordinary visit home to visit ordinary family. But there was nothing ordinary here.

"Stay. Please," Greta whispered.

Before Alice could answer, the screen door creaked open, and Elisabeth leaned out. "There you are. Come in, please. We have some things to discuss."

The sisters shared a look and headed in, Alice avoiding her mother's pointed glance. Elisabeth had also noticed the shorts.

Inside, Sam leaned against the counter by the toaster, staring down at his phone, next to Saoirse, who had a yogurt in one hand and her own phone in the other. Alice waved in her niece's direction. "Hey you."

Saoirse tucked her long hair (old-money blond, just like her father) behind her ear, but didn't look up. "Dad can't talk."

Alice looked at her watch—seven forty-five. "Are you here to interpret?"

"No . . . I kind of like that he can't talk," the teen deadpanned perfectly, enjoying the laugh she got as she made her way out of the kitchen, still riveted to her screen.

"She's funny," Alice said to Sam. "Wonder where she got it?"

He wasn't amused.

Emily and Claudia sat together on the far side of the butcher block table, steaming stoneware mugs in hand, but Claudia rose and pressed a kiss to Emily's temple almost as soon as the screen door slammed shut behind Elisabeth. "I'm going to let you guys have some time."

"Are you sure?" Alice said with a little smile. "This is definitely going to be fun."

Claudia returned the smile. "I'm sure. There's mushroom tea if anyone wants any; I left it on the counter."

"Is it hallucinogenic?" Alice whispered.

"No!" Claudia looked horrified at the prospect, which was curious, as Alice knew for a fact that her sister and her partner weren't exactly abstemious when it came to mind-altering substances.

"A disappointment," Alice replied.

"No one is drinking hallucinogenic tea," Elisabeth said, as though that were an actual option, reaching a hand out to Claudia—a movement that shocked Alice more than she'd like to admit, especially when it was followed with, "Claudia, love. You don't have to leave. You're family."

Alice looked to Sam, who was clearly annoyed by the pronouncement. In the entirety of their marriage, Elisabeth had never referred to Sila as *family*. If anything, she'd been the antithesis of it. The woman who pulled Sam's attention away from his mother. Furthermore, if Elisabeth ever called Sam's wife *love,* Alice would immediately suspect a stroke.

But Claudia, she was steady and quiet, a balance for Emily and for Elisabeth—present, but never needy. Strong, but never overbearing. And more than all that? Knew well enough to stay out of the fray.

"I have some client appointments I have to move," she said, "but I will see you for lunch—Emily said Lorraine made her chicken salad."

"Of course she did," Elisabeth said, warmly. "We know it's your favorite."

Alice's eyes went wide, and she met Greta's clear gaze, a tilt of her chin the only indication that Greta understood her surprise.

Then Claudia was gone, and their mother returned. "If we have a few hundred people coming this weekend, I cannot abide a house in chaos, you four."

Everyone looked around the impeccably tidy kitchen, perpetually prepared for an *Architectural Digest* spread. Greta spoke. "Mom. The house looks perfect."

"The pantry doesn't," Elisabeth replied. "Someone's left their luggage inside."

Alice leaned back on her stool and looked into the little room. Sure enough, there, on the far side, sat her suitcase and her canvas satchel. "It's mine."

"You have a perfectly good room upstairs, Alice. Why is your luggage in the pantry?"

Alice looked at Sam. "I don't know, Sam, why are my bags in the pantry?"

He ignored her and stared at his phone, typing. Just when Alice was ready to pronounce him the worst, the phone spoke. "How. Should. I. Know."

The disembodied voice had everyone turning to look as Sam offered a grin that could only be described as shit-eating, and he typed again. "Loophole."

Alice rolled her eyes. "Cool—can the phone help you descale the skiffs, too?"

Sam scowled.

"If the two of you are through," Elisabeth said, coming to stand at one end of the kitchen island, "I have something I want to say."

Quiet fell, everyone anticipating what bomb Elisabeth might lob. "Your father never met a stranger. People around the world loved him, and I don't believe it was for his money. Entirely. After all, I loved him, too." She paused and Alice wondered if she was considering whether or not to qualify the statement. Something like, *I loved him, too, once. For three years, six months, and eleven days.*

Evidently deciding against it, Elisabeth finished. "In celebration of that, we will open the island on Monday for his . . ." She searched for a word, settling on *community*. It came out strangled. As though she'd never really considered the concept, and now that she had, she wasn't sure she cared for it. "And I hope it will be . . . not sad."

When no one spoke, she punctuated the statement. "There."

It seemed the children were expected to respond, so they did—nothing if not receptive to their mother's expectations.

Emily started. "I love that you're setting such a positive intention, Mom. Maybe we can meditate on it later."

"Oh, I don't think that will be necessary," Elisabeth replied.

"Sounds. Good." Sam's phone chimed in.

"Dad would like that," Greta added, and Elisabeth's lips twisted, suggesting that if she'd known that, she might have said something different.

But she hadn't said anything different, so Alice added her support. "That's a pretty nice thing to say, Mom. About Dad. And for him."

Elisabeth nodded. "Good. Be sure to tell Jack about it. I've decided to get my daily requirement out of the way early."

Alice couldn't help the laugh that burst from her. "Like eating your vegetables."

A month ago, Elisabeth might have smiled at the joke. This was not a month ago.

"Hey. Speaking. Of. Requirements." Sam's phone said as he looked pointedly to Greta, "What. Do. You. Have. To. Do."

Alice inspected the inside of her coffee cup as Greta said, "It doesn't matter." Her tone was too breezy. Even if Sam hadn't known how to read Greta since birth, Franklin's assigned tasks weren't breezy. And they weren't fun.

With a smug look, Sam typed. "Sounds. Like. It. Masters. A. Lot."

As Emily would say, the universe provides. Alice couldn't help replying, "Masters what?"

Greta clung to the change of topic. "Well, when this is all over, Sam will have mastered fog bell upkeep."

"And don't forget shingles," Emily joined in, knowing this particular script.

"Duck. You."

Perfection.

The siblings all laughed, except Sam, who flipped them all off before typing furiously. "What's. He. Making. You. Do. Emily." He cast a serious look in Emily's direction, and everyone followed, including Elisabeth, who had stilled in the process of spraying the kitchen counter with organic disinfectant for the third time that morning.

The youngest Storm's hesitation was palpable. Franklin's creativity was on full creative display with the tasks at hand, and everyone was wondering what he might do to Emily, who arguably deserved his vitriol the least.

Emily took a deep breath, as Alice held hers. "Nothing."

Silence. Then . . .

Elisabeth's brows shot up. "Nothing?"

A noise was strangled in Sam's throat before he found his thumbs again. "What. The. Fuck."

"Nothing like . . . you have to stay on the island?" Alice clarified. "Or *nothing,* nothing?"

Emily gave a little, guilty shrug. "I think nothing, nothing."

It was a strange twist. Granted, Emily had never been the thorn in Franklin's side that the rest of them seemed to be, but the idea that he'd left her literally nothing to do? Not even stay? It wasn't a punishment as it was for Alice. It had come with a letter, unlike Alice's. More like . . . a gift.

And it stung.

For Greta, too, obviously. "What do you mean, *Nothing!*" she fairly shouted.

"I—" Emily looked to her oldest sister. They'd never really gotten along, what with Greta fourteen years older than Emily and the first to acknowledge that they had little in common. That said, it had always been obvious to the rest of the family that Emily vied not for Elisabeth's approval, but for Greta's. "I'm sorry, Greta."

"This is too much. Alice basically has to take a vacation for a week, you have no requirements at all, Sam has a list of *chores,* and I have to—" She cut herself off before she revealed the truth to everyone. "And none of us are guaranteed even a dime at the end of it. It's—"

She bit back the *not fair.*

Tears welled in Emily's eyes. "I'm sorry. I didn't know he was planning—"

"None of us did," Alice said, stepping in. "Dad did whatever he wanted, whenever he wanted, and without a care for who he might be hurting. It's not your fault. It's his game." She looked to Greta, now fully red in the face. "When Greta calms down, she'll see it."

"*You* telling *me* to calm down." Greta turned on Alice. "That's rich. You who *flounced* instead of being a part of this family. You don't care about this game. You're the one most likely to screw us all!"

There it was again, the suggestion that Alice lacked loyalty. "First, I didn't *flounce.* He kicked me out."

No one responded. Not that she was surprised.

"Second, I'm not responsible for Dad"—she paused, not wanting to say *dying;* why was that such a weird word to say?—"leaving us all like pieces on his chessboard. I didn't set the game. I didn't make the rules. And you're right, if it were my choice, I'd leave right now, because contrary to your analysis, Greta, this isn't a vacation for me—it's a constant reminder that when he *banished* me, not one of you actually cared."

Silence fell and she imagined for a moment that they were all finding a path to chagrin. No such luck.

"You're. Not. A. Piece. Though," Sam said.

"What's that supposed to mean?"

Greta nodded in agreement with the phone. "*We're* the pieces."

"And what, I'm not on the board?" It shouldn't matter. The *we* (plural). The *you* (singular).

"You're not," Emily said. "You're one of the players; Dad gave you all the control. Nothing to do but stay . . . and play."

They couldn't see that he'd given her *none* of the control. That he'd never let her make a single decision in her whole life, from the moment she'd had a crush on a boy in the seventh grade and Franklin had hired his father to work at Storm Silicon Valley because he wanted Alice's distractions kept to a minimum. She had grades to keep up. College to attend.

It didn't matter that Franklin hadn't graduated from college.

Alice had planned for art school. Made a careful list of the best in the world not long after that seventh-grade boy had disappeared. Worked on her portfolio for months. Begged him to let her apply to one after he provided her with his approved list of colleges, none of them art schools.

It didn't matter what Alice wanted.

Franklin had given the commencement speech when she graduated from Amherst. Made a joke about *his daughter getting lost in the art history department on the way to the computer science major he'd been hoping for* that everyone found delightful despite its singular purpose: to telegraph his disappointment.

For the day and a half she'd had left on campus, people had fawned. How charming her father was. How clever and funny. How inspirational. How lucky she was.

The truth didn't matter, either.

Every time she'd tried to make her own decision, he'd used money and power and influence as both her father and one of the wealthiest people in the world to twist that decision into what he wanted. And when she'd finally refused, and fought back? When she'd finally claimed ground? Her father had left her out in the cold and made sure the rest of them did, too.

And this week, instead of just letting them all fucking *mourn,* he'd tied her hands again. Alice could stay, or go, but either way, Franklin was writing the next chapter.

If she stayed, he won. If she left, she lost.

Maybe she'd already lost.

Frustration edged into something worse, and Alice's throat went full and tight, her skin beginning to tingle. "You're wrong. He's treating me the same way he always did. Like a child. And I'm not a child anymore; I'm thirty-three."

"Better be careful, not a great age for martyrs." Everyone turned to look at Sam, who'd spoken out loud. Alice looked at her watch. It was a few seconds past eight o'clock.

"There is nothing about leaving this house that would make me a martyr, Sam. No suffering involved." It was a lie, but she'd never admit it.

"I've had enough of this," Elisabeth said. "As much as she would like to, Alice is not leaving the island. *No one* is leaving the island. Hundreds of people are coming to pay their respects Monday, and we will *all*"— she leveled Alice with a stern look—"be present. What would it look like if we weren't? What would people think?"

A pause, long enough for everyone to fill in the words she had left unspoken. *What would people say?*

"They'd probably think the truth," Alice said.

Elisabeth didn't like that. "And what is that, Alice?"

That we're a fucking mess. But the question wasn't for answering, so she kept her mouth shut.

"You will all be here," Elisabeth repeated in the heavy silence, looking from one of her offspring to the next. "And you will all *enjoy* it."

Brows rose around the room, presumably because they were all uncertain that they would like their father's funeral, full of titans of industry, world leaders, and a fair share of weirdos.

"Are there any questions?"

"Yeah, I have a question," Sam said. The sisters rolled their eyes. Of course he did. Sam always had to have the last word. "Why is Alice wearing a University of Delaware shirt?"

A beat while everyone considered the question. And the answer.

"Because my suitcase is in the pantry," Alice said, looking first at Sam, and then at Elisabeth. "And no one told Jack that my room isn't a guest room this week."

"Well. If you ever came home, we might have thought to do that," Elisabeth said, without an ounce of remorse. "The rules haven't changed. Your suitcase belongs upstairs, as you know."

"I didn't put it—" Alice bit back the retort that sprang to her lips, suddenly nine years old and infuriated by having to take responsibility for her older brother's nonsense. "Fine."

"Proper clothing would not go amiss," Elisabeth added, her gaze tracking over Alice's makeshift pajamas with cool judgment before she looked to Sam. "Sam, I expect you have work to do?"

He pulled out his phone, stared down at it for a moment. "I've cleared the schedule for the day, so we're going to clean some boats, I guess." He looked to Emily. "I feel like you should have to help."

"Mmm . . ." She tilted her head. "I feel like—no."

"Have the grandchildren help; it will keep them occupied," Elisabeth said before turning her attention to Greta. "I have a list for you."

Greta had been waiting for the summons. "Whatever you need."

"Can I help, Mom?" Emily interrupted.

"Oh, Emily." Elisabeth turned to look at her youngest. "I assumed you'd be doing whatever you do. Lighting candles for solstice or something?"

"It's—not solstice?"

"It must be solstice somewhere, no? Or a full moon?" Elisabeth said, lifting her tablet from the kitchen counter, distracted already by the information within.

"Nope." The light had dimmed in Emily's eyes, but she pressed on ever hopeful, in adulthood as she'd been as a child, that she might get a fraction of the warmth Elisabeth gave Greta—not knowing the burden of that heat. "I'm free to help."

"Hmm," Elisabeth said. "Come with us, then."

They followed her out of the room like ducklings, just as she liked—Elisabeth's minions, not Franklin's. How many times had he stood in this very room and told them all to go help their mother?

Not that Alice was any less a duckling. She immediately made for the suitcase at the far end of the pantry—a strip of silk underwear peeking through the closed zipper. Of course. Sam hadn't even been careful with her stuff.

She leaned down to assess the damage and fiddled with the zipper, cursing her obnoxious brother and her overbearing mother and her dead father and his infuriating lieutenant whose shirt still smelled like him—a smell she had enjoyed all too much while lying in bed the night before—a truth she would never admit. To anyone. Ever.

And then, as though it weren't all mortifying enough, tears came. Why did she cry every time she was in the stupid pantry? She redoubled her efforts with the zipper—vowing that this one thing would go right if she had to sit here all day.

The house had other plans, however, and behind her, the door slammed shut and the light switched off, plunging the whole room into darkness.

With a sigh, Alice made for the door, kicking a heavy bottle of—olive oil, maybe?—before fumbling for the doorknob. She twisted and pushed. No luck. Putting her shoulder to the door, she gave it a strong shove.

Nothing. It was stuck.

On the other side of the door, she heard a chair scrape across the floor. Someone was there. Sam, no doubt.

"Hilarious," she muttered to the darkness, before banging on the door. "Let me out, you man-child." Nothing happened. "Sam. I'm not kidding around."

In the kitchen beyond, footsteps retreated into the distance.

She was locked in.

GRETA

WHEN IT CAME TO good daughters, no one on earth could compete with Greta Storm.

It wasn't just that she was the eldest, though she was a textbook eldest: emotional (aggressively caring), controlling (extremely dependable), and intense (having a sensitive stomach borne of a constant and deep-rooted concern that, at any moment, someone in the family might stray from the path).

In another timeline, Greta might have married and had a family of her own, dominating the sport of PTA. Never gone anywhere near school grounds without a cooler full of organic juice boxes and clementines. Passed down an impressive amount of anxiety to a new generation as a momfluencer of the highest order.

But that would've meant leaving her own mother.

Though she did not have them herself, Greta had always intuitively understood that children belonged to one parent or the other. Not in the flippant, off-the-cuff way the world defined them (momma's boy, daddy's girl), and not in the sense of favorites (though Elisabeth and Franklin Storm had never hesitated to identify those). This was a deeper understanding. Cellular. Synaptic.

Greta belonged to Elisabeth and had from the beginning. She'd never even had a chance, not from the date she arrived, on her mother's twenty-fifth birthday. Even Greta's birth had been a gift to Elisabeth; she'd been born with speedy efficiency, so as to prevent any undue discomfort for her mother. Elisabeth had labored barely ninety minutes, and Greta had arrived to the private maternity ward at St. Luke's–Roosevelt before her father had had a chance to do the same.

If Franklin apologized for missing the birth of his firstborn, it hadn't been passed down in the lore of the day. Instead, he'd laugh his booming laugh every January 11, toss a slim box from Cartier in the direction of his wife, and quip, "Not as good as Greta, though!" and return to work.

Diamonds might be forever, but Greta was forever and ever, amen.

And so, when Elisabeth climbed the stairs to her private study that morning, head full of the welcome distraction of a garden party summoning half the world to shower her with attentive concern (and celebrate her husband's life), it was Greta who followed closest on her heels.

Emily trailed behind, a lost puppy, never so well attuned to her mother's needs as her sister; how could she be? Even if Elisabeth were interested in training another acolyte, Greta would never have ceded the spot, the one reserved for what the world might have seen as her mother's favorite.

She wasn't her mother's favorite. That spot belonged to Sam—though Greta tried not to think about it, because she was more important than *favorite*.

Favorite was for frivolity; she'd been bred to be indispensable. For comfort. For intuitive understanding of what Elisabeth needed at any given moment.

What was *favorite* when compared to *essential*?

"The company sent a list." Elisabeth's words were crisp and clear as she crossed to the high-backed chair by the window overlooking the Bay, drawing Greta's immediate attention.

"A list of what?" Emily asked.

Their mother did not look up from the quad-res screen of her tablet (commonly referred to as the 1107—in honor of the $1,107 Franklin used to start Storm Inc. nearly fifty years earlier), where a spreadsheet glowed in a half dozen colors.

Greta answered her sister. "Attendees for the funeral."

"It's not a funeral," Elisabeth corrected, swiping to scroll the seemingly endless list. Would the island even fit all those people?

Of course it would. Elisabeth Storm would make sure of it.

"But it is, though, isn't it?" Emily asked, looking to Greta.

"It's a *celebration*," Elisabeth replied.

Greta did not miss the fact that there was nothing appended to the word *celebration*. No, *of life*. No, *of your father*. Instead, it was a celebration. As though his dying was a boon to them all, and Elisabeth herself would lead the merriment.

The eldest Storm ignored the grief that whispered from the edges of her consciousness, yes, for her father, as it should be. As it would be for a good daughter. But for something else, too—for an altogether different kind of loss that she would not be able to ignore for long.

Don't do it.

Alice's words would have echoed if Greta had let them. But she had no intention of letting them echo. Alice didn't understand; she never had. None of them did.

Greta had a job to do. "I'll call the caterers."

"Alice already did that, yesterday afternoon. When you were nowhere to be found."

Controlling a flinch, Greta refused to think about where she'd been. With whom. She controlled, too, the breathless panic that surged up at the idea that Elisabeth had needed her and someone else had stepped in.

"I'm here now," Greta said.

Elisabeth had reached the end of the list and was returning to the top. "This won't do. There's no one personal here. None of our friends."

Emily leaned in to look over her mother's shoulder. "Actually, Mom, it looks like your friends are in green. I see them . . . The Nadirs, the Silverbergs, the Nelsons, the Haskinses, the Singhs—"

"Those are your *father's* friends."

Considering they'd summered and holidayed with all of those families throughout their childhood, this was a surprise. Nevertheless, Emily reached for a notepad on the corner of Elisabeth's spindle desk. "Okay, so. Who is missing?"

Elisabeth waved a hand. "You know, the others."

Happy to have a task, Emily wrote the names as she spoke, listing the who's who of New England elite that Elisabeth had brought to the marriage.

"Mmm," Elisabeth said, turning to Greta. "Evelyn needs Social Security numbers."

Their presence on the *Mayflower* passenger manifest aside, there would be at least two former presidents in attendance, and names weren't enough for the Secret Service. Greta nodded. Before she could reply, Elisabeth added, "You'll have to call them all. I don't want to talk to them."

Emily piped up from behind her mother. "I'll help."

"No. Greta can do it."

The youngest Storm's jaw clenched, and Greta watched as Emily took a deep breath—surely meant to be cleansing. She wondered how that went for her sister. "Mom, there are, what, forty people on this list? And that's before we add our friends."

Elisabeth's brows stitched together. "*Your* friends?"

A beat. "Yeah, Mom. Our friends."

"Why on earth would you invite your friends?"

Once, at Alice's insistence, Greta had tried therapy and lasted three sessions (somehow going 165 minutes without revealing that she was a Storm as in Storm Inside™) before she'd confessed the infraction to their mother, who'd wrinkled her nose (a shock—Elisabeth never wrinkled anything on purpose) and said, *Why on earth would you do that?*

All those years ago, Greta hadn't replied to the question, but Emily replied now. "Because they support us? Because it brings peace? And balance?"

If Emily thought any argument including peace and balance would win over their mother, she had not been paying attention for the last twenty-eight years. Elisabeth returned to the Storm Inc. spreadsheet. "No. The guest list is full."

"What?" Emily stopped. Restarted. "Mom—"

Greta stepped in. "We should get started."

Emily ignored her. "Mom—aren't you . . ."

When she trailed off, Greta sucked in a breath and shook her head. *Not now, Emily. We aren't you.*

Even if Greta had said the words aloud, she wasn't sure Emily would have listened. "Aren't you . . . sad?"

Greta froze.

Elisabeth did not, endlessly scrolling her 1107. "Not particularly."

Emily's gaze went wide, and she looked to Greta, her silent *What the fuck?* as clear as a gunshot. Greta lifted a shoulder in reply, but she couldn't deny the thread of satisfaction that ran through her at the question. Emily didn't understand, but Greta did. Because she was the good daughter.

She shook her head to stop Emily from saying more—instead redirecting her to the task at hand. For the next hour, the sisters played personal secretary to Elisabeth, making phone calls while she fielded emails and texts from an array of Franklin's staff, peers, and personal friends.

Greta made two calls for every one of Emily's, because the youngest Storm couldn't seem to get through a single conversation without tears and some kind of discussion of healing energy.

And of course, Alice never turned up. Honestly, it was for the best as Greta always felt as though her middle sister was silently judging her. Maybe it wasn't true—maybe it was just that they were so different. Where Greta had (almost) always been the steady, dependable one, who attended every dinner, every cocktail party, every nonprofit ribbon-cutting, everything that required a Storm to smile and speak on behalf of their father, and remained too insignificant to rate Elisabeth's attendance, Alice . . .

Well. Alice had been the bad daughter.

"Right. See you both then, Twyla." Emily was finishing another call—the last one, if Greta had been keeping correct records (of course she had). A pause, while Emily's eyes filled with tears. "Thank you. That's really kind."

Greta returned her attention to her list, resisting the urge to roll her eyes. They barely knew the newly minted wife of the cofounder of

Storm Inc., Mike Haskins. Half his age, Twyla had been the head of marketing for Mike's most recent venture and the society pages were happy to suggest she'd been the reason for his widely publicized divorce, leaving his first wife the wealthiest woman in the world.

Emily needed to hurry this along. Greta wanted the calls done, so she could leave here. So she could see Tony. She pushed away the knot of emotion that came with the thought of him.

"Who was that?" Greta stiffened at her mother's curt question as Emily ended the call.

"Twyla Haskins. She and Mike will be here," Emily responded. "I think that's—"

"Who told you to invite them?"

The air in the room went still. Emily raised her notepad. "You did."

"I most certainly did *not*." What had begun as curt was edging into something like shrill, and Greta froze, confused and unsettled by her mother's displeasure.

"Mom." Emily stared Elisabeth down, her tone firmer than usual. Irritated. "We read the list out loud. The Haskinses are on it." A beat. "Uncle Mike . . ."

"Michael Haskins is not your uncle and I would *never* have put him on the list."

Emily's gaze snapped to Greta, silently pleading, and suddenly Emily was seven or eight again, about to take the heat for some minor infraction, begging her older sister—a grown-up herself—to come to her defense. To stand with her, shoulder to shoulder, against Elisabeth in one of her chilly moods.

Greta remained silent.

Seeing that she wasn't going to get Greta's support, Emily turned back to Elisabeth. "Mom . . ."

"Stop saying that."

"What? *Mom?*"

"Yes. I have no intention of having Michael Haskins here." Elisabeth was turning a red unbecoming of a born-and-bred New England WASP who rarely showed heated emotion. "This is exactly the reason I asked *your sister* to make the calls."

The barb landed. "Okay . . . well . . . how about this: It's Dad's fu-neral, and *I* want Uncle Mike here."

Greta's brows rose in surprise. That didn't sound like Emily. That sounded like . . . Franklin.

Elisabeth must have heard it, too. "For the *last* time." Their mother's tablet landed on the thin Turkish rug—the sound loud enough to shock everyone, because no accidental slip would cause such a clear *thud*. "It is a *celebration*."

Silence fell, fraught and unpleasant, and Greta refused to meet Emily's eyes as the youngest Storm stood, unfolding from her chair with grace that came from years of lotus position. "Right. How could I forget."

She left the room, shoving the door open and disappearing into the hallway beyond, pushing it closed with a firm hand—not loud enough to be called a slam, but definitely loud enough to make her point.

Elisabeth leaned down to pick up the tablet.

Greta cleared her too-tight throat. "Mom—"

"You can go, too," Elisabeth said, a cold, unyielding rescue, as Greta didn't know how she was going to finish the sentence. "It's obvious how you all feel."

Confusion flared, along with the familiar, unpleasant lash of her mother's disappointment. "What does that mean?"

"We're done."

It didn't feel like they were done. It felt like they were just beginning; not that Greta would say that. In forty years, what things *felt* like had never been a part of their relationship.

What things *felt* like was reserved for another place. For another person.

Greta hovered on a precipice, frozen in that too-familiar way, afraid that action would upset Elisabeth, afraid inaction would.

Elisabeth made her way to her desk, not looking up as she said, "Was I not clear?"

Swallowing the twin emotions of guilt and excitement that loomed (always intertwined), Greta did as she was told, escaping before Elisabeth could change both of their minds.

It was a trip she'd made hundreds of times in the past—exiting through the door to the north side of the island, with its views of the less exciting part of the Bay. While the port of Providence was too far to see, there was no denying that northward travel would take visitors away from the luxurious promise of the Rhode Island of legend, toward the more blue-collar communities that kept the state running with manufacturing, shipping, and, yes, fishing—but not the glamorous kind.

Maybe that was why the north end of the island had always been Greta's favorite—as unglamorous as a piece of land boasting a helicopter pad could get.

That wasn't why, though. She liked it because the helicopter pad, the trio of cedar-shingled staff cottages, and the service buildings that housed the water pumps and generators that kept Storm Island running were the most private spots on the island—specifically built out of view from the main house, designed to give the appearance that the whole of the estate ran by magic.

Of course, it wasn't magic. It was hard work, keeping the island running. The kind that was underappreciated.

Greta could relate.

Past the helicopter pad and down a set of slate steps, she approached one of the tiny, two-room cottages. Slipping inside, she kicked off her shoes and crossed the barely there space, appointed with a full-sized bed, a serviceable table for two, mini fridge, and hot plate, and exited to the back porch, tiny and perfect, with views of the water . . . and Tony.

He looked up from his book as she stepped out onto the cedar planks, worn gray from storms and salt, taking his reading glasses off to meet her eyes.

Everything loosened as she went to him; the spring that seemed ever-tightening while she was with her family disappeared with Tony, easy and comfortable and *hers*. She tucked in beside him on the wicker love seat, his heavy arm wrapping around her, pulling her close.

"What are you reading?" she asked.

"Reacher."

She deliberately misunderstood. "Research, huh?"

He smiled into her hair, and she reveled in his warmth, in the smell of him—salty from his morning swim—in the sound of his voice, rumbling in his chest. "It'll be useful when I have to strong-arm someone to keep you safe."

The words were silly, meant to be a minuscule lifting of her spirits. His spirits, too, as they were both in mourning, weren't they? And for what Tony believed was the same thing—the same man.

Tony didn't know that Greta was mourning their entire future, instead.

She wasn't going to tell him. Not yet. Not when she could stay here for a bit longer, keeping her secrets.

But she didn't laugh at the joke. Instead she pressed closer, leaning in to the words and their fantasy of them, together, on the run. Him, big and strong, olive-skinned and square-jawed and Roman-nosed, all vigilante justice like in the books. And her, at his side. Nameless.

Of course, it was impossible. Greta Storm would always be a Storm. And that meant loyalty to family, first and foremost. No matter what Alice might think.

Alice thought she was making a mistake. She'd always thought that, though, hadn't she? She'd never understood how difficult it was to be the oldest, to set the standard, to bear the weight of maternal expectation. Of paternal disapproval. To do better, think faster, and always, always put family first.

Alice couldn't see it. The burden Greta bore. Sam had never been expected to take on an ounce of responsibility, and Emily was the baby of the family—full of charm and healthy boundaries, but Alice was something else entirely. Alice had always been bright resistance, flying in the face of expectation and refusing to budge.

Not even for her sister.

They'd never been close. For all the ways Greta belonged to Elisabeth, Alice had belonged to Franklin—and while she told herself that it hadn't mattered that Franklin had clearly loved Alice best, even after she'd flitted off to start a new life, far from the rest of them, if Greta had stayed in therapy, she would have found a word to describe her feelings about it.

Resentment, probably. Maybe *jealousy*—for the ways Franklin loved Alice without her having to *do* anything. Not envy. Belonging to Franklin wasn't easy. Greta should know—she loved someone who belonged to him.

Tony Balestreri didn't belong to him anymore, though. And Franklin would break his toy before he'd let anyone else claim it.

Chest tight, she turned her face into his warmth and pushed the thought away as Tony asked, "Tough morning, hmm?" He waited for her nod. "You okay?"

When was the last time someone had asked her that? When was the last time she'd told the truth? "You should come up to the house," she replied, because she knew he wouldn't.

"I don't think your mom would like that."

"I don't care," she lied, softly, knowing he wouldn't believe her.

"I talked to Jack this morning."

Greta stiffened. *Did he know what her father had asked her to do? Had Jack told him?* "What did you—"

She cut herself off and he reached for her, his fingers tucking a lock of her hair behind her ear. "Hey. Not about you."

Of course they hadn't talked about her. Tony's loyalty was never in question; he'd seen more than anyone else in Franklin's orbit and never breathed a word of it. And still, it felt dangerous that Jack had spoken to him. It *was* dangerous. A move she couldn't counter. "What did you talk about?"

One big shoulder shrugged. "Company stuff. He wanted to know if I was heading back to the city anytime soon." He was so casual. He didn't see that it wasn't a message for Tony, but a message for Greta. A question. Had she done as her father commanded?

She swallowed her panic. "And? What did you tell him?"

"That I was around if he needed a ride."

She laughed, the sound a little hysterical.

"Greta. Honey. It's okay. I'm not going anywhere."

The words made her feel drunk—not the soft, misty kind of drunk that came with too much champagne at the company holiday party, but the whirling, everything out of control kind of drunk that came with too many vodka tonics before getting into your brother's Porsche Boxster in the Hamptons and being unable to stop him from driving it directly into a dune.

She had five days.

She pressed her hand to Tony's at her cheek. "I don't like him."

"Jack?" he said, an edge of surprise in his tone. "I don't think anyone *likes* him. Well, except your dad."

"Why did Dad like him?"

"Loyalty."

He hadn't liked Greta, though. Hadn't she been loyal? Too loyal. "Like you," she said.

Tony pressed his full lips together but didn't disagree. Instead, he nodded. "I guess so." The words filled his throat and the sound, garbled and rough, summoned Greta's tears—the first she'd shed in company.

She dashed them away as Tony cleared his throat and said, "Anyway. Jack's complicated, but he's not a bad guy."

"He's not family."

"Neither am I."

Her eyes snapped to his. "But you—" Her *are*, along with its insistence that he was wrong, stuck in her throat, refusing to come. Because of course, Tony wasn't family. If he were family, she wouldn't be here, tucked away in a secret place in a secret place in a secret place, keeping him as far from the house as possible on this island that would never let any of them free.

He shook his head and leaned toward her. "Greta. It's okay."

He kissed her, soft and warm, lingering like comfort. Greta sighed and gave herself up to it, her hand falling to his chest, where his heart beat in slow, even rhythm. Like he belonged there.

Like she did.

He'd always been able to make her feel that way—as though there was something beyond this little world, full of her mother and her father, and her responsibility to it. Something that wasn't shared. Something that belonged to Greta.

Don't do it.

Alice's words, from earlier, whispering through her.

She broke the kiss and searched his eyes, deep and dark brown and full of the understanding she would never have. "Why doesn't it bother you? That we never welcomed you? That *he* never welcomed you? You were by his side for twenty years. You could have gone anywhere. Been anything."

"You sound like him," Tony said. "He pulled me aside not long ago and told me the same thing. That I could leave. Offered me a retirement package. A great one."

She sat up. "You didn't take it."

He shook his head. "Of course not."

"You dedicated your life to him."

A pause, and then, "Not only to him."

The words weren't light, like they should have been. They weren't easy, the way they might have been a week ago. Instead, they seemed urgent, as though everything had changed, and now he had something to say.

Or maybe she had something to hear.

Don't, Greta pleaded, silently. *Don't say it.*

For years, she'd been certain that if she shared Tony, made him public, he'd be taken from her. If there was one thing people knew about Franklin Storm, it was that he didn't like to share. So, for years, Greta had kept Tony a secret and consoled herself with the fact that in doing so, she was keeping him hers. With her. Private. Safe. Comfortable.

Even after yesterday's letter from her father, she'd told herself she had time. That she could keep everything with Tony the same for another day/hour/minute, but of course, that wasn't possible. There was no savoring these moments any longer. Franklin wouldn't have it. Elisabeth wouldn't have it.

Greta wouldn't have it.

The spring began to wind again, awareness of the world on the other side of the island. Of the responsibilities there, even as Tony took her hand in his and lifted her fingers to his lips. Fingers that she'd never thought of as bare until that moment. She pulled away from the caress, smoothing over the rough stubble of beard he hadn't shaved that morning. Because he didn't have to. Stubble that matched the sleek slate gray at his temples.

Gray, like the cedar planks of the cottage, weathered by storms.

"I told him that, you know. That I had other things keeping me here."

"You did?" Her touch stuttered over the line of his jaw.

"I didn't say it was you. But I think he knew it." He pulled her close. "And he didn't stop us."

But Franklin had stopped them. He'd just waited to do it. "How long ago?"

Tony sighed. "A few months ago. Greta, I don't want to talk about that. I want to talk about—" He paused, and for a wild heartbeat, she thought he might do something crazy. Like propose.

And maybe he did. "What if I dedicated my life to you, now? To us?"

She sucked in a breath at the question he'd never spoken before, the one they'd silently agreed never to voice. Her throat was tight, working to find words. To hold them back.

"Shit," he whispered, more to himself than to her. "I didn't mean to do it today." He shook his head. "Forget it. It's not important."

It was, though.

Greta stayed quiet, waiting, the silence stretching between them until he had no choice but to fill it. "You never wanted to tell them. I understood, honey. I did. I *do*. The last thing I wanted—I *want*—is to be a burden to you. I want to be the only person in your life who doesn't ask you for something. But . . . if you wanted to ask me . . . to carry the load . . . just know . . . I can. I would."

He couldn't, though. That was the point.

Greta was in that fucking Porsche again. Soaring toward the dunes. Only, this time, it felt like she might not survive it.

CHAPTER

8

"AUNT ALICE? ARE YOU in here?"

From her place on the floor of the darkened pantry, Alice looked to the sliver of sunlight beneath the door. "Yes! In here!" she called, banging on the door. "Saoirse! I'm in the pantry!"

There was a pause, and the knob jiggled. "It's stuck," her niece said, an edge of panic in the fourteen-year-old's voice. "What do I do? Should I get help?"

"Better look for someone we're not related to."

"What?"

"Yes, please!"

A pause, and then her niece said, "Um. Well . . . don't go anywhere, I guess?"

"Funny."

Saoirse was already headed for help; Alice listened to her footsteps disappear, only then realizing she should have asked the teenager to turn on the overhead light. With a sigh, she put her back to the door and resumed waiting, wishing that she had some of Emily's skill for meditation.

Instead, she was filled with quiet dread that if Saoirse didn't come back—if she happened to glance at her phone, for instance—Alice would be returned to the uncomfortable thoughts that had consumed her in the darkness. She didn't like being alone with her thoughts. She didn't like dwelling on Griffin and how she'd stayed with him for so long, and why. Pride. Rebellion. A desire for the antithesis of this place. These people.

She didn't like dwelling on them, either. On how they had let her go. On the way her mother had kept her firmly at arm's length. And of course, on her father, who'd controlled her, pushed her, and grown more and more infuriated every time she resisted. And then . . . finally, when she'd given him a good enough reason, he'd pushed her out.

She didn't like dwelling on the time she'd been gone. Time she'd never get back. Much like the time she was stuck in this fucking pantry.

After what felt like an eternity, a knock sounded on the door, strong and sure. "Alice?" The voice came from close enough that it seemed as though the person speaking could see through the door and knew exactly where her left ear was. It was low and quiet and smooth and very annoying.

She grumbled, "Yes."

"I found Jack," Saoirse announced, sounding as though she'd returned to her texts.

"Great," Alice said, false brightness in her voice.

A pause, and then Jack said, "You're stuck in the pantry."

"Am I? I hadn't noticed."

The overhead light flicked on, and Alice flinched at the brightness. God. She was still wearing Jack's clothes. *So embarrassing.*

The doorknob rattled. "Hmm." She imagined his disapproval on the other side, as though there'd never in his life been a door that hadn't opened at his whim. Jack Dean: Master of Doors. "Stand back, please."

Her brows shot up. "What are you going to do, break it down?"

"I'm not an action hero."

An image flashed of his body, laid out on the bed at the Quahog

Quay, the gold light from the streetlamp outside casting shadows across the ridges of his torso. The thick cords of his thighs. It wasn't *not* the body of an action hero.

"Alice?" he prompted. For the best.

She cleared her throat and stepped back. "Can't wait to see how you Tony Stark this thing in."

A pause, then, distracted, "Tony Stark *definitely* can't break down a door without the suit."

"Don't discount the adrenaline boost that comes with allowing yourself to feel a feeling." Silence. "You probably don't do that, though. Feel feelings."

"Do you think annoyance would work? I could probably muster that one up."

She scowled at the door. "I think if either of us has a lock on annoyance this morning, it should be me."

"Okay, then you try breaking down the door," he said, casually, the words punctuated by a rhythmic tapping.

Alice ignored him. "Saoirse—can you go get Charlie?" There was a reason why Charlie and Lorraine lived on the island—someone in the place had to have practical life skills (Charlie couldn't bang down a door, either, but that was irrelevant).

"We don't need Charlie." Jack's irritation was as clear as if he were inside the pantry with her. More tapping. When it stopped, Saoirse said, "Cool!"

The tapping resumed. And then, with a soft *thump*, the whole door tipped toward her, into the pantry, just far enough for him to catch it in his hands. He set it against the shelving just inside and looked to her. "No feelings necessary; just a hammer."

"My father would have been proud."

Jack nodded at the sack in her hand. "No less proud than he would have been to find you in here eating licorice."

"Breakfast of champions." She tucked the bag up on the shelf and collected her suitcase. She pushed past him and looked to her niece, still scrolling her phone in a red tank top, ripped shorts, and high blond pony. "Thanks for the help, Saoirse. Maybe next time you could find someone a little more . . . generous."

"Have I not been generous enough with you?" A pointed pause, as his words landed, along with the memory of the night at the Quahog Quay, when he was very generous. Deliciously generous.

Alice ignored the hot wash across her cheeks. "I meant generous of spirit. Why are you even here? In the main house?"

Saoirse answered for him, crossing to the fruit bowl on the counter, blissfully unaware of the subtext in the room. "He was looking for you."

"He was?" Alice looked at Jack. "You were?"

"Just wondering when I could get my shorts back."

Saoirse turned back, hand to the door, bright Granny Smith halfway to her mouth as her blue eyes settled on Alice. "Are those *his* shorts?"

Alice's blush flamed brighter. "Yes."

A beat, then, "They make your butt look great."

"Thank you, Saoirse."

"No problem," her niece said with a little smirk before crunching into the apple, looking startlingly like her father as she leaned against the butcher block island, having clearly decided that Alice and Jack were more interesting than her texts (for now).

When no one moved, her eyes widened with understanding befitting a much older person, and she said, "Ohhh-kayyy . . . So. I'm supposed to meet my mom and dad at the docks. We're disinfecting boats or something."

"Descaling them," Jack said.

"Whatever." The teen disinterest was absolute perfection, and Alice wished she could bottle it.

"Have fun," she called after her niece, now headed for the kitchen door on legs that grew longer by the second. Soon she'd be taller than Alice. She was already more stylish. When had that happened?

More time Alice had missed.

Without looking back, Saoirse replied, "Yeah, I don't think that's going to happen. We're just doing it for the money."

Of course, Sam and Sila had told the kids about the game. It was so inappropriate and so completely their style. Alice put on her best aunt face. "Don't worry about the money, Saoirse. That's not for you guys to worry about."

"What do you know about it? You don't even care if we don't get the money. You don't have kids. You don't know how much we cost."

The words came out pure Sila—full of something close to venom, and Alice couldn't hide her surprise at the complete change of tone. "Of course I care."

"No," Saoirse replied, emphatic in a way only fourteen-year-olds could be. "Mom says you don't care about us. You don't care if I can't stay at my school. And you don't care about whether I can go to Switzerland with my friends over winter break. She said you can basically leave anytime you want—even before the funeral—and ruin it all, and you don't even have to do anything but stay, even though Grandpa is making us clean boats and stain the dock. But you don't care about Grandpa. You probably don't even care that Grandpa is dead."

Leave it to a teenager to really land the punch.

Alice pressed her lips together, resisting the urge to respond to the words, the way they revealed all the color commentary Saoirse had heard from her parents. The last of her niece's monologue came out on a slight wobble—just enough to center Alice—and with a deep breath, she tried again. "Saoirse, I'm not—"

"Forget it." Saoirse straightened at her name, swallowing her grief, just like they all did, and banged the screen door open. "Like I said. You don't understand."

When she was gone, Alice studiously avoided meeting Jack's gaze, wishing he hadn't witnessed the moment with her niece. He didn't need to know any more about her than he already did. Instead, she returned to the pantry to collect her bags, slinging her satchel over her shoulder and rolling her suitcase out of the narrow space, knowing it was too much to ask that he be gone when she resurfaced. She didn't need a witness to the hot embarrassment and anger and frustration that coursed through her.

Of course, he stayed. He was leaning against the island, watching her.

Don't say anything, she willed him, silently. *Please. Just leave it.*

"Are you going to thank me?"

She blinked in surprise. "What?"

"It's customary to thank someone when they've rescued you."

He was changing the topic. It was a kindness (albeit obnoxious). "Thank you."

"Cantankerous, but I'll accept it."

"Yeah. Well. I promised I'd help my mom."

"Funeral stuff?"

"It's not a funeral," Alice said, instantly.

"Of course." A pause. "He wouldn't have wanted a funeral, you know. Everyone in black, weeping and wailing."

He was right, but Alice didn't want to admit it. "Have you done a lot of thinking about how my father would have liked to be memorialized?"

"You think he *would* have wanted everyone in black, weeping and wailing?"

"Maybe not the black, but he rarely missed an opportunity for drama."

He thought for a moment. "Yeah, he might want the weeping and wailing," he said, moving to reinstall the door he'd taken off its hinges.

She watched him, knowing she should leave, distracted by the way his shirtsleeves tightened over his shoulders as he lifted the door into place. "Well, I'm not sure he'll get it, considering what my mom's got planned: string quartets, an open bar, and speeches from half a dozen international dignitaries."

"You didn't grow up in my family, and it shows," he said, focused on matching the knuckles of the hinge again. "An open bar basically ensures weeping and wailing." There was something so personal about the quip—the revelation that he had a family, and hadn't been tossed down to earth fully formed, thirty-five and broad-shouldered and full of himself. She hid her surprise as he looked over his shoulder and said, "A little help?"

Alice dropped her bag and collected the pins for the door hinges.

Approaching Jack, she played assistant, handing over the hardware, ignoring the scent of him, like cool sea air.

She backed away, watching him hammer in the top hinge. "So feelings are in your wheelhouse, after all."

"Under certain conditions, yeah." He leveled her with a look that, if she were honest, produced a very specific kind of feeling in her. One she had no intention of revisiting.

She cleared her throat, and he went back to work. "Is this what you meant when you said you put out fires? Light carpentry?"

He hammered in the final pin. "Among other things."

"I'm impressed."

"Too easily," he said, dryly.

"What's that supposed to mean?"

"Only that you should expect more from people."

Now what did *that* mean? "Excuse me?"

He opened the pantry door. Closed it. Turned back to her, ignoring the question. "Do you need help with your bags?"

"Do I—" She looked down at her suitcase and satchel. "No. I'm very capable of carrying them upstairs."

He nodded once. "Okay."

"Thank you," she said, not feeling grateful at all.

"You're welcome." Why did everything he said irritate her? Why was it all so weird? Either way, she didn't have time for it. She had agreed to help her mother—albeit under duress.

As if on cue, a shout sounded from upstairs. Unintelligible, but definitely Elisabeth, and definitely heated, if the heavy *thud* that accompanied it was any indication. Brows raised, Alice and Jack looked to the ceiling, as though it would somehow open and reveal whatever was going on.

They shared a look, and for a fleeting moment, everything between them was forgotten; something was going on upstairs, and they weren't involved, and whatever it was sounded uncharacteristically emotional for a family that did not traffic in emotions.

Her shoulders straightened, and for a heartbeat, she was consumed with the urge to flee. Maybe she could—with the drama unfolding upstairs and Sam and his family at the far end of the island, maybe no one would notice. There were benefits to a family that was the portrait of self-absorption.

But Jack would notice. He seemed to notice everything.

"You were looking for me?" she asked.

He thought about denying it. She could see it in the breath he took, a little too deep. And then, "I have a task, too."

Interesting. "From my dad?"

Silence.

"Something other than judging our performance in this new round of Storm children vie for title of favorite child?"

The way this man shut down would have been impressive if it wasn't so goddamn annoying. Fine. If he didn't want to talk, she wouldn't talk. She didn't have to know. It wasn't her business. So why did she ask, "Is it something related to me?"

"No."

Good. She hadn't wanted it to be.

"At least, not really."

Good. She ignored the thought.

"What is it?" The silence was back, but she knew better than to try to match it. "It can't be worse than all the others."

He sighed. "Yours isn't that bad, Alice."

"You didn't grow up in my family, and it shows."

He didn't respond to the repetition, the words he'd used with her earlier, instead tilting his chin in the direction of her suitcase. "You should take that upstairs."

"What do you get if you play the game?" she asked.

The words were barely out of Alice's mouth when Sila came down the back stairs and into the kitchen, clearly on a mission. She pulled up short, her tight ponytail swinging across the line of her jaw, sharp and pale despite the hours of seaside idyll she'd logged during the summer.

"Oh! You're here." She hesitated, her attention laser-focused on them as she added, in a tone that made it all sound much more salacious than it had been, "Together."

Alice was smart enough not to correct her sister-in-law, as denial would make everything even more salacious. That, and she wasn't sure she'd be able to keep her anger about the conversation with Saoirse at bay if she let herself get into it with the other woman.

Sila didn't seem to notice, pointing to the back door and saying, brightly, "I was just—the boats."

"Nice day for it," Jack said, and Alice couldn't help the side-eye she slid his way at the banality.

"Isn't it?" Sila asked, one hand on the screen door, all her attention on Jack as her tone shifted. "Do you want to walk back with me, Jack? Just to make sure we're doing everything by the book? Being trapped in this house can get so *boring*."

Ballsy to make a move in her in-laws' kitchen, but history had proven that Sam's wife was pretty legendary at shooting her shot. And making it.

Before Alice could analyze the situation any further, Jack reached for the suitcase at Alice's feet and shocked everyone in the room. "Alice asked me to help her with her bags."

The most basic of excuses. Completely transparent and somehow, wildly entertaining? Not to Jack, clearly, which made it even better. She turned her back to the others, hiding her amusement as she leaned down and collected her satchel.

As Sila left the kitchen, screen door slamming in her wake, Alice said, "I'm pretty sure I said I could take care of the bags myself."

"You did." He lifted the suitcase and started for the stairs leading to the upper rooms and the tower.

"I only say it because it seems like maybe you misunderstood me," she said, following him.

"I didn't."

"Are you sure?" she teased.

"I'm sure," he grumbled, picking up speed on the landing as he made for the next set of stairs.

She didn't speak then, following quietly, not wanting to attract attention. Instead, she took the time to marvel at the fact that the heavy suitcase didn't seem to throw him even a little off-balance. Did anything throw him off-balance?

When they started up to the third floor, she pushed. "Funny. I thought you were my *dad's* fixer?"

"Alice."

She ignored the warning in his tone. "I'm just saying, it seemed like Sila had something that might have needed . . ."

"Stop."

"Fixing."

The sigh he let out as he reached the bottom of the tower stairs was long and rewarding. She followed him up the narrow, dark space and through the door of her room feeling pretty proud of herself for that sigh.

He set the suitcase down just inside the door and turned to face her, ostensibly to leave, but instead coming face-to-face with her. "Your dad was right about you."

She ignored the way her stomach dropped at the statement. The riot of possible answers to "How so?"

"You're a pain in the ass."

She exhaled at the dry words, undeniably her father's, though warmer than he'd probably said them. Kinder. Almost like Jack liked her. (He didn't. Clearly.) "A shock, I'm sure, considering what a delight he was."

Jack didn't laugh—she had trouble imagining him laughing—but his lips did curve in one of his small, spare smiles. "Yeah."

Alice stepped aside, clearing his path to the door, knowing she shouldn't keep him there. In that room. Where there was a bed. In which they'd both slept (separately, but still, it wasn't good sense). "Why *were* you looking for me? In the kitchen?"

He stopped and looked over his shoulder, and she followed him to the door, setting one hand on the knob, meaning to tell him not to worry about it. To wave him out. To close it. Behind him. And yet.

He looked away, to the dim stairwell, as though it were an escape hatch, and she wondered if he'd just ignore her. It wouldn't have been a surprise, honestly, considering his whole vibe was man of mystery—full of secrets and a unique set of skills, like removing SD cards and pantry doors.

Skill at removing other things, too, if she was being honest. Like clothes. And good sense. And afterglow.

Close the door, Alice.

Before she could, he surprised her.

"Come sailing with me tomorrow."

CHAPTER

9

SAILING WITH JACK WAS a mistake.

The night before had been brutal, a dinner filled with long silences and strong drinks and ending with the Storms heading to their individual corners, leaving the common areas of the house empty to everyone but Charlie and Lorraine, who arrived nightly, like the fog, to tidy and clean and prepare the house for the next day, efficient and invisible (ensuring Elisabeth's hardworking Puritan roots avoided interrogation).

Alice had lingered in the kitchen, despite Lorraine's resistance to letting her help. She'd won the battle, drying enameled cast iron and ancient silverware, trading stories with the older woman whose thumbprint cookies were a staple of her childhood summers.

Maybe that was why she agreed to sailing. Maybe the memories lured her into it.

Or maybe it was curiosity that sent her stealing downstairs and out the kitchen door, into sunlight too young and golden to have burned the dew from wild thyme and clover and the little white puffs of funnel spider webs. Maybe she'd seen the invitation as an opportunity to better understand this man who held her family in such a chokehold.

Reconnaissance. That's what she told herself she was doing.

It had been years since Alice had been on *The Lizzie*—the thirty-foot yawl her father had named for her mother some twenty-five years earlier, an homage that, in hindsight, indicated that either Elisabeth had done something very right, or Franklin had done something very wrong.

The boat had been christened with a shower of Dom Pérignon and a chorus of delight that someone—possibly Greta, who'd been going through a black-and-white photography phase—had captured perfectly. The photo of Elisabeth and Franklin laughing together at the bulkhead of the sailboat had been framed and affixed to the wall of the helm, its sharp edges long faded to watercolor in salt and sun.

Before *The Lizzie*, there'd been a different boat. A yacht, bigger and tackier and less nimble, designed to prove something in that way newly wealthy men believed rampant consumerism would—buying them respect from peers in their tax bracket (and old-money in-laws). And so, for a few years, Franklin had spent money, until he'd settled into his new role as the 1 percent of the 1 percent of the 1 percent and realized that there was something more rewarding than membership at the Union Club—ubiquity.

Storm telephones and tablets made their way into the zeitgeist and Franklin's obsession with approval had evolved into arrogant resistance of the old guard. He'd changed the world. Democratized it, he liked to say, placing information and access in the hands of everyone from world leaders and celebrities to landscapers and oystermen.

Franklin's world wasn't a democracy so much as a dictatorship, however. Freedom and equality—as long as everyone behaved as Franklin wished. Politicians, Wall Street, tech developers, engineers.

His children.

The Lizzie wasn't the boat on which Alice had learned to sail, but it was the boat on which she'd learned to love sailing. Lavish and stunning, all hand-hewn teak and gleaming brass and crisp white sails that dazzled on the water, it could be piloted by one person, though whenever she'd been on it, it had been her and Franklin. It was almost impossible to believe that he wasn't there that morning, heading for the mouth of the Bay—his hair, the color of New England sand, wild in the wind as he shouted orders.

Jack was already on deck when she arrived, acknowledging her with a stoic nod as she climbed up from the skiff she'd piloted out to *The Lizzie,* anchored a short distance from the island. She eased into the familiar work of preparing the boat for sail, letting herself feel for the first time since she got to the island—the bite of the lines, the slick of the teak coaming, the snap of the crisp mainsail as they took to the sea, Jack at the helm—probably because he was afraid she'd sail them to the mainland and take off (an idea Alice hadn't not considered).

Instead, she stood at the bow, letting the sea wash over her, clearing her head. For a quarter of an hour, they remained in something like companionable silence, and she almost forgot him in favor of the splash of the water, the lick of the salt, the thick flap of the stiff jib sail—loud enough to drown out everything but the wind, the water, the sun. If she closed her eyes, she could hear her father shouting quotes about the ocean in that way people did, half-insufferable, half-charming depending upon the mood.

She didn't close her eyes. She had work to do, turning her back to the bow and setting a hip to a stanchion, watching Jack. He maneuvered the sailboat with the kind of certainty that wasn't learned in a week of sailing lessons in the Hamptons.

"You've done this before."

She shouted over the wind, but his immediate attention made it seem as though he would have heard her anyway. Not that he replied.

"Did he teach you?" It wasn't hard to imagine. Her father had loved bringing people onto the boat—training a new crew, he liked to call it.

"I grew up with boats."

Not this kind, though, Alice could tell. Wealth had a way about it, an ease that was difficult to explain but impossible not to recognize, especially if you'd spent your life around it. Though it came in many forms, from confidence to carelessness, it pervaded a person's world-view, was impossible to replicate, and incredibly difficult to hide.

It couldn't be bound up in the tattoos on his arm and the roughness of his hands, and the stern set of his jaw. Everything about the man was wound tight, as though he might at any point need to fight, and nothing about that said dinner at the yacht club. "I bet my father liked that."

He moved the wheel. Checked the mast. "I liked sailing with him."

Alice looked away from the words, from the fondness behind them, from the memories they evoked, when it had been her on the boat. When she'd liked it. She took a deep breath, letting the salt air hum through her, settle in her lungs. The sea was healing, wasn't that what the Victorians said? Taking the waters cured things.

This water brought questions.

"Were you here? When he died?"

If he was surprised that she asked, he didn't show it. "No."

"Did you talk to him that morning? Before he left?"

"Yes." It hurt, knowing that.

"Did he say anything?" She hated having to ask him, this stranger. Hated that he knew more about her father than she did. Than she ever had. Before he could answer her, she said, "Never mind. I don't want to know."

"I would tell you," he said. "If he had."

She had no reason to believe him. And yet. "Why did you ask me to sail with you?"

He was quiet for a long time. "You're the one who loves sailing."

You're the one. In comparison to everyone else, he meant. Sam hated the patience it took—not enough excitement for him. Emily didn't like open water. Greta couldn't deal with the spiders that inevitably revealed themselves (eight-legged adventurers, her father used to call them). And Elisabeth. Well. She'd lent her name to the vessel, but Alice couldn't remember the last time she'd condescended to set foot on it.

Alice *was* the one who loved sailing. "How do you know that?"

Her sharp question was beneath them both. "I know a lot about you, Alice."

The words rumbled out of him, humid with sea air and all the things he knew. The way she'd clutched the newspaper on the train, the bleed-proof white that had found its way into her hair after a too-short morning in the studio, the way her voice shook in the face of the photographers at the train station, the way it shook—different, better—when he'd run his hands over her skin later that night.

She gripped the bow rail at her back. Told the truth. "I do like sailing."

"That's my task. To sail." His truth.

As her father's tasks went, it was a pretty good one. The best one, probably. More proof that Franklin had no interest in fairness. "And what do you get? If you do it?"

He adjusted their course. "Closure."

"You can't get that from playing executioner in his inheritance game?"

"That's my job," Jack said.

"What a devoted employee," she said, dryly.

"I owe him."

And there it was. Jack was an acolyte. Just like the others on Franklin's staff, in the world, the ones who went to the developers' conferences, the ones who analyzed every statement her father made, every tossed-aside comment that could move markets. Franklin Storm didn't just change the world, he convinced the world that, without him, it had no hope of ever changing.

"Why?"

"He . . . changed my life."

"I'm sure he loved that you thought that."

Everything about him tensed at the reply, as though he had a half dozen arguments. As though, if they weren't on this boat, he'd take her to the nearest conference room and cue up a presentation replete with all the reasons he owed Franklin Storm.

"So *you* have to sail," she said, returning the conversation to smooth waters. "Why am *I* here?"

"It's been a while since I've been on the water. I thought maybe it was the same for you."

It wasn't an answer, but she hadn't expected one. She tilted her head up to the enormous mainsail, gleaming cream in the sun, and answered him like they told each other the truth. "It has been."

She didn't tell him the whole truth, though. She didn't tell him that the last time she'd sailed, she'd been here, on this water. On this boat. On this island.

In this family.

Silence for a while, and she was grateful for the mirrored sunglasses he wore, so she didn't have to feel his intent gaze when he asked, "When was the last time?"

"I was on a pontoon boat a few years back." He made a sound that indicated how he felt about pontoon boats. "They are very sturdy, you know. And skiffs. Yachts even. All safer than a sailboat. No one gets knocked off a pontoon boat by a twenty-foot boom."

"Your father was never one to be swayed by security."

"Yeah, well, considering he crashed a glider into a field three days ago, maybe he could have been a little more careful."

It wasn't kind, she knew. But somehow, this boat, which she'd been so sure would provide respite from the island, was even more constricting. She stood and made for the rear of the vessel. "I'm going to check the mizzen. It shouldn't be so—"

Chaotic. Untethered.

She didn't mean to look at him when she passed, but it was difficult not to. Even if he wasn't the kind of man who demanded attention by simply existing, she couldn't ignore that he was watching her. And then, to make matters worse, he said her name. Sturdy. Even. Like solid land. "Alice."

What was she supposed to do? Not respond? It would have been rude. So she looked at him. Under duress.

"I'm sorry for your loss." He'd said it before, to the whole family, when he'd laid out the instructions for the game. When no one had acknowledged it. She should probably acknowledge it now. Except she didn't want to. She knew it made her obstinate, but what was there to say?

Thanks, but if you were really sorry, you wouldn't be carrying out his insane final wishes. That was the kindest thing she could imagine saying. The worse one was *Thanks, but if you were, why'd you fuck me in a seaside motel?*

And then there was, *Thanks for being sorry, but I'm not sure I am.*

She settled on, "I'm sorry for yours."

His jaw tightened. She shouldn't have noticed. "Thank you."

And then, as though the gratitude unlocked her, she offered, "The last time I was on this boat, I had an argument with my father."

They were nearing the Jamestown Bridge, dozens of boats jockeying for position to pass through toward the mouth of the Bay, where sunlight gleamed in blinding reflection. "Your father was an easy man to argue with."

"This one was a long time coming," she said. He used the work of navigating the congestion to avoid looking at her. It was a move, she would later realize. A tactic to make her say more. A lifetime of media trainers felt a chill in the air when she did just that. "I'm guessing you know why we never met."

He didn't pretend not to understand. "You and I? I know what I'm supposed believe."

Franklin must have loved this man and his unbearable astuteness. "You know what I did to him. To Storm."

He nodded. "You're pretty famous."

"Don't you mean infamous?"

He shook his head once. Firm. "Do you want to tell me about it?"

"I'm sure you know the important parts," she quipped. "I have my own section on the Storm Inc. Wikipedia page."

"Is that where the important parts are?"

It wasn't.

She rephrased. "You know the parts that were important to the world. The parts that came from the women who spoke up." Alice had been twenty-six years old, working in the industrial design department at Storm, when she'd discovered that a dozen women at the company had stood together and reported the inappropriate behavior of Storm's head of operations—a man who had abused his power for years. Motivated by the sea change in the world and by each other, his victims had come forward, hoping to be heard, believed, and taken care of.

The misconduct—which ran the gamut from innuendo to blatant harassment to accusations and eventual proof of physical assault—was announced at a time when businesses across the globe were facing a social and fiscal reckoning. When Alice had heard, she'd gone straight to Franklin, only to discover that instead of standing up, turning on the lights, and cleaning house, her father had approved a spate of quiet settlements, airtight NDAs, and a tidy sweeping under the nearest rug.

Alice had been outraged. She faced him head-on, furious when he'd defended himself, explaining that she was hardly more than a child and couldn't understand the weight of the scandal. The women would be well compensated—generously—and the COO given a quick exit via golden parachute and not a lick of public punishment, but this was business, and if Alice was going to run Storm someday, these kinds of unpleasant decisions were par for the course. Couldn't she see the situation was nuanced? That this was the best solution for everyone?

She couldn't see it, though. It wasn't a solution. It was *wrong*.

When she'd left her father's office, Alice had dashed off her email resignation, called her friend Roxanne, and put the company on blast.

The piece broke in the *Journal* three days later, victim accounts alongside her own public statement of disappointment in the corporation's leadership. The news had a field day, staff walked out of Storm offices across the globe, customers threatened boycotts mere weeks before the release of the latest 1107, the COO was disgraced, then arrested . . . and the stock price had taken a hit.

All because of Alice Storm, heir to a fortune and the unlikely new face of the fight against late-stage capitalism.

"You changed the world."

She shook her head. "They changed the world; I just knew who to call."

He nodded, turning the wheel, calling the shift in the boom as it swung, making sure she was safe from it. "And your dad was pissed."

"*That*," she said, "is an understatement."

Franklin had a legacy to protect—he was a billionaire, sure, but he liked being a *relatable* one. One who'd come from his parents' garage. A guy who was supposed to understand that the people who'd run the world in the past weren't the ones who would lead it into the future.

The Storm PR team worked overtime and within hours the whole thing had been spun. How shocked he was. How devastated. How much he cared. There were massive public donations to victims' rights organizations. An overhaul of Storm HR. And an apology tour for the ages: colleges, corporations, news magazines, papers of record—Franklin sat down with anyone who asked.

Except Alice.

He'd never forgiven her.

"He punished me," she said, half to Jack, half to the water. "I shouldn't have been surprised. It was the first time I'd ever fought him." She paused. "Or, rather, it was the first time I'd ever won."

The wind died down in the wake of the words, letting Alice finish the story. "He spent two years refusing to acknowledge my existence. I would come to family dinners, to holidays—and he would look straight through me. There's this photograph that ran in the Style section a year or so after everything went down. The two of us, at some benefit, smiling brightly, looking so *normal*. And I remember how weird it was to see it, because I had literally that morning moved out of the apartment I'd been living in—the one he'd bought for me."

"He kicked you out?" The question was sharp with disbelief.

"No," she said. "That would have required him to speak to me. But that apartment reeked of his anger, and I wasn't going to live there anymore." She watched the water gleam for a bit, and then added, "Anyway. That went on for two years, until the last time I was here."

"You argued."

She nodded. "The last time I was on this boat." She waved at a passing boat, grateful for something to do with herself. "The last time I saw him."

"God. I shouldn't have—"

"No," she said, horrified by the beginning of the apology, like he was going to handle her differently now, gently. Thoughtfully. She didn't want that. "Please don't. If it hadn't happened here, it would have happened somewhere else. That's what people get for crossing Franklin Storm. The wild thing is, I never even wanted to work at Storm."

His brows rose above the aviators. "Why were you there?"

"Jack, in all the time that you worked for my dad, did you ever see him *not* get what he wanted? Hell—he's *dead* and he's still getting it." He didn't deny it, so she pressed on. "I worked there because he wanted me there. Because that was his plan." She continued, counting on her fingers. "He chose my friends, the college I went to, the summer internships I had, the apartments I lived in. I was living Franklin Storm's dream."

The others weren't for him: Greta was Elisabeth's replica; Sam was the kind of person who blossomed with money and power, but struggled with work; and Emily was sweet, but not for stockholders. But Alice—

"It didn't matter what I wanted. He was convinced I was the future of Storm. The kid he would mold in his image." She ran her fingers through the seawater on the deck rail as she spoke. "I had a fellowship in Rome all lined up. Art conservation. I'd worked my ass off to get it— an American hadn't received it in twenty years. I applied in secret, knowing it would piss him off. I was so proud of it. The first thing that really felt like it was entirely mine. And you know what he did?"

"Alice."

He knew what she was going to say, of course. She looked to him. "Why am I even telling you this? You were his fixer. You know what he did. What he was capable of doing to get what he wanted."

She'd been devastated when she'd received the letter reporting that funding had been pulled for the fellowship. She'd begged her mother for money, then begged the museum to let her pay her own way.

Six months later, Storm Inc. was listed as a major donor on its website. Her father hadn't hidden it; he'd wanted her to know that he would always win. When she'd confronted him, he'd reminded her in that superior, arrogant way he always did that she was *Class A stock, impossible to be divested.*

Every time he said it, it made her dig in more. Made her try for something further afield. Something less like him. Less Storm. "My whole life, he had plans for me. Who I was allowed to date. Where I was allowed to go to school, what he wanted me to study, where he wanted me to live, to work. And I *hated* it." She shrugged. "And the truth was, once he was forced to see that I didn't want the same things . . . he didn't really want me at all. But he still wouldn't cut me loose."

"So, you cut yourself loose."

She narrowed her gaze on him. "What's that mean?"

"Only that I'm doing the math—seven years since your Wikipedia entry, and only five since the last time you were here. So what was it? The final straw? Let me guess—the fiancé."

"Griffin." She lifted her chin. "There is no Griffin. Not anymore."

She'd been afraid it would feel like failure, to confess it to him, but when he nodded and said, "I know," it felt like something else. Like freedom.

"How?"

A hesitation. Barely there, then gone as he answered. "You don't wear an engagement ring."

She looked down at her hand, recently bare. "You're the only one who's noticed."

"I notice you."

Her eyes widened behind her sunglasses, and she wasn't sure what to say—her whole life, she'd tried hard not to be noticed, but it had never felt as dangerous as it was when this man, all strong hands and set jaw, noticed her.

As if she didn't have enough mess to contend with.

The sound of his throat clearing should have been lost in the wind, but it wasn't. Neither were his words. "Your father didn't like your fiancé."

"My father barely knew my fiancé."

"Okay," he said, focused on the water again, navigating the waves. "Did you like him? Griffin?" She didn't miss the way he said the name, like it tasted wrong.

"Obviously." Was it, though? Obvious? She looked to the sea and took a deep breath. "He was the second thing that felt entirely mine."

She'd been twenty-eight, devastated by a lifetime of battles with her father—large and small—the war unwinnable now that she'd betrayed him so thoroughly, turned her back on the road he'd paved for her from birth.

"He was handsome and funny. Had a big personality." Griffin had been all friendly smiles and belly laughs and wild stories about the time he'd backpacked across Europe during a gap year before he went to NYU and with friends everywhere, and no, he didn't have a steady job (an actor) and no one was really certain how he paid the rent on his apartment in Greenpoint (not by acting), but did it matter when he was so fun?

"I was in hiding—the whole world knew what I'd done. My father wasn't speaking to me. The rest of my family was fading away, uncertain of what was to come and absolutely not interested in getting caught in the cross fire. I had a new job, was trying to make a new life. And Griffin . . . he was just . . . different.

"He hosted a trivia night at a bar near the school where I teach." She'd never gone before that night, too afraid her colleagues would ask questions she didn't want to answer. But they hadn't. It had been fun, and she'd been happy. "When our team won, he came bounding over. I'd known an answer he'd expected to stump the room. He bought me a drink." That was a lie. Alice had bought the drinks, but she'd rewritten the night for so long she'd forgotten the truth. "I'd never met someone so—uninhibited."

"Uninhibited," he said, in the same tone he'd said *Griffin.*

"Impulsive," she clarified. "Impulsiveness isn't afforded to Franklin Storm's children. The press pays attention. Social media explodes. Wikipedia gets updated."

He ignored the point. "What was the answer that should have stumped you?"

"*Judith Slaying Holofernes,*" she said, taking comfort in the fact that he didn't respond, likely because he didn't understand the reference to the painting. Griffin had understood it, though, and where other men might have shied away from a woman with a passion for that particular painting, he'd been impressed (granted, he hadn't known her history with the vibe).

One month later, Griffin moved into her tiny one-bedroom and everyone loved him—even Gabi, who notoriously hated everyone Alice dated. Griffin was a good time, a good hang, and he was good to Alice. Who cared that he didn't have a steady job? Who cared that he didn't take anything seriously? They were in their twenties and Griffin was great entertainment.

That, and the most important bit—he was Alice's choice (for better or worse).

"Okay," Jack said, breaking into her thoughts. "So what happened?"

"I brought Griffin to the Fourth of July."

His brows rose. "Here?"

"Yes."

"With your father."

"I take it from your obvious shock that you are familiar with Storm Independence Day."

He nodded. "I haven't had the pleasure of attending, but yes."

July Fourth was a family affair for the Storms—not because anyone had a particular affinity for red, white, and blue, but because it was a glorious time of year on the island, which made it the perfect time to descend for a long weekend of croquet and bocce and sailing and oysters and lobster boils and cocktails and rounds and rounds of cards that made them all feel like they were a normal family, until Franklin got bored and the Storm Olympics began—with the patriarch of the family assigning ever more impossible tasks to his children . . . and whomever they brought for trial in this particular fire.

It was not for the faint of heart, and usually marked the final test of a newcomer to the family. Partners were only brought to July Fourth once they were a sure thing. Sila hadn't been invited until she married Sam (by then, she'd been pregnant with Saoirse, so there was no turning back). Emily broke the rules and brought a boyfriend once when she was in high school (ever the youngest child) and everyone freaked out—including the poor kid, who'd gone wide-eyed at Franklin's insistence that they all go cliff diving and called his parents to pick him up in Wickford for a well-timed "family emergency."

Emily liked to joke that she'd only dated women after that, because

men weren't strong enough for the Storm Independence Day shenani-
gans (Claudia, for the record, had aced her first time on the island—
leaped from the Moonstone Cliff without hesitation, and received
Franklin's respect as a trophy).

Not so Griffin—he wasn't strong enough for the Storm games; Alice
had known it at the time. But Alice hadn't expected him to run the
normal gauntlet. Charming, funny, never met a stranger—a lot like
Franklin, in that way. She'd expected Griffin to just golden retriever his
way through the holiday, too oblivious to be afraid.

"My father hated him."

"I assume that was the point," Jack said, as though it were obvious.

And it had been, she understood now, with the benefit of time and
a lot of therapy. But then, she hadn't been willing to admit that she'd
never really expected Griffin to be accepted by her family. "It wasn't
about him. Not really."

"Not for either of you, I would think." When she turned a sharp
look on him, he said, "It was about you getting your father to speak to
you again, wasn't it?"

It was possible that she hated this man and the way he saw everything clearly. The way he made her ask questions she was deliberately
avoiding. Had she realized what the fallout would be, would she have
done something different? Impossible to know. Impossible not to tor-
ture herself with the what-ifs now.

"And my father? What was it about for him?"

"Anger," he said. "You were the most valuable thing he had, and he'd
lost you."

Protégé or not, Jack clearly did not understand Franklin's feelings
about her. She forced a laugh. "That's funny."

"It's the truth."

Silence fell and she filled it by looking to the south, where the mouth
of the Bay opened into the Atlantic. She tilted her head toward it. "We
should head back. Around Beavertail. Up past Castle Hill."

Jack didn't respond, shifting the boat into a turn. She made for the
boom, checking the mainstays, adjusting as he made the turn. She
looked to the Castle Hill Lighthouse, high on the ragged shoreline that

rose above them, watching over them as it had done for countless other ships in the century it had been there. She'd painted that lighthouse for her father once (Davy's gray, terre verte); she'd never seen the painting again.

"We hadn't even been on the island for an hour before Dad summoned me to sail." She lifted her chin in the direction of the cockpit. "He barely looked at me, he was so irritated that I'd come. That I'd brought Griffin."

You know better than to come with someone like him. She could still hear him; could still feel the satisfaction that she'd finally provoked a rise out of Franklin. *He's a joke. Get rid of him.*

Or what? she'd asked, unwilling to back down, grateful for the fight. For the attention, for which she was starved, even then, even as an actual adult (was anyone an actual adult under the heat of their parent's disdain?). *Are you finally going to kick me out?*

No one would blame me, he said. *For what I've tolerated.*

She'd been furious. *You've tolerated me? What about me? You haven't spoken to me in years!*

What did you think would happen? he'd replied. *Did you think I'd laud you as a hero, too? Did you think I'd thank you for betraying me?*

I would have thought you'd . . . She'd changed her mind. And the words. *I'd have thought you'd be a better father.* At the time, she hadn't realized how it might have stung. But now, remembering that they were the last words she'd ever said to him—

She swallowed back the emotion that threatened. Reminded herself that it was Franklin who'd ended it.

Then we're equally disappointed.

"He told me to leave," she said, pushing her shoulders back. Lifting her chin, like she had whenever they fought. How often had she replayed his rigid, cold words over the years, holding her phone in her hand, wondering if she should call home. She never did, too distracted by the sound of them in her ears, the way they filled her up and resurrected her own rage. Her own unwillingness to bend.

Even masked behind aviators, she could see Jack's surprise. "In those words?"

Get the hell off my island.

It had been quiet and dismissive, somehow worse than if he'd shouted it and dropped her in the nearest harbor himself. He hadn't cared, and it had hurt. There'd been a part of her that had been grateful for that pain. For what came next. For the way it made her brave.

It had never occurred to her that it would be their last conversation. She'd never imagined he would die; Franklin Storm wasn't the kind of man who died.

She nodded. "That was it." The boat felt infinitely smaller in the wake of the embarrassing confession, and she didn't like it. She looked to Jack, his lips pressed into a firm line, and a spark of that old anger flared again, this time for Jack.

"Was it worth it?" Jack interrupted her thoughts. "Leaving?"

"It's always worth leaving when someone doesn't want you to stay." Her therapist would be really proud of that answer.

Griffin wasn't worth it, but Alice's freedom? The knowledge that she could thrive without them, that she could be more than Alice Storm Inc.? That was worth it. As for her family . . . was it worth them ignoring her? Forgetting her? Was it worth her father not having final words for her? No letter, no phone call, nothing.

A final punishment. No answers. Only questions. She watched the water for a long moment, filled with them, and finally turned to him. "That night. On the train. At the Quahog Quay."

If Jack was shocked by the wild change of topic, he didn't show it. It was his job not to be surprised. "For what it's worth, I didn't intend to sleep with you. Not at the start."

"That's funny, as you could have avoided it by telling me the truth about who you were." He'd barely opened his mouth to reply when she raised a hand and said, "It's my fault for insisting on no names. I brought on an irrevocable case of vocal paralysis."

"No." His reply came curt and unyielding. "By the time you said no names, that was fine with me."

Her brows shot up. "It was?"

He did look at her then. "What do you want me to say, Alice? That I wanted to fuck you?"

Yes. The response shot through her—surprising and unexpected and *real.* Alice was not the kind of woman men wanted to fuck. At least, she wasn't the kind of person men told they wanted to fuck. And if someone had asked her a week earlier if this was the kind of thing she would have liked to hear, she would have said, *Absolutely not. No thanks.*

Apparently, she would have been wrong.

Luckily, the question was rhetorical. "Okay. I wanted to fuck you. And I knew that if I told you who I was, that wasn't going to happen."

Her jaw went slack, but he was still going. "Maybe I was sad, and maybe I was angry, and maybe I was in shock, and maybe, in the moment, I wasn't interested in facing real life. And neither were you. You wanted it as much as I did."

He was right. Her grip tightened on the smooth edges of the boat. She'd wanted it. And if she let herself, she still did.

As though he heard the silent confession, he said, "Like I said: You should expect more from people."

Her gaze fell to his hands, strong and sure at the helm, that compass with its beautiful lines inked across his forearm. It was the first time she had seen it in the light, and so it wasn't until that moment that she noticed that it wasn't only a compass. There, embedded in its fine-lined face, was an equally fine-lined sextant—an ancient sailing tool, used to navigate the sea using the stars. The kind of thing only someone who'd sailed for a lifetime would care enough to have permanently inked on their skin.

Who was this man? And why was he here, with her?

This man who noticed her. Who asked questions and made silent space for her to answer them, luring her into bad decisions. He wasn't good for her.

"When I expect more from people, I'm disappointed," she said to the water. "I expected more of my family. Of my siblings. Of my mother. Of my father. More of Griffin." She looked to Jack. "Of you."

For the first time since she got on this boat, she could see the words strike him.

"You were supposed to be a good guy. You told me you were."

He nodded. "You're right."

"My father isn't the only one playing a game, is he?"

"Alice."

"No," she said. They were approaching the east side of the island, the sun had moved higher in the sky, casting a deep blue shadow of the cliffside on a tiny cove there—Prussian blue, sharply delineated from the gleaming ultramarine of the Bay in the sun. Low tide had revealed the tiny beachhead that was one of Storm Island's best-kept secrets.

"You're playing a game, too. Aren't you?"

Jack shook his head. "Not that night."

"But now?"

Silence. Alice couldn't help her laugh—shocked and full of the realization that she'd just told him more than she ever would have if she'd known. "Oh my god. We're not just his pieces. We're yours, too."

"Alice—"

She cut him off. "You knew who I was. You knew I had to get to the island. You knew I had to stay here. You were the *only one* who knew I had to stay here. He didn't write me a letter. He sent you." She looked at the island, her father's domain, full of memories. Whatever Jack was up to, it was a test, just as everything here always had been—impossible to pass. "Everyone thought we got a reprieve on the first day of the game. Seven days, but you didn't arrive until day two. Except you did arrive for me."

If his jaw clenched any tighter, he'd break it.

"*We're* not your game. *I am.*"

He didn't reply. He didn't have to. She was right. "You're not just here to judge the game, and your task isn't just to *sail*. You're my keeper. You're supposed to keep me on the island because, what, he thought I might leave and ruin the fun? That's it, isn't it?"

A long moment passed, during which he looked absolutely furious. Triumph surged in Alice's chest; she'd figured it out. And then she was moving—heading for the mainsail.

"Alice!" Jack shouted. "Let me explain."

"Nah," she said. "Now that I know this is the game, I know how to play." She slipped the line with ease, loosening the massive triangle of fabric as she called out, years of experience on the water making the words instinct. "Heave to."

Luffing the sails would slow the boat enough that when she dove into the water, she wouldn't get caught up in its wake. Not that it would have deterred her, as she was pretty drunk with momentary power and something much more dangerous—grief.

She kicked off her sneakers and climbed up to the edge of the boat.

"What the—" Jack was heading for her, fast.

His expletive was lost to the water as she dove off *The Lizzie,* the cold whoosh of the Bay welcoming her like an old friend.

Like home.

She surfaced to the sound of her name, deep and angry, and moved immediately into freestyle, aiming for the little beach, letting the knowledge that she'd shocked and enraged him flood her with smug delight. Even if he wanted to stop the boat and scream, there was no way he could; there was no turning off the wind. Stopping sailboats with precision and speed required practice that came with hundreds of hours on the water (and no small amount of paternal castigation).

She made it to shore in less than five minutes, emerging from the water onto the little beach with her heart pounding and her breath coming in full, lung-expanding gusts. She pushed her hair out of her face and smiled.

Jack might think he knew about her and this family and her father's boat, but he didn't know everything. If her calculations were right, *The Lizzie* would already be out of sight, headed toward the northern tip of the island, around the cliff's face. If he wanted to follow her, he'd have to circle the island once again. And by then, she'd already be up the hidden steps, headed for the house.

Alice looked to the water and stilled, surprise and no small amount of admiration coursing through her.

The Lizzie wasn't out of sight. It was stopped, pointed into the wind, mizzenmast anchoring it on the gleaming water, closer to the shore than it had been when she'd dived off.

He'd heaved the boat to like a seasoned sailor.

No. Not like a sailor. Not while he stood on the edge of the boat, arms crossed over his stupidly broad chest, watching her.

Like a pirate. If pirates wore sunglasses.

As though he heard her, Jack reached up and pulled the aviators off, tossing them away, not caring where they landed.

And then he dove into the Bay and headed straight for her.

CHAPTER

10

"You didn't just grow up with boats."

She spoke first, because she didn't want him commandeering the moment, and she didn't want him noticing how much she'd enjoyed the view as he'd executed a perfect, Olympic-level freestyle before emerging from the sea, his casual linen button-down clinging to him in a way some might consider a clear nod to Mr. Darcy.

Not Alice, though. She was definitely not likening this man to a beloved romantic hero. He was the opposite of romantic heroes.

I wanted to fuck you.

Definitely not something Darcy would say.

That, and no Austen hero had tattoos inked across his chest. She'd seen them in the dark the other night, but she hadn't lingered on them—everything about that experience had been frenzied, as though they both knew everything would change the next day.

Only Jack had known how much, however.

She straightened at the thought, pushing her curiosity about the inky shadows beneath his wet shirt aside and reminding herself of the truth: Jack was the villain of the story.

Keeping her gaze fixed on his face as he stalked from the sea, she lifted her chin and said, "You can actually sail." It came out like an accusation.

"Was that unclear?" There was no hint of the earlier calm in his voice now. He was furious—like he loathed being manipulated.

They had that in common. "You stopped that boat on a dime."

"Aside from being taught to do that when someone jumps overboard into an active waterway—" Oh. He didn't like that. "Yeah, I know my way around boats. I told you I grew up on the water."

"I was perfectly safe. I didn't do anything I haven't done a hundred times before."

For a moment, she wondered if she'd pushed him too far. "I don't care what you did on boats piloted by your foolish friends while you were growing up, rich and stupid. When I'm at the helm, you take better care of yourself."

She resisted the way that gruff concern made her feel warm inside. And the way it made her want to—very vaguely, barely at all, really—do as she was told.

He was obnoxious and domineering, speaking to her as though she'd never set foot in the ocean. Was he wrong about swimming across the Bay being dangerous? Not *really*. But it wasn't as though she'd been paddling around out there—she'd headed straight to shore. Just as he had.

"I thought I made it clear that I don't need a keeper."

"If the last three days have been any indication, you absolutely need a keeper."

"Had I known that you'd been hired for the position, I would never have agreed to sail with you."

"Is that supposed to upset me?" He was breathing heavily, and Alice had the feeling it had nothing to do with the swim.

She narrowed her gaze on him. "For the record, I was never stupid."

"Of course you were," Jack said, refusing to give her quarter. "You were young and rich and the whole world was yours for the taking. A recipe for stupidity."

"Isn't that how every young person feels?" Alice was feeling petulant, like the young rich kid in his example.

"Yeah, but the rich ones don't just feel it. They know it's true."

She pressed her lips together at the words. At the judgment in them. Righteous? Maybe just right. "And you? Was the world for your taking?"

"What do you think?"

She could imagine him, tall and good-looking—probably the best-looking boy in his class, probably born broad-shouldered and overbearing. Captain of some team, probably. One of the ones girls flipped over. Lacrosse. Or with the way he swam, something to do with water. Diving. Water polo.

"Did you play water polo?"

He exhaled, still exasperated. *Good.* "No."

"Diving?"

"No."

"What did you play?"

"Nothing." He looked up at the cliffside. "Where are we?"

"The back side of the island, past the giant oak." She paused. "Theater kid, then."

He cut her a look, a flash of amusement there for a split second before it was gone behind his too-handsome mask and she ignored the little zing of triumph that came with it. "I didn't have time for . . . extra stuff."

"Too busy making your first million?"

"Too busy—" He considered his words. "Too busy."

Something about the response gave her pause. Something like truth. Ignoring the pang of curiosity that came, she looked to the boat, unmoving despite the wind. "My dad would have been impressed with the way you handled that boat."

"I didn't do it to impress your dad. I did it because we weren't done."

"Aren't we?" she asked. "I'm done. I'm done talking to you. Telling you things I shouldn't have." She paused. "Or is that part of it, too? Making sure I embarrass myself by telling you all about my mistakes?"

"No—" He ran a hand through his hair. "Yes. I'm supposed to help keep you here. But I'm not the fucking enemy."

He believed it, but she wasn't so sure. "Weird. If you're not my enemy, I might start thinking you like me."

"I'd never dream of liking you," he said, the words curt. "I wouldn't want to scare you off."

Another observation she would have resented if she hadn't been so surprised by it. While she wasn't sure what his deal was—where he'd come from, who he was—she did know that he wasn't like the other men in her life. He wasn't goofy and sweet like the guys at work, or unserious and emotional like Griffin, or dark academia like the men from the New York art scene, or born with a platinum spoon in his mouth like the ones she'd grown up with. At least, he didn't give off the impression of being any of those things. He gave off the impression of being strong and steady and smart . . . and able to hold his own in a fight, physically or mentally.

He wasn't the kind of man who made a person comfortable, and Alice wasn't feeling anything close to comfortable in that moment.

"You scared the shit out of me, Alice. Diving off a moving boat."

"Worried you wouldn't get paid if I drowned on your watch?" It wasn't kind, but she didn't care.

"Jesus Christ."

She ignored the way her pulse sped as she moved away from him, staring around the small strip of sand, keeping her eyes on anything other than him and all his edges. The ones in his words, and at his jaw, and in the muscles visible through his white shirt, and in his unrelenting focus on her.

"I'm an excellent swimmer."

"Yeah. I noticed."

"Always," she said, and they both heard the surprise there, the memory of the other times he'd noticed her. On the train. At the station. At the clapboard motel. In her room two nights earlier—when she was naked.

Well. She didn't want to think about that (at least, not with him *right there*).

"Fine. What *do* you get? For keeping me here?"

Silence for a long moment. And then, "I told you. I owe your dad."

"Right," she said, bending down to select a perfectly round, white pebble from the sand. "For changing your life."

He nodded. "Exactly."

"What does that mean?"

"He was on my side long before I was valuable on his." It was a strange thing to say—while there were dozens of adjectives to describe her father (*trailblazing, genius,* etc.), people were rarely moved to describe him as helpful. Or supportive. Or loyal. Or kind. At least, not after first blush.

"How long did you know my father?"

A pause. Long enough for her to wonder if he'd tell her the truth. "About ten years."

"How long have you worked for him?"

"I've worked for Storm for five years."

That wasn't what she'd asked, though. "And for my father?"

He faced her. "Longer."

"You're not going to tell me what you did, though, are you?"

He bent down to the sand and selected a perfect match to her white pebble. When he stood, he extended it to her on his broad palm. Like a peace offering. "He wanted you here. You're here. The rest is up to you."

Why? It didn't make sense. Franklin had everyone else leaping to do his bidding even now, dead. But Jack was, what, supposed to enjoy a vacation? Impossible.

"And if I stay? The whole week? What's in it for you?"

"I think the question is—what's in it for you?"

It wasn't a reply, but she didn't push him. He was a brick wall; no point bashing her head against it. "And if I don't stay?"

"You lose the inheritance. So do your siblings."

"And what do you lose?"

"Do I have to lose something?"

"You won't admit to an incentive," she pointed out. "So, yes."

"If not carrot, then stick?"

She reached behind her and shoved her hands in the back pockets of her shorts. "The Franklin Storm way. In the case of his family, both carrot and stick."

Jack nodded, not looking away from her. "What if the incentive was this?"

Heat coursed through her at the words. He couldn't mean— "This, what?"

"Sailing." He waved a hand across the glittering blue Bay and recited, "*On a day when the wind is perfect, the sail just needs to open and the world is full of beauty.*"

She recognized the words her father had repeated enough that everyone in their orbit would. Replied, dry as sand, "If my father ever read Rumi, I'll give up the entire inheritance right now."

Dark brows rose. "I thought you wanted to give up the inheritance right now anyway."

She swallowed around the knot of frustration in her throat, and he seemed to notice, changing the subject, waving a hand across the small beachhead. "I didn't know this was here."

Alice clung to the new topic. "It's not always here."

He took in their surroundings—wet sand, the green wash on the gray slate steps at the base of the cliff nearby. "Low tide."

She nodded, unable to keep the pride from her voice when she said, "One of the island's best secrets." There were few things she loved more than the little strip of sand, dotted with treasures churned from the seafloor, left to be discovered for a heartbeat before they were returned to the mysteries of the Bay.

Out of the corner of her eye, she could see Jack advancing. She straightened, hesitating, heart in her throat. "I bet you brought all the boys here," he said.

She couldn't stop the laugh at the idea, as though there were any way boys would end up on the island and not be decimated by her family. Hadn't he been paying attention? "Oh sure. Tons," she said, bending to pull a bright white shell from where it peeked out of the wet surf.

He indicated the slate steps. "Where do those go?"

"Up to the woods behind the big oak."

"Along the cliff face? I'm feeling better about having to swim back to the boat." He punctuated the statement with a grimace, one she knew was for show. She'd bet this man could climb those steps without breaking a sweat.

"Then it will be a race back to the house," she said, leaning down to rinse her find off in the ocean.

"I don't love the home team advantage." Jack was close enough to see her treasure now—the most perfect sand dollar she'd ever found. "I'm not sure I've ever seen one of those in the wild." The words were quiet, a momentary respite from whatever it was they were doing.

"They only look like this when they're dead." She extended her hand, the flat shell filling her palm. "Still cool, though. Prehistoric."

He reached for it. "May I?"

"Sure."

A slight graze of his fingers over her palm, warm and sure, before he lifted it for inspection. "One summer, when I was about nine or ten, this was my Storm Olympics task."

His gaze snapped up from the sand dollar. "What does that mean?"

"He dropped me here at low tide." She pointed up the cliffside. "The test was to find my way back to the house."

"What?" He was horrified. "You were nine?"

"Or ten."

"Well sure," he scoffed. "That's totally different and not at all unhinged."

"That was my dad." She shrugged, considering the cliff wall, suddenly realizing how unhinged it was to leave a child here, alone, to face it. She shook it off. "It wasn't that hard. I just had to climb."

"And if you'd fallen? If you'd been hurt, and the tide had come back in?"

"I didn't. I wasn't."

"But you could have been."

She couldn't help her little smile, her pleasure at his outrage. "But I wasn't. I hung around here for a while. Explored until the tide returned. And then I climbed up and went home."

The memory of that afternoon flashed bright and clear, the blue sky, the green trees, the triumph she'd felt when she got to the top of the steps. When she'd come through the woods and approached her father's glass-walled office from the outside and banged on the window. He'd turned, phone to his ear, and nodded through the glass, the closest she'd ever gotten to his approval.

She pushed the memory away. "Anyway, I like it here."

Jack looked like he had something to say—to her, maybe. To Franklin. To the rest of the family—but he stayed quiet.

Pointing to the sand dollar he still held, forgotten, she said, "They're weird little dudes. In calm waters, they stand up on their sides, vertical. And usually in groups."

"And what about when it's rough seas?"

"They lie flat and isolate themselves. For protection." She paused. "The best way to weather storms." He wasn't looking at the round white disc any longer. Alice cleared her throat. "You should keep it."

"A peace offering?"

The question came with a little tease, and she matched it, grateful for the way he let her change the subject. Tossing him a smile as he pocketed the sand dollar, she turned away. "A suggestion."

She could have sworn he laughed, but the sound was swept out to sea before she could be sure. What she was sure of, however, was that he was watching her—she could feel his eyes on her, hot and focused, as she collected two pieces of sea glass and another perfect sphere of a rock. Time and silence stretched between them, and she grew more and more aware of him. Was he noticing the way her wet shorts clung to her? The way her white T-shirt showed—she looked down—pretty much everything?

She did not have the ridges he had, but at least she was wearing a decent bra.

Hyperawareness consumed her, making her question everything. When the tide started coming back in this time, what would she do? The path wasn't as easy now as it had been when she was a kid. When she got back to the house, there would be a different test. Questions. Where had she been? Should she pretend she hadn't spent the day with Jack? Or tell her family the truth? How would she respond to the other question—*Why?*

Because he asked, didn't seem like enough.

Because he wanted to fuck me that one time, was definitely too much. Would she ever forget he said that? Definitely not. But it wasn't relevant. At least not to her family.

Because I wanted to get the hell out of here. The truth.

"Why does everyone think you're going to leave?"

The question broke into the cacophony of her thoughts, and Alice couldn't help the surprise that flared when she realized Jack had somehow followed them. She shouldn't have been, of course. That was what he was paid for—to know what everyone was thinking.

She shrugged. "I'm the only one who ever has."

He watched her carefully. "Not enough reasons to stay?"

"There are a few hundred million of them, I hear," she said, unable to keep the sarcasm from her words.

"It's not nothing," he said.

"It isn't—"

"Alice. Please don't say the money doesn't matter."

"I wasn't going to," she replied. "Of course the money matters. If my father were an accountant or a carpenter or a teacher, do you think we'd all be here, playing his stupid game?" She paused, but he didn't take the bait, forcing her to continue. "Do you think you would be here? Feeling like you owed him for some perceived generosity ten years ago?" She didn't wait for him to argue about the truth of his debt. "If he were any of those things, it would *all* be different. But he was Franklin Storm, trailblazing genius, beloved for his vast influence, prized for his brilliance, forgiven for his faults, and renowned for his unwillingness to fail."

She was on a roll now. "Franklin Storm, force of nature. Unstoppable. And who would want to stop him? He was changing the world."

"He did change the world."

"Yeah. I know." She couldn't keep the snark from her voice. "It was hard to miss."

"Do you resent that?"

"What's the value of that? It would be like resenting the color of your hair or the air you breathe," she tried to explain. "My father's success was just . . . there. Like the ocean. It was all we ever knew." She paused. "Well, except my mom. She probably resents his success."

"She didn't leave, though." He left the second part unsaid. *Not like you.*

"I wasn't going to say the money didn't matter," she said, defensively. "I was going to say it isn't enough."

His brows rose, but he stayed quiet. She looked back to the shore, desperate for something to distract from the conversation. A small crab trundled along in the shallow water, unable to stop itself from being clumsily tossed around.

Same, crab.

She spoke to the little blue creature. "The money can't give me what I want."

"And what is that?"

"I'm not proud of it," she whispered.

"Good thing I'm not interested in judging it."

She believed him, and maybe that was why it was so easy for her to say, "They didn't care when I left. They were surprised to see me the day after he died—like they'd forgotten about me. And now . . ."

He nodded. "Now, they only want you to stay because there's money in it for them."

"Exactly."

"There's money in it for you, too."

"I don't want it." He laughed. She liked him less. "Why is that funny?"

"It's not. Not really," he said. "But it's exactly the kind of thing a girl like you would say."

She blinked. "A girl like me."

"The money doesn't matter to you, because you have never had to worry about it."

Irritation flared, and a tiny bit of disappointment that he, too, thought of her as Alice Storm Inc. "Not that I should have to explain it, but when I moved out of his apartment, he cut me off. Killed all my accounts. I pay my own way now, Jack. No sailboats. No helicopters. No private island."

"Watching roaches climb the wall, huh?"

She didn't miss the reference. Knew the next line of the song about the poor little rich girl. Resisted the urge to tell him to go fuck himself. "I was never going to call him to come rescue me."

"He still pays your siblings' bills."

"Yes. And they let him dictate the terms of their lives. When I say my father wanted control, I mean he was furious when we crossed him. And he punished me the only way he knew how."

"He took the money away."

She shook her head. "That was the easy part. Honestly, considering my age, it was long past time for that. He should have done that for all of us—and maybe we wouldn't be at each other's throats thinking about inheriting instead of grieving our father." A pause. Then, "It wasn't the money. It was the access.

"He took it all. And he took all of them, too." She was lost in thought for a moment, the memories of the months after he'd exiled her, waiting for someone to reach out. No one had, not for months. "They chose him. He made sure of it."

He shifted, and for the first time since they'd met, Jack seemed uncomfortable.

"So you can see why they'd be concerned that I might leave. Because they know I can survive. But they don't want to discover whether or not they can."

"You do want to find out, though. If they can survive the consequences of you leaving."

"No. I don't want them to have nothing. I want—" She paused. Turned the shell over in her hand, running her thumb over the smooth inside, thinking about mixing paint there, blues of the sky and the sea. She searched for the right words. "I want them to want me to stay."

I want them to want me back.

But was that even it? Did family ever feel right once you'd left? Maybe Thomas Wolfe was right. Maybe you couldn't ever go home again.

God, death was so weird. And having this man around, with his sculpted jaw and his stern looks and his tattoos and his ability to sail did not make it any less weird. In fact, he definitely made it more weird. As though the underpainting of a watercolor was wrong.

For the record, an attraction to your dead father's second-in-command was definitely bad underpainting.

Alice took a deep breath and looked out to *The Lizzie,* perfectly anchored in the distance, freedom and a trap. A thought occurred. "Didn't I break the rules?"

"What?" The question was curt, like he'd been lost in thoughts he wasn't going to share with her.

"I'm not supposed to leave the island." She indicated the boat with a tilt of her chin. "Isn't that what my dad decreed?"

Jack followed her attention. "I figured the boat didn't count. It's basically the island. I knew you liked to sail." He'd said it before, but this time was different. Softer. Less damning. With a hint of something that she might like if he were the kind of person she could like. "That, and you're with me."

He closed the distance until there was nothing but the two of them and the wind, and the smell of the sea and this place that she loved so much. His advance shouldn't feel so good. It should feel dangerous and contrived. Threatening. And whatever it was, she shouldn't *show* him how good it felt. She *definitely* shouldn't let him reel her in like a well-weighted line.

But he was excellent bait. And what was the worst thing that could happen?

It was already happening, of course. She was already imagining that it wasn't bait.

She tilted her face up to meet his gaze and lied. "What if I don't want to be with you?"

"Hmm." The sound rumbled from him, straight through her. "It's a little late for that."

Her breath was shallow, and later she would blame the wind coming off the Bay for how the moment felt, like it might blow part of her away.

"I've never brought anyone here," she whispered.

He was close enough that she could feel his warmth even before she lifted a hand and touched him. Close enough that he didn't have to raise his voice for her to hear him say, "Good." The gruff satisfaction in the word was more appealing than her feminist roots should find it. "You should be careful."

Something flared in her. Hot. Certain. "*They* should be careful."

His jaw hardened in response, lips flattening into a firm line, somehow making him more handsome. "Yeah. They should be."

She reached up without thinking, stopping herself from stroking her fingertips over his mouth just before they made contact. She detoured at the last second, her touch stuttering down his arm along with her courage, to his hand, clenched at his side. She looked down at his knuckles, healing. Soon, there'd be no evidence of how he'd punished people who should have done better with her.

She reached for his hand, and he gave it up easily, letting her stroke over his skin. "You were angry then. At the train station."

"They were disrespectful."

Alice couldn't help her little laugh. "That's a pretty old-fashioned way of thinking about it. They were doing their jobs."

Just as he'd been doing. But Jack didn't see the comparison. "Fuck their jobs."

A gust of wind punctuated the crass reply, gifting Alice with an excuse for the lush shiver that thrummed through her. She didn't stop touching him. Instead, she turned his hand over in her own, running her fingertips over the rough hills of his palm. "Thank you," she whispered, too soft to be heard over the wind. "That night you exceeded my expectations."

He sucked in a breath at the stroke over his skin, hand lifting, cradling her face, thumb stroking over the swell of her cheek. Tilting her face up to his.

It was a bad idea. But history was littered with women making bad decisions about men.

He kissed her. Or maybe she kissed him. Later, she wouldn't be able to decide, because she wanted to kiss him so much in that moment, on that beach, where she'd spent the majority of her childhood imagining kissing someone, she couldn't remember what was truth and what was fantasy.

Whatever the truth, Jack made it feel like fantasy, slanting his kiss over hers like the pirate who'd dived into the sea, leaving his ship behind, to follow her to shore. Except he'd been furious then. She'd seen it in his controlled, perfect motions.

This wasn't controlled. It wasn't furious. But it was perfect.

He tasted like salt from the sea, and Alice licked into him, loving the way he pulled her closer to him, stroking over her back, down her spine.

Alice was five-ten and clear-minded enough to know that she was not the kind of woman men lifted off the ground. She'd dated enough to have put any dreams of being swung around like a Disney princess directly out of her mind (anyone paddling around the New York City dating pool understood the need for reasonable concessions).

But the moment Jack's big hands slid into the back pockets of her shorts, activating any number of as yet undiscovered neural pathways, clear-mindedness was lost at sea. And then he did it—lifting her off the ground with a firm grip, with an ease that she would marvel at later, when she wasn't enjoying it so much. She had no choice but to cling to him, wrapping her legs around his hips, breaking the kiss with a wild gasp. "Oh my god."

"Mmm." One hand—how was he holding her up with *one hand*?—slid into her hair and brought her lips back to his as he turned to walk her to the cliff face, where an outcropping of rock made the perfect place for her to balance as he broke the kiss and brushed his lips across her cheek and down her neck, his tongue sliding out to taste the salt on her skin.

She sighed; he groaned.

"We shouldn't do this," he said to the place where her neck met her shoulder. "I don't want you to think . . ."

"That you want to fuck me again?"

He lifted his head and met her gaze, his eyes hot on hers. Irresistible.

"That you scoped out this spot"—she wiggled against him, extremely pleased with the gruff sound he made—"the moment you set foot on this beach? Waiting for your chance?"

He didn't respond. Instead he took her face in his hands and kissed her again, stealing words and thought and breath until she had nothing left but the taste of him, and the feel of him, and a deep, wild *desire* for whatever was to come. Whatever he was about to do.

And he was about to do something—she could feel it in the way his muscles tightened and strained beneath her touch. In the way his tongue stroked along hers. In the way his thumb ran across her cheeks. In the hard press of him where he stood, between her thighs.

In the slide of his impossibly warm hand under the hem of her T-shirt, against the cool damp skin of her torso, pushing the wet fabric up as he searched and she held her breath and waited for him to touch her where she wanted him.

And then he was there, big and strong, testing the weight of her breast, his thumb stroking over the pebbled tip. She gasped into his mouth as he smiled, all triumph. "Cold?"

She shook her head. "Not even a little."

Oh . . . this was dangerous.

She wasn't supposed to like him. Maybe she could keep herself from that. But she categorically would not be able to keep herself from wanting him. How could she? The man was a walking (and sailing, and swimming, and *very excellently kissing*) bad decision.

Which was a problem for Future Alice.

She'd tackle that in a minute. Just as soon as Present Alice was finished.

And then she was, because he was pulling away from her, breaking the kiss, leaving them both breathing heavily, like kids caught making out in the back of a movie theater.

Alice reached for him as he stepped away, in a move that was instantly mortifying, like she couldn't bear to lose him.

It was a problem he didn't seem to have. He was back to being stern and controlled, like the man who'd walked into her childhood living room and sent her family into chaos.

If he hadn't cleared his throat, she might have thought she'd imagined the whole thing—a fever dream of sexual frustration with this man who was too handsome for his own good.

Definitely too handsome for hers.

Yikes. She yanked her shirt down as he ran that big hand—the one that had been heavy and warm and perfect on her—through his hair. "I should—go back to the boat."

She scrambled off the ledge, feeling clumsy and bare, and not a little bit stupid for all the ways she'd gotten lost in this day—on the boat, on the beach, in that kiss—as though real life weren't looming like the cliffside above them.

"Right," she said, trying for effortless cool, reaching for her sunglasses on top of her head, grateful for the reflective lenses that would hide her thoughts from him.

Except her sunglasses weren't on top of her head. Of course they weren't. Because they'd been on her face when she'd dived from the boat into the water. And now they were at the bottom of Narragansett Bay.

So now she was just standing there like a buffoon, his attention on her hand patting the top of her head.

Horrifying.

Without taking his eyes from her hand, he cleared his throat again. "I shouldn't have—"

Oh no. He was going to apologize. And there was surely nothing worse than that. "Don't," she whispered. *Don't ruin it.*

"No?"

She shook her head. "No."

He didn't look so sure, probably because she was already skulking away, pointing in the direction of the steps. "I'm going to—yeah. Anyway. Thanks for the—" She cut herself off. "Yeah. Thanks."

He looked to the steps, his brow furrowing as he considered the slate steps, green with sea algae. "Be careful."

The directive was firm enough that it should have annoyed her. She wasn't a child, after all, and even if she were, she'd climbed those stairs a thousand times. But instead, a warmth spread through her, something close to the same pleasure she'd taken in his outrage over her unscheduled swim. "You too."

He nodded, but didn't reply, and she turned, heading for the steps, telling herself not to look back. And she didn't. Even though, as she climbed the steps to the house above, it was Alice who felt like the one at sea.

"YOU'RE PAINTING."

Alice turned from the view of the Bay through the tower windows to face Emily in the doorway. "Hi," she said, softly, beckoning to her younger sister. "Do you want to come in?"

"It's only six-thirty." Emily stepped into the room, pausing just inside the threshold. "I thought you were still asleep."

A shake of the head. "I'm a teacher; we don't sleep in."

"Right," Emily said, as though she had never considered the daily schedule of a public school teacher. "Well, that's good—morning sunlight is the best light for aligning chakras. Before all the messy stuff pollutes it. I can give you some crystals that would help—a tumbled citrine, maybe?"

"I'd been thinking I was missing a tumbled citrine," Alice replied with a smile.

"Funny." Emily threw her a look. "You could use one. Maybe a rose quartz, too." Before Alice could ask what a rose quartz would do, Emily craned to look at her notebook. "You're so good at that."

Alice followed her attention. "My version of a tumbled citrine."

Emily reached for the journal. "Can I—"

Alice nodded, moving aside so her sister could flip through it, reversing time—the morning bay (ultramarine, cerulean, dioxazine purple), the sunrise in the east (lemon, rose, cadmium orange), the island in the dark (indigo, Vandyke, the raw sienna of the lights in the upper half of the boathouse).

Jack had steered clear of her the night before, his regret for that kiss palpable even at a distance. Of course, she'd done the same, locking herself away in the tower when she got back from the beach, carefully resurrecting the ancient palette of watercolors she found at the back of her closet. Yes, she'd painted and made plans to avoid him for the rest of her time on the island, but that was *her* decision to make. Not his.

Unaware of Alice's thoughts, Emily turned another page, revealing a collection of studies. A sand dollar. A crab. A set of slate steps, green with algae at low tide. *The Lizzie,* once more anchored offshore, sails returned to their tight rolls, not even a hint that she'd sailed that morning.

"These are beautiful," Emily said, her fingers stroking across the swoops of Alice's brush, the deep Prussian blue of the hull, the teak woodwork. The sea, viridian and phthalo blue.

Alice had a more critical eye. "They're not what they could have been," she said, waving at the collection of quahog shells, full of the paints she'd mixed. "I couldn't get the gray right." Emily didn't respond, lost in her perusal. Alice filled the silence.

"Do you remember when we used to paint here?"

Emily nodded. "On the docks. You were always better."

"You only ever wanted to paint flowers. Flowers are deceptively difficult," Alice said, remembering Emily's waning patience. "You always got frustrated and ruined my brushes."

"I'm not going to apologize for that," Emily retorted. "You were boring. Always trying to match the ocean—like it wasn't constantly changing."

"And look, that's still my problem," Alice replied with a little smile. "That's why I paint New York City now." In her moderate success as a painter, she was best known for her watercolor cityscapes, galleries and collectors fascinated by the way she merged a medium best known for nature with urban landscape. Still, when she was alone, painting for herself, Alice always came back to the water, full of secrets, impossible to capture without leaning in to chaos. "Too hard to get the ocean right."

Emily's gaze lingered on the dozen or so quahog shells strewn across the dresser. "I remember when you had the idea to use them as mixing trays. You made me collect them with you."

Alice shook her head. "I don't remember that."

"All I wanted to do was get ice cream, and I wasn't old enough for my sailing license and you spent three days up here mixing blue in clam shells."

"No one else could take you?"

Emily shook her head. "Greta and Sam were grown up and Mom and Dad were who even remembers where, but honestly, I just wanted to go with you." A pause. "That was back when it was us. A team."

"Emily—" Alice said, the name tight in her throat as she searched for something to say. Something better than, "I'm sorry."

"Don't apologize," her sister said immediately. "You made choices. Forged a new path. I just wish you understood that I am not . . . that I wasn't ever . . . the enemy."

She wasn't. Not really. Of the whole family, it had been Emily who'd been caught in the cross fire. "I know that. I'm so sorry I missed your wedding."

"Not just that. You didn't come to the Fourth of July." The words were threaded with accusation, enough to set Alice on edge. "I asked you to come."

In June, Emily had reached out for the first time since Alice had declined the wedding invitation, asking Alice to come to July Fourth. *Everyone would love to see you,* she'd written.

It had been such a blatant lie, Alice hadn't even considered it. "Emily. You know I couldn't come."

"Yeah. You were busy."

Alice hated the words and their lack of understanding, as though she'd been the problem all along. Before she could defend herself, Emily changed the topic. "Anyway, we need you downstairs."

Alice hesitated at the *we*. "Why?"

"Mom called a meeting."

"What about?"

A little shrug. "The Secret Service is due later for a site visit. She's on a tear, Greta's vibrating, Sam's being . . . Sam. And they sent me up to get you."

"Sounds like real Storm family fun," Alice said dryly, dropping her brushes into a jar of water nearby. "I'll be right down."

"'Kay."

Emily started down the steps, getting halfway before Alice reached the landing and called after her, "Em?"

She turned.

"Are we okay?"

Her sister tilted her head. "Could be worse, right?"

A beat. "Could be better, though."

Emily gave a little nod. "Yeah. Could be better."

Great.

"I'll be down." She needed to put on her armor.

Descending the central staircase a few minutes later, hair pulled into a tight ponytail, wearing a black tank top and black flared yoga pants, Alice decided to skip coffee (a mistake) and head straight for her family, who had collected in her father's office.

She paused outside the open door, just out of view, and listened as her mother delivered marching orders the Storm children had heard dozens of times over their lives . . . hundreds of people coming . . . the eyes of the world on them . . . and above all . . .

"No time for theatrics. We needn't perform for an audience."

Alice sucked in a breath at the familiar words, and the way they were designed to preempt emotion of any kind. If there was to be grief, if there were to be tears, if anyone was going to even *consider* causing a scene, it would not be on Elisabeth Winslow Storm's watch, dammit.

Something moved in Alice's peripheral vision, and she found Tony at a distance, down the shadowed hallway looking . . . disheveled. Gone was his ever-present suit, his perfectly combed hair, his freshly shaven face. Instead, he wore jeans and a white button-down, the fabric pulling across his wide chest, as though it didn't know what to do without a jacket to contain it. And all that before the furrow in his brow.

Worry for Greta, no doubt. Alice smiled with a little shrug and a head tilt in the direction of the office. *Storms, am I right?*

The hand he raised in greeting was hesitant, as though he wasn't sure he should be interacting with her at all. It was only then that she realized she hadn't seen him since she arrived on the island—despite him being a near-constant presence for years, her father's shadow in cars, on helicopters, as he walked through crowded rooms and busy streets.

Alice had always liked Tony—it was hard not to. He was quiet and calm, had borne witness to their familial foibles for years without (vocal) judgment, and had shielded Alice from overzealous attention in public more times than she could count.

But now, without Franklin, Tony was relegated to the shadows.

Unless Greta brought him into the light. Which, if Elisabeth drill-sergeanting inside the room was any indication, wasn't going to be that morning.

So, Alice did what they both knew her sister wouldn't. She pointed to the door, the universal sign for *Join me?*

He shook his head, a strange look in his eyes, as though he'd never dream of intruding.

If only she had the same freedom. With a little wave, she stepped through the open door.

Alice hadn't been in her father's office since she'd returned to the island—the result of studious avoidance, not that she would admit it. Once she stepped inside that morning, however, it was impossible for her to avoid the memories.

Greta stood with her back to an enormous Victorian fireplace, so large that she could have been standing inside it, arms crossed over her chest. An enormous Picasso leered down from the wall above her.

Franklin had purchased the piece with several of his first millions in the early 1980s and hung it in the living room of the family's New York City apartment where anyone who happened by would know Franklin Storm was so wealthy he could own a Picasso.

Alice had hated it almost since birth—not only because of the basic reasoning behind the purchase (did everyone see how successful little Frankie Storm had become?), but also as she grew older, because of her inability to see the art divorced from the artist. Franklin had no doubt sipped his scotch and stared at the cubist masterpiece and bemoaned the artistic taste of his daughter—who couldn't possibly have been a decent artist herself.

Her father had never thought much of her art, not when she'd won prestigious awards in high school and college (she didn't need to be an artist to work at Storm, which was his plan), and certainly not when she chose to teach it after her exile (those who couldn't, taught, didn't they?), so she'd kept her public art private—never telling her family that she was on her way to becoming a respected artist in her own right.

That part of her life had blossomed in the years she'd been estranged from the family, and it didn't belong to them. It didn't even bear their name—she painted as Alice Foss, a name far enough back on the family tree that neither family nor fanatics (there were a few of those after she'd upended the Storm Inc. stock price for a few months) would think to look for it.

At the base of a wall crammed with photographs, plaques, and accolades, Sam sat on the buttery leather sofa, facing Emily, who was in lotus position across the room in one of Franklin's prized Arne chairs. Behind her, the enormous floor-to-ceiling windows boasted one of the most beautiful views in New England—Narragansett Bay in its full glory, spread out beyond the centuries-old red oak their father claimed was the reason he'd chosen that particular spot for his office.

No one was looking at that view right now, though. Instead, they were focused on Franklin's massive mahogany desk, heavy and dark and the absolute opposite of the steel and chrome and sapphire glass that had made his fortune. It was impossible to ignore, already intimidating, and made more so by Elisabeth, her steady gaze fixed on the tablet there.

". . . as you all know, I don't like mess." She finished her sermon, looking from one child to the next, before letting her gaze land on Alice in the doorway. "Good of you to join us."

Alice's back was up, instantly. She took a step into the room from where she hovered in the doorway. "I didn't realize we had a six A.M. family meeting."

"Considering tomorrow is a fairly big day, I would have thought you'd set an early alarm," her mother replied, as though everything were perfectly ordinary.

"I was up, actually," Alice couldn't help the retort, even as she hated the way it made her sound like she was twelve again. "What did I miss? I assume the greatest hits?"

"What's that supposed to mean?" Elisabeth asked. "I don't have greatest hits."

"Don't embarrass me in front of the guests," Sam said, dryly.

"Don't embarrass me in front of the Secret Service," Emily added.

Even Greta played. "Embarrass me in front of the first gentleman at your peril."

Elisabeth didn't like any of that. Especially not when Alice added a little laugh. "Come on, Mom. You've read us this particular riot act a thousand times."

Her mother pursed her lips for a moment. "And yet, it did not seem to sink in when you embarrassed your father in front of the whole world."

The whole room went still in the wake of the words, and Alice did her best to ignore the way they struck, hard and hurtful, made worse by the fact that no one said anything in her defense.

Before Alice could speak, Claudia entered. "Emily thought you might like some tea, Elisabeth."

As though everything were perfectly normal and Elisabeth hadn't just landed a wicked blow, she said, "You know, I would like tea." Claudia poured and handed over the cup. "Claudia, you really are the best of the children."

"The tea was my idea," Emily pointed out as Sam said, "She's not your child."

Elisabeth smiled and patted Claudia on the arm. "Best of the in-laws, then."

Everyone's eyes went wide. Remarkably, Claudia found her voice first. "Well, I'm sure that's not true," Claudia said, tossing an amused smile in her wife's direction, and receiving an eye roll in return before she slipped from the room.

Elisabeth lifted the cup to her lips, but did not argue. "Thank you. Where was I, Sam?"

"You were giving it to Alice," Sam said, letting his mother's comment slide.

"Are you sure?" Greta jumped in. "It seemed like she was giving it to Sila."

Before Sam could retort, a chorus of alarms sounded throughout the room, and Emily and Greta looked to their watches. "Oooh. Bad luck, Sam," Emily said, her delight palpable. "It's 6:59, you've got to give it a rest for a bit."

"Set an alarm for 8:59," Greta said, staring pointedly at Sam.

"That's diabolical," Alice said.

"Isn't it?" Greta asked.

"I wish I'd thought of it."

"I still have one minute to tell you to fuck off," Sam interjected.

The words were barely out of his mouth when Sila appeared in the doorway. "Good morning," she said with a smile that did not reach her eyes. "I set an alarm for five minutes till, just in case Sam needs me."

"And . . . the outlaw, right on time," Greta said, under her voice.

Sam heard, and didn't like it. He lifted his phone and typed as Sila crossed to sit next to him on the couch. "Have. You. Done. It. Yet." The robotic voice spoke as he stared Greta down.

"Done what?" she asked.

His phone didn't have to reply. His face said plenty.

Greta spun on Alice. "You told him?"

"I absolutely did not," she protested.

"It sure sounds like you did."

"Greta. I—"

"No one told him." Sila leaped in, quickly dismissing any possibility that she might be defending Alice with, "We found your letter."

"*Found,*" Emily said, her disbelief palpable as she came out of her chair and slid into a deep side bend.

Alice couldn't help her scoff. "Went looking for it, I think you mean."

Sam had the grace to look guilty but was surely grateful he was forbidden to speak (apologize) as Sila's brow furrowed. "It's only right that we all know how everyone is getting on with their tasks—we're very public about ours. Sam isn't speaking. We're descaling boats and fixing fog bells." She sat back and crossed her arms like she was Elisabeth's favorite in-law. "We're right to check in. It's our inheritance, after all."

"Sam's inheritance," Alice said.

"What?" Sila snapped.

"It's Sam's inheritance. Not yours."

Sila narrowed her gaze on Alice. "Sam has children, Alice. I speak for them."

"Could someone please tell me what Greta must do?" Elisabeth interjected, clearly irritated. "I loathe it when you all gang up on me."

As though they weren't all ganged up on Greta.

Sila was on a roll. "Greta has to end her relationship with Tony."

One did not have to be a mind reader to know that everyone in the room was thinking some version of the same thing: *Why didn't Franklin shut you up, too.*

"Sad, of course," Sila added in the silence (not a mind reader, apparently), "but we can all surely agree the inheritance is . . . most important?" As though the inheritance wasn't on everyone's mind, all the time. "If she doesn't do it, there is no inheritance."

"Thumbs-up emoji." Sam's phone, having the last word.

Alice ignored it all, focused on Greta, still consumed by the carpet. Silent. Of course she was. Greta's truth was always lost in silence, and there were moments when Alice couldn't bear it, wanting to shake her into action. "Greta," she urged. "He was just here."

Greta looked up at that. "Where?"

"In the hallway. Probably to make sure you were okay. And not being gaslit. You should go see if he's—"

"Greta isn't going anywhere," Elisabeth said. "And no one is gaslighting anyone."

"Of course not. You'd never do that, Mom," Alice said.

"Careful," Emily said, the words echoing inside the forward fold. "She doesn't like being called that."

"Called what?" Alice asked.

"Mom."

Elisabeth put a hand to her brow. "Oh for God's sake, Emily. Would you stop being so dramatic? This is exactly why I am concerned people won't believe this is a functioning family."

For a moment the siblings were unlocked, the wild statement bringing them together for a heartbeat before Elisabeth decided she'd had enough of whatever was going on between her children.

"I am having two hundred people on the island *tomorrow,* many of whom are *extremely private* and I simply cannot have you *emotional.*" She fairly spat the words at Greta before returning her attention to the 1107 in front of her. "I expect you to handle that." Before Greta could respond, Elisabeth moved on. "We have the team from Storm and the Secret Service coming today for security sweeps, by the way, so I hope you don't plan to disappear again today, Alice."

"I'm not disappearing. I'm here."

"Where even were you yesterday?" Greta asked. "You were supposed to help us." The question was sharp with accusation in the most familiar way—Greta, searching for a way to shift the spotlight from her. A lifelong trait.

Alice lifted her chin. "I spent the afternoon in my room. It was pretty clear everyone was busy without me."

"And in the morning? When you were supposed to be helping?" Greta prodded.

"She. Was. With. Jack." Alice closed her eyes at the sound of Sam's phone.

"What?" Elisabeth, Greta, and Emily spoke in unison.

Alice spun on her brother. "I wasn't—" Sam cut her a look, daring her to deny it. "How do you even know that?"

"Saoirse was in the boathouse when you took the skiff out," Sila said. "She thought you might be leaving, so she came to find us . . . And then we all saw you."

"I wasn't leaving."

"Saoirse thought you might be. But then you were sailing, and we realized you were just . . . vacationing."

"Alice was on a boat yesterday?" Elisabeth asked.

"Yes. The sailboat," Sila said, happily. "We were all at the fog bell— taking it apart for cleaning and oiling, per Franklin's orders. We've been very diligent, as you know, Elisabeth." Sila paused for effect, then pressed on. "I don't blame you for going sailing, of course, Alice. We would have done the same if we hadn't received a letter from your father. *But we did.*"

Alice hadn't been raised a Storm for no reason. She did not rise to her sister-in-law's bait. Not even when Emily said, "Chill, Sila."

"Why on earth were you with Jack?" Elisabeth Storm, always very good at staying on topic.

"Jack and Alice are spending lots of time together," Sila said, sounding like a teenager who'd just learned how to deploy gossip, the expression on her face best described as gleeful. "Saoirse said he rescued her from the locked pantry on Friday morning."

Okay. Alice had to get this situation in hand before it went fully off the rails, even if it meant defying family tradition and telling the truth. "Dad gave him a task, too. He's supposed to sail."

Everyone shared a look.

"Why?" Greta asked.

"On *my* boat?" Elisabeth asked sharply, as though she'd been on *The Lizzie* in a decade.

Sam shot forward. "Is he—"

Everyone turned to Sam, who immediately realized his mistake. He lifted his phone and typed furiously. "Is. He. Getting. A. Ducking. *Cut. That. Mother. Clucker.*"

"Samuel," Elisabeth said firmly. "Language."

Emily snorted a laugh at the other side of the room.

"Don't worry about it, Sam," Emily said. "You can console yourself with the ridiculous bonus that comes with that CEO job you're getting."

Sam went back to typing.

"Well. This waiting is irritating, isn't it?" Elisabeth opined as they all hung on the *click-clack* of his phone.

Alice and her sisters shared an amused look before Sam added, "We. Should. Know. If. He's. In. The. Mix." More typing. "And. If. Alice. Is. Working. With. Him."

"I'm not working with him," she defended herself. "Not that I am sure what that would mean, but I'm sure you've cooked up some conspiracy theory about it. Have I not made it clear I'm not interested in this stupid game that is a guaranteed trap?"

"Why *were* you with him then?" Sila asked.

Sam dropped his phone and flung a hand in his wife's direction, as though they'd really done something. Alice rolled her eyes and looked around the room, only to discover that the whole family was waiting for an answer.

"He asked me to go sailing," Alice said as Sam's eyes narrowed to slits and he picked up his phone, typing furiously. "That's it. Nothing happened."

Greta's brows rose, and Alice resisted the urge to wince at the unforced error. But Greta wasn't in a position to probe on exactly what kind of *nothing* might or might not have happened. Instead, she asked, "Why did you go?"

"I—" Alice stopped. "I don't know."

"Just casual friends on a leisure cruise?"

She looked to Emily. "We're not friends."

Her sister laughed. "No kidding. Jack doesn't seem the type to have friends. He's so stern and difficult. You know I once offered to do his birth chart, and he told me he didn't have time? He wouldn't even tell me his birth date, so I can't even tell you his sun sign, though I suspect he's a Capricorn. Virgo rising." She looked to Sam. "That would explain why Sam can't stand him—Aries."

"Doesn't Alice have a fiancé?" Sila asked, suddenly alert.

"We're not lovers." She paused. "Jack and I. Obviously. Not Griffin and I." This was getting messy. "The point is, I'm not sleeping with Jack."

Shut up, Alice.

The entire family was staring at her.

"I should hope not," Elisabeth said.

No one replied for a moment, and Alice went warm with embarrassment at the silence until Sam saved the day, albeit unwillingly. "This. Is. Bull. Ship." A pause. "Ship." Another. "Ship." He groaned his frustration.

Emily deadpanned. "It's a sailboat, Sam. Not a ship."

He shot her a deadly look.

"It's a mess, is what it is." Elisabeth looked from Alice to Greta. "Think of what people will *say*. Your father's silly game, Alice catting around with Jack—"

"Okay, well, once again, we are not *catting around.*"

Elisabeth was still speaking. "Greta moping about because she won't simply end her . . . adventure . . ."

It was a brutal thing to say. To diminish what Greta and Tony obviously had.

"It's not an—" Greta started to defend Tony. Stopped under Elisabeth's cool gaze, knowing better than to argue.

"You know, I'm beginning to think your father knew what was best with these games." Elisabeth twisted the knife. "Get it done, Greta." Once she delivered the directive she looked to Alice. "And you. I expect you to lead with discretion when speaking to your *journalist* friends." Her mother said *journalist* the way she said *politics.* Or *carbohydrates.* "It's bad enough there were photographers at the train station."

"How did you know about the train station?" Alice asked, but she knew the answer. She looked to Greta, who was staring at the floor, consumed by the thick sapphire pile. Of course, she'd told their mother. And with no expectation of loyalty in return. "It doesn't matter." Alice straightened, steeled her tone. "I didn't talk to them."

"You're sure?" Alice faced her mother again, betrayal hot in her chest. There was strain on the older woman's face. The faintest shadows underneath her eyes. The tightness at the corners of her lips.

"Yes, Mom, I'm sure I didn't happen to mention that my father had planned an elaborate inheritance game to a bunch of people paid to take my picture. Nor did my sister's yearslong secret love affair come up."

"Well," Elisabeth retorted. "You can't blame us for considering it. You aren't exactly part of the family anymore."

Alice froze, the words not entirely unexpected and still cutting sharper than she would have imagined. It wasn't the words that hollowed Alice out, though. It was the silence that followed them—no one willing to refute them. Emily staring out the window at Franklin's tree. Greta chewing her lip, consumed by her own worry. Sila's eyes wide. Sam's phone silent.

They didn't have to speak. Their agreement was loud enough. Whatever had happened when her father had exiled her from the island and the family, had been at best Alice's choice, and at worst, her fault. "Really? None of you . . ." She shook her head. It wasn't worth it. "Well. Whatever you think, the truth is the same. I didn't tell anyone anything."

"Mmm." The sound wasn't comforting, nor was the way her mother leaned back in her chair and exhaled, as though she'd fought a battle.

Alice was vibrating with frustration and anger. All she wanted was to *go*. What was the point in staying? It wasn't for mourning or shared grief. It was laughable that this family would be able to access either of the two.

She didn't need this. Or them. Or the money. She had a life. Friends. A future. The inheritance wouldn't do anything for Alice but ruin what she'd built for herself.

With it, she would always be Alice Storm Inc. Without it . . . maybe she would find someone to love her for more than her name. To appreciate her for more than the requirements of her birth. For more than what she could give, unlike this roomful of people who couldn't do anything but take.

You aren't exactly part of the family anymore.
No one had corrected Elisabeth.
Get the hell off my island.
No one had stopped Franklin.
Nothing had changed.

She might have walked out then and there, if Greta hadn't taken that moment to speak to the floor, the words soft and broken. "Please, Alice." Her sister lifted her gaze, and Alice saw it all—the sorrow, the grief, the frustration, the loss. Greta, whose task was the worst of the bunch. Greta, who'd never been able to walk away. Greta, who was wrecked.

For a heartbeat, unable to look away from the tableau, her sister in the foreground, and that fucking Picasso in the background, Alice wondered if they were all wrecked . . . a little bit . . . in their own way.

"Please," Greta repeated, softly, something in the word, as though she knew she'd disappointed Alice and still was asking for help. She didn't have to say the rest. Alice heard it anyway.

Stay.

A beat, before she nodded. Offering Greta an anchor. Because they were sisters. And it was what sisters did. At least, it was what Alice had always imagined they did. In normal families.

Whatever they were like.

CHAPTER

12

IT MIGHT HAVE BEEN five years since Alice had been an officially recognized member of the Storm family, but she knew the basics of the job, including an essential one: When the Secret Service was coming to the house, you looked sharp.

She descended the central staircase an hour later, having used the ancient hairdryer and applied actual mascara to discover her mother, Claudia, and the rest of the Storm siblings huddled together in a way that could only be described as suspicious. As far as Alice could tell, they were looking at a painting on the wall of the foyer, which was odd on a normal day, let alone on a day when several presidents' security details were on their way.

"What are we doing?" Alice asked, before Greta shot her a meaningful look and tilted her head toward Elisabeth.

Their mother was standing very still, staring at a painting that had hung in the rear of the foyer since before Alice was born, a Belle Époque oil of autumn in Arles, all golden poplars and sarcophagi. Elisabeth was flanked by Emily and Greta, with Sam a few feet away, leaning against the wall, framed by classic Victorian blue (cobalt) and mahogany wainscoting.

"Mom?" Alice prompted, confusion flaring when Elisabeth did not reply. Looking to Greta, Alice asked, "What happened?"

"Do you know why your father succeeded so well in business?" Elisabeth asked, dreamily, riveted to the painting. She didn't wait for a reply, instead speaking to the tiny dark-clad people on the dirt path in the painting. "He behaved as though nothing mattered. No wonder people threw millions at him. He was endlessly compelling in his belief that everything would simply . . . happen. Like he could will it." A pause, and then she looked to Alice. "Not you, though, Alice. He couldn't will you to do anything. Hello."

Weird. "Hi?"

Elisabeth looked back to the painting and spoke to the poplars. "Trees are very soothing."

"What on earth?" Alice asked, meeting her siblings' shocked expressions. "What's wrong with her?"

"Nothing's wrong with me," Elisabeth said.

"Something is very wrong with you," Alice replied.

"I think I shall take a walk," Elisabeth said. "Maybe a swim."

Greta let out a high-pitched half laugh that might have been pure panic. She was having a bad day. "Um. The Secret Service is coming for a security sweep. And Dad's team from the company is coming for prep and pregame. We've got a list a mile long, Mom. Two hundred very important people here tomorrow, remember?" Greta said. "You can't go for a swim."

"You say that like it's a product launch," Alice said.

"It kind of is, if you think about it," Sam said at a distance.

"Well. Whatever else is happening today," Emily said, calmly, sliding an arm around Elisabeth's shoulders, "Mom is taking a break."

"A . . . *break*?" Greta repeated the word as though Emily were speaking a foreign language, which made sense, as in her whole life Elisabeth Storm had never taken a break.

Emily nodded. "Exactly."

Elisabeth turned to face her youngest. "Emily. You have lovely eyes. You look so much like me."

"Yup!" Emily said, "Maybe we could go get some water or something? Are you thirsty?"

Elisabeth smacked her lips, testing her answer. "Maybe?"

What. Was happening. It was almost like . . . "Ohhhhmygod," Alice said, staring. "She's *high*."

The entire gathering went still.

"That's impossible," Greta said, taking Elisabeth's other arm. "How could she be—"

"I am?" Elisabeth asked, seeming fairly disinterested in the answer.

"What the *fuck*, Greta?" Sam said, coming off the wall.

"What do you want from me?" Greta said. "I'm sure Mom didn't mean to get high, Sam." It was an understatement almost beyond comprehension. Elisabeth Storm would *never*.

"She did it on your watch," he said.

"I'm not her keeper," Greta snapped back.

"You sure about that?"

"Okay, Sam. You're being unhelpful and obnoxious," Alice interjected. "It doesn't matter how it happened—"

"What happened?" Claudia entered from the hallway to the kitchen.

Sam spun to face her. "You!"

Claudia's brows rose. "What about me?"

"You dosed our mother!" He looked to Emily and spoke to everyone. "Of course she did. They brought a fucking pharmacy with them. I can smell the two of you getting high every night; my room is directly below yours, Emily."

"Oh, I know," Emily shot back. "I can hear the two of *you* screaming at each other every night. You might remember you have children with working ears, Sam."

Yikes.

"You're such a little bi—"

"Hey!" Claudia stepped in. "Watch it."

"Or what, you'll drug me, too?"

"Don't tempt me with a good time," Claudia said, surprising them all.

"Claud." Emily set a hand on her wife's shoulder. "It's okay."

"You know what?" Sam said. "You're also a bi—"

"Sam." The single syllable cut through the small space, shatteringly quiet and full of warning. Everyone looked toward Jack, by the door, standing in a pillar of mottled light—the sun finding him through a massive stained-glass window high on the wall, making him look like a marble statue, set there to pass judgment on them all, his opinion clear in the set of his jaw.

Alice ignored the response that tumbled through her in the beat that passed, no one speaking, the full focus of Jack's taciturn gaze on her brother. "That's enough."

Sam went silent, as though Jack had sped up time and Sam's silence was required.

"Good morning," Jack said to the family before meeting Alice's gaze. "Alice." Why did he have to say her name like that? In that deep rumble, as though he'd been standing here in the dark, waiting to say it?

She lifted her chin. Made sure she did *not* match his tone. "Jack."

"The Secret Service will be here in an hour and a half," Jack said calmly, looking at his watch. "They make it a point to be on time."

"You're meeting them?"

"I had planned to. It's not the first time I've managed these visits for Storm."

"I can manage it," Sam said, petulant. "I'm a grown man."

"Be that as it may," Jack said, "it will take a few hours."

Which meant Sam would be rendered silent for part of the time they were here.

Sam's gaze narrowed on Jack, his knuckles going white on his phone. He couldn't possibly be thinking of having a run-in with Jack—a man well out of his league. "You did that on purpose."

As though on cue, Greta's alarm went off. Emily smiled broadly. "One more minute."

"You can't speak, Sam," Elisabeth said dreamily. "Whoever meets with them should probably be able to speak. They protect the *president*."

"You know," Sam said, spreading his hands wide, "maybe it's for the best—then I don't have to explain to the Feds why Mom is high as a kite."

"Which brings us back to . . . why *is* Mom high as a kite?"

Everyone looked at Emily and Claudia, who knew better than to deny it. Emily began. "There may have been a miscommunication. Regarding the tea. Earlier."

"Oh, you mean the tea Mom's *favorite* brought in this morning?" Greta said, looking to Claudia.

"You didn't tell them?" Claudia said to her wife.

"I didn't think it would . . ." Emily waved a hand. "I thought it would calm her down!"

"Well, to be fair, it has done that," Alice said, before adding, "Emily, I mean this in the best possible way, but what were you thinking?"

Emily's eyes were huge in her face. "Honestly, I really did think it would just . . . chill her out."

"She was up all night worrying about your mother's anxiety," Claudia defended. "About making it easier for everyone. Especially Greta."

"Why? I'm fine," Greta insisted, as though they hadn't all witnessed her near emotional meltdown. "I don't need it to be easier."

"Hmm," Claudia filled the disbelieving silence that fell after the pronouncement. "I must have misjudged the quantity she could handle. Have you been eating, Elisabeth?"

"Of course not," Emily and Greta replied in unison.

Claudia made a pained noise and addressed the room. "I'm so sorry."

"Don't be, darling," Elisabeth said softly, taking Claudia's hand in her own. "I feel *fiiiine*."

Alice was the only one who laughed.

"Okay, Mom," Emily said, all calm, measured action. "How about we skip the visit from the Feds and go sit under a tree?"

"Maybe Franklin's tree." She turned to look at Claudia. "Oh! We'll have a picnic! There's that chicken salad you like!"

Claudia nodded and met Emily's gaze. "Perfect. I'll get it."

Her sister-in-law's willingness to do anything to get the hell out of there was admirable, and Alice's laughter returned.

"Jesus, Alice! This isn't funny!" Greta said, sounding like she might vibrate straight out the front door.

"It's a little funny," Alice offered.

"It's really not," Greta snapped. "Now I have to take care of her!"

"No, you don't," Emily said. "I'm literally taking care of her right now."

"*You?*" Greta said. "You can't be trusted to pour her a cup of Earl Grey, Emily. I mean, obviously. Because you've never had to worry or think or take responsibility once in your whole life."

It was a cruel thing to say, and Alice stepped in. "Greta."

"Don't." Emily straightened, looking much taller than her five-two. "I'm not a child, you know. I can take care of Mom. If you would let me, I could actually relieve some of that weight you're so fucking proud of carrying around."

They stared each other down, and for the first time, possibly ever, Alice understood Emily. She wasn't frivolous or flighty. She was a grown-up. It was a strange thought, considering the current situation, but maybe this was exactly the kind of scenario that tested maturity. A mistake, out in the open rather than turned into a secret.

"Claudia." Jack spoke, reminding everyone he'd been watching. "You've used this tea before?"

"Oh, of course." She waved a hand. "I wouldn't have made tea with something unknown. I'm not an amateur."

"Understatement." Sam's phone.

Alice let out another little bark of laughter and Greta shot them all a withering look. Alice shrugged. "Maybe you let them handle this one."

An eternity passed before Greta nodded, barely. "Fine."

The air shifted, and Emily couldn't help a joke. "You wanna try some, Greta? You might enjoy the ride."

No one in the universe would enjoy the ride less than Greta.

"No, thank you." Greta looked at her watch. "Dad's whole team is about to turn up alongside the *Secret Service,* Mom is *high,* and tomorrow half the world will be here to take stock of how we're handling our grief. God. *Someone* ought to be sober through the fallout."

"Oh please," Alice said. "You think the Secret Service hasn't seen this before? The entire C-suite at Storm Inc.—including Dad, I might add—spent the first ten years of the company on coke. And besides"— she waved a hand toward Jack—"that's what we have Jack for. To fix stuff." She met his gaze. "Right, Jack?"

The only sign of Jack's surprise that she'd referenced him was the slight rise of his brows. "Correct."

"Jack. Is. Not. In. Charge," Sam's phone said.

Greta nodded. "Sam's right. This isn't his family. This isn't his fune—" She stopped. "*Celebration.* It's Mom's." It was Franklin's actually, but no one corrected her. "One of us has to be a grown-up and handle this if Mom can't because she is—"

"Sitting under a tree," Alice helped.

"Franklin's tree," Elisabeth clarified again, dreamy.

Greta scowled. She looked at Emily. "How long is she going to be like this?"

"She'll be fine. It just has to wear off."

"How long will that take?" Alice asked.

"Not long. She'll be fine by tomorrow."

"By *tomorrow*!" Greta shouted.

"Chill, Greta. There are worse things than microdosing." Emily looked to Jack and said, "Jack can handle the Secret Service. I mean, look at him."

His brows shot up. "That sounds like an insult."

"I mean, it's not a vibe I personally search for in friends," Emily allowed. "But I'll admit it's handy now and then."

"Jack should handle it. And you, Greta," Elisabeth interjected, not noticing the storm clouds on Sam's face as he registered his exclusion from the sentence. "I'm not interested in meetings today."

Alice and Emily shared an amused look. "If you're sure, Mom."

"No." Sam cut in, his thumbs tapping furiously, the manual equivalent of raising his voice to the decibel level of Man Vying for Control. "Jack. Shouldn't. Meet. The. Secret. Service. This. Is. Storm. Family. Business."

Everyone looked to him.

"There will be a Storm with them, you jag," Emily spoke first. "Greta. *We're all Storms.* Why don't you say what you really mean?"

He watched her for a moment, anger clear. And then typed, "It. Should. Be. Me."

The girls all laughed, the way only siblings could.

"Sam," Greta said. "You're the least reliable of all of us, and Emily just dosed Mom. Come on."

Elisabeth, who had been watching the volley between the group, took that moment to speak, as though a vital thought had just occurred to her (drugs were excellent at convincing people they should say things they absolutely should not say). "You know, listening to the four of you, if I could do it all over again—"

The opening was a trigger. Greta stiffened. Sam rolled his eyes. Emily looked away.

Alice faced her head-on. "Yes, Mom. We know."

"Know what?" Jack asked.

"If she could do it all over again, she wouldn't have children."

"It's her favorite thing to tell us," Alice said. "That if not for us, she might have . . . what is it, Mom? Been more?"

"I'm not sure what more there is, considering her influence," Emily added.

"It was your father's influence," Elisabeth said. "No one ever noticed that I was the one who made him who he was. I made all of you who you are."

For better or worse, she wasn't wrong.

Their mother had been vocally regretting their existence for decades, and there'd never been anything to say before, so why should there be something now? For all the ways he'd been a controlling ass, at least their father had never seemed to regret them.

Except for that one time he exiled Alice. She felt a pang of something she didn't want to inspect, and she ignored it.

Sam broke the silence, knowing he was outmatched. "Fine. I'm. Going. To. Oil. The. Fog. Bell. With. My. Kids." He straightened his spine and met Jack's gaze, something there reminding Alice of an old nature documentary. Sam jockeying for position over a man who had absolutely no doubt of his own strength. Embarrassing really.

Alice looked to Greta, then Jack, registering the cool irritation on his face, and wondering to whom it was directed. And then he spoke. "Elisabeth, may I suggest—"

"You never call me Mrs. Storm." When he tilted his head, his silent question an echo of everyone else's, she went on. "Everyone else at the company calls me Mrs. Storm. Even Tony calls me Mrs. Storm, and he's sleeping with Greta."

"Oh god." Greta sounded like she might shrivel into a husk, but no one was paying attention to her. Instead, they were all waiting for Jack to formulate an answer.

He didn't need time. His response came quick and honest. "Would you prefer I call you Mrs. Storm?"

"No," she said, after thinking about it for longer than anyone should. "No."

He nodded. "I didn't think so."

"I suppose you'd like me to say something nice about Franklin." She paused. "As per the rules."

"If you'd like," he said, again, a sliver of frustration in his reply, as though he, too, was growing tired of the game. As though he'd like to be more serious.

Alice couldn't blame him. Who knew what her mother would say at this point? The older woman looked as though she was considering her words very carefully.

"He was generous." Well. That was a pretty nice thing to say if slightly arguable. Maybe the mushrooms weren't so bad. And then her mother added, "In bed."

"Oh. No." Emily spoke without thinking.

"Ew." Greta.

"Let's never discuss this again," Alice said. The suggestion was unnecessary. Everyone had taken a vow of eternal silence on the matter.

"You may not like it," Elisabeth said to everyone and no one, "but it's true."

"All right." Jack passed over the statement as though it hadn't been said, adding, "I was going to suggest that you enjoy your day with Emily. You don't have anything to worry about."

That was nice, Alice thought. The kind of thing a person said to a grieving widow who wasn't Elisabeth Storm.

But Elisabeth Storm wasn't Elisabeth Storm in that moment, and maybe Jack saw that. Maybe he knew that she'd reply. "I know, you'll take care of it."

"I will."

"Thank you," their mother said, turning to her daughters. "And thank you three."

"Of course." Greta spoke for them.

"That's why Franklin liked you the most."

Pain flashed across Greta's face. "If he liked us the most, Mom, he sure didn't show it."

"Maybe not," Elisabeth said, distracted by another painting. "But maybe that's why he didn't. Didn't want to play favorites."

It was patently false. Franklin had loved to play favorites, pitting the children against one another and watching them fight. He'd pushed Alice out of the family and made no attempts to bring her back. And he'd left Greta the indisputably cruelest task in the inheritance game. But Emily . . . maybe she was the real favorite.

Or maybe it was all a mindfuck.

Whatever it was, Emily was practicing radical acceptance. "Come on, Mom. Let's get some water. You need to stay hydrated."

"I don't need water," Elisabeth said, the words trailing into silence for a beat before she added, "I think I might be thirsty."

Unbelievable.

Emily spread her hands wide in the universal sign for *See?* The two women disappeared down the hallway, Alice and Greta watching with wide eyes.

"I cannot believe . . ." Greta trailed off.

"I know," Alice said.

"You're sure they'll be okay?" Greta said, the panic in her tone obvious. Not that she would admit to it. "What if she—"

"She's going to be fine. Emily and Claudia are pros," she quipped, laughing at Greta's face before turning serious. "You should let people help. You don't have to handle her all by yourself."

Greta shook her head, her throat working, as though she had something to say.

When she didn't, Alice added, teasing, "Think of it this way: If you go with her, I'll have to deal with the company. And you know how I get around the company."

Greta forced a little laugh. "The stock price is already down."

"Exactly."

Greta stood on the precipice known to children throughout time: Honor thy father? Or honor thy mother?

Or honor thyself?

It was Jack who tipped the scale. "I think it's important for someone who knows the ins and outs of the approved guest list to be with Tony and Storm security for the walkthrough. Who is the best person in the family for that?"

The invocation of Tony made the decision for Greta, though she didn't look to Jack. "If you're sure."

"I am."

Greta tilted her head in Jack's direction. "Are you okay with him?"

Dark brows snapped together. He didn't like that. "Of course she's okay with me. Why wouldn't she be?"

Considering the way he consumed Alice's thoughts despite him having lied to her multiple times, there was no *of course* about it. Ignoring him, she spoke directly to Greta. "I'll be fine. Let me know if you need anything."

The eldest Storm sibling wouldn't need anything. Greta made it a point of pride not to need anything from anyone. Still, she nodded, and took off, through the back hallway, past the kitchen, and presumably out the rear door to the house to find Tony, who wouldn't be far. He might not have Franklin to protect, but the look on his face earlier that morning had been proof that he was more than willing to stand as Greta's protector for as long as she would have him.

Not long, Alice feared.

They were all so willing to roll over for Franklin.

"So. It's the two of us again." Jack hadn't moved from his place in that pool of sunlight.

"You're pretty good at that," she said, closing the distance between them, telling herself she wanted to keep their conversation private.

"At what?" He straightened in that way she was beginning to notice, going tight, as though he were on the cusp of movement.

She took another step toward him. "At getting my family to do what you want them to do."

"I had nothing to do with it." He paused. "Well. Maybe Sam."

"Definitely Sam." She tilted her face up to his. "It hadn't occurred to me how useful it might be to have a fixer around."

"It doesn't take a fixer to know you don't put the loudmouth in the same room as the Secret Service with an old lady high as a kite ten yards away."

For a single, strange moment, the situation overwhelmed them, and they smiled at each other. "Your family," he said finally, shaking his head, as though it meant something.

It did. "I know."

"Why haven't you told them you're not engaged anymore?"

He was good at that, too, asking questions out of the blue, setting someone on the back foot. Making them feel like answering.

Making her want to tell him things. "My family doesn't respond well to failure."

A beat, and she could see him choosing his words. "Was it a failure?"

"I was engaged, and now I'm not, so . . ."

"It feels like it would have been more of a failure if you'd married someone who couldn't see what he had."

She ignored the thrum of excitement that came at the words (so smooth). "Access to the Storm inheritance?"

He shook his head. "Don't."

She looked away, wanting to tell him she was kidding. That it was a joke. Embarrassed that it wasn't.

"You weren't the failure," he repeated. "And if he made you feel that way . . ."

Her gaze fell to his right hand. "Are you going to defend my honor?"

He lifted it, flexing it in the light, which restored red to his now-healed knuckles. "My reputation speaks for itself."

She couldn't help her smile at that reply, teasing and serious at the same time. Not that she was interested in such a thing right now. She'd just gotten out of a very serious relationship, and that was before her father died. What was it they said about grief? No major decisions for a year? Well, letting Jack Dean mess with her head . . . or any of the rest of her . . . was a major decision. And she wasn't about to allow it to happen.

Starting now. Clean slate. No major decisions.

And definitely no Jack.

"Are you flirting with me?" Now, hang on. That wasn't the kind of thing she should say if she was committing to *No Jack*. That was a clear violation of the *No Jack* rule.

But she couldn't take it back. Not when he had already answered. "Not intentionally."

No Jack. No Jack.

"In fact, I have been feeling like I should apologize for yesterday . . . at the beach."

That was the last thing she wanted him to do. "We did more than flirt, Jack."

His voice slid into a deeper register. "I noticed."

Okay. Apparently *No Jack* would begin later, as this was all feeling very *Jack*. "That was intentional flirting."

"It was," he admitted, with something in his eye that might have been described as sweet if he were literally anyone else. "I don't know what's wrong with me."

Bad decisions abounded that day, and he could easily be the worst of all of them. *Get it together, Alice.* "I should go. I should see if Emily needs help. I should get Mom . . . a banana or something."

His brows rose. "A banana. I've never heard that particular remedy for . . ."

"Tripping balls?" Alice offered.

He laughed then, a low rumble that she shouldn't have liked so much. "Yeah." He ran a hand through his hair, the first sign all morning that he might not be as in control as he liked everyone to believe. "Christ. This is . . ."

"I would remind you that *you're* the one who decided to spend the week with *us*."

"I didn't really have a—" He cut himself off, but she heard the end.

An irony, that. Considering he seemed to be the one with all the choices. The arbitrator of what was acceptable, who was properly following the rules, where they could go, when they could speak, with whom they could interact.

"As far as weeks go, I've had worse." Everything tingled at his words, so soft, like a secret, her scalp, her fingers, the skin of her neck that could still feel the rough scrape of his late-night stubble.

What was he offering?

What if she took it?

No. God. This was not—*No Jack*.

"You know, Jack," she said, to them both, really. "The more time I spend with you, the more I understand why my family is unsettled around you."

"Why is that?"

"You're a lot like my dad. It feels like you're one step, two steps, eight steps ahead of us—that makes sense. You learned to play his game, and you're here to finish it for him. That, I understand. But there's a part of you that isn't like my dad. And that's the part that scares me."

He frowned. "Why?"

"Because he sent you here, made you our common enemy for a reason." She took a breath, wishing it were deeper. "I've been waiting for the other shoe to drop. And here's the thing . . . I'm afraid you might be it."

"I'm not." The denial was instant.

"I don't believe you."

He sighed. "Alice. Your mother's high, your sister is about to ruin her life, your brother is blaming everyone around him for his own problems, and tomorrow the island is hosting two ex-presidents, half the *Fortune* 100, a Nobel Prize winner, and a real live duke. Aren't there enough shoes dropping?" He closed the distance between them, until he was *right there,* leaning down, so close that if she lifted herself onto her toes, just barely, she could press her lips to his.

Fire exploded in her belly—desire. It took everything she had not to do it. Not to lift her hand and set it on his chest, broad and warm and so familiar for all the time she'd spent imagining it when she absolutely shouldn't have been.

"I know you don't trust me. I know it's too much for me to ask you for that. But I swear . . ." A pause. "I'm not the enemy."

It was somehow both the exact right thing for him to have said and the absolutely wrong thing at the same time. Because if Alice knew one thing, it was that trust was not part of whatever game this was. Trust was how everyone got hurt.

Wasn't it how she'd been hurt again and again?

And still, when Jack looked down at her, his gray eyes seemed to be full of something that was a rare find in the circles she'd run in— honesty.

Or maybe he was just really good at the lie.

SAM

"I STILL DON'T UNDERSTAND WHY we have to be here."

Saoirse Storm didn't look up from her phone as she cycled cellular access off, then on again, in the futile search for a pocket of service never before found on Storm Island.

As she groaned her frustration to the world, her father dipped a cloth deep into the can of lubricating oil stored in the corner of the island's fog bell house and returned to his task. "The situation hasn't changed; we're here because your grandfather asked us to be."

A delicate snort from Sila. "We're here because we *have* to be."

Sam clenched his teeth and focused on the grease he was cleaning from the large gear, which was a critical piece of one of the island's most curious features.

"Ew. What is *that*?" Nine-year-old Oliver spoke at his shoulder.

"Do you want to help?" Sam offered a rag in Oliver's direction.

"Don't get dirty, Ollie," Sila said, fixing her hair in the front-facing camera of her phone.

"It's summer," Sam said, as Oliver ignored his mother and sat on the dusty floor to assist. "They're supposed to get dirty."

"I know you think this is romantic or something, Dad, but there are so many *spiders* in here," Saoirse said, staring up at the corner of the bell house.

"You could clean the cobwebs off the windows," he offered.

"Absolutely not," Sila said.

The categorical refusal shouldn't have surprised him, but Sam still gritted his teeth and worked his way beneath the cast-iron base of the fog bell machine wishing, for the first time since he'd opened the letter from his father, that it was an odd-number hour, so that he would not be required to speak.

"I hate it here," Saoirse said, dropping her phone to her side for the first time in—was it possible it had been years since Sam had seen his daughter beyond the glow of her phone? "There's no cell service and the Wi-Fi doesn't reach over here and I'm missing everything at home and we've been stuck here *forever*."

"None of us are having a good time, Saoirse," Sila snapped.

"Why can't we go home and come back tomorrow? That's what helicopters are for!"

She sounded like her mother.

"You know, when I was your age," Sam began, the cliché making everyone in the bell house groan. "There were no helicopters taking us to and from the island."

"What'd you do?" Oliver teased. "Ride a dinosaur to get here?"

"Funny," Sam said. "We figured out something to do. We went swimming. We . . . explored the island." He stopped, embarrassed by the way the words made it seem like this place was anything more than a prison they'd been desperate to escape during the summer, Elisabeth and Franklin barely ever there, and the kids barely interested in each other. Emily and Alice were young enough that they were just pains in the ass, and Greta had never been much fun. He wiped down the cast-iron legs, checking the bolts. "We took a boat to the mainland."

"Cool. Can *we* take a boat to the mainland?" Saoirse wasn't giving in. "And stay there?"

"No," Sam replied, sliding back out and grabbing the rag from Oliver, moving more quickly to clean the gear. "But you can help me with this if you'd like."

"Pass," Saoirse said.

"Same," Sila said, perching gingerly against the opening in the wall where the enormous bell stood silent. "I prefer to watch."

"What else can I do, Dad?" Oliver asked.

"What else can I do, Dad," Saoirse singsonged.

"Shut up, Saoirse!"

"You shut up."

"Both of you shut up," Sam said, setting the gear back onto the machine and standing to consider his next step.

Sensing the limits of her father's patience, Saoirse came forward and joined him. She reached out and touched the enormous metal drum, wrinkling her nose at the grime there. "When was the last time anyone cleaned this?"

"When was the last time anyone *used* this?" Sila asked.

"It gets used," he said, frustrated and defensive.

"Have *you* ever used this?" Oliver asked.

Sam nodded. "This was one of your grandfather's favorite things about the island." Seizing the moment, he pointed out the important parts of the machine—the gear, the drum, the cable attached to a heavy weight, the crank, the hundred-year-old hammer that would strike the enormous bell in fifteen-second increments when they were done. "If we're here and there's a storm, we'll wind it, and it will run for hours."

"Not annoying at all!" Sila said.

Miraculously, the kids ignored her.

"Dad?" Saoirse asked, earnestly, for the first time in what seemed like forever (she was very good at being fourteen). "No offense, but why do you know all this?"

A memory flashed—one he hadn't thought of in ages. It must have been twenty years earlier—god, closer to twenty-five. He and Greta had been teenagers, Alice only eight or nine, and Emily so tiny it was hard to imagine his parents had let them take her places unsupervised.

"Once, we were on the island for your grandfather's birthday," he said. "And your Aunt Greta had this idea . . ." He reseated the gear on the machine. "None of us had bought Dad—Franklin—Grandpa—a gift."

"Relatable," Saoirse quipped.

"Aunt Greta thought it would be fun if we got this thing working. It had been broken for as long as any of us could remember, but Charlie knew a guy on the mainland who serviced lighthouses, and so . . ."

The memory came back bright and clear. That weathered old man with his white hair and his rheumy eyes explaining the machine. The Storm kids listening like it mattered.

Sam shrugged. "He came and taught us." Finishing his work on the gear, he turned his attention to the machine itself, where the drum required a new cable. "How to clean it, how to attach the cable here"—he showed them—"how to wind it carefully." He turned the crank, watched as the rope coiled in even lines.

"Your Aunt Emily was so little, the drum was too heavy for her to even wind."

"Can I?" Oliver asked, and Sam stepped back to let him. Saoirse set her fingertips to the winding cable, and Sam watched, feeling an immense satisfaction—one he hadn't experienced since . . .

He couldn't remember.

"This is cool, Dad," Saoirse said. The greatest of compliments.

Something burst in his chest. Embarrassing. Something like pride.

He kept it secret. Instead, he grinned at his daughter. "I'm glad you like it."

"It's cool that you did this when you were a kid, too." Something about the words, so simple, so obvious, settled in him.

Whatever happened, he had this. *He had them.*

The roar of a helicopter distracted him from the thought, and he pushed it aside as they all looked out the window, toward the south, where the Bay lay gleaming into the Atlantic, the sky dotted with two massive White Hawk helicopters.

"Who is that?" Sila asked, coming off the windowsill, interested in something, finally.

"The Secret Service."

"Cool! Like, the president?" Oliver asked, his excitement palpable. Infectious, if one weren't a Storm, conditioned to eschew excitement.

"The president isn't with them today, but yes, like her."

"Can I go watch?"

"Don't get in their way."

"Can I go, too?" Saoirse jumped to ask. "Unless you . . . need me to stay?"

It was thoughtful enough to feel like a trap. "Go."

Her face, in that awkward place between the adorable kid she'd been and the beautiful woman she was going to become, split into a bright smile. "Thank you!" She followed her brother out of the bell house, leaving Sam in a quiet that should have felt like a relief, but seemed strangely empty instead.

"The Secret Service are here?"

Not so quiet, after all.

"That's what I said."

"And you're in here. Fixing the fog bell."

"That's right." The words came out clipped. He knew what she was getting at. He'd thought it, too, and he didn't want to. He should be out there, just as his father would have. And instead, he was in here, oiling a 150-year-old machine that no one needed to use anymore, because maps existed. Computers existed. Because boats didn't run into islands anymore.

"Don't you think you should be out there? Being, you know, a man?"

She wanted a fight. "What is that supposed to mean?"

"I am certain *Jack* is out there, meeting those helicopters," she said.

"Jack is managing director at Storm, so yeah, I would think so."

"Who cares about managing director when you're going to be goddamn CEO?"

He ignored the question and the way it opened something unpleasant in him. In her, too. Instead, he circled the machine attaching the weight required for the mechanism to work.

"Are you hearing me?"

"You make it difficult not to hear you, Sila." He returned to winding the drum again, the tension of the cable making the task more challenging and deeply rewarding. The mechanics moved smoothly as he set the machine back in order, returned a series of pins to their proper places, and stepped back. "That looks good," he said. And he meant it.

Sila didn't like sincerity. "God, you are such an asshole."

He looked to her, enjoying the way the words rolled off him for the first time in a long time. "What do you want from me, Sila?"

"What do I—" She looked like she might lose her mind. "I want you to *win*, Sam. I want you to be furious that there's even a possibility that you might not. I want you to *close*."

Sam had never much liked Sila's father, even before he was convicted of scamming millions off his wealthy friends and colleagues. Franklin had loathed him—something Sam had always imagined Sila knew, considering how committed she'd been to becoming a Storm in the first place, and the ease with which she'd turned her back on her own family when her father had been sent to prison. But now, with her spitting the word *close* at him, Sam was reminded that his wife carried no small amount of her father in her heart.

That, and it was clearer than ever that she didn't care for her husband.

Which was fine, as it had been a long time since he'd cared for her. "You don't want me to win," he corrected her. "*You* want to win."

"It's expensive to live our life, Sam. It's expensive to keep you happy."

He doubted Sila had thought about his happiness in years, if ever, but he didn't push back. "I know," he said, hating the way the reply sounded, petulant. Like she was his mother. God knew she felt like his mother sometimes with the way she ran the show, as though he couldn't be trusted.

He could, of course. That wasn't why she kept such close tabs on him. She had one path to money and power, and she wasn't about to let it out of her sight.

"I had *everything* when I met you," she said. "Do you realize who I could have married? What kind of life I could have had? I could have married a Saudi prince! But no, I chose you."

He'd never wanted to marry her. She'd been pretty and tempting, wild in the way rich girls at prep school could be—in that prepared-to-post-pics-to-the-feed kind of way, risking only so far. Sex that didn't muss hair or makeup, drugs procured from the best physicians on the Upper East Side, never going below Fourteenth Street without Daddy's driver, let alone taking the subway to Brooklyn.

But now, Sila couldn't afford to be wild.

It wasn't his fault, but she loathed him for it anyway.

Maybe she'd loathed him from the start, from the moment she'd left a pregnancy test on the marble bathroom countertop in his apartment in Back Bay. And—as he stood there, blood rushing in his ears, ready to call the family doctor and get things discreetly taken care of (was there a way to do it without the press finding out? Without his *father* finding out?)—she'd appeared behind him in the mirror, bright smile on her face and said, *When should we tell everyone?*

They were going to be New York City royalty, she'd told him, before putting an appointment at Harry Winston on their shared calendar. Nine weeks later, the prenup was signed and Sila was walking down the aisle (custom Vera Wang).

She'd always been the one in charge. Even now, even when she said, "Everyone thought I was the lucky one. Marrying into Storm. No one realized *you* were the lucky one. You were some rich kid when I met you. And now? I'm the reason you're going to be CEO. I'm the one who made you something your father thought was worth investing in."

He didn't have to ask what she meant. Franklin had never considered Sam a serious person. He'd never been smart enough for his father. Never clever enough. Never a good enough athlete, or speaker, or manager, or fucking driver. Sam had never had the right friends. Wasn't dependable like Greta, or sharp like Alice, or a delight like Emily.

If he closed his eyes, he could see Franklin's disappointment in myriad locations. The headmaster's office at Dalton (solved with a large check). In a meeting with the dean of students at Harvard (another large check). At the Tiverton police department late one night the summer before his junior year (okay, they were all large checks). In Franklin's office in the main house, when his father had informed Sam in no uncertain terms that he was going to marry Sila because she was pregnant and no Storm child would be born without protection (that might have been the largest check of all—the one that came written into the prenup).

Five and a half months after that, Saoirse was born (private room at Lenox Hill), and Franklin was pulling Sam aside (another private room at Lenox Hill) to tell him in no uncertain terms that this was his future. Time to get his head on straight.

It should be said that Sam didn't need the note from his father. He'd taken one look at that baby and known the truth—he would do what he could to make the marriage work.

Because it had always been about the kids.

To help, Franklin had opened his wallet more times than Sam could count, happily (not really happily, but *willingly*) paying for Sam and Sila's extravagant lifestyle, to supplement the boredom of Sam's mediocre work at Storm. Franklin kept Sila in style, Saoirse and Oliver in school, and Sam in entertainment.

Until nine months earlier, when Franklin stopped signing checks. *The well's dry, kiddo.* Kiddo. Like Sam wasn't thirty-seven and a father of two.

Until two months earlier, when his father had called him into his office here, on the island, and finished the job.

"Well, Sila. I'm sorry to tell you, but your plan has gone to shit. I'm not going to be CEO."

She turned sharply. "What?"

"He fired me."

She was frozen, her lips barely moving as she asked, "When?"

"The Fourth of July." *Time for you to figure out life without me, Sam.*

It had been a long time since he'd seen Sila shocked, and he liked it more than he should have. "You didn't tell me."

"Can you believe it?"

Her eyes narrowed to slits at his sarcastic reply. "Fuck you, Sam. You fucking joke. What am I supposed to do with that? You have *kids*."

He supposed he deserved that. It didn't matter what he did—he was never enough for Franklin, or Sila, or anyone else. He was name or money or the nepo baby who worked at the company. But nothing more. Even now, Franklin had figured out a way to shut Sam up.

Strangely, Sam hadn't been surprised that Franklin had put limits on his ability to talk. If there was one thing Franklin had always hated, it was Sam talking. Everyone else was fine—Greta was always helpful and Emily was always cute and Alice was the one who'd gotten out.

Alice, who'd somehow never lost their father's respect. Not when she studied art in college. Not when she refused to go to business school. Not when she fucking *blew up Storm*.

Even then, as Franklin railed at her, isolated her, insulted her, he'd never stopped respecting her. And he'd never once turned his attention to Sam. Not even after their father exiled her, and Sam came as close as he ever would to screaming, *Put me in, Coach!*

Of course, if he had, it would have been a disappointment; Franklin had already tapped Jack as his new favorite. A better son than Sam had ever been. Able to predict Franklin's needs, solve his problems, and run his empire. Even now, after he was gone.

And Sam, what good was he?

He looked to the fog bell, his final task. His father couldn't have made it clearer that this was what he saw in Sam—not a legacy. Not the next CEO of Storm Inc.

Not even a son. He was just some asshole who couldn't be trusted with anything more important than a make-work job.

Sam reached out and cranked the machine which, fully wound, would ring every fifteen seconds for fourteen hours. Long enough to see the island through a long, dark night.

When he released the crank, the mechanism groaned into action, clicking and moving in little jerks.

"Congratulations," Sila said, not meaning it. "You got it working."

He nodded. "Not such a joke now, am I."

They watched it together, each wondering if it would do what it was supposed to. And then, with a mechanical *thud,* the hammer let fly and struck the massive bell, loud enough for them to lurch backward.

"Are you *smiling*?" Sila looked to him, horror replacing the panic and shock that had flooded her earlier questions. "Jesus Christ, Sam, whatever this is . . . you need to get it under control. If we're going to win, you cannot let your"—she waved a hand at him—"*grief* . . . get in the way."

Grief. What a bullshit concept. Sam wasn't grieving. Normal people grieved. What was there for him to grieve? His father was still there, looming like a specter over the whole damned place. Over the whole damned family. And they were damned, he thought as he watched the gear turn again.

This wouldn't end on Wednesday. It wouldn't end ever.

Franklin would always have more to say, and he'd always be able to shut Sam up to say it. Even now. Even dead.

So, no. Sam wasn't feeling grief. He was feeling fury, that he'd let this place run him for so long. And that he couldn't stop.

The hammer hit the bell again.

"I'm getting out of here," Sila said in the echo.

"For good?" he asked, turning to look at her. Hating the panic that flooded through him at the question. At the answer.

She froze, and he watched a dozen emotions cross her face before she turned on her heel and left the building.

He caught up with her at the ancient stone wall that marked the meadow at the top of the ridge, the bell still ringing from the south, his father's enormous oak looming in the distance. That damn tree, bad enough before, now tall and green and beautiful, with his kids underneath it, a fourteen-year-old sister and her nine-year-old brother usually from different planets, now laughing together.

Another memory. A million years earlier, under the same tree with his own sisters—nothing else to do on the island but figure each other out. A million years was right. He couldn't remember the last time they were together.

He didn't want that for his kids.

"Sila—"

"You'd love that, wouldn't you," Sila said, like she was the heroine of the play, like a character the Internet would lose their minds over, beautiful and strong and cold (queen!). She stared him down, her face smooth and sharp and perfectly sculpted, her dark-brown hair turned a warm gold that cost him thousands every six weeks. "If I left. If I took the kids."

"No," he said, the reply harsh and unyielding. "You're not taking the kids."

He knew instantly that it was the wrong thing to say. That he'd given her too much. That she'd use it to punish him. "You owe me, Sam. The Storms owe me. For every time your mother side-eyed mine. For every time your sisters act like they're better than me. For your father, who loved to gloat that he paid for everything, including your salary, which now you tell me he took from you? For making me sit in the fucking *fog bell house*. Your well may be dry, Sam, but you can be certain mine is getting refilled."

"So that's it. You'll stay for the money."

"What am I supposed to stay for? Love?" It came out like a hilarious joke, and for a moment, Sam remembered a time when they teased at love. When they might have been happy.

Sam turned to look toward the Bay, gleaming and beautiful.

He'd never thought about love. It had always been a transaction with his family. There one day, gone the next, back another time, when someone earned it. And love hadn't been a part of his marriage. Attraction? Yes. Fondness periodically, respect even (though not right now, clearly). But he didn't stay in the marriage for her.

She didn't stay for him, either. Neither of them were perfect. The years had been filled with boredom and disinterest and infidelity on both sides, though Sila had been careful to keep hers devoid of strings and scandal—a lesson Sam had struggled with, until his parents had reminded him of the power of their disappointment.

So he'd stayed in the marriage, partially because of Franklin's will and partially to avoid Elisabeth's disappointment. But he'd also stayed because he had known that while he wasn't a great father, Sila was a terrible mother.

"I know you don't want to say it out loud," Sila pressed on, unaware of his thoughts. "Because those old-money values of your mother's make sure you never mention money in polite company, but one of us has to think about it. One of us has to think about how we get the life we want, and the kids get the lives they want, and we all get to live the future we were promised."

The wind picked up, as if on cue, as if she had summoned it. She might have been beautiful then, if he didn't hate her so much. "I'll do whatever it takes to make sure your family doesn't ruin what I've worked for." She paused. "And your family will do what they have to do to activate the inheritance."

"How do you know that?"

"Because you're not as fucking special as you think you are. You're all just assholes and idiots, like everyone else. And you'll choose the money, just like everyone else. You'll stay quiet when you have to, and get that stupid bell working, and Greta will choose your mother over Tony, and Emily and Claudia will do nothing and get everything just like usual, and your mom will tell you whatever she has to in order to make sure everyone gets their cash, because she's a shitty mother, but she knows the job."

Jesus. She'd thought it all through. And she was right.

"And you will get your head out of your ass and do what you need to do to get your cut, and then I will get my cut. And everyone will live happily ever after."

"That's my family, Sila." The only one he had. The only one his kids had.

"*Your family,*" she emphasized, the words punctuated by the fog bell clanging in the distance. "They don't like me and I don't like them, and I have smiled and sucked it up for *years.* So yes. I am making sure that we win this time."

"I win, you mean."

"What?"

"The inheritance. It's mine. He was my father." He waved a hand toward Saoirse and Oliver, who were hanging off a low branch on Franklin's tree, legs swinging over Elisabeth and Emily, who were now lying flat on their backs and staring up through the canopy.

The kids didn't seem fazed, even though Elisabeth wasn't the kind of grandmother who lingered under the canopy of a tree. But they were young enough and open enough to accept this strange new grandma and their fun aunt in a tableau from an old-timey lemonade ad. If old-timey lemonade were made with psychedelics.

"Their grandfather," Sam added.

"Fine. Then get it for them."

She didn't care what his reasons were, as long as she got what she wanted. And she would get it. Greta would choose to make their mother happy, as she always did. Emily and Elisabeth would fall in line and make sure everything turned out right.

Alice . . . she was the only one who might need a nudge in the right direction. The only one who had nothing on the line. The only one who had proved she could survive without the money. The only one who could survive without the Storms.

What a skill.

"If you fuck this up, Sam—" Sila said, deploying her final weapon. "The kids come with me. And not just because they have no idea who you are without this place, and everything that comes with it."

Sam didn't misunderstand. There was no saving the marriage—it had likely been doomed from the start. But with the inheritance . . . he'd see his kids. That was her offer.

Turning away from his wife, he started back up the long slope toward the house, along the centuries-old stone wall to his father's tree, where his mother and his kids and his sister giggled and ate bananas.

Sila didn't follow.

The only thing that followed him was the sound of the fog bell, loud enough to be heard by boats all around the island, every fifteen seconds, warning the entire Bay of coming storms.

CHAPTER

13

I T WAS A BEAUTIFUL day for a ~~funeral~~ celebration.

Their mother had pulled it off. Between the gorgeous blue sky, the calm waters of the Bay, the collection of crisp white canvas canopies artfully arranged across the great lawn on the southern slope of the island, designed to provide shade but not shelter (it was a party, not a camping excursion), and the string quartet at the far corner, there wasn't a whiff of grief to be found.

Elisabeth had vetoed anything that might even remotely be referred to as funereal, so there were no photographs, no programs, no speeches planned—a late-hour decision that obviously hadn't been passed on to the numerous dignitaries who were in attendance (two former United States presidents, three former and two current prime ministers from members of the G7, the first gentleman of the United States, and a pair of European princes from the same royal house who, if the tabloids were to be believed, did not speak, though Alice was planning on asking Roxanne to confirm that rumor when she arrived).

And then there were the others—standing out from the crowd— a handful of locals, Charlie and Lorraine, the owner of Skipping Stone

Farm. Two members of the Wickford town council. The septic guy, literally feet away from the president of France.

Funerals were weird.

Alice slipped on the Wayfarers she'd raided from her mother's beach tote that morning and joined her siblings against the low stone wall that marked the northern boundary of the lawn. "Should we know all these people?"

"I know all of them," Sam said, all bluster. "Dad expected me to."

Alice rolled her eyes. "Right. Tell me, Sam, how are you going to CEO all over this place during odd-numbered hours?"

Before Sam could retort, Greta stepped in. "I'll hand it to Mom, the universe gave her what she wanted." A stream of mourners made their way from the helipad, through a break in the wall and down into the meadow. "Oh look, there's Uncle Mike."

Michael Haskins, her father's first business partner. Childhood neighbors, Mike and Franklin had built the Storm prototype together in Franklin's parents' garage (Mike had also offered up $1,107). While Franklin had been consumed by the project, Mike had been in it for excitement and profit, and when they received their first injection of venture capital, he'd taken his cut and headed for greener (and richer) pastures. Since then, Haskins Enterprises had been the incubator for a half dozen companies, each one more integral to modern culture than the last. If Franklin was one of the ten richest people in the world, Mike had been far and away number one—for a time.

That rank had slipped a few notches three years earlier, when he'd left Julie, his wife of nearly forty years, with no choice but to split his massive fortune with her. Her replacement was on his arm that afternoon, thirty years younger and clinging tightly to Mike's hand.

When he saw the siblings on the wall, looking down on the gathering of people below, he lifted his free hand in greeting. "Young Storms!"

Everyone waved as Emily called out, "Hi, Uncle Mike!"

He pointed to their mother and then back to them in the universal sign that he'd see them once he'd kissed the proverbial ring—and returned his attention to his new wife.

"I guess Mom changed her mind, after all," Greta said.

Alice looked to her older sister. "About what?"

"She flipped her lid about us putting them on the list," Greta said. "She and Emily had it out."

"Really?" Alice was shocked. "I can't imagine him not being here. But I guess all that emotion Mom has been bottling up had to go somewhere."

"She didn't change her mind," Emily said, watching Mike cross into the great lawn. "Dad wanted him here, and I made sure he came."

Everyone looked to Emily.

"Uh," Sam began.

"What do you mean?" Greta added.

"*Dad* wanted him?"

Emily didn't miss a beat. "No question."

Chalking it up to Emily's crystal-shop vibes, the siblings turned to watch as Mike and Twyla made their way down the meadow toward Elisabeth, holding court in summer white, beneath a wide-brimmed hat. As they drew closer, she stiffened almost imperceptibly, and looked up the slope to her children, her gaze hidden behind dark sunglasses.

"She's hexing you, Em," Sam said.

"Why didn't she want them here?"

"Probably because of Twyla," Greta said, her verbal shudder straight from Elisabeth's training. "Access to a billionaire's credit card, and *that's* the dress she picks?"

"Greta . . ." Alice admonished.

"Oh, please. You were thinking it," Greta defended. "Admit it."

"I admit only that I enjoy every time I open my phone and see that Julie Haskins has donated another half a billion dollars to a worthy charity and made the rest of them look terrible."

"Twyla's really very sweet, you know," Emily said.

"I've never met her," Alice said. "But how do *you* know that?"

Emily shrugged one shoulder. "Claudia and I went to a gathering of yogis in the Hamptons during the eclipse last month; Mike and Twyla have a house there, so I asked if she wanted to come."

"*Twyla?*" Greta tilted her head. "Why?"

A little shrug. "I don't know. I thought maybe we should know her better. Considering. We meditated."

"You could have invited me," Greta said, sounding left out.

"Would you have wanted to meditate during an eclipse?" Greta's face answered for her, and everyone snickered while Emily spread her hands wide. "You see?"

They fell silent for a few minutes, watching the stream of people coming down the rise on the path from the helipad and up the lawn from the docks. After the third helicopter left, Alice asked, "Did Dad *like* all these people?"

"Absolutely not," Sam said. "He would have had something to say about everyone here."

"And walked away with them all in his pocket, nonetheless," Alice said. "Franklin Storm never met a person he wasn't able to control."

"Including us," Sam said.

Silence fell and they watched the throngs of people crisscross the meadow, lingering at a distance from Elisabeth, who was more than ready to accept their condolences and attention. No one looked up to the children, along the stone wall.

"She's avoiding making a scene, at least," Greta said, tilting her head in the direction of their mother, a false, patient smile pasted on her face as she listened to Twyla.

"I cannot believe this is the first I'm hearing of her not liking them."

"Well, maybe if you hadn't disappeared for so long . . ." Sam trailed off, and Alice bit her tongue, knowing he was aiming to get a rise out of her.

"Sam, stop. She would have known if she hadn't been trapped in the pantry with Jack all morning when it happened . . ." Emily said, an edge of teasing in her voice. "Where is your friend, speaking of?"

"First of all, I was trapped in there by myself. Second, he's not my friend," Alice said, raising a hand to silence her sister. "Why would I know where he is?"

He was two-thirds of the way down the lawn, beneath a large canopy, in effortless conversation with a group of men, each in perfectly tailored menswear and still not looking even close to as handsome as Jack in a sleek navy pinstripe—bespoke as hell and worth a small fortune.

Why did he always have to look so good?

And worse, why did she have to notice all the time? Weren't fixers supposed to be unassuming? Charming and effortless and seemingly harmless before they did whatever her father had paid Jack to do? Seduce people, probably. That was clearly one of his top skills.

As though sensing her attention, Jack looked up toward the house and found her. Lingered for a heartbeat while she felt immense relief that her dark sunglasses hid the fact that she had found him first.

Not because she'd been looking. Alice had done her very best to avoid him since the moment in the foyer the day before. She'd steered clear of the boathouse, of her father's office, of being alone in the common spaces of the house.

No Jack, she'd decided, and she was sticking to it. Every time she was alone with the man, she lost her way. If he wasn't making her think about the kissing they'd done (more than that, but she was doing her best to put it out of her mind), he was being kind to her.

Asking her to trust him.

Making her *laugh.* Ugh. That might be the worst of all the infractions, because she was such a sucker for a guy who could make her laugh. And he'd been that guy on the train platform—but she'd convinced herself that it had been a lie. That there was no way this man, who'd lied to her and betrayed her trust, was in any way the thoughtful, funny guy who'd joked about being a Boy Scout with her.

He was the kind of guy who knocked out a photographer. That behavior made sense. It was boorish. Brutal. Criminal.

Sexy.

That was her reptilian brain talking. Jack was her father's fixer, here exclusively to fix. And when Franklin Storm fixed things, it wasn't kind. It wasn't funny. It wasn't safe. It was extremely serious.

"Fuck that guy," Sam said, as though he'd been a party to her thoughts. *Yes.* Alice agreed. (Metaphorically, at least. Literally was not a good idea, for the aforementioned reasons.)

"Where's Claudia?" she asked Emily, who pointed in the direction of her wife, deep in discussion with a group of Elisabeth's friends. "Wow. She really just fits right in with Mom's crew, doesn't she?"

"Don't say that," Emily replied with a laugh. "Sometimes I really do worry that Mom would sell us all for a dollar as long as she got to keep Claudia."

"Is that Mrs. *Austin*?" Sam interrupted, tipping his chin toward one of Claudia's companions, an older woman who'd been a part of long-ago summers on the island. Her husband had owned three hundred acres of ice-wine vineyard in the Sakonnet Valley.

"Who's Mrs. Austin?" Emily asked.

"My god," Alice said. "I haven't seen her since . . . God, Em you must have been two or three."

"I've never seen that woman before."

"Because Mom sent her packing after she hit on Dad," Sam said, waving over a server headed into the fray with a tray of wine.

"No!" Alice's excited utterance was loud enough to carry, and to make the server nervous.

When Alice cast a look behind her to the path where the caterers were working, Sam said, "It's okay. Think of us as the kids' table." He collected a glass of champagne (Greta), two rosés (Emily and Alice), and a white from the tray. "Keep those coming all afternoon."

"What he meant to say was, *thank you,*" Alice called after the young woman.

"I'm not a dog, Alice. I don't need correction," he replied.

"You absolutely are, and you absolutely do, though," she said.

"Can we get back to that lady and Mom sending her packing?" Emily asked. "What does that mean? Did Dad have an affair?"

"You guys," Greta snapped. "It's his funeral."

"Exactly," Sam said. "Our father's funeral, filled with more than two hundred people, fewer than ten of whom we actually like. What are we supposed to be talking about?"

Greta opened her mouth to reply, then stopped. "I don't really know."

"Great. So did Dad bone Mrs. Austin or not?"

Alice burst out laughing at the rude question, drawing the attention of three men from the C-suite at Storm Inc. She raised a hand in greeting, and the trio shared a look among themselves that Alice did not miss. She turned back to her siblings. "Oh no. Quick. Look like we're talking about something serious so they don't come over."

"How is this not serious?" Sam asked, smirk on his face, and Alice snickered.

"You're both being inappropriate." It was Greta's turn to admonish. "We're not kids anymore."

"You guys," Emily said, urgently. "*Did* Dad have an affair?"

"You sound pretty shattered, considering this is Dad we're talking about," Sam said. "Alice isn't the only one who knows about men and money and power."

"Terrible combination," she said into her wine.

"Ruins lives and companies, right?"

"Not companies run by our father, surprisingly," Alice retorted.

"Hey!" Emily shouted for their attention, and got it, along with the attention of a half dozen other people at a distance. She lowered her voice and turned her back to them. "Did he have affairs or not?"

"What does it matter?" Sam shrugged. "Ask Alice."

"Why not me?" Greta asked.

"Because you'll never admit the truth."

"Alice?" Emily did as she was told, her blond hair glistening in the sun, and Alice imagined her enormous blue eyes behind her mirrored sunglasses. Because it seemed important to Emily, she considered the question.

She was inundated with memories: her parents on *The Lizzie*, laughing as they took her for her maiden voyage; Elisabeth and Franklin dancing at the Metropolitan Club on New Year's Eve, kissing in the elevator as it zoomed to the penthouse apartment in New York City; his arm wrapped around her when they waved goodbye to Alice on her first day at Amherst.

And then, one weird, hazy conversation they'd had, at a diner uptown for some reason—just Alice and Franklin. He'd asked her if she was dating anyone, and she'd wrinkled her nose and bemoaned the state

canvas canopies, and beautiful tablescapes that had been brought in that morning. "Never."

"Where *is* Mom, anyway?" Sam asked, looking to Greta.

"How would I know?" Greta's reply came sharper than anyone expected.

Sam's brows shot up. "You always know."

Alice was smart enough to stay quiet, even as Emily shrugged and said, "He's not wrong. That's kind of . . . your thing."

"Well. Fuck that."

Everyone gasped.

"Greta. *Language.*" Sam's response was mocking, edging on unkind. "Seriously. Relax."

"Oh boy," Emily said.

"No. I hate it. I hate the way you talk about me as though I'm just an extension of Mom. I have my own life, you know."

"Yes, we know," Sam said, digging himself deeper. "You're in a long-term relationship with a man you're about to fire."

Everyone followed the direction he indicated, to the far end of the lawn, where Tony stood alongside a collection of other broad-shouldered, barrel-chested men in suits and sunglasses—a half dozen body men who had ceded protection for the day to the Secret Service detail lining the perimeter of the island.

"How's that going, by the way?"

"Shut up," Greta said, suddenly fifteen again, at odds with her brother.

"I ask because I'm doing my thing."

"If you mean keeping your mouth shut—" Alice began, censure in her tone.

"You can't threaten to tattle, Alice. I've got a pass for the funeral. I can talk as much as I want to whomever I want. And it's time for her to make some sacrifices for the rest of us."

"I have made sacrifices my whole life for you, Sam," Greta said. "Someone had to compensate for the disappointment Mom and Dad had in you."

"Whoa . . ." Emily spoke for both her and Alice.

"*I'm* the disappointment?" Sam said with a laugh more cruel than amused. "That's rich. I'm the one who gave them grandchildren."

It was a direct hit, and Alice jumped in as Greta turned red. "Okay, Sam. Why don't you go spend some time with those grandchildren?" She tilted a head toward Sila in the distance, giggling with her companion. "Or maybe stop your wife from running away with her new movie-star friend."

"Can't blame her." Greta finally found her voice. "When this is what she married."

"Both of you, stop," Alice said quietly, stepping between them and staring Sam down before he retaliated. "Look around. The whole world is watching." With a glare, Sam turned away from them, and headed for the guests. And the bar.

Alice sighed, her gaze tracking over the crowd, a who's who of the wide world, all vying for attention themselves, no time to watch the errant Storm kids doing what they were famous for doing. No one was looking. Except . . .

Of course. Jack had seen it all.

And, considering the way his jaw had set, he was about to come and handle it. *Fix it.* As though her family would allow that. She shook her head, barely. Warning him off, knowing that later she'd pay for revealing that she was watching him as much as he was watching her.

"Storm sisters!" came a familiar voice at Alice's back, saving her from having to dwell on *that.*

She spun around, joy and relief rising in her chest as she threw herself into her best friend's embrace. "You're here!" Pulling her close, Alice whispered into Gabi's ear, "Thank god."

"It looked like we might be interrupting," Gabi said, turning to embrace the rest of the family.

"You were not," Alice said. "We're always a heartbeat from each other's throats. It's how we were raised."

"Basically feral," Emily said. "Very bad at feelings."

"Today will be harder than most," Gabi said, hugging Emily tightly. "It's the finality of it." She moved to Greta. "The last time you'll be with all these people. The last time your father will feel so present with so many."

While Gabi spoke, Alice turned to Roxanne, hugging the tall Black woman. "I'm so happy to see you. Thank you so much for coming."

"We wouldn't have missed it."

In Roxanne's ear, Alice whispered, "There are so many people here whose names I don't know."

"Don't worry, I'll be your wingwoman," Roxanne whispered back. "I know them all."

"I'm going to hold you to it."

Roxanne pulled back and searched Alice's face. "How are things?"

Alice raised her brows in a silent, *How do you think?*

Her friend nodded. "Checks out."

Alice pushed her sunglasses up onto her head, so she could look into her friend's eyes and tell the truth. "I'm better now."

"Good." Gabi leaned in and joked, "Jesus, Alice, I knew you were rich-rich, but this is a *lot*."

Alice gave a little laugh-sob. "I'm so glad you're here."

"Us, too."

"We saw three separate helicopters arrive and leave while we were sailing over," her friend added. "*Fancy*."

"Twenty minutes straight shot to the Hamptons," Alice explained.

"Kind of you to make it so convenient," Roxanne said. "Are the Gatsbys here?"

"No," Alice said, lowering her voice to a gossipy whisper. "Didn't you hear? He died, too."

Gabi and Roxanne choked back laughs; Emily snickered. Greta looked horrified.

"Oh, please. Dad would have loved that joke," Alice said.

"So, aside from the tight ten minutes Alice is workshopping . . ." Gabi looked to the other Storms. "How's it going?"

Everyone hesitated, searching for an answer. Emily found it. "I don't know, I thought it would be more . . . exciting?"

Roxanne nodded. "Like the movies? Uncle Carl gets drunk, knocks over an ice sculpture?"

"Yeah. Something like that."

"Do you have an Uncle Carl?" Gabi asked.

"No, but"—Alice waved toward an elderly woman with a collection of dachshunds—"that lady has dogs."

Roxanne followed the direction of her gaze as though it were very normal. "Oh, that's Bitty Foster. She doesn't go anywhere without those dogs." They all watched as a silver fox attempted to extricate himself from a web of leash.

"It's amazing what you know," Gabi said to her wife before tossing Alice an amused look. "Maybe that's her way of catching men."

"Mmm," Alice said. "She's obviously too clever to knock over an ice sculpture."

Another group laugh, and Alice looked back to the crowd. Jack had moved from where he'd been earlier. He had a drink in hand now. Something clear and cold in a highball glass as Justin Mill—the young billionaire recently named the richest man in the world—bent his ear while a dozen others pretended not to notice.

Alice didn't have to pretend. As a host of the afternoon, it was expected that she keep an eye on the proceedings.

Her mother, for example, had reappeared on the great lawn, and was receiving the condolences of the first gentleman (so sorry for your loss). Sila and Sam were on the far side of the lawn, having some kind of argument that Alice hoped they sorted out before Elisabeth noticed and sent them both to time-out for causing a scene. Claudia was with a circle of women in flowing linen—obviously friends of Emily's from the crystal/aura alignment/meditation world.

See? Alice was just paying attention. Like any good hostess.

"Did you guys have a good trip?"

Gabi knew the Storm personalities well enough to address Greta directly. "It was all so easy. The train to a car to the docks."

"You know you're welcome to stay here for the night."

"Oh, that's really kind," Gabi rushed to say, "but we have to get back—"

"Gabi has work tomorrow. Roxanne, too," Alice said, lowering her voice to a stage whisper. "By the way, if my mother questions whether

THESE SUMMER STORMS 223

or not I spilled all the family secrets to you, please tell her I absolutely did, and started with hers."

Roxanne burst out laughing. "I do not need Elisabeth Storm as an enemy, Alice. You fight your own battles. Though I am interested in what happens when you all cause trouble?"

"We're not allowed," Emily said. "Jack won't let us."

"Who's Jack?" Gabi asked, looking to Alice.

"He's Alice's sailing partner," Emily replied. "Stern. Handsome. Worked for my dad."

"Is he?" Gabi asked, suddenly very interested.

Alice scrambled to triage the moment. "The fact that he's handsome is irrelevant."

"I wouldn't go that far," came his deep voice, sending a shiver through her—not that she would ever admit that. Gabi's and Roxanne's eyes went wide as he leaned in and extended his hand. "Jack Dean. Nice to meet you."

"Is it, though?" Alice said, under her breath.

"Gabi Romero-Jiménez," she said before turning a knowing gaze on Alice, the kind that only decades-long friends could deploy. "And you didn't even have to trip over a dog leash on the way up. I'm impressed."

CHAPTER

14

"Y OU DIDN'T GET A letter?" Gabi said around a mini lobster quiche from the little plate she'd piled high with canapés before suggesting they take a walk along the eastern side of the island, away from the crowds.

"He didn't leave them for everyone." Alice paused as another helicopter—would they ever stop?—flew overhead, low and loud as it descended to the landing pad. She looked at her watch, knowing it was wishful thinking—helicopters had clearance to arrive and depart Storm Island until seven, still hours away.

The sound of the helicopter abated, and Gabi said, "Who else didn't get one?"

"No one. Just me." Alice raised a hand. "It's not a thing. I'm fine with it."

"Okay, well, it's a very big thing," Gabi said. "What the fuck, Franklin? Are you sure?"

"I'm sure."

"Maybe your mom just . . . overlooked it? She's grieving and—"

"First, Elisabeth Storm wouldn't let a little thing like widowhood in the way of doing her duty. But in this case, it wasn't her duty. It was Jack's."

"Jack, the hot fixer?"

"Is he hot?" The question came out way too casual to be for real.

"Oh please, we don't have time for this. The hotness is empirical— the height, the thighs, and the jaw," Gabi said. "Also hot: the way the two of you circled each other, so I'm definitely planning to get into that on Friday night—you're coming for dinner."

Alice smiled. "Deal."

"In the meantime, though," Gabi continued, "I'm only here for three hours so stop bullshitting me and please explain why your dad gave the letters for each of you to some guy he works with."

"He's not just some guy. Jack was my dad's second-in-command. And not just the letters—he's in charge of the whole inheritance game Dad left for us."

"But couldn't he have given them all to Sam, who he also worked with?"

"Instead, he told Sam he couldn't speak for twelve hours a day."

"With love, Alice, your dad was an asshole."

"This is what I've been *saying*," Alice said.

"So, everyone has something to do."

Alice nodded and gave Gabi the short version, proving that old friends really are the best kind, because she immediately understood the delight of Sam having to shut up and the pain of Greta having to end it with Tony, and shared the vague sense that whatever truths Elisabeth was required to tell would be uniquely unhinged, and understood the confusion they all felt over Emily's not having a task at all.

"She got a letter, though? From your dad?"

"Yup. And no task. Unlike me. I got a task, but no letter. I have to stay until Wednesday."

"That's it?" Gabi extended her plate to Alice. "Two more days and . . . Alice Storm, billionaire?"

"Yup."

"And you don't want to stay."

"I—" She heard the gentle judgment in the question—barely there because Gabi was trying to be a good friend. "I know it sounds ridiculous."

"Not at all. I mean, seven days on a private island in the closest thing New England has to paradise, and you only get a *billion* dollars? Who *would* take that offer?"

Alice laughed. "Spoken like someone who doesn't know my family."

"Spoken like someone who has a healthy understanding of late-stage capitalism," Gabi said. "Don't take this the wrong way, but it's giving poor little rich girl, my friend."

"And you, without your guillotine."

"I'll have to make do with brutal honesty."

A beat. "They don't want me here."

"On the contrary, I imagine they want you here very much."

"They want the money. Not me. And he only wanted me here so he could get the last laugh of controlling me."

They walked in silence for a few moments, before Gabi said, "Yeah, that's probably true."

For Alice, there was immense relief in Gabi's honesty. Tears welled, and Alice blinked them back, refusing to cry.

Gabi reached for her, and Alice shook her head. "Don't. I can't."

A nod. "Okay."

And it was. And that, somehow, summoned more tears, pushing a fat one down her cheek. She dashed it away. "I'm going to ruin my makeup."

"It looks so good," Gabi replied immediately. "I noticed it right away. Assume it was for Jack?"

"Stop—"

"Okay, okay. Back burner again." A pause. "So hear me out, what if you say, fuck it, and *don't* stay? Come back with me and Roxanne. Hell, hitch a final helicopter ride with a billionaire—you shouldn't though, helicopters are death traps, did you read that piece in the *Post*?" She shuddered. "Anyway. You've got a job, an apartment with original hardwood that any realtor would call *cozy,* friends who love you, and that's before we talk about the art galleries that love Alice Foss. Who needs the extra zero in their bank account?"

It was a lot more than one extra zero, but that wasn't the point.

Alice shook her head. "I can't."

"You don't need it."

"I know. But if I leave—no one inherits."

Eyes widened. "*No one?*"

"No one." She paused. "And I think that was his point. Summon me back to the family fold only once he was too dead to apologize for pushing me out in the first place."

"And them? Have they apologized?"

No, and they wouldn't. "They haven't even thought about me for a second, except to make sure I'm present and accounted for."

"Jesus," Gabi whispered. "They could all murder you!"

"I don't think they inherit if they murder me."

"Okay, well, I don't love that *think*, and I don't have the same faith in rich white people two days from losing their inheritance, but . . . fine. Then play it the other way. Stay until Wednesday. Get your billions, and walk." Gabi shrugged. "Doesn't seem like the worst plan. You can take me on a trip."

They stopped on the edge of Moonstone Cliff, a limestone precipice that fell into a deep swimming hole close to the secret beach. Gabi watched Alice for a while, and then asked, "May I change the subject?"

Alice slid a nervous look at her friend. "I don't know."

"What's the deal with Jack?"

Nothing.

"Don't you dare say *nothing*," Gabi said. "Even if you hadn't been weird when he came over and introduced himself—"

"I wasn't weird, how was I weird?"

Gabi's side-eye required no additional explanation.

"Okay fine, but my dad just died. Maybe I was weird because of that."

"Yeah, maybe," Gabi said, "but this was a different kind of weird. This was sex weird."

"What is sex weird?"

"The kind of weird that comes when you've had sex with someone. Am I right?"

Alice should have said no. She was going to say no. But then she'd hesitated too long (any hesitation was too long, clearly), and Gabi pounced. "Oh my god, I *am*." A heartbeat while she took in the news. "*When?* Was it *great*? I bet it wasn't." She tutted. "The hot ones never try hard enough."

This one did. This one was great.

"Gabi, this is a funeral."

"Please. Funerals are for this." She paused. "Oh my god, *Alice*. You slept with the executor of your father's trust, who is running an inheritance game for your family, for which he should really be remaining impartial? Incredible. Ethically, extremely messy, but I honestly could not be prouder."

"I thought this was tabled for dinner on Friday."

"Oh, we'll talk about it at length then."

"I'm happy that this is all entertaining you," Alice said. "But it's actually not just ethically messy, it's also personally messy. For what it's worth, I didn't know he was a managing director—"

"I bet he managed to direct you."

Alice rolled her eyes. "I didn't *know*."

She trailed off, but Gabi had no trouble picking up the conversation. "He's the guy from the motel!"

"Gabi, we're not exactly in private here."

Gabi lowered her voice. "Sorry. I'm just fascinated. You had a one-night stand at a seedy motel—"

"It's not seedy."

"I'm staying there, my friend. It's kind of seedy, which is not at all relevant. You had a one-night stand thinking you'd never see him again and then he turned out to be the man standing between your family and a massive inheritance." She paused. "It's like a romance novel."

"It's not like a romance novel," Alice said. "In romance novels, it's all a surprise to everyone. This wasn't a surprise to him. He knew it was me!"

Gabi's mouth went slack. "A *snake*."

"Yeah. So it doesn't matter that the sex was great."

"It was! I knew it!"

"You literally said you bet it wasn't."

"Irrelevant. The point is, *you* didn't know who he was, so plausible deniability is in play here."

"Thanks, counselor."

"Getting back to it, then—when we say, personally messy . . . is that because you had some great sex and now it remains . . . something you want to do?"

Alice heaved a giant sigh. "I have terrible taste in men."

"Agreed."

"And this man is not ideal."

"For, like, a dozen different reasons. Including the fact that he lied about knowing who you were. Did he tell you why he did that? Why he didn't come clean right away?"

I wanted to fuck you.

Alice swallowed. She wasn't going to tell Gabi that. "I kind of urged him to . . . keep it anonymous."

"*Filthy,*" Gabi said in a way that made it sound not at all filthy. "Did you tie this man up? Was he rendered speechless in some way, as you are such a smokeshow?"

"Me being a smokeshow never came into it."

"Devastating."

"I didn't want it to be more than one night," Alice said. "At least, not then."

"And now?"

"Having a friend who is a star in the courtroom isn't so fun sometimes, you know."

"I know. Answer the question."

"Yes. I want to do it again."

Gabi nodded, as though she'd known it all along. "No further questions."

It wasn't as funny as it should have been, because it really did feel like Alice had confessed something damning. "He's a very bad decision."

Gabi tilted her head. "Maybe you don't need a good decision this week. Maybe this week is about bad decisions. You know, stay with your family, sleep with the wrong guy . . ." She pointed to the water below. "Is this the cliff we jumped off of when we were in college?"

Alice nodded. "I haven't done it in, I don't know, a decade?"

"Well, maybe you should try it again. It's safe, right?"

That was the question, wasn't it? *Safe* didn't feel like it did when they were young and invincible and there were people to hold her hand when she jumped. Gabi. Her sisters. Her dad.

That tightness in her chest was back.

"Does he feel safe?" Gabi asked, pointedly.

Alice was saved from having to answer by the sound of laughter behind them. They turned to find Roxanne and Claudia headed toward them.

"We've been found." They turned to watch the duo clinging to each other and making their way down the slope.

"Be careful, you two!" Claudia called. "You don't want to fall in!"

From the looks of them, it seemed like Roxanne and Claudia were the ones at risk of falling in. "Glad someone is having a good time," Alice said.

"Yeah," Gabi agreed. "I figured she and Claudia would get along." She raised her voice as they approached. "What are you guys doing? Roxanne, you agreed to be our cover when we snuck out!"

"I know! I know! And then Greta disappeared with some guy—"

"Tony," Claudia cut in, with a meaningful look at Alice.

"Is she doing it?" Alice was shocked by the possibility.

"Oh shit," Gabi said, understanding. "Do you think she'd do it now? With all these people?"

"I can't imagine she would," Alice said, feeling suddenly guilty that she'd left before she could tell Greta that now was not the moment to break up a decades-long secret relationship. "But maybe? Safety in numbers?"

"I don't think she's doing it. They were headed to the fog bell house."

"Ah," Alice said.

"Okay, so Greta's having sex with a man built like a sturdy oak in the fog bell house," Roxanne said, as though it were perfectly normal. "But what is she *supposed* to be doing with him?"

"I guess you'll never know," Gabi teased, knowing just where to strike—gossip. "That's your punishment for bailing on your one job."

"Oh, come on," Roxanne protested. "I promise I told countless people that you and Alice were just over there, on the other side of that crowd of elderly white men, but then Claudia came over and offered to introduce me to some of the fun people here and . . . honestly, it was pretty great."

"What good are you?"

"Wait, there are fun people here?"

Claudia tilted her head. "Okay, maybe not fun in the traditional sense, but there are definitely people who are *more interesting* than others."

"Like who?" Alice asked.

"Well, my favorite is Nealy Twill, who told her that great story about the time she got stoned in the Azores with two members of the Beatles."

"Would you believe she wouldn't name them?" Roxanne sounded affronted.

"Nealy Twill has been around lawyers long enough to know that you shouldn't name real people when you're telling fictional stories," Alice said before looking at Claudia. "I didn't know that you had favorites."

"Of course I do. I'm just smart enough to stay quiet about it— drawing attention to yourself as an in-law in this family has never ended well."

Alice nodded. "I've always liked you best."

Claudia grinned. "Your mom agrees."

Alice was delighted that Claudia replied, open and chatty in a way she rarely was when alone with the family (a brilliant play). "I like all the weird ones—but don't tell your mom that I called them weird." Her sister-in-law reached down to take off her heels. "Anyway. It's my fault Roxanne left her post. There's only so much Storm I can take alone." She raised a hand in Alice's direction. "No offense, Alice."

"None taken," Alice replied. "I feel the same way."

Roxanne was still going. "And then, Claudia introduced me to this *incredible* man."

Claudia grinned. "Your dad's friend Tom."

"Ah," Alice said. "I bet you liked him."

"I did," Roxanne said.

"Who is your dad's friend Tom?" Gabi asked.

"Well," she started, "we've always been told he was a polo player."

"Yeah, I don't think so," Roxanne said. "We cover polo now and then, and I'm pretty sure that guy is a polo patron. Which means he's just a rich dude who pays for all the real players to drink and party while he hangs around the stable in jodhpurs or whatever."

"Are they called jodhpurs in polo?"

"Whatever." Roxanne waved a hand. "The point is, that's not all he does."

Alice immediately understood. "Oh! No. That's not. He has a fascinating hobby. One he can't stop talking about."

"What is it?" Gabi lowered her voice. "Is it porn? I bet it's porn."

"God! No! Why is that the first thing you thought of?" Alice said.

"I don't know!" Gabi defended herself. "Once again, I don't know what you people get up to on your private islands and helicopters and shit, but I've read some biographies."

"Tom doesn't do porn," Roxanne said. "He collects flags."

Gabi tilted her head. "Is that a euphemism?"

Roxanne laughed. "It is not."

"What do you mean, flags?"

"Historical flags," Alice clarified.

"Like, Betsy Ross?"

"Oh!" Roxanne said as though she'd never been so disappointed. "I should have asked him about Betsy Ross! Anyway, it was very sweet. He was so excited to tell me about his flags! He just bought one from the Roman Empire."

"Did they even have flags during the Roman Empire?"

"I know someone who will tell you all about it!" Roxanne replied, laughing.

"This place is too much," Gabi said to Alice. "How did I become friends with someone who knows a flag collector?"

"Just lucky, I guess," Alice replied.

"There are honest-to-God real problems in the world. And here we are with an island full of people who can solve most of them. And they collect flags and lie about the Beatles."

"What a country," Alice added.

"I mean, sure, it seems like a waste," Claudia replied, dryly. "But at least he's keeping polo well-funded."

Everyone laughed, and for a moment, Alice was consumed with an immense sense of gratitude that even in this, the strangest, most unsettling time of her life, she had these women by her side. Eventually, she returned to reality and her sister-in-law. "Okay, but where was Emily during all this?"

Claudia shook her head. "I left her with Mike Haskins—he was telling her some story about when he and your dad were twenty-two and it was the two of them and your mom against the world. It was sweet but felt . . . private."

"You're a good wife."

"Nah," Claudia said. "She is."

Something thrummed through Alice at the words. Something like envy. Maybe it was because Emily was the youngest—the one with the most distance from the intensity of young Franklin and Elisabeth Storm—but there was no question that she'd found love in a healthy, honest, wonderful way. Sure, she and Claudia ran a crystal shop, and they took sound baths, and smudged homegrown sage in hotel rooms, but she couldn't help but envy their connection. If soulmates existed, Emily and Claudia were it.

Of course Alice was envious. Who wouldn't be? They had a person. A safe space. Someone who was on their side, no matter what.

Is someone with you?

On the train, before she'd known who he was, Jack had asked that.

What would it be like to say yes to that?

The quartet popped out of the woods at the eastern edge of the house, where a flagstone patio had been commandeered by the caterers. The stretch was overrun with people—waiters and chefs and a half dozen others from the events team at Storm Inc.—in a portrait of organized chaos.

No one paid the women any notice as they stepped onto the white seashell path that ran past the house toward the great lawn, around the glass-enclosed sunroom that had been added to the house sometime before Franklin and Elisabeth bought it. No one ever used the room—the old glass paneling made it blazing hot in the summer and bitterly cold in the winter, and so it became what many of those ancient sunrooms became—a modified greenhouse, watered weekly by Lorraine and left empty the rest of the time.

Because of that, the raised voices that came from within were an unexpected surprise. The quartet froze, nearly toppling a young waiter with a tray full of scallops as they exchanged wide-eyed looks.

"He asked me to be here, specifically," a man was saying, loud enough to be heard through the glass. "And so, I am here."

Without speaking, everyone took a step closer to the greenhouse, and Alice turned to peer through the enormous monstera in the window, grateful for a stranger's gossip, less serious than her own.

No luck.

"I don't care if Franklin came back from the dead to fly you in himself. I want you gone."

Alice's brows shot up. That wasn't a stranger. It was her mother, in the greenhouse, where Alice wasn't sure she'd ever been.

"Who's she with?" Gabi whispered, obviously having had the same revelation.

Alice shook her head and shifted to find a better view. "I don't know." Through the collection of bromeliads, she could see a sliver of her mother's silk shift (purple lake), and the legs of a man in a glen check suit (moss gray).

"It doesn't matter what you want," the man said in a voice Alice couldn't place. "He wanted me here."

"Exactly. To punish me."

"I don't think that was the case. He loved you, Lizzie." A pause. "And he loved her."

Alice's eyes were wide. She'd never heard anyone but Franklin called her mother *Lizzie*. And even then, not for decades.

"You can't kick me out. He left me a letter."

Alice sucked in a breath. Another letter from her father. Another person he'd thought of before he thought of her. Tears stung at the back of her throat. This stranger in the greenhouse had been more important than his own daughter.

"Of course he did. Anything to make sure he stirred up trouble before going directly to hell."

Alice stiffened.

Gabi took her hand. "Oh *shit*."

"I'm here for him," the man said.

"He doesn't have a say anymore," Elisabeth argued.

"She does, though."

Gabi and Alice shared a look. "Who's *she*?" Gabi mouthed.

Alice shook her head. It could be anyone. But before she could think, her mother spoke, the words so cool that Alice was vaguely surprised that the contents of the entire greenhouse didn't immediately frost. "This isn't his island anymore; it's *mine*."

"I'm not here to take any of it from you," came the reply, and Alice could hear the thread of frustration in the words. Whoever this man was, he'd had enough. "It's not a zero-sum game, Elisabeth."

What did that mean?

"Good," her mother said, the words harder by the second. "Because I am through letting him decide my future. All these years later, and he's still punishing me for one night. For one mistake, which I never would have made if he'd been around."

"For all that night was a mistake, this isn't," the man said, and Alice stiffened, watching him move closer to Elisabeth through the wall of houseplants. "And I promise you, when we spoke, it didn't feel like punishment. It felt like he was giving her a gift. And me, too. A gift you have to understand."

"It wasn't his to give!" The wobble in her mother's voice set Alice on edge. She stiffened and looked to Claudia, who was listening just as intently, her lips pressed tightly together.

Silence from inside the greenhouse. And then, "He gave it nonetheless. And I'm taking it. And you'd be a monster if you didn't let her do the same."

"I'm calling security," Elisabeth said in a tone Alice recognized from a lifetime of speaking her mother's language. The stone wall of her mother's resolve. "I want you off my island."

"You're not calling anyone." The man's reply was so dismissive; it must have destroyed Elisabeth. "You'd never cause that kind of scene."

"We should get Tony," Claudia said, softly. Alice didn't misunderstand. This wasn't for Storm security or the Treasury Department or the myriad bodyguards who'd arrived with their billionaire bosses that afternoon.

This was a family affair.

"No," Alice said, turning away from the group to head for the house. Later, she'd tell herself she said it because Tony was in the fog bell house with Greta, and it was too far away. But in the moment, she acted on instinct, already moving upstream through the throngs of white-shirt-black-tie waiters, toward the door to the house.

"Get Jack."

And then she headed inside, to face another one of the island's secrets.

CHAPTER

15

EVEN THOUGH SHE TOOK the shortcut through the caterers' staging area, by the time Alice arrived, Elisabeth was alone, standing in profile at the center of the greenhouse, still and poised like a John Singer Sargent portrait. *Lady Storm.*

Alice peered down the long, dark hallway that led into the house to the foyer, everything within made darker by the bright sunlight outside. It was empty. Whoever her mother had been arguing with had disappeared.

Taking the two steps down into the solarium, she scanned the room, empty except for her mother. "Mom?"

Elisabeth Storm was best in large groups of people, preferably those with whom she had to put on a face. While she didn't think her mother particularly disliked her children, Alice knew better than to imagine that she enjoyed being around people who could see her truth. A quiet sigh was the only indication that she'd heard Alice.

"Everything okay?"

"Yes," she said, turning her attention to her dress—the purple silk shift that had somehow avoided even a single wrinkle in the windy, eighty-degree seaside humidity. "I'm fine. Why wouldn't I be?"

How many times had she heard those exact words—*I'm fine*—over the years? Her mother never acknowledging a single moment of stress, of anger, of wear, in any way.

Perhaps it had taken until now, until the irrefutable knowledge that something worthy of her mother's concern had happened—something upon somethings upon somethings (the death of her husband, for example)—for Alice to realize that in suppressing every negative emotion, her mother had succeeded in suppressing the good ones, as well.

But there was something else, in that moment, frozen in time and space and the unbearable heat of the solarium (how was her mother not sweating? How was she not even *dewy*?). A realization that Alice, too, had done her best to hide her emotions, for fear of being seen, of being known, of being rejected.

Not good enough to be a Storm, not good enough to be anything outside of one.

In the past, Alice would never have argued with that clipped *I'm fine*. She wouldn't have dared. But they were all in uncharted territory. "I heard you in here," she said. "There was someone with you." A pause as she tried to be gentle. "It sounded serious."

I'm here. If you need me.

That felt like too much to say.

Her mother didn't look at her. "You shouldn't be listening at keyholes."

Tears sprang, unwelcome and angry and sad and a dozen other things, burning Alice's throat as she searched for the right thing to say.

She settled on, "Mom, I'm so sorry."

She saw the words strike Elisabeth, making her impossibly stiffer. "What are *you* sorry for?"

Sorry for your loss. For our loss. (The truth.)

But she wasn't going to say that. "I'm just—sorry."

"There's no need to cry."

"Right." Alice agreed with the experience of a kid who'd had this conversation a thousand times, built by cool emotion that came from four hundred years of New England winters, always threatening to ice out the other 50 percent—the undeniable heat of her arrogant, over-bearing father.

It wasn't until that moment, standing in the brutal humidity of the greenhouse, that Alice realized the truth. Elisabeth and Franklin had somehow existed in strange, perfect balance.

Until last week.

And now, without fire, there was nothing but ice.

Elisabeth inhaled sharply, the sound startling Alice from her thoughts, releasing words she might not have said if she'd thought about them. "Mom—this is terrible. You're allowed to say that."

"Why would I say that? People seem to be having a lovely time."

Alice's brows shot up. "A lovely time—" She stopped, unable to keep the horrified laugh from bubbling up and still measuring her words as she'd been taught. "You remember why everyone is here, don't you? He *died*, Mom. He's *gone*. And we're all sad. And people are *sorry.*"

Innocence morphed instantly into anger, Elisabeth's blue eyes nar-rowing, the skin around them—so carefully preserved—pulling tight into lines. "I know he died, Alice. *I was here.*"

Elisabeth didn't have the same rules of battle as Alice; she deployed the words without hesitation. Without even a moment of considering the edge they would carry. Or maybe she was aware of it all along.

"I wasn't here, you mean."

Elisabeth did not reply, her gaze flickering past her, to the exit and the dark hallway that yawned beyond.

"What do you want from me, Mom? I came as soon as I heard," Alice said, the words turning to dust on her tongue. "I came as soon as you called."

"Precisely."

"What, I was supposed to ignore that he never reached out? That you never did?" She knew she shouldn't say anything. That even if it was the right time for this conversation, it wouldn't end in anything new or fresh or healed. She shook her head. "He told me to *get the hell off his island* and I did as I was told—as I had done for my whole life, I might add, right up until I couldn't anymore—and this entire family wrote me off."

"Don't be silly. You were always welcome to come home." She said it so firmly, like it was settled law.

"Tail between my legs, begging to be let back in," Alice said. "Because God forbid any of us stand up to him. God forbid anyone tell him he was wrong. Even now. Well, Mom. He was wrong. And you let it happen."

"You're being dramatic."

God, she felt dramatic. She wanted to scream her drama into being, in this room made of glass and terra-cotta and flagstone. "Am I wrong?"

"Yes, you are." Her mother turned on her, something like fire in her eyes, like Alice had finally knocked her loose. "I fought your father all the time."

"Not for us," Alice said. "Not for Greta so she could actually love her person, not to make room for Emily, not to ensure that Dad respected Sam. Not when I *begged* you to convince him to let me have a life outside of Storm. You never once fought for us. You fought for *yourself*. And that's different. You never stopped him from any of it. Not even when he pushed me out and turned his back on me."

"No one ever stopped your father from doing anything. We lived according to his whim." A convenient lie, as though Elisabeth had been a jellyfish in Franklin's ocean rather than queen of storms (Storms?). Her tone went bitter as she waved a hand toward the south-facing window of the solarium and the crowd beyond, in the distance. "Even this week."

"Right," Alice said, her voice growing louder, angry and hurt and frustrated. "Because he died and you couldn't even find your way to having a goddamn funeral. Instead, we're passing mini quiches and champagne at a fucking *celebration*."

Elisabeth froze, and Alice wondered at the shock that flashed over her mother's face, even as Alice's words reverberated through the space, banging against the glass, passing through it. And when it dissipated—

leaving the caterer no doubt reminding the staff nearby that they'd signed NDAs—the only evidence that she'd heard Alice at all was the slight rise of her perfectly shaped brows.

Something whispered through Alice at the expression, cold and unpleasant and incomprehensible. Before she could say anything, Elisabeth's attention slid past her again, over her shoulder to the entrance to the room. Alice knew who was there before she followed her mother's gaze. Claudia had found Jack. Told him Alice needed him. And he'd come.

Like a fucking Boy Scout.

"Elisabeth." He acknowledged the older woman but didn't look at her, his focus entirely on Alice. "Do you need something?"

Alice shook her head, but he didn't leave. Of course he didn't leave, stepping into the room, the sound of his oxblood loafers like gunshot on the flagstones. Her gaze tracked over him, sliding over his broad shoulders, down the pristine line of his jacket, the length of his sleeve, to the gleaming white cuff peeking out at his wrist, liked he'd been dressed by a personal valet.

His left hand was fisted when her eyes found it, and he flexed his fingers almost immediately, as though he could feel her notice. He shook it, barely, and she tracked the movement. Jack had come ready to fight. To fix.

Of course, there was no fixing this.

"Are you—"

Elisabeth cut him off. "We're perfectly fine, Jack. You needn't chase along after us all day. We're not Franklin; you don't work for us."

His gaze flickered to Elisabeth, and back to Alice. "No, ma'am."

"We've lingered long enough," Elisabeth said. "I'm returning to the guests." She pushed past Jack and into the house with a smooth grace that Alice had never mastered, and certainly wasn't able to even approximate in that moment.

As Elisabeth disappeared down the dark hallway, Alice looked to the floor, wishing she were anywhere but there, on that island.

"Alice—"

"No," she whispered. "Don't."

He was already moving, though, coming for her. And she thought he might close the distance this time, for a wild moment, she imagined he'd reach for her. Pull her into his arms.

She played out the fantasy, imagining what it would be like if she let him. If she leaned in to his embrace and let him keep the world at bay.

It did not escape her that she'd told Claudia to get him. Not Tony. Not Sam. Not half a dozen Storm Inc. security guards. Jack.

And he'd come. And he'd stayed.

But even now, he kept himself at a distance. "You always do that," she said, "come for me like you have no intention of stopping, and then . . . you stop."

Silence fell between them, and he ran a hand through his thick dark hair. "I have to."

"I understand. Maybe someday you'll realize that he doesn't control you anymore."

A long silence. "Yeah. You too." There was no rebuke in the words, instead, only comfort. Like they'd walked through the same fire. He exhaled harshly and unbuttoned his jacket. "It's hot in here."

"We don't have to be here," she said, tilting her head toward the door. "We can go back."

He didn't move. "Why did you send them to get me?"

"My mom was—" She stopped. Restarted. "There was someone—" Another pause. A shake of her head, feeling like she shouldn't say. Like it was a secret. Just like everything else. "I don't know; I shouldn't have."

After a long moment, she looked up to find him staring at her, his gaze heavy on hers, as though if only he looked hard enough, he would be able to see her thoughts.

"Nothing about this makes sense, you know." She flinched at the words, even as he added, "The day, the week. The future. And nothing about how you're feeling is wrong, either."

"That doesn't feel true," she said. "It feels like it should make more sense. Like I should understand it better. Nothing about this is special. Everyone dies. Shouldn't we all be better at it?"

He shook his head. "We don't get better at it. It doesn't get easier."

"How do you know?"

"Because I've done it." He said it so simply, the way someone might say *I've been to Paris* or *I play tennis.*

Her brow furrowed. "I'm sorry."

Maybe that was obligatory, but it didn't feel that way. And when he nodded and said, "Thank you," that felt real.

She clung to it. "Can I ask—"

"My father." He said the words carefully, as though, if he didn't, they would come out mangled and strange. She understood that. "He died eight years ago."

"Oh." It was all she could find as she searched for the right thing to say—struggling to imagine that other people had experienced this strange, uncomfortable sensation.

"I wasn't there," he said.

She hadn't been, either. "That's hard."

He nodded. "You understand."

"Was it sudden? Was it like—"

"He was sick," he said, clipped, like he regretted bringing it up, but now the words were coming and he couldn't stop them. "I wasn't there. For a lot of reasons—he wasn't the best man. He tried, but he brought a lot of pain to the people around him. And I was young and angry, and he was all I had. It was easy to disappear, and honestly?" He ran a hand through his hair, disturbing the dark waves. "I wanted to disappear. It wasn't hard for me to leave, but it was too hard for me to go back."

She nodded. "I understand that, too."

He met her eyes. "I think you do. But if I learned anything from that, it's that this day—the days to come—they aren't for him. They're for you. Today is an end, but it's also a beginning. Who were you before, and who will you be after?"

She lifted a hand, not knowing if she should touch him. If this kind of connection was allowed. For all the ways they'd touched, all the things they'd done with and to each other, this was somehow more intimate. "Considering how close you were to my father . . . this must be difficult."

He gave her one of those fleeting half smiles that she was beginning to like. "Careful. Things like that will make me start to think you like me."

She was starting to think it, too, but she wasn't ready to admit it. She dropped her hand. "On the boat," she said. "You told me you were sorry for my loss."

He nodded. "I am."

"You shouldn't be. I lost him a long time before that."

"I'm sorry for that loss, too," he said. "That's the one that doesn't go away."

Alice's chest went tight, suddenly full of truth, and strange relief—that someone understood. Maybe it was the relief that made her say, "And then I lost the rest of them."

"Are you sure?" He was so close, and she was aching for something that wasn't the rawness of the day. The unease of the week. The uncertainty of what was to come. And this man, so steady he unmoored her, leaving her whispering his name, barely there, almost lost in the heat of the solarium. In the stillness of the moment, stolen from the chaos of the day.

He heard it.

"Alice, I'm coming for you." A warning. A promise. "This time, I'm not stopping."

She lifted her chin as his fingers grazed the side of her neck, setting her pulse pounding. "Please."

A dark rumble came from deep in his chest. Approval. "That's so pretty."

The words tumbled through her, and she closed her eyes as his fingers stroked over her jaw. "What is?"

"Knowing you want it like I do." His touch left fire in its wake, back down the column of her neck, finding purchase. He pulled her close. "I'll give it to you," he whispered, tilting her face up to his, lowering his lips until they were a hairsbreadth from her, the scent of him enveloping her—sand and salt and sea. "Just a little. Just for a second. And then we'll stop."

"Just for a second," she agreed. "Just a tiny bit, and then we'll—"

He swallowed the rest with his kiss.

They'd kissed before, obviously. Hot, wild kissing that felt fierce and desperate and explosive, like they were racing against some unseen rival for pleasure. The kind of kissing that made you forget.

But this . . . this was for remembering. This was for holding close for a lifetime, for hiding away for late nights and long afternoons when there was time to relive it. That time he'd found her in pieces no one else could see, and honored her. This was for exploring in secret, again and again, just as they explored each other now, slow and sinful and perfect.

And it was an exploration, his tongue stroking over her lips as she sighed into his mouth, opening for him, pressing herself to him—somehow hotter than the room itself as his hands came to her face, holding her with steady certainty, like he had plans for her. She couldn't resist touching him in response, her hands sliding beneath his open jacket, chasing up the ridges of the torso she knew was kissed by the sun.

He grunted at her touch, and she loved that sound, the proof that he was as beholden to the moment as she was, their kiss stopping time with its slow, sinful movements, firm and impossibly soft, setting fire to them both when his thumbs stroked over her skin and he tasted her, savored her.

When he finally stopped it, lifting his lips, making her want to fist his lapels and pull him back for more, Jack stared down at Alice like he was admiring his work, memorizing it.

Memorizing her.

Jack whispered something, too soft for her to hear, and then said, "This isn't the right place for this."

He was wrong. Alice honestly couldn't think of a better place—an unused solarium hotter than the sun and full of dirt and growing things. It was perfect, and if he would just kiss her again, she'd prove it.

In fact . . .

She pulled him down for another kiss, and he groaned into it, claiming her again, long and slow and lovely. When they broke apart, he pressed his forehead to hers and said, in that delicious rumble, "Alice. It's *definitely* not the right time for it."

"Okay," she whispered. "But what if it was?"

That won her a low laugh, and for a wild moment, she wondered what it might be like to make him laugh regularly. "Sweetheart, if I thought you wouldn't regret it, I'd take you upstairs to your tower room and make it the right time."

Now, why did her heart race at that *sweetheart*? Why did she want him to say it again?

This was dangerous.

He was dangerous.

The little whisper, deep in her gut, telling her she should run, because this man, whoever he was, however he'd come into her life, was sure to send it spinning out of control—far beyond the careful boundaries she'd built for herself.

And she might like it.

And that, alone, was enough for her to stop.

"You're right," she whispered.

She recognized the emotion in his eyes—a twin to her own. *Disappointment.*

Unable to stop herself, she reached up and ran her thumb over his lower lip, smeared with her barely tinted lip balm. "You have—"

He grabbed her hand and turned it, pressing a kiss to the soft skin at the inside of her wrist. "Thank you."

The movement flustered Alice with its easy familiarity, as though he'd done it a thousand times before. As though she were his to touch. To kiss. But before she could find her footing, he dropped her hand and stepped back, waving a hand in the direction of the door leading into the house. Alice sucked in a breath, feeling as if she were on a precipice—like the moment she left this room and its peace and Jack's protection, everything was going to turn to chaos.

It was a silly thought; everything was chaos already.

They'd barely left the house before proof appeared. Elisabeth had paused on the rise of the great lawn, looking down on the crowd as Greta and Tony approached her from below.

Whatever was about to happen was not going to go well. The least Alice could do was make sure it didn't happen in full view of the whole world. She headed for her mother, quickly, eager to intercept before Elisabeth decided to—

"Where've you been?" Elisabeth's question carried on the wind across the lawn.

Greta sped up in response to the subtext of the question. *I needed you. And you weren't there.* Her gaze tracked from Elisabeth to Alice, closer now. "Why? What happened?"

The question set Alice on edge, the crisp meaning impossible to miss. *What did you do to her?* Alice lifted her chin, her shoulders pushing back. Armor on. "Nothing."

Greta didn't believe her. That much was clear. "Mom? Is everything okay?"

Elisabeth ignored the questions, her gaze sliding like an accusation to Tony, then back to Greta. "I see you haven't done it yet."

Everything stilled. Greta, Tony, and Alice faltered in their approach, shocked by the words. The sound of the crowd dropped away, Elisabeth's cool words echoing around them. The wind, ever constant on the island, seemed to die down, like even the weather couldn't quite believe what was happening.

Greta scanned the area around them and dipped her head. "Mom," she whispered. "Please stop."

"You've had days to do it, Greta. And instead you're sneaking off to do God knows what with him during *your father's funeral.*"

Greta went ashen at the words, her mouth falling open in shock. As for Tony, he was turning red, and Alice wondered if it was out of embarrassment or anger.

Alice stepped in, keeping her voice low as she drew close. "Mom, don't do this."

"I'm not *doing* anything," Elisabeth said calmly, "except what I have always had to do. Clean up your messes." She looked to Tony. "You're not a fool, Anthony."

"Mom. Are you kidding? Here?" This was the antithesis of Elisabeth Storm's life lessons—never complain, and never in front of people. Absolutely not in full view of two hundred people whose opinions mattered—not only to the world, but to Elisabeth herself. "Now?"

She didn't reply to Alice, instead holding steady, facing down Tony, who did not cower or shrink, meeting her gaze with his own stern look, his shoulders square, his chest barreled and his arms like tree trunks. "No, ma'am. I am not."

"Please." Greta inserted herself between them, her back to Tony. "Don't do this. Not now."

"You should have thought of that before you disappeared with him and embarrassed us all in front of the world," Elisabeth said.

Greta went beet red. "No one was looking."

"You're wrong. Everyone is looking." The words were guaranteed to cause the scene Elisabeth had been trained for years not to make. But loss did strange things, made people cling to what remained. Elisabeth didn't see that what she was about to do would guarantee more loss. A deeper cut.

Alice searched for her siblings. Sam was a million miles away on the other end of the meadow with Saoirse and Oliver. Too far.

Closer, Emily was extricating herself from a conversation, Claudia at her elbow, watching them, knowing something was wrong—an outsider with a clear view to the truth. But there was no time to wait for them. Greta couldn't seem to find words.

It was Alice, alone. "Please, Mom. You need to let this go."

"I'm not interested in discussing this with anyone but you." Elisabeth's words were a weapon, leveled directly at Tony.

He lifted his chin.

"No." Greta put her foot down (as much as she ever did that with Elisabeth). "Leave him alone."

"Tony," Elisabeth said, refusing to look at her daughter. "I do not believe your services are required here any longer."

Greta made a noise that might have been a keen if it hadn't been strangled in her throat.

Alice opened her mouth to speak, not sure what she'd say, knowing she had to say something. Elisabeth cut her off. "You understand what I mean, don't you?"

"I do," he said.

"You've known since Wednesday."

"I have."

Elisabeth nodded. "And you understand why you're not welcome."

"I do."

"That's bullshit," Alice said, instantly, though it did not escape her that she was the only one to say it out loud. "Tony, of course you're welcome. This isn't okay." She looked to her sister. "Greta—for fuck's sake—say something!"

Greta was staring at him, eyes wide. "Why did you stay?"

He stayed for you, you dummy. It took all Alice had not to say it.

She didn't have to. Tony might as well have shouted it for the way he looked at Greta. The ache of his desire, his anguish, his fury was impossible to ignore. He would walk through fire for her.

This whole game—Franklin's, Elisabeth's—it was nonsense. It was time to be done with it. If no one else would say it, Alice absolutely would. "Greta, don't do this. It's not worth it. We'll figure it out." She looked to Jack. "We'll figure it out, Jack, right? She doesn't have to do this."

He didn't reply, and she realized it was beyond him.

This was something he could not fix.

She cast about to do it herself. Inelegant. "It doesn't matter, Greta—the money, the expectations, whatever the press says—it's not important. Not like this. Not like your happiness."

"Don't be ridiculous," Elisabeth said. "You lose everything if she doesn't do this. You and Sam and Emily. Greta would never do that to the family."

"And you, Mom," Alice snapped. "You lose, too."

"I couldn't possibly forget, Alice," Elisabeth matched her tone. "Your father made sure of that."

There it was again—*father,* spat like it was foul-tasting. "And so, what, you punish Greta to stick it to Dad?"

"I am not punishing anyone," Elisabeth argued. "I had nothing to do with this stupid game. I continue not to have anything to do with it; this is your father's doing. And his." She pointed to Jack. "I'm just a bystander."

"Innocence personified."

"Exactly, and your father is dead now," Elisabeth said, as though they weren't surrounded by the proof of it. As though they weren't consumed with the proof of it.

"She can't fire me," Tony said, surprising all of them.

"What does that mean?" Elisabeth's affronted utterance would have been a delight to experience if they weren't all having the same thought.

"You can't fire me," Tony said, simply, turning his steel gaze on her. "Even if you had the power to fire me, I don't work for Storm any longer."

Oh, shit!

Everyone looked at him. "What?" Greta asked.

"I gave my notice on Thursday." He looked to Jack, standing at a distance, and everyone followed.

"You were involved in it," Alice said.

"I'm a managing director at Storm," he said, dryly. "So yes. I was involved."

Before she could reply, Greta spoke, surprise and something like hurt in her words. "You met with the Secret Service. You worked with the company security team today."

Tony was silent for a long moment, long enough that Alice wondered if he would answer. And then, finally, he said, "I don't have to be on the payroll to want to keep you safe."

Alice's chest went tight at the words, the beautiful simplicity of them. Tony was staring at Greta like she was the only thing in his world, like she was the sun—so raw and honest that it felt wrong that anyone was there to witness it.

It was an undeniable profession of his love for her. Of what should come next. Greta's loyalty. Her love. Her future.

But that wasn't so freely given, as it had been claimed already. Long before Anthony Balestreri had arrived on the scene. Greta's gaze was glued to the grass at her feet, lush and green and fragrant with wild thyme. "Tony," she whispered, and Alice looked away, knowing what was to come. Not wanting to watch.

"I've had enough." Elisabeth waved a hand between them, apparently having no difficulty hearing it. Watching it. "This secret love affair that has consumed you for *years* and was never going to give you a future. Your father only wanted what was best for you and the family," she began, knowing how to push Greta's buttons. "And now he's gone, and it's time for you to assume some responsibility."

It was monstrous. As Alice watched, a collection of Storm staff whispered among themselves. A few of Greta's old-money friends from the East Side of Providence tried for unobtrusive stares.

They might as well have been obtrusive—the entire assembly would be whispering about it before Elisabeth was through. And that made Alice even more angry. Two hundred people here to center her mother—to coddle her and care for her and console her—and she still couldn't see her way to doing the same for her children?

If Greta needed Tony to get through the day—this day, of all days—was that so bad? Couldn't they have put the world on hold for twenty-four hours? Alice met her sister's eyes, full of deep indigo sadness, and willed her to stand up. Finally.

Tell her no. Claim your space.

"You can finally put it all behind you," Elisabeth said. "Close the door. Again."

Now, why did that *again* sound so ominous? Why did it spark a flash of regret in Greta's eyes? A shadow of shame so obvious that it seemed like a physical blow?

Next to Alice, Jack was still, the heavy weight of his presence setting Alice on edge. He could stop this right now. She looked to him, and he deliberately avoided meeting her gaze, as though he, too, understood that whatever this was, it wasn't fair. And it wasn't right. And her father was dead, for God's sake, so who would know?

No one. Jack would know.

And he shouldn't care.

But he didn't say anything, and he didn't move, and just as the scream woke in her chest and crawled up her throat—threatening to release and scorch him with years of pent-up anger—Alice looked to Tony, and the fight in her faded.

Because he had already accepted what she refused to.

Greta wasn't going to defy their mother. She wasn't going to push back. And he respected himself too much to stay and let her break his heart.

He nodded once. "Okay."

He shook his head and looked to Greta, who wouldn't meet his eyes. It was heartbreaking. This man loved her so much, and he was still Greta's secret. She still couldn't find it in herself to walk away with him. To stand in their truth, together.

Her sister took a deep breath, and for a moment, Alice thought it was to shore up her courage, knowing what she had to do, what she had to say.

And then she turned to steel, her face going sharp and angled, like Elisabeth's. Her hair gleaming, old-money blond in the late-summer sun, like Elisabeth's had once done. Her shoulders tipping back, spine straight, like Elisabeth's.

In the silence that fell, Tony was gone, crossing the lawn toward the path that would take him to the helipad, Greta and Alice watching as Elisabeth made a show of surveying the mass of people below who didn't realize what had happened up on the hill—something that might have been tragic if they weren't all here to mourn a different tragedy (or at least pretend to mourn one).

They didn't know they'd witnessed a decimation.

Alice took a step toward Greta, who was looking out to the water, where the sun gleamed on the waves in a thousand tiny, blinding lights. "Greta. You can stop this. Hell, I can stop this. If I leave—"

"Don't you *dare*."

Alice was shocked by the venom in Greta's reply. "I— This wasn't my fault."

It was true. *Wasn't it?* Or had she pushed her mother into this in the solarium? Had she gone too far?

"Just—" Greta looked as though she might scream. Held it in. "Just—you'd better not leave. Not after this."

Alice pulled up short. "I wasn't—"

"Not after we've all made sacrifices. You'd better fucking stay." Greta's fury was palpable, directed squarely at Alice. And then the eldest

Storm sibling was spinning away, down the hill, toward the party, where she could don her costume as doting, grieving daughter, and hold her emotions at bay.

"Well," Elisabeth said, as though everything had gone according to plan. As though she hadn't been the architect of Greta's broken future, and her animosity toward Alice. "That settles that."

Alice came undone. "How could you do that? Push him away like that? Force Greta to end it? Now? Today?" Alice was facing her mother now, unable to keep her tone measured. Unable to keep herself still. She advanced toward Elisabeth, who stayed still, an immovable force. "Do you realize how cruel that was? How much you'll regret it when you see what comes of it?"

"*Cruel?*" Elisabeth blinked in that practiced innocence that Alice was beginning to loathe. "How? I did it for her. I took the task from her. I handled it. Like I have always handled everything with her, and with all of you. Sam's through with his tasks, Greta with hers, and you certainly won't leave now . . . not now that it's all resting on you."

Alice's jaw went slack. "What?"

"And as for regret—I shall simply add it to all the rest. I've more than enough."

So that was it. Her mother was going to play martyr. And to think Alice had worried about her earlier. What a stupid thing to do. If there was one truth in the world, Elisabeth Storm *survived*.

Jack stepped in, the words low and quiet and threatening. Unyielding. "That's enough."

"Thank you, Jack," Elisabeth said, as though he'd come to her rescue. "It's nice to know there is some chivalry in the world."

Alice bit her tongue.

"You should return to the party, Elisabeth," he said.

"I think I will," she said, firing a cool retort at Alice as she started down the rise. "I'll find someone who enjoys my company."

Jack let her get a few feet before saying, "Elisabeth."

She stilled, looking over her shoulder, a false smile on her face, like Jack was her new favorite person. The portrait of a gloat, as though she'd won. "Yes?"

"You're wrong. Your task isn't complete; you're still not telling them the truth."

"I don't know what you mean."

"I think you do," he said. "But if you're struggling, you're welcome to complete your other task for the day now." They all understood. Immediately. And still, Jack clarified, sharp and clean. "Do you have something to say about Franklin?"

Alice couldn't help the little laugh that came at the question, at the knowledge that every one of them could happily predict what Elisabeth *would like* to say about Franklin.

Elisabeth turned her narrow gaze on her middle daughter. Without missing a beat, she replied to Jack. "He would have been proud of Alice."

It was supposed to sting as it sailed through the loophole Elisabeth obviously believed she'd found, but it didn't.

Instead, Jack met her eyes and said, unironically, "Perfect."

Before Alice could enjoy the satisfaction that came in the wake of his word, Elisabeth's brows shot together and she threw Jack a look best described as deadly (she must have been *furious,* as she allowed herself the wrinkles). Pressing her lips together in a thin line, she turned on her heel and left.

Alice and Jack stood watching as Elisabeth headed back to the festivities, where those assembled did their best to pretend they had not noticed any of the proceedings (laughable, that—if there had been cell service, the texting would have already begun). The wind picked up, sending a perfect late-summer breeze, dry and delicious, around them, like a gift. Like a message. She turned to look at Jack, her hair rising on the wind toward him.

He lifted his hand at the same time she did but stopped as she pushed her hair behind her ear. His hand hovered in mid-air, and she resisted the urge to claim it. To lace her fingers through it and pull him closer, this man who had been the enemy and now . . . didn't seem to be that at all.

"Thank you," she whispered instead, the words caught on the wind, stolen away like a secret.

She met his gaze, serious and something else . . . something rich and humid, like if she did touch him, he'd be the one to pull her closer— back to the house, to privacy. To a place where he could lay her down and prove that he was nothing close to the enemy.

A wild thought followed. What if she asked him to do all that . . . but somewhere else? Somewhere far from here? What if she asked him to leave with her? To be free of this place? Of its secrets? Of its burdens?

Would he do it?

"Jack," she began. "What if—"

"Alice!"

Gabi's urgent call came from closer than Alice expected, as she hurried up the garden slope toward the house, a look on her face that was decidedly un-Gabi. Like whatever it was, she didn't know how to handle it.

Now what?

Dropping her hand, she took a step toward her friend. "What's happened?"

"So, I can tell some shit is going down, but . . ." Gabi waved a hand in the direction of the meadow, her attention flickering to Jack, then back to Alice with absolute focus. "Griffin is here."

CHAPTER

16

"ALLEYCAT."

Alice didn't hide her distaste as she stopped in front of Griffin McGill, the man who'd promised her, again and again, that he didn't care about this place, or these people or her past, because he was going to be her future.

Liar.

Two months away from him hadn't cleared Alice's instinct to find him in a crowd, tall and blond and blue-eyed, the kind of white guy who'd been prom king in high school. Reality TV handsome, Gabi liked to call him, but the truth was, he was handsome enough that two months ago, her heart ached to look at pictures of him, this man who was supposed to have been the love of her life.

She'd been so desperate for someone to love her for something other than her name, and now, all she could think about were all the ways he'd been just like her father, trying so hard to convince her that what he wanted, she wanted, too. She'd paid for his whole life—supported him when he told her he couldn't search for a full-time job because he'd be giving up on his dream, and didn't he deserve a dream, too?—made room for him in her apartment, with her friends, paid for the joint trip to Prague where he'd proposed, turned the other way when he'd charged their joint credit card for her engagement ring, telling her of course she didn't have to pay for it—he'd pay for it, eventually.

In the end, he'd never paid for it. God, she'd been so stupid.

But she'd said yes, anyway, and she'd planned a wedding on her own, and she'd believed him when he told her he loved her. And then he'd left.

And now, he was back.

After the week she'd had, Alice was furious. "What are you doing here?"

"*Babe,*" he said, as though nothing had changed. As though he deserved to be there. He reached for her hands, claiming them with ease. "Of course I'm here." Griffin's brilliant, wide smile flashed until he seemed to remember that this wasn't a time for smiles. "I knew you'd need me."

"She doesn't need you, you asshole." Gabi spoke up from where she stood, at a distance, having refused to leave Alice alone after revealing Griffin's arrival. Knowing, in that way best friends did, that Alice might need her. Standing, in that way best friends did, at the ready, perfectly able to both tell Griffin off and procure a shovel if a body required burying.

At least there was someone on Alice's side.

Jack had tried to come, too. He'd gone big and gruff when Gabi had announced Griffin's arrival, but Alice had shaken him off, too embarrassed to face the shame of having been with this obvious buffoon while Jack looked on. She'd urged him back to the gathering, even as his gaze had turned stormy, and she'd followed Gabi to the far end of the lawn, where Griffin had been parked at the bar since his arrival.

"Gabriela!" he said, big and boisterous, designed to draw attention—a tactic Alice recognized as the protective shield he used whenever anyone called him on his bullshit. "Is that how it's going to be?"

Gabi looked to Alice for a cue. Or maybe permission.

No. Alice wanted the fight herself. "Again, Griffin," Alice said, "what are you doing here?"

Nearby, heads began turning, stopping just before they could gawk.

Griffin got nervous, casting looks around the assembly, obviously searching for allies. Of course, if he'd listened to Alice even for a moment during their time together, he'd have known the truth—there were no allies for him here. There were barely allies for her.

His smile disappeared and he lowered his voice, dipping his head toward her. "I was invited."

"Not by me."

"Alice." He laughed in that patronizing way men did when they were about to gaslight the hell out of a woman. "I would have come even without an invitation. Of course I came. Babe . . . I wouldn't have left you alone in this place."

"She's not alone," Gabi said.

"Don't call me babe," Alice added.

He ignored Gabi and searched the space, packed with people. "Can we go somewhere? To talk?"

"Hi!" Emily appeared at her elbow, Claudia at a distance. Alice gritted her teeth at her bright greeting—a greeting she would have been so grateful for two months earlier. "Griffin, it's been a really long time."

It was so *authentic*. Where were Greta and Sam when you needed them? At least they would have treated Griffin like garbage even without knowing the whole story.

"Oh, shit," Gabi said, softly, immediately understanding.

"It's really nice to see you," Emily added.

"No, it's not," Alice said.

"It's not?" Emily's eyes went wide.

Alice returned her attention to Griffin. "We don't have anything to talk about."

Emily's mouth dropped open. "You don't?"

Alice turned on her sister. "I didn't put him on the list."

"We did," Emily said.

"Of course." Alice looked away, across the crowd, to where Greta played young Elisabeth, the perfect hostess, as though her heart hadn't just been fully broken. She would have noticed the oversight. Rectified it. "I wish someone had asked me."

"Asked you—" Emily's brow furrowed. "We thought you—Alice, he's your *fiancé*. Of course he was invited."

"You haven't told them?" Gabi interjected.

"Em, maybe we should . . ." Claudia trailed off, clearly understanding, her hand on Emily's elbow.

"We're not together anymore," Alice reported. It was a kind way of saying it. Less mortifying than *Griffin left me. Alone. With no explanation.*

"*What?*" Emily's shocked reply was loud enough to summon the interest of a dozen people nearby, all of whom immediately pretended they hadn't heard.

Alice lowered her voice to a whisper. "Jesus, Emily, I thought you were supposed to be the portrait of subdued balance."

"You have to admit that's difficult in this family," Claudia pointed out, dryly.

"What happened?" Emily asked.

"Griffin turned out to be a fucking asshole." Gabi, from the gallery.

"Thank you, Gabi," Alice said.

"You should tell the whole story," Gabi said. "Everyone will agree with me." She turned to Griffin. "You're a fucking asshole."

"Gabi—" Roxanne said, materializing nearby. "I'm not sure this is quite appropriate for—"

Griffin looked to Gabi. "You're a menace."

Roxanne's brows rose and Gabi grinned. "Glad you've finally noticed."

"Alice, please." Griffin returned to her. "Let's talk. Alone."

She took him in, so familiar, blue eyes in his perfectly symmetrical face, his clear skin the product of hundreds of dollars of skincare (she'd paid for that, too), the deep-set dimples in his cheeks that she'd always thought were charming. The night she first met him, everything about him had seemed so *different.* He'd been so full of feelings and emotions and used words like *authenticity* and *truth,* and it had been like a drug. She'd been wildly attracted to his promise—someone who put her first.

He broke that promise when he broke their engagement.

And now he wanted to claim part of her here?

Today is an end, but it's also a beginning.

Jack's words threaded through her. Who had she been before, who was she going to be after?

Whatever it was, it wasn't going to be with Griffin. He ended today.

"Ten minutes. And you leave." Without waiting for him, she headed through the break in the stone wall, to the edge of the garden overlooking the southern tip of the island, where the fog bell house stood sentry over the mouth of the Bay.

"First," he said, running his hands through his wild hair. "I'm sorry for your loss." *Lie.*

"Please don't," she said. "You left me, Griffin. Why would I *ever* want you here?"

He looked confused, as though it had never occurred to him that she wouldn't want him there. "I am sorry about that," he began, and she saw the actor in him, working to find the right lines. "It was a mistake. I didn't mean to leave you."

"And it took until my father died and my inheritance came into play for you to realize that?"

"What? No!" She took it all back. He wasn't a good actor after all. "I just—I know you had complicated feelings about your dad, and I didn't want you to have them alone."

There they were again. *Feelings.* Invoked to lure her in again. He'd done it so many times over the course of their relationship, always when she came to a precipice and considered ending it.

He'd lure her back in with words like *love* and *trust* and *happiness.*

And she'd stayed. Because those things tempted her more than her father's money ever could. And the truth of that was tied up with her pride and her constant rebellion. If only Franklin could have seen her then—so happy with Griffin. Happily ever after.

Except, she hadn't been happy with him.

"My relationship with my father is no longer your business."

"I didn't ghost you," he said with a complete lack of embarrassment. Not even a sliver of chagrin.

"You're right," she said. "You left a note. *It doesn't feel right,*" she repeated, disgusted all over again.

"Alice," he said, her name sounding like *calm down*. "You don't understand."

"You're right. I don't. I would *never* have done that. Five years we were together. And you packed up your shit and disappeared." She sucked in a breath, tears hot in her throat, behind her eyes. Not *sadness*. *Embarrassment*.

She knew the difference now.

"It's time for you to do it again, Griffin."

"Wait," he said, quickly, laughing, like she'd missed the joke. Like the joke wasn't him. "Alice. Think about it. We can try it again, now. With your family's blessing. Your dad isn't around anymore. You're free of him, and all the strings that came with him."

Gabi was right. He was a bridge troll. "You mean the money is free of him. Of the strings. You mean, the inheritance is free of strings."

Truth flashed in his eyes, something that might have been guilt in another man. He hid it with another stupid laugh. "No. Of course I don't. I mean *we* are finally free."

Since her childhood, Alice had known that she was cloaked in her family's money—her father's money. She'd spent a lifetime keeping her distance from other people, holding herself back from making friends, from dating, from living, out of the fear her father had instilled in her—that people would always choose the money over her. That she was nothing on her own. Nothing but her last name. Her father's net worth.

She'd spent a lifetime trying to be more than her name and this place and these people and just when she'd convinced herself that she had it, with this man and his handsome face and his instinct for gaslighting, he'd left.

And now he was back, sensing new opportunity. Thinking he could lure her in again. Thinking he finally, *finally* had Alice Storm Inc. on the hook.

She thought of Gabi and Roxanne. Of Emily and Claudia. Of Greta and Tony. Of how any one of them would change everything, do anything, be anyone for the other. And then she looked to Griffin, who'd never even tried.

She shook her head. "No. We're done."

"Alice." He reached for her as she spun away, his grip tight on her arm, fingers biting into her flesh until they hurt, bruising as harshly as his tone when he drew close and hissed, "You're making a big mistake."

She looked back at him, pulling against his touch, but he didn't let go, something she didn't like in his eyes, like anger and desperation and punishment. Shock coursed through her and panic rose in her chest. Would he hurt her? He couldn't. Not here—not in front of the whole world. Not in front of—

And then Griffin was gone, his whisper replaced by a high-pitched shout as he stumbled backward, and Jack stepped between them, his hands fisting Griffin's lapels. "You don't touch her."

Another shout, sharply cut off, Jack's broad shoulders hiding what happened from her and everyone else surely gawking at this drama (Elisabeth was going to be *horrified*), but Alice didn't have to see it. She heard the *thud*, followed by the pounding of her own heart. "Jack—"

He didn't look back as he shook Griffin. "Do you understand me, now?"

"Jack," Alice said, reaching out to touch him, her hand landing high on his shoulder. "Stop. It's okay." He didn't respond, but he did release Griffin, sending him scrambling backward for balance. And then Tony was there, too, catching Griffin from behind, spinning him to face away from onlookers (bloody noses didn't make good mourning viewing).

Impossibly, Jack went broader, straighter. As though his body suddenly understood its task. To protect her. He pressed closer to her, making it impossible for her to see Griffin. She liked that, for a moment (she wasn't proud of it).

"Fuck you, Dean, I wasn't going to hurt her." Griffin spoke as Alice was about to leap into the fray, so focused on defusing the situation that she almost didn't hear the name.

Dean. Jack Dean.

"Wait. What?" Griffin knew Jack's name. Which should have been impossible, because *Alice* hadn't even known Jack's name until five days ago. She looked at the two men as they faced off against each other. The storm clouds returned to Jack's face. "You know each other."

They both went still, seeming to understand the weight of the words. Griffin's gaze went from defensive to shifty.

Jack didn't have the same kind of difficulty. He said, "I wouldn't say that."

Alice narrowed her gaze at the cleverly phrased non-answer. "I would, though." She looked to Griffin, then, and it was obvious.

They'd been together for five years. She could tell when he was lying, unable to meet her eyes or Jack's—studiously avoiding Jack's, actually, as though he were prey hiding from a predator.

He struggled in Tony's firm grip. "Let go of me."

Tony's grunt of refusal was enough to end that.

"You know each other," she repeated, chest growing tight with something . . . fear? Doubt? Panic? When Griffin didn't respond, she looked to Jack, knowing he would tell her the truth.

He did, not even having the grace to look chagrined. "We've met."

Whatever that emotion had been, it evolved with instant clarity into anger. "When?"

A muscle ticked in Jack's jaw. Unfortunate, that, as it made her want to punch him in it. "When did you have cause to meet Griffin, Jack?"

His gray eyes flashed. "A few months ago."

Another secret, brought to light by the island.

Suddenly, everything was clear. Red-tinged with rage, but clear nonetheless. She rounded on Griffin. "How many months ago?"

His gaze flickered to Jack, nervous. Barely landing before he had no choice but to answer her. "In July."

"*July*," she said, panic rising alongside recognition. "July what?"

"Alice." Jack's soft tone made her want to scream.

"If you say *calm down* . . ." she said, letting an edge of laughter into her voice, not caring that it sounded slightly hysterical.

"You don't want to get excited," Jack replied. "Not here."

This fucking man.

"Funny, because you just barreled in here and almost started a fight."

"That was different."

"Why?"

"Because that was to keep you safe."

She couldn't help the laugh that bubbled out of her—unhinged, honestly—at the words. As though whatever was going on here weren't making her feel a dozen kinds of unsafe . . . far more at risk than she had felt with Griffin's hand on her arm. "Is that the kind of bullshit tone you take when you're playing fixer?" She rounded on him, her voice rising. "Is this your attempt to *fix* me?"

He didn't break. "It's my attempt to make sure you don't make a scene."

"Make a *scene*? Haven't you spent the last five days trying to remind me of who my father was? My father, the king of scene-making? Franklin Storm, who rappelled from a helicopter into the middle of Times Square to launch a new cellphone?"

Tony pulled Griffin back, giving Alice more space.

"If you think I'm afraid of a scene, you've forgotten the family into which I was born. One you have absolutely no hope of *fixing*."

Jack wasn't backing down. "Ask the question, then."

Gabi appeared at her elbow, Emily not far behind. "Hey . . . as much as I'd like to watch you fuck up some rich assholes, this seems like something that might be for . . . another time?"

"It's not," Alice replied, not looking away from Jack.

Her friend didn't hesitate. "Cool. Who are we starting with, then?"

"When in July did you meet Griffin, Jack?"

"Wait—what?" Gabi caught up. "Wait. These assholes know each other?"

"Yes. And I'm guessing that this asshole"—Alice pointed to Jack— "met that one"—she waved at Griffin—"a day or two before that asshole"—Griffin again—"moved out of our apartment with a note written on a food delivery receipt."

A beat of silence while the words landed.

And then, "Oh my god," Emily said, softly.

Gabi took a step back. "Then by all means, fuck up some rich assholes."

It wasn't worth it. Alice knew that. No matter how much she wanted to exact revenge. She looked to Tony. "Let him go."

Tony's gaze flickered to Jack, behind her. "No. Don't look at him, Tony. This isn't about him. This is about me. About my life. I get to decide."

Tony let Griffin go with a firm enough push that he had to catch his balance again.

Alice couldn't enjoy it. She was rounding on Jack. "Was that my dad's plan? To stop my wedding?"

"Alice . . ." he began, and she hated him for the lie he was thinking about telling.

"You owe me the truth."

"He just wanted to . . ." He paused. "It was a test."

And like that, she understood. She couldn't help the laugh. "Of course. It was the Fourth of July." She looked to Emily. "You didn't invite me to come. *He* invited me."

Emily had the grace to look chagrined. "Yes."

Coward.

Alice nodded. "And when I couldn't come, he sent the Storm Olympics to me. Or, rather, to Griffin." She looked to Griffin. "And you lost." She looked to Gabi. "What an asshole."

Her best friend didn't miss a beat. "Which one?"

"Honestly? All of them."

Gabi pointed to Griffin. "That one the most, though."

"Fuck you, Gabi."

Alice wasn't paying attention. She was too busy asking Jack, "So, what did you do, fixer? Threaten him?"

"No. I didn't." He crossed his arms over his chest in a sign she was beginning to recognize as frustration. He'd done it on the boat. At the beachhead. Yesterday in the foyer with Sam.

"You sure?"

"If I'd threatened him, Alice, he wouldn't have shown up today."

"So, what?" she asked. "What did you and my father do?" He didn't have to answer, though, because the answer was obvious. "Oh my god."

And he knew she knew. "Alice."

That was the confirmation. She looked to Griffin. "They paid you off."

He hesitated. "I didn't—"

"Don't. Don't lie to me," she said, softly, hating the intrusive thoughts that were consuming her. Hating the ache that punctuated them. "You said you didn't care about my family's money. I never should've believed you."

He shook his head, but it wasn't a denial.

"You need to leave. Now," Jack said, looking ready to do murder.

"Fuck you," she said. "I'm in charge. I want to know what he has to say for himself."

"He took the money," Jack said. "We offered it—"

"*You* offered it," she corrected him. "It was my father's money, but you wrote the check. Or was it a shoebox of cash? More? A duffel bag?"

"Hell yes I offered it," he said.

"So happy to be my dad's lackey."

"No," Jack said, angry and rough. "I was happy to get this jackass out of your life." He looked at Griffin, his disgust palpable. "Fuck this guy. I'd do it again and wouldn't hesitate. He doesn't deserve you. He doesn't deserve to breathe the same air as you."

Something rushed through her at the gruff words. She pushed it away. "Cute that you think you have a say."

"Goddammit," Jack said, looking to the sky with a frustration that might have looked dramatic on another man. "You cannot be serious. He walked away from you without a fight. Did I pay him off? Yes. But *he took it*. And you deserve someone who would have taken a swing at me for even suggesting he didn't love you with everything he had."

She'd rather see Griffin drop-kicked into the Bay than resurrect their relationship. But it didn't mean Jack had the right to insert himself into her business. "I should have had the chance to decide that."

"You *did* have a chance," he said, clipped. "Your father gave you five years to take it."

"And when he didn't like my decision, instead of talking to me, instead of asking me to come home, instead of reaching out in any way, he sent you in to fix me." *Like I was broken.* The thought rioted through her, leaving an ache deep within. "You've been pulling the strings of my life since before I even knew you existed. My father, I expected. But you—I didn't see you coming."

Jack didn't have anything to say.

She won, but it didn't feel like it. She looked to Tony. "Tony?"

"Yes?"

"I know you don't owe us anything . . ."

"No problem," he replied. "I was leaving anyway. This helps." Later, Alice would admire the emotion in the words. Grown-up. Nothing like the squeal Griffin let out when Tony grabbed the collar of his jacket and hauled him away.

She looked at Jack. "I don't suppose I can get you to go, too."

"Alice—"

"Don't." She looked to the sky, where the sun sank low in the west, setting the water aflame.

A trickle of mourners flowed toward the docks, ready to leave. It had happened—everyone had come and had their drinks and eaten their canapés and spoken in hushed tones about what a loss the world had suffered. And now they were going home to their lives, grateful that they weren't the ones left on the island, changed forever.

It had happened, and Alice had missed it. Hadn't she?

She was still changed forever, though.

She'd borne the brunt of her mother's disdain. Watched helplessly as Greta sacrificed her happiness for this place. This family. And then discovered that her father had been the instrument of her heartache. Her father, and Jack.

A single thought ran through her head. "God, I want off this island."

"We can do that," Gabi said, waving toward Roxanne. "You can come with us."

Emily was silent. Was that approval? Would she let Alice leave?

"Alice," Jack called after her.

She stopped. Turned. He was coming for her, closing the distance between them, and she took a step back, not wanting him close. Not trusting him close. Her sisters—by blood and friendship—flanked her.

He froze. And the movement (or lack of it) reminded her of the night on the train platform, when he'd seemed so decent. Not at all like the kind of man who would pay someone to break off their engagement.

"You deserve better," he said.

"You mean someone who doesn't lie to me?"

The muscle in his jaw flexed before he nodded, stiffly. "Bare minimum, yes."

She turned and made her way into the dwindling crowd, full of condolences and farewells and promises that no one would keep (were there any other kinds?). Emily peeled away, and Roxanne and Gabi pointed in the direction of the docks themselves.

"We've got you," Gabi said.

She shook her head. "If I go with you, they'll see. They'll stop me."

Greta, who'd lost everything, and made it clear she wouldn't stand for Alice leaving. Sam and Sila, who were willing to do anything to secure their bag. Elisabeth, who would have nothing left if she didn't have the money—at least, nothing she considered to be of value.

"Alice," Roxanne said, carefully. "If you stay, will you be safe?"

What did that word even mean in the context of this family?

"I take it back," Gabi said. "You don't have a responsibility to them. You don't need them. Not when you have us."

In the wide world, there was nothing like a best friend. Alice grabbed Gabi and hugged her, matching the fierce tightness of her friend's grip. "I'll be home soon."

"When?"

She pulled back. "Dinner Friday, right?"

A slight hesitation while Gabi searched her eyes. Then, "Okay."

Hand in hand, Roxanne and Gabi headed for the dock, and Alice turned to face the house, growing darker and more ominous in the setting sun, and considered what Gabi had said. *Responsibility.* She'd been raised on it—loyalty to family first, above all. No matter their selfishness, their chaos, their manipulation.

No matter the way they broke her down.

Responsibility was to others. Never to herself.

"Alice?" Mike Haskins spoke at her shoulder, startling her from her thoughts. At her little jump, he smiled. "Sorry. I didn't mean to surprise you. I just didn't want to leave without saying hello. And goodbye."

She shook her head and focused on him. Aged, like her dad. Laugh lines on his face, salt-and-pepper hair. He must be seventy, too, now. A trailblazing genius in his own right. And still, for all the millions he made without Franklin, he still made time for Alice. The kindness didn't escape her, and was a welcome distraction. "It's good to see you, Uncle Mike."

He spread his arms wide, and she stepped into his earnest embrace. Warm. Paternal. Smelling like cologne and sea air, just as her dad had. And it occurred to her that she hadn't had this kind of embrace in a long time. That she might never have it again.

She didn't want to let go.

"I'm so sorry, kiddo," he said quietly. Just for her. *Truth.*

Tears came instantly, shocking her. She stepped back, dashing them away with a self-deprecating laugh. "I'm sorry. It's just . . ."

He produced a folded handkerchief from his jacket pocket. An old-fashioned move that made Alice tear up all over again. "Overwhelming."

She gave him a little smile of gratitude. "Thanks."

"You know, I talked to your dad a few weeks ago?"

He sounded as surprised as Alice was. "Really?"

"Yeah, he called me out of the blue," Mike said, thoughtfully. "It had been years; I was so surprised, I picked up, even though I was in a meeting."

She smiled. "I bet he liked that."

"He did," Mike agreed.

"What did you talk about?"

He looked toward the sea for a moment, like he might say something, but shook his head, instead. "We talked about you kids." He paused. "He told me about your art. Tried to get me to commission a piece from you."

Her eyes went wide. "I didn't even know he knew about my painting."

"Oh yeah," Mike said. "Couldn't figure out how you got your talent.

Must have come from Lizzie, he said. I thought you might like to know that. He was always proud of you, kiddo. Even at the worst of it." He tilted his head. "He was pretty pissed at you then, too, but . . ."

She laughed softly, the joke washing over her.

"You did the right thing, Alice. You were always the one who did the right thing."

The words crashed through her, a gift and a punishment. She'd heard it a hundred times. A thousand. Read about it in magazines and newspapers and the comments sections, which she knew no one should ever read. Alice Storm, who'd stood up when wealthier, more powerful people hadn't. Who'd spoken truth to power. Who'd won.

But she'd never really believed it. Because the people who said that, that she'd done the right thing, hadn't known that standing up had been about her own truth, as well. Her father's power.

And it hadn't ever felt like the right thing, because the fallout had been so wrong.

But in that moment, hearing it from Mike, her father's friend, a man who knew him, who had stood in Franklin's shoes (albeit, without a child of his own, perhaps the Storm kids were good birth control), it didn't feel wrong. It felt like, maybe, Franklin had seen her. And maybe he'd felt something more for her than disappointment.

Even if it wasn't true, it was kind of Mike to say. "Thanks." She extended his handkerchief, and he accepted it, sliding it into his trouser pocket.

Moss gray. Glen check. She knew those pants. Knew that suit.

He'd been in the greenhouse with her mother. *Why?*

Well. She certainly couldn't ask.

This place. Full of ever more secrets.

Unaware of her thoughts, Mike filled the silence. "I was really happy to get to talk to him before—" He stopped. Cleared his throat. Shook his head. Changed the topic. "I hope we see each other more. Come see me. With Emily sometime, maybe. It goes without saying, if you need anything . . ."

She nodded. "I will."

He turned away, toward the north end of the island, to the helipad, and she watched him go, a little slower than she remembered. A little slimmer. Had her father been that way? She'd never know.

Add that to all the rest she wouldn't know. All the rest she would have to cobble together from people like Mike, who were willing to speak to her. To tell her their truths—things she could choose to believe.

You did the right thing.

The right thing. It seemed impossible, considering all the wrong things that had happened this week. All the backbiting and infighting and arguing and jockeying for position. All the ways they'd hurt each other. *Greta.* And others. *Tony.*

And for what?

She inhaled, sharply, returning her attention to Mike, farther away. Almost to the house.

"Mike!" she called, and he turned around to face her as she jogged toward him. "Actually, there is something you can do."

Twenty minutes later, Alice was descending the main stairs of the manor, suitcase in hand, satchel slung over her shoulder, full of clothes and toiletries haphazardly shoved inside.

Once on the main floor, she turned away from the front door of the house, heading down the dark hallway toward the kitchen—the exit closest to the helipad, where Mike and Twyla Haskins were waiting for her.

She moved quickly, feeling like a criminal, skulking through the halls, eager to leave without being caught. And she almost did it.

"Aunt Alice?" Saoirse met her as she entered the foyer, a few feet from the kitchen.

Alice froze. "Hey you."

"Are you leaving?"

For a moment, she considered lying. But, god, this family lied enough, to themselves and each other. With a deep breath, she said, "Yes."

"But if you leave—doesn't that—" She paused. "If you leave, what will happen to us?"

"You're going to be okay," Alice said, setting her bags down. She repeated herself. "Saoirse, you're going to be okay. You're going to have a life with a family who loves you, and parents who choose your happiness and a brother who isn't constantly looking for ways to sabotage you."

"Is this because Dad locked you in the pantry?" It was such a strange question—asked from such a distance, a lifetime ago, and Alice's confusion made her silent for a moment. Before she could answer, Saoirse jumped to add, "Because it wasn't him. It was me."

It took Alice a moment to understand. "What? Why?"

"Oliver and I thought you were going to leave. We heard you say it, and everyone was freaking out. Like we were going to be poor."

Alice resisted the roll of her eyes at the words. She could hear Sila, furious with panic, screaming that at Sam, like it was his fault, not thinking for a moment that her children were there, listening. That they'd panic, too, and not with anger, but with fear.

And then Saoirse confirmed it. "Aunt Alice—Mom is going to divorce Dad if we don't have any money."

Alice couldn't hide her shock at the words, so matter-of-fact. "What? Honey—" she started. Not knowing how to finish a denial of something that seemed so true.

She didn't have to. "Oliver took your clothes, and it was so stupid— like not having clothes was going to keep you here. It was so childish." Alice hid her smile at the assessment. "But I guess thinking that I could lock you in the pantry and that would make you stay was, too."

"Not that childish," Alice said. "After all, I thought it was your dad."

"What about me?" Sam entered the conversation from a distance as he came through the front door of the house. His gaze fell to Saoirse. "Your mom is looking for you and your brother."

Saoirse looked to Alice, who read her nervousness—the universal fear that a grown-up would tell your parents about your mistake. Alice shook her head. *Don't worry about it.*

"Go," Sam said. "I have to talk to your aunt."

Saoirse pressed her lips together, like she had more to say. And then she nodded once, and said, softly, "Okay."

She left the room, feet dragging.

"Where are you going?" Sam asked Alice, nodding at the bag on her shoulder.

She straightened her spine, knowing what she was in for. "I'm leaving."

He shook his head. "No, you're not."

"Yes. Sam, I know you think you need the inheritance. But you don't."

"I do, though. *You* don't, but I do need it." He tilted his head in the direction of Saoirse's departure. "Do you know what it costs to keep them happy?"

"They'd be happy if you loved them."

"Please." He scoffed. "You were raised smarter. You can't leave. So Dad sent Jack to buy off your idiot fiancé. So you had a bad week. So you don't like us. Alice—" He paused. "You're not leaving."

"I don't want to be manipulated anymore." Surely he could understand that. "I don't want Dad running this show anymore. He's controlled us for our whole lives. He's controlled *my* whole life. And I'm done."

"So get the money and get gone; what's a day or two?"

How many times had she thought that herself? A week was nothing in the grand scheme of things. In another family. In another circumstance. "What if these are the days that matter?" she asked herself, as much as Sam. "What if letting him control us now, like he did before, is the thing that makes it impossible to chart the After?"

"Then we have all the money we need to pay for therapy." It was supposed to be funny, but it wasn't.

"You'll already have the money you need for therapy, Sam. You're going to be CEO."

"Actually, I'm not." She went still as he slashed a hand through the air. "I'm not going to be anything. Because he fired me. I'm fucking *fired*."

"What? When?"

"The Fourth of July. Would you believe it? Summoned us all here for the usual nightmarish games, and on the last night called me into his office and *fired* me. I worked for that asshole for twenty years, and there it was, his dying wish."

Oh, shit.

She couldn't believe it. No. Actually, she really, really could. "Jesus, Sam." A beat while they stared each other down. "This game isn't good for us."

"And still, it is the game."

"What if it isn't? What if he died, and we're supposed to choose a new path?" She sighed. "God, I'm so sick of the secrets, the lies, the constant hope, the ever-present disappointment. I just want to be done with it. With the doubt. With the past."

While her thoughts rioted through her, Sam stayed silent, and she couldn't read him. Defying instinct, she spoke, pleading with him. "Sam, please. Try to understand. I don't want the burden of it. It feels wrong. You have to feel that, too, right? How wrong it feels?"

Silence stretched between them, long enough that Alice gave up, grabbing the handle of her suitcase and heading past him, making for the kitchen, heart pounding.

He might never speak to her again, she thought, but he hadn't spoken to her in five years, so it wouldn't be much of a change.

He didn't have a choice. But she did.

She was barely past him when he caught her from behind, one hand sliding over her mouth to muffle her outrage as he dragged her down the hallway, deep into the house.

17

WHEN FRANKLIN STORM BUILT his office off the southeast-
ern corner of Storm Manor, the architectural world lost
its collective mind. It was a chrome and glass addition to
the gothic Gilded Age home, all windows and modern angles, but with
several nods to history, including a rare-book vault built in the style of
the one at the Morgan Library, beautifully lit and full of manuscripts
and first editions, not because Alice's father liked books, but because
her father liked walking in the footsteps of magnates of yore.

As children, the Storm siblings loved playing inside the vault, risking
their father's wrath—sticky fingers and rough play were poor companions for manuscripts and ancient leather bindings.

But now, Alice had trouble remembering a time when she loved
the inside of this little space—as Sam shoved her and closed her in, ignoring her shout and the way she banged on the door.

She shouldn't have been surprised that her brother's plan was as
well formed as his daughter's had been. As though he wasn't eventually going to have to let her out, and she wasn't going to immediately

leave this island, without a thought for the inheritance he cared so much about.

Evidently, Sam had also not considered the likelihood that when she got out of there, she was going to murder him, and then there wouldn't be any more Sam to inherit.

"You are the *worst!*" she finished, the words punctuated by the low muffled drone of a helicopter above. Her ride.

She spun away from the door to take in the tiny room, shelves full of leather-bound books, a small hexagonal mahogany table, adorned with nothing but a Tiffany reading lamp.

And there, on its side, on the floor of the vault, a painting.

She stilled.

In Progress.

The painting was an enormous watercolor landscape in four panels, fused together, each a work in unfinished progress, intended to be a commentary on the artist, on the viewer, and on the moments and places that made people who they were.

The panels were left in varying states of underpainting and over-painting, each more lush than the one before. Grays and browns gave way to yellows and greens and eventually blues and bright whites, crisp, clear colors, in imperfect lines, as though the artist couldn't get them right.

As though it was rendered from memory and will, just as humans were.

And it had been rendered from memory; Alice had painted it, cob-bling together remnants of the island.

She'd been so incredibly proud of it—her first large-scale work, the centerpiece of her first solo gallery show. She could still feel the sense of wild achievement that coursed through her as she witnessed it there, hanging like something of value, not because she was Alice Storm, of the Storm Inside™ Storms, but because she was Alice, a painter on her own merit.

And then, the intense joy that had come when it had sold for more than she'd ever imagined, to a mysterious buyer. *An anonymous patron,* her agent had said. *Only a checkbook and compliments.*

Alice had been so thrilled—knowing that she'd done this alone. Without her father.

It turned out she hadn't done it alone. Her father had done it for her, another in a long line of controlling events designed to keep her from making her own decisions and keep her under his thumb . . . or worse, to punish her for going against his wishes.

And it was punishment. How could it be anything but? Franklin had known the sale of that painting would have marked a powerful moment in her life—one that she would have held close. He would have known that she'd wonder where it hung and who admired it, and the idea that he'd bought it with money he might have found in the cushions of the old couch in his office, and left it here on the floor . . .

The discovery diluted her fury with Sam (though the full force of that emotion wouldn't be gone for long).

Now, she was pissed at her dad.

Again.

And then there was Jack.

Jack, who had probably bought it in another moment of devotion to her father, just as he'd bought Griffin. Without hesitation, without regret.

She closed her eyes, embarrassment and shame coursing through her. He'd paid Griffin to leave her. He'd borne witness to the utter lack of loyalty she inspired in a man who'd sworn he wanted to spend his life with her.

It was horrifying. But she refused to feel bad about it. Everyone else should feel bad about it. Alice, though, she should be furious.

Which she was, for an hour or so, as helicopters flew overhead, until the vault locks turned with several loud thuds and Alice came to her feet ready to fight. She was expecting the battle to be with Sam, who'd remembered to free her now that everyone had left with their various modes of transportation (as though she wasn't prepared to swim if she had to).

The heavy door scraped open.

It was Jack. He wasn't wearing his jacket or his tie anymore. The top buttons of his shirt were undone, and the cuffs were rolled up in that effortless way men had—like they didn't know how it triggered women's reptilian brains.

Alice's reptilian brain was busy being angry, thankfully, preventing her from noticing his tanned forearms or the tattoos inked across them. She certainly didn't remember the feel of the left one with the compass, strong and sturdy as it held her to the cliff wall the other day.

"Are you okay?" The question came quick and gruff, like if he weren't so unreasonably muscled, he might have been out of breath.

She ignored the curl of something she would not name and reminded herself that she was angry. "Of course it's you."

"What does that mean?"

"Only that it's always you, right there, pretending you're just . . . wandering by."

"You mean, always rescuing you?"

"I don't need your help, Prince Charming," she argued. "Go play savior somewhere else."

That muscle in his jaw that she shouldn't even notice clenched. "Do you want me to close this again so you can bide your time waiting for the oxygen to run out, or . . ."

Her brows rose at the edge in his tone, the first time she'd heard him anything but calm in this uneasy house. Something flashed through her. Relief, maybe? Gratitude that he, too, could come unraveled. Desire for it. Willingness to poke the bear.

"The oxygen isn't going to run out. It's temperature-controlled, not vacuum-sealed. Sam isn't a murderer; he's just an asshole." She pushed past him, painting in hand, and propped it against her father's desk.

He waved toward the vault. "Hey, if you'd rather stay in that gilded cage . . ."

"It's funny that you think the vault is the cage," she replied. "You'd better watch out, Jack, because you're trapped in here with the rest of us, and you're beginning to act like it."

He didn't like that. "What's that supposed to mean?"

"Weren't you the impartial judge? A referee for this stupid game?" He stiffened, sensing the blow before she delivered it. "How was that going to last when you slept with me before it even started? When you accepted Tony's resignation before Greta could make her own decision?"

"I tried to tell you—"

"Yeah, you worked really hard to tell me," she said. "I must have missed the part where you told me you were the reason Griffin took off."

He ignored the words. "Tony's resignation didn't impact Greta's decision. If anything, it would have made it easier for her to refuse to do your father's bidding."

"So what, you're the good guy, now?"

"I never said I was a good guy."

"Good, because you're not. And the wild thing is—I *knew* it. You've been orchestrating this game from the beginning, manipulating us all on behalf of my father, for whom manipulation was like breathing. And still, I thought—"

She cut herself off, and he leaped in. "I wish you would stop doing that."

"What?"

"Stop yourself from saying what it is you really want to say. Stop yourself from being honest." Her words remained stuck in her throat, angry and desperate to get out, and Jack pressed on, his own frustration clear. "Say it, Alice. What did you think?"

"I thought—" She stopped again, and this time he let the words hang there, waiting. Listening. And it was too tempting. "I thought there was something between us. Something like the truth."

He took a step toward where she stood at the corner of her father's enormous desk, empty of everything but a hunk of glass, some humanitarian award bestowed for millions in tax write-offs.

"But this has never been honest. Not from the moment you got on the train and asked if the seat next to me was taken."

Except he hadn't asked that. He'd asked something worse. Something more tempting.

Is someone with you?

The first words he'd ever spoken to her. As though if the answer were no, he would make it right. *Liar.*

No one had been with her. And no one was now, either.

"You've been playing me from the start. From before the start, when you paid Griffin to leave me." She stopped, giving him time to speak. When he didn't, she said, "This is the part where you apologize."

He took another step toward her, stopping just far enough away that she didn't feel confined, but close enough that if she reached for him, she could touch him.

She searched for something that would stop her from doing just that. Found it. "How much was I worth?" He shook his head, looking away, avoiding her, and that did the trick, restoring her anger. "Tell me," she said, raising her voice, willing him to give her the fight. "How much to give me up? What was the market value of my future happiness?"

The question hung between them for a bit, long enough that she thought he might not answer. And then he looked back at her, and she recognized the anger in his own gaze. "You want to know?"

"I do."

"Not enough." The words were clipped and tight, soft where hers had gone loud. "I met him certain that it was a waste of time. No way would someone take your dad's money—when *you'd* chosen them. The girl who took on Storm and won? I didn't know you, but I knew you were talented and decent and brave as fuck. And I knew that anyone you loved would tell Franklin to get bent rather than leave you. It was unfathomable to me that Griffin would even hear me out."

"Must have been a lot of money."

"There's no amount of money worth it."

The pronouncement took the wind out of sails, a verbal heave to.

"Tell me something," he said.

It felt like a trap. "Why would I tell you anything?"

He shrugged. "Might be fun to speak the truth."

"I've never found that to be the case," she retorted, and they both would have laughed if it didn't feel so serious.

"Did you love him?"

The question surprised her. *Love.* What a strange word. Sure, people used it all the time—*I love that restaurant, I love those earrings, I love that movie, that song. I love my kid, my dog, my sister, my mom* (now it was getting into dangerous territory). But love wasn't the kind of thing that she'd grown up with. Elisabeth never referenced it; admitting to love would've felt as exposing to Alice's mother as attending a New York Public Library gala in the nude.

And her father . . . well, he'd never had time to tell them anything but what he expected them to do.

Alice wasn't a monster. She had experienced love. She loved Gabi unconditionally. Roxanne. Her students. Her art. And she wouldn't be here on this island if she didn't love her family in all the weird ways they allowed themselves to be loved.

But Griffin? He'd been charming and free and so different from anything that had been even possible for her when she'd imagined her future. A person who embraced life and emotion and never tried to tell her what to do, so different from everything she'd grown up with, she'd told herself it had to be love.

But she'd forgotten the most important part.

"I loved what he represented," she said, finally. Jack's attention didn't waver, but he didn't speak, so she added, "He was not my dad. He was the antithesis of my dad. He made me feel"—she paused—"ordinary."

"Right there—that's why I should have destroyed him when I had the chance." Her eyes were wide on his as he spoke, his anger palpable. "There are many things that keep me up at night—any number of which I will spend a lifetime apologizing for; but that is not one of them. I will never apologize for paying that asshole to get out of your life. The only thing I regret about it is that I didn't end him as well as your engagement. Don't you ever let yourself feel *ordinary* again."

Oh. "You didn't even know me."

"You're right. That was before." Anger had slid into fury. "Now, I do know you. And if I can muster up another emotion for that asshole, it would be gratitude, because if he'd been a better man, we wouldn't be here now."

She was having trouble breathing. "I don't want you to pity me."

He closed the distance between them, so she could feel the heat of him. "Alice, if I pitied you, I would be able to keep my hands off of you."

The words came out desperate, like he ached. Like she ached. One of his hands came to her waist, fisting her dress, and she came off the edge of the desk willingly, toward his heat and the scent of him—like a shipwreck. His voice went lower, darker. "Tell me some more of that truth you're trying out."

She looked at him for a long moment, those eyes that seemed to see everything, that marble face that made him look like a superhero—stern jaw, straight nose, and those cheekbones that were stupidly perfect. He was all wrong. Too handsome, too strong, too sharp, saw too much.

Too dangerous. And yet.

"I'm not okay," she said, softly, shocking them both with her honest confession. But she'd liked telling him the truth. Liked that he held it. Believed it. Accepted it.

Even now. "I know."

"I hate all of this."

"I know," he said again, softer, pulling her a bit closer.

It felt good, being known, and Alice went willingly, looking down and taking his hand in hers, running her fingers over the compass on his bare arm. She spoke to the ink as she traced it. "I hate that it feels like you have to be here. That you're only here to fix things. That you're going to realize that I can't be fixed."

"You don't need fixing."

It was a lie, but she liked it too much to call him on it. Her fingers stroked over the inside of his wrist, his fingers curling with the pleasure of the touch, and she turned his hand over in hers.

She looked up at him. "How did you find me?"

"Saoirse came to get me. You know, your niece might be the most honorable of the whole family."

The kids were all right. "Sam'll make sure that doesn't last," Alice joked, softly. "He would have let me out, eventually."

"Sure. Wednesday afternoon." Alice shouldn't have found the reference to the family's ticking clock funny, but she couldn't help it. He understood the game, and it felt like he was on her side. She tilted her face up to his.

That big hand landed at her hip again. Flexed. "I should go."

"What if I told you I still needed a hero?"

He shook his head. "I'd tell you that I'm not a hero. Not by any metric."

"Villain, then."

"Maybe." And then he kissed her, and it didn't matter which he was, because all she wanted was this moment, all heat and strength and—how was it possible this stern man was such a tremendous kisser?

He set her on the edge of the desk, and she pulled away from the caress for a moment. "I'm still mad at you."

"I know." He knew it was a lie, and they were kissing again, her hands in his hair, his on her dress, pulling it up past her ass.

"I haven't decided if I'll forgive you," she said, gasping as one hand slid into the back of her underwear—was she wearing cute underwear? That hand grabbed her flesh and pulled her to the edge of the desk, and she realized she didn't care.

"Understood." They kissed again, his tongue stroking deep as his free hand slid down the outside of her thigh. "Is there anything I can do to help that decision along?"

She spread her thighs and he moved between them, pressing against her, strong and hard and—"That might help," she said.

The sound he made was close to a growl.

He hooked her leg around his waist and returned his hand to her face, stroking his thumb over her cheek and running his fingers into her hair, tangled from being in the sea air all day. He swallowed her gasp with another long kiss—no one had ever kissed her like this. Had anyone ever kissed anyone like this?

"You should take your time deciding." He slid a kiss across her cheekbone to her ear. "I'll tell you a story while you do."

"Okay," she whispered, her fingers tangled in his shirt, chasing his buttons.

"On the beach," he said. "When I kissed you?"

The words were hot at her ear, sending a shiver of anticipation through her. "Yes?"

"Those jean shorts." The hand at her ass moved, tracing up, under her dress, stroking the skin there. Singeing it. "As though it wasn't bad enough that I had to watch you on the boat wearing them—they were too fucking short for public view, Alice."

"It's not my fault you can't control yourself." The words were reed thin, their volume caught with her breath.

"I can, though," he rumbled. "I'm paid to control myself. I controlled myself so well—when all I wanted was to take those shorts off. And that shirt. White and wet and fucking transparent."

"You seem very angry at my clothes."

"I am," he said, pulling up the hem of her dress, drawing her tighter to him. "I'm fucking furious at them for being on."

He sounded it, too. Like he wanted to tear them off her. Like he would, if he weren't holding himself on such a tight leash.

She didn't want him on the leash, though. She didn't want him controlled. She wanted him out of control.

"So take them off."

He leaned down and kissed her neck, hot and lush. "Stay right here."

He went to the door and flipped the lock before activating the electric privacy shades on the windows. She watched him move around the room with the same intensity he did everything, and everything in her coiled, as she considered what else he might use that focus on. Thinking about where he might put his hands, his lips. Other things.

When he returned to her, she said, "Thank you."

"For what?"

"For keeping me safe."

He looked like he might say something in the moment but changed his mind, instead kissing her again, slow and delicious, as though now that he'd ensured their privacy, he had all the time in the world.

And then she was naked, pulling him toward her, suddenly desperate for him.

"Wait. I want a look," he said.

Alice was on fire, aware of his gaze tracking over her skin, as she resisted the urge to cover herself—all the soft bits that should have been muscled, the puckered bits that should have been smooth.

When she couldn't take it anymore and moved to cover herself, he let out one of those low, disapproving growls and stopped her, touching her himself, instead, stroking up her legs, over her ankles, tracing the insides of her thighs, the soft swell of her belly, the undersides of her breasts.

He pressed a kiss to the base of her neck, inhaling deeply before he pulled back and said, "You smell like summer." His tongue licked over her pulse. "Like salt and surf and the sun. Like long days and lazy nights."

She sucked in a breath, covering the way her stomach flipped at the words with an attempt at humor. "That doesn't sound like something a villain says."

"It is when it's the truth," he replied. "Fuck, Alice—" He lifted a hand and shoved it through his hair, a small, secret smile ghosting over his face, like he'd just won a prize. "You're perfect."

His hands stroked over her skin again, the backs of his fingers finding the hard points of her nipples. When she thought she might scream out of frustration, he leaned down and took the tip of one breast into his mouth, sucking gently until she thought she might scream from pleasure.

Silence was not easy, however, and he lifted his head, beautiful eyes flashing, to say, "There is nothing I want more than to hear every noise you've got, but if you're going to let me do this to you—you're going to have to be quiet, sweetheart."

The rule shouldn't have been so sexy. She threw him a little, questioning smile and whispered, "What are you going to do to me?"

His brows shot together, focused, and she wondered if this was Jack Dean, legendary fixer. He leaned in and kissed her again, rough and deep.

She unbuttoned his shirt, stroking over the dusting of hair on his chest, the ink spread over it—she still hadn't had time to look at those tattoos—it had been too dark the night in the motel, too frenzied. But now, there was so much to look at. And she would. She was already making plans to look at it. But first, her touch slid down to his waistband, her fingers tucking inside—

"Not yet," he said. "I have other plans."

"Are you sure?" she asked. "My plans are pretty good."

"I think you'll agree mine are better," he said, and then he lowered himself to his knees between her thighs. He was right. His were better.

His hands were tracing over soft skin, pressing her wide. He was watching her open to him, and she'd never seen anything so sexy. Never seen anyone look so hungry.

Unable to stop herself, she flexed, tilting her hips, adjusting to the nearly unbearable ache within her, and his attention shot to her face as his hands stroked again, rougher now, back and forth, until they found the tight curls at her core, and he teased her, "You need something?"

She flexed again, and his touch lightened.

"Say it."

"You. I need you."

Another low rumble as he rewarded her with long strokes over her straining flesh, back and forth, too light. Too smooth.

"Are you going to stay quiet?"

Considering the things that question did to her, she wasn't sure she could, but she wasn't about to tell him that. "Yes," she said, grabbing his wrist and pressing him closer. "God, yes, Jack. Now stop teasing me."

This beautiful man did as he was told, tucking his broad shoulders between her thighs, holding her open as he set his mouth to her, his tongue tracing along her soft heat.

And Alice, no longer embarrassed, no longer anything but aching and needing and so fucking humid for him, gave herself over to this man who had been tempting her for days. And it was different this time, because she knew who he was, and she didn't care, as long as he didn't stop. Her fingers slid into his hair again, clenching, as she urged him on, rolling her hips against his sinful, skilled mouth, loving the feel of him there, as he closed his eyes and groaned his pleasure in a long, low sound that set her on fire.

"Yes," she cried out, and he lifted his mouth from her, making her want to scream.

"Shh," he whispered to her core, the sound making everything hotter, more achy. "What did I say?"

Later, she would be horrified at the way she whimpered, "I'll be quiet, I swear."

Actually, she wouldn't be horrified. She'd like the memory of what came next too much, when something wicked flashed in his eyes and he said, "Good girl," just before finding her clit and stroking over it with a rough urgency that made her whisper, "Holy shit," to the ceiling before she closed her eyes and let her head fall back and rocked against him, one of his arms coming to brace against her stomach, somehow increasing the pleasure, focusing it, like bright light.

"Jack," she whispered to the big room, her hands scrambling for purchase and strength on the heavy desk. "Please . . ."

Don't stop.

She didn't have to say it.

He wasn't going to.

Instead, he worked her over, fucking her with his hands and his tongue, in the slow rhythm she had never known she needed until she was coming against him, taking her pleasure, using him, controlling him, riding him, his name on her lips as she whispered her pleasure to the room and lost all her strength, falling back on the desk, undone.

And he stayed there as she came down from her pleasure, his fingers stilling, his tongue gentling, stroking in long, slow licks that sent delicious tremors of pleasure through her until she returned to the room, to the enormous windows overlooking the Bay, the walls full of priceless art, the heavy oak at her back.

She sat up as he released her and came to his feet, meeting her kiss as she reached for him, shoving his shirt over his shoulders and setting her hands to his waistband. "Is this okay?"

He gave a little laugh. "Yes. Fuck. Whatever you want."

She smiled up at him as her hand slid into his boxer briefs and he groaned his pleasure. "*Whatever* I want?"

"You don't scare me, Alice," he said, the words sounding more honest than sex had ever been for her as he pulled her to him and kissed her again. "I can take it."

The words lingered, wrapping themselves around her for a heartbeat, making her wish they were true—that this man might be the one who would give her what she wanted. That he might be the one she could trust. The one who would stand by her side. Fight for her.

Like everything he'd done for her so far was just a taste of what they might have in the future.

She liked that thought too much to let it stay, and she pushed it out of her mind with another kiss while she stroked his hard length. Breaking the caress, she whispered, "Tell me you have a condom, Boy Scout."

He gave a low laugh and reached for his wallet. "In fact—"

She made quick work of his clothes, pushing them past his lean hips to the floor as he sheathed his heavy cock and slid his hands over her again, stroking and kissing and worshipping her in all the spots he'd discovered before, until she was desperate for him again. And then he lifted her, positioning her on the edge of the desk once more, pressing into her, strange and familiar and *oh yes* and *right there* and *slower, longer,* giving her everything she asked for, letting her control the pace, the movement, the strokes, him, until their breathing had gone ragged and she was having trouble with words and she whispered, a broken "Please."

And then he was fucking her in heavy thrusts, hard and smooth and perfect, like they'd been doing it for a lifetime. Like they would do it for a lifetime. And she was biting back her pleasure because he was whispering how quiet she had to be, how anyone could hear them, how she was so good, and so perfect, and he loved the feel of her, and did she want to touch herself? Did she want to come?

She did, coming hard around him, and he was with her, falling over the edge, his own groan loud and welcome and absolutely audible outside the door, but Alice didn't care, because it was all so perfect, and all she could think was that she'd never felt such pleasure, and she'd never wanted anything so much, and then, as he pulled her in for a final kiss, wrapping her in his embrace as their breathing began to slow, a tempting thread of something like belonging coiled through her, and she realized this was what she'd remember about this day forever.

And what a gift that would be.

CHAPTER

18

"WHEN DID YOU GET THIS?"

They were on the couch on one side of the room, Alice leaning back against one tufted arm, her legs draped over Jack's lap as he sat back on the camel-colored leather. They were wrinkled but dressed again (they weren't raised by wolves), though Jack's shirt was mostly unbuttoned, and he'd pocketed her underwear (maybe a little raised by wolves).

One of his hands traveled the inside of her leg in a lazy, possessive slide, lingering just inside the hem of her dress, like he wasn't ready to let her go, which was fine, because she wasn't ready to go. Night had fallen, heavy and dark outside, and for those stolen moments, it seemed like they controlled time—if they didn't leave each other, they could keep everything at bay.

Jack's free arm was draped across Alice's lap, and she tracked the patterns of his tattoo. "It was the first thing I noticed about you."

"Really?"

"Actually, no. The first thing I noticed was that you were stern."

His brows furrowed. "Were you unsettled?"

"I was too distracted to be unsettled. You just looked so serious. Like you took everything seriously."

"I was serious that day." He'd lost Franklin. And come for her. "I was taking you seriously."

She traced the circle of the compass face. "I know. I like that. That you take me seriously."

"I'm not always serious."

"Were you serious when you got this tattoo?"

"You really want the story."

She smiled. "It's not every day a girl who grew up sailing meets a guy with a sextant on his arm." He offered a tiny laugh, and she said, "It was between that and *You know what they say about guys with sextant tattoos.*"

Another laugh rolled out of him. "I don't, actually."

"Me, neither. Which is why I want the story."

"When did you notice it?" He leaned back against the couch and looked down at her, his dark lashes at half-mast—long and lush enough that she'd be jealous of them if she weren't so happy to look at them.

"You rolled up your sleeves on the train platform, while we were waiting for our cars." She shrugged. "I like tattoos."

"You don't have one," he said, his confident tone a reminder that he could speak on the issue with authority.

She shook her head. "I like them in the way an artist appreciates art—precision detail work on an uneven surface. I can acknowledge the challenge in it and admire the skill it takes to make one as beautiful as this. But I've never had anything that I loved so much I wanted it tattooed on me."

"Well, that's your first mistake," he said, squeezing her thigh just enough to make her breath hitch. He pretended not to notice. "Not every tattoo is about love."

"No?"

"You're an artist," he said, tilting his head toward the painting she'd leaned against the desk. "Is all your art about love?"

"The stuff I finish is," she said. "But *your* mistake is believing that love is an inherently good thing all the time."

"That's pretty cynical."

"Maybe. I think it's pretty honest." Her attention flickered to the painting on the floor. "I wonder if it's been here the whole time—tucked away in the vault as a constant reminder that he remained pulling my strings."

They were silent for a moment, and then Jack said, "It hung in his office in New York."

"It did? Really?"

That tiny smile that she found absolutely too charming flashed. "When do you think you'll be able to take for granted that I'm not lying to you?"

It was hard to do. The idea that her father had liked her painting enough that he'd displayed it in a room where he met with—everyone—she looked to it, still perched by the desk. "Why is it here, then?"

"He brought it with him when he came at the start of the summer."

"But he didn't hang it here," she said.

"No."

"I hate that he bought it," she said, the words coming on a whisper, like a confession. "That night—I can remember every minute of it."

"Tell me," he said, like he really wanted to hear.

"It was just all so perfect—the golden light coming through the windows of my bedroom while I got ready, the taste of the champagne Gabi and Roxanne brought over to pregame. Griffin was—" He hadn't been there. He'd been busy with something more important, not realizing that, for Alice, that night had been the pinnacle of importance. She pushed the thought away. "I remember we even had luck with the subway . . . the trains came immediately. No waiting."

"No car?"

She slid him a look. "From Brooklyn on a Friday night at rush hour?"

"I don't live in Brooklyn." The realization that she didn't know where he lived was strange—it felt like it violated some kind of rule that should exist: If you've had sex in your childhood home with someone, you should know where they live. But also, it was impossible to imagine Jack at home. He didn't seem like the kind of person who had downtime. If he were a character in a novel, he'd be one of those eccentric mystery men who lived out of hotel rooms. Nothing but high-quality menswear and a toothbrush to survive.

Except—he didn't seem like that kind of person now. Not while they were cloaked in the quiet of the island, his sleeves rolled up like he might have a book to read. Or a woman to kiss.

A zing of pleasure shot through Alice at the thought. *Pick me.*

She held it together. "Where do you live?"

"Flatiron."

"Weird."

"I can walk to work."

She shook her head. "I say again, it's really no wonder my dad loved you."

He lifted her hand and pressed a kiss to one of her knuckles. "You were telling me about the night of the gallery show." Another kiss, and another, in a row, as she talked.

"It was incredible. One of those perfect fall days, sunny and sixty degrees in the day, with that bite in the air that makes you want to put on your long coat and pretend you're in a rom-com."

His brows went up.

"Haven't you ever wanted to pretend you're in a rom-com?" she teased.

"I can't say I have, no. My life doesn't exactly lend itself to the genre."

"Mine, either," she allowed, though the knuckle-kissing was nice. "As you might have noticed. Anyway, the show was packed and wine was flowing and there were all my paintings hanging in this gallery and no one knew I was *Alice Storm,* they just thought I was Alice Foss, the painter, and it felt . . ."

"Good?"

"Amazing. And that was before my agent told me someone had bought *In Progress.*" She waved a hand in the direction of the piece. "The largest of the paintings, and the one that had taken the most time—different from all the others. Bigger in scope and terrifying, because what if no one liked it? I'd asked my agent to deliberately overprice it, because then I could convince myself that if no one bought it, it wasn't a referendum on me. No one would possibly take a risk like that on a young, untried artist. An art teacher from Brooklyn."

She paused, thinking, then gave voice to her disappointment. "And it turned out no one did. He couldn't even give me that. One night of success, all to myself. He had to be involved. Had to control it." She looked to Jack.

"I know."

"You're not going to try to convince me that I'm wrong? That he bought it because he loved it?"

"No. But I don't think he bought it because he didn't love you."

"Maybe," she said, looking to the painting. "I guess we'll never know."

To his credit, Jack looked like he wanted to say about a dozen things she might not like. Instead, he asked, "Have you painted all your life?"

She relaxed—this was a question she'd answered a thousand times. No loopholes, no tricks. "When I was thirteen, I did the after-school program at MoMA. It was a few blocks from my school, and it gave me something to do that didn't involve following my family around. That, and it set me apart in some way. It was something that could be mine."

"Isn't there a Franklin and Elisabeth Storm wing at the Met?"

"Sure," she said. "But Franklin and Elisabeth like tax write-offs and charity balls, not art."

"There's a Picasso on the wall of this very room," he said.

They both looked at it, and Alice scrunched her nose. "I hate that painting so much. It was the first one my dad ever bought at auction. Did you know that? So he could show it off to his friends." She scoffed. "*Picasso.*"

"You don't like any Picasso?"

"Cultural appropriation, hypermasculinity, misogyny . . . what's not to like?" He didn't argue with her, which was nice in its own right. "My father *loved* that I hated it. He loved to mock me with it in public. *This is my daughter, Alice. She's an artist, but do yourself a favor and don't ask her about Picasso.*"

Jack gave a little laugh. "For what it's worth, he never mentioned your loathing of Picasso to me."

"Why would you like Picasso when Jacqueline Marval is right there? Goncharova? Kahlo? Gentileschi?"

"Is this my chance to impress you with my knowledge of *Judith Slaying Holofernes*?"

She slid him a look. "My personal history suggests I shouldn't be impressed, but I confess, I am."

"Don't be," he said. "I had to look it up."

Somehow, that made it better, that he'd listened to her story and been interested enough to learn more. For her. "I like a man with a working knowledge of the Internet."

They shared a little private smile, one that set off a tiny explosion of pleasure deep inside her. Alice looked to the painting on the wall and made her decision, doing her best to ignore the way his touch lingered as she rose from his lap, following her until she was too far away. She had something to do.

"If he bought it, it can hang on the damn wall as intended." Lifting her painting, she walked it to the fireplace, leaning it against the edge of the hearth before reaching for the Picasso already there.

"Wait—" Jack said, the words coming urgently, like he hadn't expected this. To be fair, very few people would have expected her to yank a master down. "Let me—"

"No," she said. "I got it."

And with that, she heaved the painting off the wall and lowered it to the ground (he did help, it was a Picasso after all) before lifting her own painting and hanging it in the empty space. It was done in such a seamless, fluid way, without even an ounce of concern that she might not find the hooks—as though the hooks wouldn't dare defy a woman so hot about patriarchy, artistic or literal.

And they didn't.

She stepped back and looked at her handiwork, hands on her hips, and Jack joined her. With a renewed sense of confidence, she spoke to her painting. "Were you there?" A beat. "At the gallery? Did you come with my father's checkbook?"

"No." The answer was quick and honest, and Alice appreciated that he wasn't offended by the question (he'd bought her fiancé, after all), and still, she did not deny the relief that coursed through her at the categorical denial. And what came next. "But I wish I had been."

The words summoned the worst kind of memory—one that had never happened. Jack at that opening, not at a distance, not mysterious. But by her side. Celebrating her. Happy to be there. Her cheeks went hot at the thought, and she dipped her head. "That would have been nice."

He took her hand in response, leading her back to the couch, where they resumed their position.

Pressing against his thigh, she returned her attention to the ink on his arm. "While this was all a very good ploy to get me to stop asking about your tattoo, you forget that I was raised by the man who trained you in the art of deflection."

"Excuse me, but I was a pro at deflection long before your father hired me."

"A dream employee," she quipped, tapping the compass. "Did you put it here, on your forearm, so all the ladies would swoon when you rolled up your sleeves?"

"I've heard that about sleeve-rolling." His fingers slid a little higher than they had before, along the inside of her thigh. "It's not a new story. I got it after my father died."

It wasn't a surprise—he'd told her that afternoon. "You said he was sick."

"He was," he said.

"Your mother?"

He shook his head. "She left when I was young. I don't remember her."

The words singed, too casual. Like it was normal. Like it was okay. Alice stiffened, angry for this man and the boy he'd once been, but she knew better than to say so. Instead, she laced the fingers of one hand through his. "And you weren't there."

He nodded, the movement stiff, like he wasn't quite sure how his body worked. At least, the part of his body that wasn't touching her. That hand at her leg was still moving. A balm. Maybe for both of them.

They sat in silence for a bit, until she couldn't bear it anymore for him. "You don't have to—"

"I didn't want to be there," he said, quickly, like he wanted to get it out. "I hated it there."

Alice's thumb stroked back and forth over the beautiful mechanics on his arm. "Tell me about sailing," she said, thinking she was changing the subject. That she was giving him a port in whatever storm he was facing.

"I didn't grow up sailing. Not the way you did. My father was a fisherman. There isn't really time for sailing when you're up at three to clear as many crabs as you can before the fish market opens. He had a motorized fishing boat, a rotating crew of whichever misfits were still awake at the bar by the docks when he was heading out, and afternoons and evenings free and clear to spend at that bar himself."

She didn't stop touching him, didn't dare change anything for fear he'd stop talking.

And he didn't, as though floodgates had opened. "When I was a kid, I'd go on the boat with him."

"That's how you learned."

"He taught me everything he knew. *Someday this will all be yours,* he'd say. And I wanted it, then. I wanted the fishing boat and the boys on the pier and the harbormaster who gave him shit anytime he was the last one out. His kingdom."

Like the one they were all vying for.

"Dads are like that," she said, softly. "They're the first kings we know, for better or worse."

He returned their hands to her lap and said, "Mine was for worse. By the time I was in high school, he wasn't getting on the boat most days. There wasn't any money, and I was desperate to get out." He shrugged.

"You took over the business." Somehow, she knew the story.

He nodded. "If I was up early enough, I could be out and back before school started. A guy at the fish market would sell my crabs for a percentage."

She sat up, annoyed. "You were a kid."

"One who understood exactly how business works before I was in the eleventh grade. I worked my ass off to make sure I got into the University of Delaware, because it was close enough to home that I could run the boat every day until graduation." He paused. "My dad didn't come to it. He meant to—at least, he said he was going to—but he didn't. And so I never went back. To the boat, or to him." He paused. "Not even when his liver gave out. Not even at the end."

She tightened her grip on his. "You were angry. You can't blame yourself for that."

He was still for a long time, and then he took a deep breath and turned his arm face up, revealing the tattoo again. "By the time he died, the boat was long gone. And I didn't know what to do to grieve him— I wasn't really sure how to grieve him. How do you grieve someone who you don't really know? And who you don't really forgive?"

The question was familiar. "I don't know."

"I got a tattoo."

She traced the lines of it again. "Keeping you on course."

When she looked up, he was watching her. "I might want a new course."

A shiver went through Alice at the words, at the tease in them, the possibility. As though he might have found another direction to chart his course. And though she had not known Jack Dean for long, she had no doubt that he was the kind of man who got what he was aiming for. "What would Franklin Storm say?"

He stiffened at the words and she immediately regretted saying them, bringing her father into this moment. "He would be pretty pissed at me tonight."

"Yeah, but he's dead, so . . ." The words were so unexpectedly inappropriate, they both laughed louder than they should have, loud enough for it to turn into a secret, locked away in the walls of the house. When they stopped, Alice said, "God, I can't believe he *died*. He was so enormous. It's impossible to imagine what comes next, without him."

"He wasn't easy," he replied, reaching for her, his thumb stroking over her cheek. "Alice, don't forget, your dad brought me into the inner circle five years ago. I saw the best and worst of him. I know how he was. I know how furious he could get. How entrenched. How controlling."

"Then why—" Confusion flared and she cut off the rest of the question. *Then why are you doing this?*

He heard it anyway. "I don't know. Maybe it's a little loyalty to him for taking a chance on me when I wasn't sure I was worth it. Maybe it's a deep-seated obsession with doing my job well. At the beginning it was. But now"—he squeezed her knee—"maybe it's because I want to make sure it all works out."

She thought about that, about the fact that without him, the trust would still be in play, the game would still be afoot, and there would be a different referee—someone else to play judge and jury. If the Storm family knew how to do anything, it was manipulate a situation to get what they wanted. They'd been trained by the best.

Because of that training, Alice still struggled to believe Jack wasn't in it for some other, nefarious reason. Franklin would have been, wouldn't he? But the thing was . . . she didn't want to believe that Jack was their new puppet master, pulling all the same strings.

Before she could say so, he spoke, his gaze focusing on hers, the hand at her thigh going still. "Can I ask you something?"

"Of course," she said.

"This thing. Between us."

Her heart began to pound. "Is there a thing between us?"

"Yes, Alice," he said, his voice lower than it had been, "if the events of the last hour are anything to go by, I'd say there is."

Good. Her, too. "Go on."

"Is it because you think your father would have disapproved?"

The question should have made her angry—the thought that she might sleep with someone just to get back at her father, her mother, the whole family. But it wasn't out of the realm of possibility in a family like theirs, anything for attention from the patriarch. Even the negative kind.

She'd done it before, hadn't she? Hadn't she chosen Griffin, at least partly, to spite her father? "You are a very bad decision on paper, Jack

Dean. By all accounts, my father adored you, I watched you work a room today like I've only ever seen Franklin do, my family can't stand you, and I've seen you punch two people in less than a week."

"Justifiably."

"Fair," she allowed. "Maybe it's because of all that, and all the strange, unexplored shit that's coming up this week, that I can't stop thinking about you and—worse—how much I could like you."

He nodded. "Maybe."

"But also"—she shrugged one shoulder—"maybe it's simpler than all that. Maybe I just like you."

"Maybe I just like you, too," he said.

"Yeah, that's the part that worries me most," she replied, quietly. "Everything is out of control. I just want to feel in control again, and this isn't that."

"Sweetheart," he said, that word warming all the corners she'd planned to reserve. If he was playing her, he was great at it, and she was done for. "This can be whatever you want. No matter what happens. That's the truth."

God, what a gorgeous promise that was.

Alice couldn't help herself, leaning forward and kissing him, tasting him again, fresh, with all these new revelations between them. It was slow and soft and he lifted her onto his lap with ease, so he could kiss her back until they were both out of breath.

She broke the kiss and set her ear to his chest, listening to his heart beat heavy and fast. Jack leaned his head back on the couch and they stayed like that for long minutes before she finally said, softly, "You're much sweeter than you'd like people to know, Jack Dean. Not at all the villain you set out to be."

"I didn't set out to be a villain," he said.

"No?" She deepened her voice, mimicking him. "*I never said I was a good guy*."

That raised brow again. "Okay, first, you do a terrible me."

"I thought I did you kind of well, actually," she teased.

"Watch it or I'll make you do it again," he warned, toying with a lock of her hair.

Yes. Please. She put her head to his chest again, and they lingered there, in silence, before she said, "What's the worst thing you've done?"

"Ugh." He winced. "You don't have to ask it like I've been roughing people up and making unscrupulous deals all day."

"Is that not what you do?" she asked, all innocence.

"Mostly, I do things that would keep me out of prison."

"Ah, you see? *Mostly.*" She flipped his hand over and ran her thumb over his knuckles, raw again. For her, again. "There's this, too, though, isn't there?"

His hand fisted and flexed under her touch, and she committed the movement to memory as he raised it to run it through his hair, embarrassed. "Yeah, a little."

"You can take the boy off the docks, but you can't take the docks out of the man," she replied. "I shouldn't like it, but I do."

His gaze cut to hers, something flashing there. "Yeah?"

Alice nodded. "Did you threaten Griffin before he left?"

"Hell yes, I threatened Griffin." She couldn't help her laugh at that, like he was offended by the suggestion he might have sent weaselly Griffin on his way without striking fear in his heart. "He won't bother you again."

"Or he'll answer to you?" she joked.

"Damn right he will."

She laughed. "So, tell me, Jack Dean, fixer extraordinaire. What *is* the worst thing you've done?"

Jack's gaze flickered to the dark windows at the far side of the room, the night beyond so black that the glass had turned to mirrors, reflecting them there, on the couch, wrapped in each other like they'd sat just that way, together, a thousand times. "I don't think I've done it yet."

The grandfather clock in the foyer punctuated the statement, pulling them both away from wherever the conversation might have gone. Jack looked at his watch.

"What time is it?" Alice had lost track in the vault, and not thought about it once she'd gotten out. (There was plenty of time to get back to being pissed at Sam later.)

"Midnight."

Late enough that the whole family was asleep, likely. She looked to the door and said what she knew she should say. "I should go to bed."

"You're not leaving?" Jack asked.

The question surprised them both. Alice, because at some point she'd forgotten that she wanted to leave, and Jack because—well, she wasn't sure, but he looked like he wished he hadn't mentioned it.

"Are you . . . suggesting I leave?"

"No," he said, quickly. "But if you want to . . . I won't keep you here."

"Isn't it your job to keep me here?" she said, coming to her feet at the reminder that however real this night felt, the game was still afoot. Sam had locked her in a vault to keep her playing. "I should go."

"Alice," he said, coming to his feet, close enough that she was already regretting leaving their cozy embrace. He captured her face in his hand, stroking a thumb over her cheek. "Listen to me. If the only thing that's keeping you here is the inheritance—you should go. Let them figure it out."

"My father wouldn't like that."

"Well, maybe my loyalty to your father only goes so far."

Her brows rose. "How far, exactly?"

Jack was quiet for a moment, his eyes on hers, making promises as tempting as the heat of him wrapping around her, filling her with desire and memories. "How about this; sleep on it. And if, in the morning, you want to leave, I'll help you."

It was a generous proposition—one that would make him the villain of the play as much as it made her the villainess. But for a wild moment, she imagined it might not be so bad to be the bad guy . . . if you had a partner in crime. "Do you have any ideas about where I should sleep on it?"

That sexy smile again, slow and perfect, like he'd won the only game he cared about. "As you know, I'm always prepared."

She exhaled a little laugh, and took his hand, letting him lead her from the office through the main foyer, out of the house. In silence, they crossed the great lawn, now empty of mourner-revelers and family and chaos and drama, to the boathouse, dark and perfect, three tiny skiffs the only thing left of the day's events. Three skiffs that could be her exit strategy in the morning, once she was done with this man.

This man, who pulled her into his arms and carried her up to the lofted guest quarters above the boathouse before laying her down on the bed, drunk on the sound of the sea and the wind.

"Wait," she said, loving the way he stopped the moment she said it, like he'd do whatever she needed. Give her whatever she needed. The truth spread through her, bright and undeniable, and she spoke it, knowing it was the kind that would get her into trouble. "You feel like the kind of guy who might break my heart."

He pulled her to him and kissed her again, lush and lingering, like they had all the time in the world, and it felt like they did.

Neither of them noticed the storm rolling in.

CHAPTER

19

SAM WAS ON THE porch swing off the kitchen when Alice rounded the back side of the house, soaked to the bone from the heavy rain, hoping to sneak in unnoticed.

The storm had arrived in the middle of the night with lightning brighter than she'd ever seen and thunder rolling up through the Bay. When she'd jerked awake, Jack had been there to pull her into his arms and press a hot kiss to her neck. He then found his way to pressing hot kisses in a dozen other places while she discovered that thunderstorms kept secrets even better than old houses.

After they'd caught their breath, the two of them lay tangled in his sheets and tracked the storm as it moved closer and closer, like a friend, keeping everything at bay.

Making Alice wish it would stay forever.

When she'd woken again just before dawn, it seemed like it might do just that, the rain still coming in sheets, turning the light in the boat-house gray-green and rocking *The Lizzie* in her berth. In the distance the fog bell rang, muffled by the rain and the wind and the island.

Alice slid out of Jack's warm bed for the second time that week, not wanting to and still knowing she had to; if her family discovered where she'd spent the night, they'd have ammunition for years.

That, and she wanted to keep her memories of that night pristine—not just the sex (unmatched), but all the rest . . . the stories, the quiet laughter, the lingering touches (perfection). And the companionship, different from anything she'd experienced before, and enough to make Alice wonder if there was more than a night between them. More than a week.

Even as she knew it was impossible.

Nothing that began on this island, in this chaos, would survive away from it.

So, she left him warm and sleeping, his guard down, and decided to restore her own armor, vowing to protect herself as she prepared for whatever this new day—the first day of the rest of the Storm family lives—would bring.

The fact that it brought Sam first was inauspicious. Alice's stride barely broke when she noticed her brother, and she was pretty proud of the way she corrected, deciding immediately to ignore him.

Her eyes trained on the screen door, she didn't look over, not even when Sam called out, "I'm sorry."

"I don't care," she said, pausing on the porch to shake off the rain.

"I couldn't let you leave."

"Of course you couldn't. You're consumed by greed and you're an asshole," she said, finally looking at him. "But you look like hell, so that's something."

"I didn't sleep."

She narrowed her gaze. "No? Did you finally realized what a shitty brother you are?"

Sam winced. "I'll make you a deal—you don't bring that up, and I won't bring up the fact that you're doing the walk of shame from the boathouse at six A.M."

"I'm not doing the walk of shame," she said. She wasn't ashamed, so she won on a technicality.

She reached for the screen door, already charting her path to the foyer to grab her bags, and then upstairs to shower and change. At which point she'd have to think about what came next.

And where.

And with whom.

She'd barely pulled the door open when Sam said, "I couldn't let you leave because Sila left." Alice stopped and looked back to see her brother's defeated look. "With the kids. After the funeral."

She let the door slam into its seat even as she slid in next to him on the swing. "I saw you guys fighting yesterday but . . . I don't know . . . she's always pissed at you for something."

"Sometimes I'm pissed at her, you know," he defended.

"Yeah, but I always thought that was your deal—just . . . two terrible people being terrible to each other."

He flashed his middle finger, but his heart wasn't in it.

"Oh, Sam." She took him in, looking despondent and totally unlike her brother. "Do you—want a hug?"

He recoiled like she'd smacked him. "Absolutely not."

At least they could laugh about it all falling apart. "I'll tell you what, there is no scenario where we ever behave like a normal family."

"What the hell is a normal family?" he asked. "There aren't normal families. They don't exist. All unhappy families are unhappy in their own way."

"Tolstoy would be impressed."

"Why do I care what Tolstoy thinks?" Sam said, and when she opened her mouth to explain he raised a hand. "I'm kidding. I took comp lit in college."

"You did?"

"How else was I going to meet girls?" he asked, kicking the porch swing into movement. "Anyway. I think this *is* the normal stuff. A bunch of kids home for their father's funeral."

"Celebration," she said, and they both smiled. It made absolutely nothing better, but it felt nice. "I told you my story. Your turn . . . where've you been?"

She didn't want to share. "I went for a run."

"Training for a marathon during monsoon season?" He paused. "Without shoes? In the dress you wore to Dad's funeral?"

"I'm eccentric," she said.

"You're fucking the help, is what you are," he replied.

Jack wasn't the help, but Alice bit her tongue and stayed quiet, knowing that if she said anything, she'd give too much away. Pretending he hadn't said anything, she pulled her feet up onto the swing. "You want to tell me what happened?"

He sighed and leaned back on the swing, staring up at the porch ceiling. "Nothing happened. She doesn't like me. She's never liked me. And I think she'd be much happier if we weren't married."

Alice nodded. "And . . ."

"I think I would be, too."

They didn't speak for a bit, and then Alice said, "So, not like last time."

The family avoided discussion of *last time,* which Elisabeth only ever referred to in hushed whispers as *Sam's peccadillo*—like that was a word people used in the twenty-first century.

While their parents had never told them the whole story, as Alice understood it, Sam had given an interview to a fresh-faced journalist about his view of the Storm legacy, and it had gone on longer than the allotted hour. Weeks longer. The young woman made a mistake too many young women in the same situation had made before her (largely, believing the wrong man, one who accidently sexted the family text thread instead of her). Sila found out, packed her things, and moved out.

For his part, Sam had thought about letting her go, but Sila was nothing if not clever, and she knew exactly how she was going to make sure she and four-year-old Saoirse got what she felt they were owed. She'd made a call, Franklin and Elisabeth had lost their entire minds at the idea that their grandchild was living on Long Island, and Sila returned to the family fold within weeks. The whole thing had lasted just over five months, and once she was home, it took just under five months for them to conceive Oliver.

"No," Sam said, and it was impossible not to hear the bitterness in his tone. "I learned my lesson on that. She never trusted me again." He paused. "And never around you all. She thinks you all whisper behind her back."

"We don't," Alice said.

He threw her a disbelieving look.

"Okay, fair," she allowed. "But in my defense I haven't whispered behind her back in five years."

They both laughed, because what else could be done?

In the distance, the fog bell rang and Alice's eyes went wide. "You got the bell working! Sammy! Amazing!"

"Oh." He dipped his head, pretending not to be proud of himself. "You don't have to make it seem like I've never been able to complete a task. Do you remember when we did it for Dad? With Charlie and that old dude from Newport?"

She thought for a moment. "I don't think so?"

He smiled. "Maybe you were too young. Emily was barely out of diapers."

"It's hard to believe we were ever young like that here," Alice replied. They both looked out to the rain. "I wish I remembered."

Silence, the only sound the rush of water, and then Sam. "Maybe we come back sometime. Maybe I bring the kids. Maybe we make more memories."

It was a nice idea, but Alice couldn't shake the thought that it was the kind of thing another family would do. "Yeah. Maybe," she allowed. And then, "She really left you? Like . . . *left you*, left you?"

He nodded. "If she gets her cut, she won't fight me on seeing the kids."

"How tidy," she said.

"The lawyers will find a way to make it messy, I'm sure. Assuming you don't leave and screw us all." Alice turned her head and set her cheek to her knee, watching him as he explained the night before, again. "I needed you to stay. I'm sorry I locked you in the vault, but I need the money, Alice. So I'm kind of also not sorry."

Alice let the words settle, along with her anger. "God, Sam. Sometimes, you're really decent, and other times . . . you deserve it."

He exhaled. "I did it for a good reason."

"You mean, so Sila can continue to buy new clothes instead of laundering the ones she has? Don't fret, Sam—if I do leave, she can always get a job as the poster child for conspicuous consumption."

He ignored her. "I did it for the kids."

"Oh, please." Alice wasn't buying it.

Later she would feel bad about the reply, but in that moment, she was feeling pretty pissed off, and Sam knew it. "Dad cut me off, Alice."

"I know, you told me. You'll get another job."

"No. You don't understand. I mean, he cut me off. Stopped cutting the checks."

Her brow furrowed in confusion. "Cut you off how? Weren't you a senior VP? That's not exactly below the poverty line, Sam."

"Do you know how much it costs to have a family in New York City in our circles? The schools, the clubs, the designer clothes, the trips, the drivers, the apartment?" He shrugged one shoulder. "I didn't make enough, and Dad covered the extra. You know how it is."

"I don't, actually." It had been years since she'd accepted Franklin's help. "Believe it or not, I live in an apartment that I can mostly afford, thanks to my job, which I do daily. A job which is another reason why I have to leave this place, if you're keeping score. A bummer, I know. And to think I also make do without a personal driver."

She could hear his eyes rolling. "You say that like you think it makes you better than us. Being poor isn't a virtue, Alice, it's just less fun than being rich."

"Yep. Being rich has been a real picnic for all of us," she said, pointedly.

He ignored her. "He told me it was time to make my own way. Just like he had."

Alice grimaced at the last, knowing the way those words must have come out—no one loved to talk about how hard they worked more than a billionaire.

"And then he fired me." He fell quiet again, and then he said, "Sometimes I think Sila's smarter than all of us. I've got no job and no wife, and she gets thirty percent of my inheritance."

"If there is one."

"Exactly. But that's not what matters. What matters is that she gets the kids." At Alice's shock, he laughed, bleak and humorless. "I know. I was real fucking dumb."

"That's crazy. Why do you think she'd get the kids?"

"Because I signed them away at the start. It never occurred to me it would matter. She gets the apartment in New York and full custody. All of it." His throat worked as he considered his next words. "Turns out, I love my kids more than I expected to."

Alice winced at the words, like he'd just discovered the truth. "Sam." It might have been disapproving, or it might have been sympathetic. Sympathetically disapproving?

"God, Dad would be so pissed," he said. "Yet another reason to be disappointed in me."

"Well, Dad's dead," Alice replied. "What about *your* son? What about being proud of him?" She paused. "What about giving him something to be proud of?"

He was silent for a long moment, and then said, "What does that even look like?"

She shook her head. "I don't know; we didn't exactly have a great role model."

"You know," Sam began, leveling her with a serious look. "He wanted you to run Storm."

She nearly choked on her surprise. "No, he didn't."

"He did, though. Once, I overheard him and Mom talking about which of us would be the obvious one to work at the company. It wasn't going to be Greta—apparently that year she spent in Geneva was proof she didn't have the focus—and Emily was still a kid. But Dad made it clear that there was only one answer. And it was you."

"Well. I showed him," she joked. When Sam didn't laugh, she said, "Sam. You can't play this game."

He returned to the rain, easier for confessions. "I confronted him once—I thought he'd appreciate my courage. I told him that it should be me. That I was the right choice, because I did want it, and you didn't. And you know what he said?"

She didn't dare guess.

"He said, *Disappointment is what happens when you eavesdrop on private conversations.*"

Anger flared in her. Sam was far from perfect, but he didn't deserve this. "Dad was an asshole. I know we're not supposed to say stuff like that now, but it's true." She reached for her brother, setting her hand on his arm. "And still, we all rushed to do his bidding."

Thunder rumbled, loud and close, and they sat quietly through it before Sam replied, "We still do."

But what if they stopped?

Jack had been right the night before—her family would figure it out. Her mother remained in possession of multiple properties, accounts, and funds, and a life to return to full of fundraising lunches and questionable friendships.

Her siblings were Storms, yes, but maybe if she made the decision for them, taking the inheritance off the table, they would choose a life outside of this island. Maybe Greta could win Tony back. Maybe Sam could find a way to build something of his own. Emily was turning out to be the most balanced of them all—she and Claudia would land on their feet.

And Alice . . . maybe Alice could go back to the real world. Maybe Jack would go with her.

She didn't dare think too much about it, because after the previous night, and all the ways he'd made her laugh and sigh and hope, she realized he might be exactly what she wanted.

She liked him. Which was terrifying.

But even more terrifying was the prospect of him liking her, with her family and her father and the money in the way. The only way to guarantee that she had a shot at something real—that any of them had a shot at something real—was for them to get off Franklin's ride.

She looked to Sam. "What if we didn't do it?"

He looked at her as though she'd suggested dragging out the garden tools and doing a little light thunderstorm yard work. "What, not play the game?"

"Exactly.

"We don't have a choice."

"We do, though," she said. "We've always had a choice."

"To walk away from a few billion dollars?" Sam scoffed. "It would be colossally stupid to walk away from it."

Maybe.

He shook his head. "No. I need the money. My god, I locked you in Dad's vault."

"That was pretty bad," she said, teasing him. "I could have died."

"You could not have died. I'm an asshole, but I'm not a murderer."

"I said those exact words to—"

His brows rose when she cut herself off. "To . . . ?" She shook her head. "Okay, we'll play this game, I guess. I came to get you, but you were already gone. How'd you get out?"

Alice's biggest failing was this: hope that this time, her family would be different. She answered the question. "Jack."

He looked at her. "You're sleeping with him."

"I don't know what you're talking about."

"Mmm," he said, obviously not believing her. "Why didn't Griffin spend the night?"

A mighty crack of lightning struck the ocean in the distance. "No way did Emily not tell you everything last night. She's incapable of keeping secrets."

When Sam didn't reply for long minutes, she finally turned his way, ready for him to gloat or laugh or tell her all the ways he had hated Griffin. Instead, he said, "Are you okay?"

The question hung between them, honest and grown-up, and it occurred to Alice that if this was the beginning of something new, the start of After—after Franklin, after Griffin, after estrangement, after control and responsibility and everything else her family represented—someone had to start telling the truth. "I am. If a little embarrassed that Dad paid off my fiancé. That Griffin took it."

"Don't be," he said like it was inconsequential. "I mean, I'm sure he considered it with Sila back when—" He cut himself off, loyal enough to his daughter not to voice the extenuating circumstances of his relationship with his wife. "How much?"

Not enough. The echo of Jack's words the night before filled up the spaces in her that threatened to empty with doubt and disappointment. She cut her brother a stern look. "A *lot,* Sam. A fricken fortune. *Obviously.*"

He raised his hands, defensively. "Sorry. I shouldn't have asked." Leaning forward and stopping the swing, he propped his elbows on his knees and met her gaze. "Do you want me to kick Griffin's ass?"

She tried not to smile at the question, so serious, from a man she doubted could handle loading a dishwasher. "That's sweet, and very big brotherly, but no, Sam."

"I could, you know."

"I don't doubt it," she said, keeping the laughter from her words. "But maybe you just don't know what to do with yourself right now. You and Sila could still make it work, maybe."

"I'd have to want that," he confessed. "But honestly, at this point, after this week? All I really want is to know my kids. I don't know my kids."

"Well. They're nine and fourteen," Alice replied. "Are kids that age really . . . knowable?"

"It's not like I tried that hard. I never really knew how to be a dad with them. And it's not like Sila wanted me to be. They were security for her. Assets." He paused. "What a fucking mess."

Alice sat with that for a while, thinking about love and how messy it could be. How partnership and connection were so tenuous. And how hard it was to unlearn the ways they'd been taught to think about love.

Sam added, "No wonder we're all so terrible at relationships."

Maybe not forever, though; maybe that was another thing that could be new to After.

Sam's watch began to beep, the sound barely audible over the rain, now coming down so hard on the roof of the porch that it was hard to believe the structure would hold. 6:55 A.M.

Sam took a deep breath, sounding tired. "Here we go again."

The words were barely out when the screen door blasted open, swinging back hard and fast with a heavy crack against the weathered cedar shingles. And then Jack appeared, in a white tee and the trousers from his suit the day before, looking . . .

"What the hell is wrong with *you?*"

Jack turned toward Sam's question, his breath coming hard and fast. "I thought you left."

"I don't think he means me," Sam said, dryly.

She dropped her feet to the porch with a *thud* and stood up. He didn't mean Sam.

Jack advanced, eyes locked on Alice. "Christ, Alice," he said, stopping just before he reached her, making her simultaneously grateful that he wasn't about to show Sam just how intense their relationship (were they using that word?) was getting, and disappointed that he didn't pull her close. Because now that he was here, she realized how much she regretted leaving him that morning.

They were definitely using the word *relationship. Thing* no longer covered it.

"What happened?" she asked.

He shoved a frantic hand through his wet hair, pushing it out of his face. "I thought you were gone. I woke up and you were—" He stopped himself with a quick look at Sam, then went on. "The skiffs are all gone, and the storm is—" A wild rumble of thunder rendered the rest of the sentence unnecessary.

Alice's brow furrowed. "The skiffs are gone?" She'd been so focused on getting to the main house that morning that she hadn't paid attention to the docks, but there had been three of the small white boats moored there the night before. She looked to Sam, skeptically. "You?"

"No. I draw the line at locking you in the vault. And no one in the family would try sailing in this," Sam said, waving a hand at the rain cloaking the house. "The Bay has to be churning." He looked at Alice. "Someone cut the boats loose."

She understood immediately. "To keep me here." When Sam nodded, she added, "This family is one bad accident away from a true-crime podcast."

"This fucking place," Jack said, combing his fingers through his hair again, focused on Alice. "I thought you were in danger. I couldn't get to you."

Something went raw and tight in her chest at the words, and she stepped toward him, reaching out to grab his free hand. She squeezed it, reveling in the warm strength of the grip that met hers. "Jack," she said softly, squeezing his hand. "I'm here. I didn't leave."

The sound of the rain blocked out everything else, and for a heartbeat it was just the two of them. He'd worried about her. He'd seen she was gone and had come to find her. To protect her.

It was a real hero move, which made Alice—

She blocked out the rest of the sentence. The word that came to mind, a word that evoked thoughts of windswept islands and tempestuous seas and wild kisses and happily-ever-afters.

It wasn't a word for that moment or that audience. The house. The island.

Sam's phone, which broke the silence.

"Like. I. Said—Fucking. The. Help."

CHAPTER

20

ALICE DIDN'T UNDERSTAND FEAR of thunderstorms.

Maybe it was because she'd spent the summers of her childhood in her tower room on Storm Island, as close to the clouds as anyone could get, watching enormous storms sweep up Narragansett Bay from Long Island Sound only to be coaxed into staying there by the Atlantic Ocean to the east.

Maybe it was because of the way the rain tapped and sighed on the glass like an Edna St. Vincent Millay poem, or the way the clouds roiled above the sea, clearing the Bay, sending boats to harbor and birds to nest and people inside, leaving nothing but the magnificent drama of a summer storm.

The storm that raged atop Storm Island that day was pure spectacle, the largest Rhode Island had seen in years, drowning out everything, including the power, and leaving only the distant sound of Sam's fog bell—it belonged to Sam now, not Franklin.

Lightning flashed again and again across the salt water, chased by thunder that didn't roll so much as it tumbled, shouting over itself as three different storms came together in one place, each fighting to be the biggest, the loudest, the most damaging. Together, they upended the Bay, pulling down long-dead branches and bringing up long-lost detritus from the ocean floor and depositing it to be cleared away, leaving what remained stronger and healthier than what it had been.

It was doing the job.

When Alice entered the library later that afternoon, the storm was still raging outside, notwithstanding the absolute stillness within.

Greta and Elisabeth were seated in wing chairs by the west-facing stained-glass windows that spread mottled light through the room on sunny days and an ethereal glow through the room on days like this one.

Greta had a book in her lap but didn't seem to be reading, and Elisabeth was already drinking, a gin and tonic dangling from her hand (90 percent gin, tonic for propriety, lemon twist). They were not speaking, which Alice supposed was to be expected.

She looked at her watch. Four P.M. Whatever was going on here, it was going to be a treat.

"Hello, Alice," her mother said. "I haven't seen you since the funeral."

Alice didn't miss the omission of the word *celebration*. Apparently Elisabeth hadn't enjoyed the events of the preceding day any more than the rest of them.

"I've been helping out—Charlie needed the stuff from yesterday secured until it was safe for the planners to come pick it up; and I helped Sam reset the fog bell now that the storm doesn't seem to be letting up." She refrained from adding that she'd gone to the boathouse to tell Jack it wasn't safe for sleeping with the storm roiling—and been distracted by not-sleeping for a while before they separated for the rest of the day.

"Good that Sam is keeping busy," Elisabeth said, like they were discussing less-interesting weather. "I heard Sila left with the kids."

Greta snapped to attention. "She did? When?"

"Last night. The helicopter took them back to the city before the rain started."

Silence fell as Greta's lips pressed into a thin line at the reference to the helicopter, piloted no doubt by Tony, whom Elisabeth had evicted from the island, like they were on some reality TV show.

Of course, their mother didn't notice. "They couldn't leave fast enough."

Greta cleared her throat and looked to Alice. "So, she just went home?"

"Didn't even say goodbye," Elisabeth replied, sipping her drink. "Not even my grandchildren said goodbye. I suppose now that your father's gone, that's how it's going to be. Everyone will ignore me."

Greta got as close to rolling her eyes as she ever did. "Yes, Mom. I'm sure that's why they didn't say goodbye, and not the fact that their family is in chaos."

"Oh, you're speaking to me again?" Elisabeth shot back.

"Well," Alice said into the silence that fell, "as fun as *this* all seems, I really just came in to grab some of Dad's lanterns—the power is out, and it's going to get dark soon."

"I'll help," Greta said, dropping her book and leaping from her chair.

Elisabeth waved a hand in the direction of a low cabinet in the corner of the room and Alice extracted her phone, turning on the flashlight and crouching to reach into the cabinet and pull out a box of small votive candles. "These aren't going to be very useful if we lose power all night."

"They'll do for now," Greta replied, and the duo settled into a quiet assembly line, filling the little picturesque lanterns with tiny candles in a woeful lack of preparation for a night without power.

Greta and Alice shared a look before Greta asked, quietly, "What's happening with Sam?"

Alice looked to her and mouthed, "She left!"

Greta's eyes went wide. "*Left,* left?"

Alice shrugged. "I think?"

"Oh shit!"

"I wish the two of you would stop whispering. If you have something to say, you can say it to my face," Elisabeth interjected sharply from across the room.

Oh, boy. Alice recognized this Elisabeth, cantankerous and sharp, the product of what Alice would guess was a wicked hangover from the night before, and too much hair of the dog.

They were saved from having to reply by Sam popping his head into the room. "Here you all are." He looked to Elisabeth. "Mom, I see we're starting early."

"What else should we be doing with this ice before it melts?" she quipped, raising the ice bucket in his direction. "Be a darling and go fetch some more, will you?"

He crossed to collect the bucket. "I'll join you."

"And that is why you are my favorite son."

"I'm your only son, but I'll take it."

Elisabeth met Greta's gaze, cool and assessing. "And you, Greta? Would you like a drink?"

It felt like a test, because it was one. Was Greta willing to concede that what had happened with Tony was unpleasant, but necessary? That Elisabeth knew, as ever, what was best?

Alice and Sam pretended the question didn't hang heavy like the rain outside even as they held their breath for Greta's answer. Pretended, too, that when it came, it wasn't a portent of what was to come. "No."

Elisabeth stiffened imperceptibly (to anyone other than her children), and triumph must have coursed through Greta, because she added, "Considering we don't know how long the power will be out, we should probably leave some ice for food?"

A hit. "Why would we do that?" Elisabeth said, her cool tone going arctic. "We don't need food. You've had plenty of food this week."

Greta did not reply to the obvious swipe at her weight—the Waspy mother's weapon of choice since Martin Luther took a hammer to a church door. Alice leaped in. "Traditionally, humans eat daily, Mom. Three times."

Elisabeth thrust a jar in Alice's direction from across the room. "Here. Have an olive."

All hail gin o'clock.

"Tempting, but pass."

Greta snorted a little laugh, and opened an old wooden cigar box that had been the home of playing cards and matches for as long as they could remember. She removed a matchbook and two decks, brandishing them toward Alice . . . an invitation for distraction.

Distraction was good. Cards would be good. If they were trapped, cards would be great. "We should tell Emily." The words were barely out of her mouth when Emily and Claudia appeared, arms laden with tall glass votive candles.

"Tell Emily what?" the youngest Storm quipped.

"Cards?" Greta asked.

"Oooh." Emily approached. "Yes."

"We thought people might need these," Claudia said, brandishing the candles.

Emily lowered her voice and looked at Greta. "I also thought maybe you'd like a buffer from Mom."

"You are *whispering* again!" Elisabeth said.

"Thank you," Greta said to Emily, and the two small words felt somehow immense, as she relinquished the reins to Elisabeth.

Emily pasted on a smile and turned to face the room. "They're fixed candles I had made by the priestess at my favorite botanica, which means that once they're lit, they have to stay lit, but I figured we've got time." One by one, she set them on the table, speaking their promise aloud: "Wisdom . . . positivity . . . grace . . ." She looked down. "More grace . . ." Again. "Clarity . . . protection . . . creativity . . . love . . . *more* grace . . ."

Alice slid a look at Claudia. "So this is your trick for dealing with the in-laws?"

Claudia smiled. "I'll never admit it." She set the two in her hands down. "Health and abundance."

"Good that you got that one," Greta said. "Where else would we find abundance in our family?"

"Abundance isn't only about money," Claudia said, assertive in a way she usually was not. Maybe a week with them had changed her, too. "It's about getting what we need. Filling up with what's good for us. That's what I wish for you." She lit a match. Lit the candle. "With *who's* good for us, maybe."

"Alice is definitely doing that," Sam said, coming through the door with the ice bucket.

"You're gross," Alice replied immediately, sitting down and opening a deck of cards. Minutes later, with more candles lit (wisdom, protection, clarity, grace), the family was gathered like a perverse Rockwell around the mahogany card table at the center of the room. Claudia curled up on the sofa in the corner with her 1107, her own candle (love), and her own G and T, having been through enough Storm family card games to know they were not for the faint of heart.

There was no discussion of what they would play—it was Take, an obscure game that Alice had never encountered outside of this place, allegedly passed down from Franklin's side. It was played in rounds with two decks and a level of cutthroat competition that had been bred into them all from birth by their father. They'd learned the rules at Franklin's knee, and when they made mistakes, weren't paying attention, forgot the card count, or grew too chatty, they'd borne the brunt of his competitive spirit.

The game began as though they were in church, the first round played in silence with the exception of a periodical call-and-response to the only word the game required. *Take.*

The second round was Emily's deal, and she shuffled the massive deck with expert skill once, twice. On the third time, she said, "I wonder if I'll ever shuffle cards without thinking of him."

Of course, it was Emily who broke the seal. Emily, practiced in meditation, in having a thought and letting it flow through her without judgment or panic or frustration or rage, who had a thought about their father and just . . . let it out.

Around the table, the energy stuttered.

Elisabeth recovered first, tossing out a card. "Are we going to do this, now?"

Everyone looked to her.

"Do what?" And just as it hadn't been a surprise that it was Emily who invoked Franklin's name first, it was no surprise that it was Emily who pushed their mother to explain what they all already understood.

Emily, forever hopeful that she might crack Elisabeth's icy exterior.

Not yet, though. Not until Elisabeth was ready. "By all means, let's talk about him. What would you like to say?"

"About who, Mom?" Greta asked, poking the bear.

Elisabeth turned a cool gaze on her. "Your father, Greta."

"He hasn't even been gone a week," Emily said, softly. "I'm not sure any of us know what we'd like to say. But I wish—" Her voice caught, and she looked past the table, to Claudia, no longer reading. Instead, watching her wife, nodding her encouragement. Holding Emily, even from a distance. "I wish I could play cards with him again."

A fat tear spilled down Alice's cheek, liquid fire, and she wiped it away as quickly as she could, even as she reached for Emily's hand.

Sam cleared his throat. "When we were kids, you were always desperate to play Take with us. Do you remember?" Emily nodded with a little laugh. "God, we *hated* it. You weren't good. You never paid any attention to the cards. But any time any of us teased you or complained, Dad would tell us to shut up and pull you onto his lap to play your hand with you."

"Oh my god," Greta said, her voice thick with memory and emotion. "That's right."

Emily shook her head. "I don't remember that."

"Like I said," Sam teased. "You weren't paying attention."

"Hey!" she defended herself. "I was little!"

"What's your excuse now?" Alice asked.

"I can wipe the floor with you, now," Emily replied, firing cards around the table like a Vegas dealer. She wasn't wrong.

Three more rounds went by over two hours, these not at all silent (though Sam's phone made an appearance in the five o'clock hour)—instead, full of memories. Surprisingly good ones. The time Sam tripped and cracked his forehead on an enormous rock, and Franklin had to take him by boat to the Wickford urgent care. The time he'd found sixteen-year-old Greta and friends two bottles deep in champagne under the oak tree, laughing so loudly they'd woken the whole house. The time Alice had accidentally picked up a shell and brought it home only to discover she'd brought home a living hermit crab, and she'd screamed until Franklin came bursting into the tower brandishing an 1107 prototype (which he did not use on the unsuspecting animal).

It was all so normal. The kind of thing that happened after the overwhelming shock and chaotic mess of the first week of someone's death. The kind of catharsis they'd all been longing for in their own way.

Well. Not all of them.

Not Elisabeth. As they spoke and laughed and told their stories and poured more drinks and tossed more cards, Elisabeth grew more silent, if that was such a thing. Until it seemed as though she was screaming.

And instead of remembering their training—ignoring the stony silence of their mother as she spiraled into resentment and anger—Greta checked in on her (old habits and all that). "Mom? Are you okay?"

Everyone sucked in a breath at the question, Elisabeth Storm's purest trigger—the suggestion that she might be less than completely and utterly okay.

"Of course I am. I'm fine. I'm just shocked by how you've all forgotten the truth about your father."

Alice unfroze first. The idea that she might have forgotten her father's flaws was honestly laughable. "No one has forgotten, Mom."

"Seems like you all have," Elisabeth said, tossing her cards to the table and standing. "You've been so busy playing his little game, completing your tasks"—she looked at Greta—"or had them completed for you. But I still have mine left. Your father wanted me to tell the truth. And maybe I will."

Sam looked to his sisters. "Fun."

Elisabeth crossed to the bar and mixed another drink, her movements uncontrolled for the first time in—possibly as long as Alice had been alive. "The *truth* is, I am sick of hearing all the wonderful things that man did. Changing the world. So clever, so fun, so brilliant." She opened the ice bucket. "No one noticed that it was me who held his life together. I was clever, too. Brilliant. Fun."

A vision flashed. The photograph at the helm of *The Lizzie*, weathered and curled. Elisabeth laughing in a shower of champagne.

"But there wasn't room for two of us to be clever and brilliant and fun. Someone had to hold it all together. The house." She waved her glass in a wide arc, indicating the house. "And the company. And you all. And that's *the truth*."

She slammed the lid on the ice bucket. "You all want to know how I am feeling? If I'm okay? I'm furious. Even in death, he couldn't take anything seriously. How dare he play with my future? With yours? He left you *nothing* if you don't play his goddamn game, and you all seem to have forgotten that *truth*."

"No one has forgotten," Alice said.

"Not you, maybe," Elisabeth shot across the room. "You're the only one who's actually told the man to fuck off." Everyone's eyes were wide.

"Mom!" Sam said, unable to keep the admiration from his voice. "Language!"

Elisabeth didn't have time for the joke. She was busy telling her truths. "Instead, it's all card games and holding you on his lap and taking you on the boat and rescuing you from horseshoe crabs. *I don't remember any of that.*"

Hermit crabs, Alice thought, the distinction somehow incredibly important in the moment, but she held her tongue.

"And the goddamn lanterns," Elisabeth said, indicating the three on the card table, now casting more light as the afternoon gave way to unseasonably early darkness, thanks to the storm outside. "*Dad's lanterns.*" She scoffed. "Who do you think made sure there were enough of those lanterns on hand if we had guests? Not your father, whom you insist on canonizing. It was me." She paused. "There's more *truth*. He liked to play the hero and get all the accolades when the power went out."

She said it like they didn't know that her father's role was master of ceremonies whenever guests were in attendance, and even when they weren't. Controlling and demanding and critical—but the leader of the Storm family circus.

And now, without him, they were all working without a net, having to learn a new way. And in many ways, none more than Elisabeth.

"Mom," Alice said, taking to the tightrope, "we know all this. We lived it. But what's the value in resurrecting the worst of it? He's gone."

"I know he's gone!" The near shout shocked them all for how out of character it was, but Elisabeth wasn't stopping. "He's gone and he won't come back, and he left you all. And he left me." She paused. "But I'm not the villain. I'm not perfect. I have made mistakes."

The siblings all shared a look. Whatever this was, it was uncharted territory. And while no one at the table would call it growth . . . it wasn't nothing.

She pressed on. "But I will not stand by while you all hold him up like he was a hero. Franklin Storm wasn't a hero. And that's the *truth*."

Sam dropped his cards and leaned back in his chair. "Yeah, Mom. We know."

"Some of us more than others," Greta added.

"If you're making T-shirts, Greta, I'll need one," Alice joked, and they all snickered.

Everyone but Elisabeth. "There's nothing funny about it."

"We know that, too, Mom," Emily said, quietly. With grace. Too much of it (it must have been the candles). "But he was still our father."

Elisabeth's whole body went quiet at the words, as though there'd been frenetic chaos in her head that was now just . . . gone. And all four of them knew instantly that whatever was about to happen would be unforgettable.

What they could not have known was that it would be irreversible.

"Do you have other things you'd like to say?" Emily prodded, and it was like watching a lion tamer. Terrifying. "Other truths?"

"A lifetime of them." Elisabeth considered her children, one after another. Landed on her only son. "I don't care for Sila, Sam. You're better off without her."

Sam's brows rose. "I'm afraid you're oh-for-two on surprises, Mom. No one cared for Sila."

"Not even Sam, it turns out," Alice said, dryly.

"But it feels good to say it, doesn't it?" Emily asked Elisabeth.

"Stop treating me like a child, Emily," Elisabeth said. "I see what you're doing. I won't be tricked into talking about my feelings."

"No one is tricking you into—"

"Oh, please." Their mother turned on her youngest. "Your dream is for me to unravel." She stood over the table, looking at each of the children. "I've noticed it all week. Sam in the kitchen, Greta during the presentation of your father's idiotic game, you while we planned for the funeral. Claudia got me high, for God's sake!"

"Once again, that was a miscommunication," Claudia replied from her place on the couch. "I'm really very sorry, Elisabeth."

Elisabeth waved it off. "I just wish you would all stop asking me if I'm *okay*. Alice couldn't even let me get through the goddamn funeral without running me down to ask me. I am *fine*."

"Oh yeah, you seem it," Sam said, heavy with sarcasm. He could always get away with it when the rest of them couldn't.

"I only asked because I heard you talking to Mike, and it sounded—" She stopped when her mother whipped around to face her.

Everything about Elisabeth tensed, and they all noticed. Alice had overstepped.

"Whatever you heard—it wasn't what you think," Elisabeth said. "And it certainly wasn't your business." Apparently, there were some truths that were not for this storm. These Storms.

"What happened with Mike?" Sam asked, looking to Alice.

"Nothing," Alice said, suddenly wanting very much to keep whatever secret she'd stumbled into. She reached for the deck of cards in front of Emily, who set a hand on top of them before Alice could take them.

"No," Emily said, and everyone looked, finding her perfectly calm. The youngest Storm looked to the oldest. "That's a truth that needs to come out."

Something flashed on Elisabeth's face, there and gone almost instantly. But they all saw it. *Shock.* "You know."

Emily nodded. "I do. He told me."

"Mike?"

"Dad."

"*When?*"

The rest of them followed the volley, riveted.

"It's time to turn on the lights, Mom. You want to be in control? So do I. Here's where it begins. We tell the truth. Together." Emily looked to Claudia on the couch, her tablet cast aside, wound like a spring, ready to fight for her wife. Emily returned her attention to the family and took a deep breath. "So, weird thing . . . Mike Haskins is my father."

The house went silent, nothing but the sound of the storm outside and the pounding of hearts within.

And then everything exploded.

"Oh my god," Alice said.

"What the *fuck*?" Sam.

Greta was frozen, eyes wide, staring at their mother. "What?"

Claudia came off the couch and headed for Emily.

"Em . . ." Alice reached for her sister. Grabbed her hand across the table, tighter than she should. "Jesus. Are you—what?" She looked to Elisabeth. "Is that true?"

"It is," Elisabeth said, stiffly, like a stick of premium-grade dynamite hadn't just been lobbed into the family tree. "Though I don't see why it's anyone's business but mine."

"I can see how it would be *Emily's*," Sam retorted. "Jesus, Em."

Emily shook her head. "It's okay. I've known for a while."

Alice's mind raced, a dozen pieces from the last week clicking into place. Emily's insistence that Mike attend the funeral, her defense of Twyla, her fascination with Franklin's possible infidelities, Mike's invitation to Alice—the inclusion of Emily.

The conversation Alice overheard in the greenhouse. Mike's words. *He was giving her a gift. And me, too.*

And then Mike's story the night before. Franklin's call, out of the blue.

Something else, just out of reach. Like the corner of a watercolor that wasn't quite connected to the rest. Bad underpainting.

"This is true?" Greta asked, the question barely there. "Mom?"

"I already said it was true." That was it. Nothing more. No explanation. And Alice realized that it was entirely possible that was the last she'd ever say on the matter.

Some things stay secret.

"Holyyyy shit." Sam, ever eloquent. But right, honestly.

Alice squeezed Emily's hand again. "How are you so . . . *chill*?"

Emily smiled and met Alice's gaze. Her eyes—so blue—a perfect match to Elisabeth's—gleaming with tears. She turned her hand over in Alice's, her grip tight enough to hurt. "Practice, I guess."

Emily, the fun one. The unserious one. The delight.

As unraveled as the rest of them.

Claudia was hovering behind Emily's chair by then, hands on Emily's shoulders, worry etched on her face. Alice nodded to her sister-in-law.

"Okay," Claudia said. "We're done here."

"It's okay," Emily said, quiet. Focused.

"It absolutely isn't," her wife replied. "We're done, and I think we should go home."

No one could argue with that.

Except Sam, apparently. "You can't leave."

"Of course we can." Claudia had lost her patience, and honestly, it was a miracle it had taken so long. But apparently, when she decided to make herself known, she did it with impressive power. "You all may be prisoners on this island, but I'm not. And I'll make damn sure Emily isn't, either."

"Claudia. It's *okay*." Emily turned to face her wife.

"No. It's not. No one deserves this. Can't you people see what this place, that man, this family has made you? This money? You should be ashamed of yourselves."

"Listen, you're not wrong," Sam said. "But you literally can't leave. Even if there wasn't a storm, there's no way off the island. We can call you a skiff in the morning."

"Where are the boats?" Claudia asked.

"They're gone," Sam said.

"Gone where?"

"They came unmoored in the storm." The answer, from Elisabeth, who had never cared one way or another about the workings of the island, roused suspicion in them all.

"Three boats don't just come unmoored at the same time," Sam said.

"Then someone must have untied them, Samuel. And whomever it was, you should thank them. Because now Alice can't leave."

"We were talking about Emily leaving, actually," Alice said.

"Fine," Claudia said, no longer caring one way or another; whatever Elisabeth had done prior to the events of the last few minutes was nothing compared to the breaking of her wife's heart. "The helicopter, then."

"Claudia."

"Don't tell me it's okay, Em," Claudia said, her voice shaking with care and no small amount of anger. Good. Emily needed someone always in her corner.

"The helicopter left with Sila and the kids and—" Sam looked to Greta, who had gone full statue during the chaos. Tony had taken the helicopter back to New York.

Thunder crashed outside, startling everyone. Except Emily, who seemed remarkably serene (was this what meditation did for a person?). "It doesn't matter," she said, softly, to Claudia. "Love, we couldn't have flown in this, anyway."

"Okay, but we can leave this room still, right? Our feet still work?"

Emily gave her wife a little smile. "Yes."

Claudia snatched a candle off the table strewn with cards—another game in shambles—and reached out a hand. "Then let's do that."

"I suppose I'm the bad guy again," Elisabeth said, a truly unhinged response to the situation at hand. She plucked the lemon twist from her gin and took a bite out of it, and for a wild moment, Alice considered ripping the glass from her mother's hand and throwing it into her face.

"Good night, Elisabeth," Claudia said, the words sounding more like *Go straight to hell,* and they left the room, Claudia taking palpable joy in slamming the door behind them, the house groaning under the weight of her ire. Without thinking, Alice followed, wanting to get to Emily before she and Claudia closed themselves away. Wanting to apologize. Wanting to tell her she was loved. That she was essential.

Wanting to be her sister.

She'd just opened the door when she heard it, the sharp crack. For a moment, she thought it was the house. Ancient rafters unable to keep another secret. But when she looked back on the tableau, lit only by the candles around the room, it was clear that it was worse than the house breaking.

It was Greta breaking.

Elisabeth had a hand to her cheek, her eyes enormous with shock that was, for once, not feigned, her mouth hanging open.

"Greta, what the hell?" Sam said, coming around the table as Alice took a step toward them. "We're all pissed but—"

"You manipulative *monster*."

Sam and Alice froze. Whatever this was, it was big.

"You sent me away," Greta said, all her focus on Elisabeth, who suddenly couldn't seem to meet her eldest daughter's gaze. "You told me I'd shamed the family. You took away my friends, my family, my future. To protect the scandal, you said. To protect *Storm*. And the whole time— Emily was *here*. *In this house*."

Oh no.

"Greta," Elisabeth said with a little laugh, bordering on manic, as though she'd finally, finally begun to see what she had wrought. "We had to make sure no one found out—it would have ruined all the plans you had for your life."

"It was an abortion, Mom. Plenty of people make that choice. Women make that choice every day, and live their lives, no ruin in sight."

"Not in our circle!" Elisabeth said. "In our circle, you call a doctor. You handle it quietly. You walked into a *public clinic* in Union Square and did it without telling us! Your father was *furious*. What if someone had *seen*?"

"My *father*?" Greta shot back.

"Yes."

"Not you? You weren't consumed by fear that I might have made my own decision and decided I liked the taste of being in control of myself? Of living outside of your shadow? Of having a future of my own making?"

Elisabeth's gaze narrowed. "It wasn't *your* future, Greta. It was none of your futures. You're *Storms*. Your future was in this family. We couldn't risk another mistake."

"I didn't make a mistake!"

"You got yourself knocked up by some . . ." She waved a hand. "I don't even know."

Sam and Alice shared another look. *Knocked up* was not a term anyone had ever dreamed Elisabeth Storm would use.

"Well, Mom. Turns out you did, too," Greta shot back. "And no one sent you away for a year to sit with your choice in a foreign country, alone, until you begged to come home and swore you'd never make another *mistake* again."

Alice's mind raced. When Greta was nineteen, she'd taken a gap year and gone to Switzerland. The story had always been that she'd worked in Geneva and bummed around Europe on the weekends, too busy to come home. The rest of them were in school—Sam was a senior in high school and as self-absorbed as millionaire homecoming kings could get, Alice had been in middle school and as self-absorbed as twelve-year-olds could get, and Emily . . . she'd been seven years old and attached to Elisabeth. A little duckling.

Greta had returned serious and chic: thin as a rail, speaking perfect French, ready for a degree in existentialist philosophy at Brown and a lifetime as Elisabeth's shadow. She'd been almost unrecognizable to Alice, who, if she'd given it any thought (she was twelve, she hadn't), would have chalked it up to the fact that she hadn't seen her older sister for a year.

"You convinced me that I'd never have another chance of happiness after that. That I'd never have love. That I'd never have a family, unless I did as I was told. Unless I was a good soldier in your little army." Greta shook her head. "All to keep me here. With you. Like your prize."

Alice's heart ached along with her sister's, and she raised a hand to her chest, as though she could make it stop. Across the room, shock was written all over Sam's face, and he opened his mouth to say something. Recognizing the horrible idea, Alice shook her head once. Firmly. *Not now.*

Her brother really was showing growth, as he listened and kept his mouth shut.

The same could not be said of Elisabeth, who seemed to have finally realized that she was in deep. Once Greta was lost—Rome had fallen. She scrambled. "Your father—"

"*Stop,*" Greta said. "You don't want us to rewrite history? You don't get to, either. And you might not have been the one to send me away, but you were absolutely the one to keep me here."

Before Elisabeth could reply, Greta added, "You owe Emily an apology. And honestly, if she never forgives you, I wouldn't blame her."

"He never said a word about it, until he died," Elisabeth said. "Saved it up to punish me with it, just like he punished me with it every time she ran to him. The moment she was born, she was his favorite." Elisabeth was searching for a way to hurt them. To bring them down into her muck. "And she wasn't even his."

It was a deeply shitty and deeply false thing to say. "How exactly did he punish you by loving her, Mom?" Alice couldn't help the retort.

"Your father didn't *love,* Alice," Elisabeth said. "You know that better than anyone."

The words should have hurt, but they didn't, lacking the power they would have had a day earlier. An hour earlier.

"Neither did you, Mom." Greta hung her head and stared at her hands, fingers knotted together tightly, like if she released them she might fly away. "All those years I hid the truth, thinking you were right. Thinking no one could ever know. Being so sure that my choice, the right choice, would ruin me. I was too ashamed to tell anyone, even the one person . . ."

Greta trailed off, unable to speak the end of the sentence.

. . . who loved me unconditionally.

Alice's throat tightened, tears springing again as she stared at her older sister, shattered as much as their younger one, no sound in the room but the rain pounding against the windows, a slow, devastating cyclone, depositing the driftwood and secrets it found, not at a distance, but right here. Inside.

"It was for your own good," Elisabeth said.

"Jesus Christ. No. It wasn't," Sam said, finally, unable to keep silent, his own voice full of sadness and horror and something like fear when he looked to their sister. "Greta . . ."

Greta didn't look away from their mother. "I hate you."

The words snapped, falling brittle and broken at Elisabeth's feet, and the older woman lifted her glass in a mock toast. "Join the club."

Greta left the room, spine straight as steel, head high, somehow, despite it all. She closed the door behind her, firm. Resolved.

Alice looked to Sam. *And then there were two.*

At a crossroads.

The choice had never been clearer, and it was made before Elisabeth said, "Go, then." But they let her pretend she'd released them. A moment of grace to a woman so broken she could do nothing but break the things around her.

Sam opened the door and let Alice through first—both of them quiet, reeling from what had just happened. She stepped into the hallway, consumed by what would come next. Terrified of it.

And there, in the hallway, leaning against the wall, bright electric lantern at his feet, was Jack.

A stern, steady port in the storm, who had heard everything.

Sam looked at his watch. "I don't fucking care what time it is."

"Neither do I." Jack didn't look away from Alice. He'd seen everything. Heard everything, ever the silent judge. But he was no longer an impartial one, given the firm set of his jaw, the way he came off the wall, searching her face. He didn't have to ask the question in his eyes.

The answer was clear. None of them were okay.

He opened his arms, and Alice went willingly, stepping into his embrace, the thunderstorm raging outside.

Astraphobia. The word whispered through her as he tightened his grip on her, pressing a kiss to her temple, whispering her name, keeping her safe. *Fear of storms.*

Maybe she understood it, after all.

EMILY

THERE WAS SOMETHING INCREDIBLY freeing about the truth finally being out.

At least, that's what Emily would have said if one of her regulars had arrived at the studio above the shop and told her this story. *This isn't your burden any longer,* she would have said, before burning some sage and offering a Reiki session (essential oils diffused free of charge). *It changes nothing about the footprints you leave in the sand.*

She would have said that to a client and believed it.

It was a wonder that she'd never had a client turn to her and say, *Honestly, Emily? Fuck the footprints in the sand.*

"The candle isn't working," Emily said as Alice pushed a gallon bucket of ice cream across the scarred butcher block table in the dark kitchen and slipped into the chair opposite her and Claudia.

Her sister extended two spoons, her gaze falling to the word emblazoned on the label of the flickering candle. *Peace.* "Hard to believe," she said, dryly, poking her own spoon into the ice cream.

"Mom would be pissed that we aren't using bowls."

"Yeah, well, we'll call this an act of resistance," Alice replied.

"Your mom can deal," Claudia added, her anger still palpable. "God, this family."

"Amen." Alice saluted her with her spoon.

"You must really love me," Emily said to her wife. "To put up with them."

Claudia leaned close to her, her dark curls falling forward as her hand came to Emily's face, holding her attention. "Hell yes, I really love you. Forever."

Emily's heart pounded at the words, at the truth in them, unflagging. Undoubtable. Healing. She smiled and lifted herself toward Claudia's kiss. "I love you, too, forever."

And she did. She'd loved Claudia almost from the moment they'd met, in a philosophy class at Smith (yes, they were aware of the cliché). They'd been assigned a group project that had turned into a violent crush on Emily's part, helped in no small amount by Claudia being captain of the rugby team (yes, she was aware of the cliché).

Claudia was the opposite of the Storms, quiet and steady. Thoughtful and measured. And endlessly kind. Emily had set her sights, and within a month, they were inseparable. They hadn't spent more than two nights apart since graduation.

Growing up with Elisabeth and Franklin Storm made a person deeply question the existence of true partnership, but Claudia had changed all that. And Emily thanked the universe for her daily.

"Ugh. Get a room," Alice retorted. "I cannot face your relationship goals right now."

They all laughed, and Emily reached for the ice cream.

Silence fell, companionable. Like when they were kids, *Alice and Emily*.

Finally, Alice said, "Jeez, Em."

It was as good a thing to say as anything else. "Right?" Emily took a bite of ice cream, memories flooding through her as the familiar flavor burst on her tongue. Cherry vanilla, Franklin's favorite. She let it melt on her tongue before she said, "It's weird to think that his ice cream is still in the house."

Alice nodded. "He loved you." A pause, then an urgent, "You know that, right? That he loved you?"

Emily smiled. "I do. Don't worry."

"Good," Alice said, and she meant it. "More than he loved the rest of us, I think."

It wasn't true, of course. Emily didn't have children—it was a maybe, on the list to discuss down the road, once she'd finished processing the family she already had—but she understood love. Maybe better than everyone else in the family. "Parents don't love some kids more than others."

Alice took another bite of ice cream. "Even ours?"

"Even ours," she replied, turning back to the candle. *Peace.* "Though . . . maybe ours *liked* some of us more than others."

"That's definitely true." The fog bell rang in the distance, and thunder crashed, loud and impossibly close, startling them.

Claudia sprang out of her chair, and went to the kitchen door, staring into the pitch-black night. "This is a huge storm."

Alice nodded. "Franklin had one last point to make."

Lightning flashed, throwing the kitchen into stark light for a split second before it went dark again, Alice's lantern on the counter, that candle flickering on the table.

"I knew," Emily said to the candle. "I knew he wasn't my father."

Across the table, Alice froze, spoon halfway to her mouth. She set it back into the container. "You mean, like, before?"

"Maybe always." Emily had always felt out of place in the constellation of the family, telling herself it was for any number of reasons— being youngest, and by so many years, never having Greta's compulsive instinct to keep their parents happy, or Sam's rich-kid swagger, or Alice's disinterest in the whole thing.

Emily had been different. No one else seemed to think twice about it, so she'd ignored it, and played her role as the quirky one, who meditated and ran a holistic healing shop on the mainland that their father paid for, obviously, because Emily was very sweet but not ever to be taken too seriously.

Only Franklin had known the truth—that Emily had paid back his investment in the shop in full (with interest) only two years after he'd put up the capital. No one needed to know about the time she'd met him for lunch at the taco place he loved in Union Square and presented him with a check. He'd flashed her a bright smile and told her he was so proud. She'd never seen him more delighted than when she paid for lunch.

And no one needed to know that nine months before he died, he'd reciprocated—taking her to lunch, and offering up different truths. Different secrets, which belonged to them both. Secrets that Emily had kept with Franklin, heavy on her heart, as time had marched, knowing there would come a time when she would be responsible for keeping them alone. Or revealing them.

"I just knew," she said, looking to Alice, the sibling closest to her in age, and the one she'd claimed first as a child, whenever a teacher or a friend would ask about her family, it was *Alice* she'd talk about. Because of this. The two of them, here, at this table. On each other's side.

"It's all bullshit, though," Alice said, before she shot forward, like they were kids again. "But can we talk about Mike Haskins? And *Mom*?"

Emily laughed. "Weird, right?"

"Is this too soon?"

"No!" Emily said, loving the release of it. "I have wanted to talk about it with someone for *so long,* and Claudia is great but—"

"Excuse me if I took this revelation to be a bit more serious and a bit less salacious gossip," Claudia cut in.

"Yes, it's very serious," Alice said. "And *also* . . . oh my *god.*"

"*Right?*" It felt so good, this moment. This honesty. Living this out loud.

Alice set her palms to the table. "You see Mike and Twyla! Is it, like, a thing? Are you on the hunt for a new family? Not that I would blame you."

Another laugh. "No."

"Not for lack of my trying," Claudia quipped, returning for more ice cream.

"Can I come?" Alice asked.

Another laugh, making Emily feel a little lighter. "Mike didn't know."

"Oh my god." Alice's eyes went wide. "I guess that makes sense, though. He doesn't seem like a guy who'd just disappear if he knew."

He had disappeared, though. And now they knew why. Because Franklin and Elisabeth had kept the circumstances of Emily's birth a secret from everyone. "Dad told him not long ago."

Alice nodded. "A few weeks ago."

"How do you know that?"

"I know things," Alice retorted before confessing, "He mentioned a phone call to me. Said he hadn't heard from Dad in years."

Emily nodded. "He's been really cool, though. He called me right after he talked to Dad. Invited me out to their place in the Hamptons. It was nice. He said he didn't know, or he would have—"

"For the best, probably. It would have made holidays awkward."

Emily chuckled. "That's what I said."

"I'll give it to you, Em. Having not one but two billionaire dads and still finding space to be remotely down to earth . . . a feat."

"Would we say I'm down to earth?" She waved in the direction of the candle. "I'm burning a Peace candle."

"Yeah, but it's not working, so . . ."

Emily let herself laugh, and let herself like it, let it roll through her like the thunder outside. "He's not my dad, though. Mike."

"Nope." Alice offered her the ice-cream bucket. "He can't have you," she said. "Dad or no Dad, you're a Storm. You were his. You are ours."

Ours.

She loved that word, especially coming from Alice. Tucked it away for safekeeping. "I'm glad you came back," she said, finally, looking to Alice. "I missed you."

Alice reached for her hand, holding it tight, as tight as she had in the library. "I missed you, too. I'm sorry I was so . . . distant. I didn't know how to be in with you and out with everyone else."

"I didn't know, either." Emily nodded. "I could have done better."

Something flashed in her sister's eyes, turning them glossy with tears. "Jesus, Em," Alice said. "You really are the best of us."

It was Emily's turn to tear up, and she dashed it away with a little laugh. "Yeah, I kind of am."

"What a secret they kept," Alice said with a shake of her head. "I mean, I knew the family was full of them—no one loved privacy like Franklin and Elisabeth Storm—but still."

"I can't believe they never told me the truth. Not until . . ."

Alice nodded. "I hate to break it to you, my friend, but you're going to need therapy for this one. For a while, probably. Unless you're even more balanced than I thought."

Another surprised laugh bubbled out of her. "I'm not."

Another wicked crash of thunder punctuated the thought as Emily considered what she would say next. Whether it was time.

"Where did everyone go?" Emily asked.

"Sam went after Greta," Alice replied with a wince, and Emily nodded. That was good. It had always been Sam and Greta, and if Alice's story were even a fraction of the truth of what had gone on with Greta and Elisabeth, she would need him.

"And Jack?"

"He's in Dad's office. Finishing up some stuff while I—" Alice cut herself off when she looked from Emily to Claudia and discovered them both smiling at her. "What?"

"Only that he's finishing up some work or whatever while you come hang out with your baby sister is pretty . . ." Emily teed up her wife. "What's the word, Claud?"

"Domestic?" Claudia offered, reaching for the ice cream. "Like, sexy domestic. Did you see him waiting for her in the hallway earlier? Hot."

Emily smiled and leaned in to Claudia. "I mean, you basically told my family to fuck off, so that was pretty hot, too."

Claudia blushed and gave a little shrug. "You deserved it."

"We sure did," Alice said, setting her spoon down on the table and crossing to the fridge. "You're a real still-waters-run-deep girl, aren't you, Claudia? Everyone asking why you don't talk more, why you're so silent in the corner." She opened the door and groped around inside for a moment, bottles clanging together in the darkness within. She found what she wanted and closed the door. "You're just waiting to jump in and pull some touch-her-and-die shit."

Claudia didn't respond, but she didn't have to. Alice was right. Emily considered her. "Speaking of touch-her-and-die shit . . ."

Alice put two cans of seltzer on the table as her own blush rose high on her cheeks. "I don't know. I keep having to remind myself that he remains Dad's lackey and the judge and jury of this stupid game . . .

Which is over tomorrow, and since I am now trapped on this island by the universe, congratulations, Em. Your first billionaire father's inheritance looks like it's coming through." She lifted her own can in a toast.

Emily calculated the days. Her sister was right.

"It's over."

"Assuming we're not blown off the island, yes."

Another heavy rumble of thunder startled everyone, Claudia the most. "I don't know how you all put up with these," she said. "We don't have these on the West Coast."

"This one isn't normal," Emily said, reaching for Claudia's hand. "They're not supposed to last this long."

Alice drank deep from her can, then said, "Maybe Dad's not ready to go."

The words were light. Meant to be funny. But Emily couldn't help the memories that came with them. Claudia caught her eye, understanding. She nodded, and Emily took a deep breath. "He wasn't ready to go," she said. "He told me so."

Alice's gaze grew sharp. "What do you mean, he told you so?"

"My letter—the one Jack delivered?" She winced as she said it, remembering that Alice didn't receive a letter. That she didn't have the strange closure the rest of them had. Or, at least, the closure Emily got.

Emily's letter had said two words. *Thank you.*

"It wasn't a task, because I'd already finished my task."

The room was still, cloaked in the ever-present rain outside, and the near-constant rumble of the storm overhead. Alice watched her carefully. "Go on."

"I kept his secrets."

Alice nodded. "You don't mean Mike Haskins."

"No," Emily replied, looking to Claudia, ever supportive, encouraging her.

"Tell her," Claudia said.

"Tell me what?"

Another memory flashed, her father in his office in New York, pale. Sweaty. "Nine months ago, I let myself into the apartment in the city for some reason—I can't even remember now—thinking he and Mom were out. They'd had tickets to some fundraiser or whatever, and I had to pick something up." She paused, remembering. Hearing the muffled sounds from his office. "It doesn't matter. What matters was, Mom wasn't there, but he was. He'd stayed home because he wasn't feeling well. When I found him, he was on the floor of his office, because he was having trouble with his balance."

Alice's eyes went wide. "Was he—"

"He told me he was fine, but other things seemed off. Nothing obvious—only stuff that you'd notice if you were looking. And I was."

"Emily, what—"

"He wasn't as quick on his feet. At first I thought it was age . . ."

"Seventy isn't that old anymore. Not for someone like Dad."

Emily nodded. "Not long after that, he told me. He was sick." She took a deep breath. "Very."

"He knew." Emily's chest tightened as she watched Alice take in the information. "That's why he wrote everyone letters." Alice paused, her lips twisting into a wry smile. "Well. Not everyone."

"Alice," she said softly, wishing she could make that better. Wishing he hadn't punished her that way. And also, understanding. She'd been furious at Alice for years after she left.

Alice waved away the pity in her voice. "So, what . . . it was on purpose?"

"I don't know." Emily shook her head. "He kept it a secret from everyone. He didn't want people to see him failing. So, yes. Maybe? But I don't know." The tears were falling now, faster than they had since she'd heard the news. "Honestly, I don't think so. I can't imagine he would have—" She cut herself off, and Claudia took her hand, squeezing tight. Emily looked to Alice's hands, free on the table. No one holding them.

She reached out and rectified the problem. "I don't think he would have done it without more time with you, Alice." They were both crying. "God, I'm so sorry. I should have . . ."

She trailed off, and Alice reached for her. "No. What could you have done? Predicted this?" Alice gave her a little shake. "Emily. Has anyone in the history of Franklin Storm been able to predict what he would do? All we ever knew was that he'd try to control us."

That was true. "I think he loved us, too."

"He did." Claudia spoke up then, the certainty in her voice a comfort to both sisters. "He loved the shit out of you both. God, Em, think about it. We were so shocked when we found out about your biological father . . . because Franklin loved you so much. Because he chose to love you. He worked at it. He controlled it."

Another flash of lightning followed by an immediate crack of thunder.

"Maybe it was an accident," Alice said. "Or maybe it was Franklin Storm, trailblazing genius, choosing his way out, so he didn't have to give up control even once." She gave a little, humorless laugh. "We'll never know. Another secret, one we can never unravel."

The fog bell clanged in the distance, punctuating the reference as Alice continued, "You know, everyone was so concerned about it not seeming fair. It felt like the sky wasn't falling for all of us. Only for Sam, having to face the truth of his marriage. Only for Greta, having to choose between Tony and Mom."

Emily sucked in a breath at that. "That one was brutal."

"More brutal than watching your father die and not being able to tell anyone? The sky fell for you nine months ago."

"More brutal than not being here when it happened?" Emily responded. "The sky fell for you the longest."

"Well. That's a Storm Olympics I'm not interested in winning." Alice went quiet, lost in her thoughts. "He had nine months," she said, a tremor sliding into her voice. "And he didn't try to reconcile. Didn't even write me a letter."

"Alice, he . . . he didn't know how. He'd never had to work for anything like you."

Alice nodded. "That's why he invited me to the Fourth of July. Why you did."

"I'm so sorry," Emily said. So many apologies that night. How many more would there be before the ledgers were all balanced again? "I should have told you—that he was sick."

"No." Claudia stepped in. An observer. "I mean, yes, Alice should have known your dad was sick. But Em, none of this was your fault."

"Exactly." Alice nodded. "This isn't your failing. *He* should have told me. He should have told all of us. He shouldn't have made you carry that water alone." A tear spilled down her cheek and she dashed it away. "He could do *anything*. And he couldn't do that. Couldn't be honest with us. Even at the end. And I don't understand."

Emily shook her head. "I haven't understood for months. I think that's part of it."

"Some things stay secrets," Alice said, simply.

"That's the worst, isn't it?" Emily asked.

They shared a little laugh, and Alice tilted her head back, looking at the ceiling, somewhere in the darkness above. "Fuck," she whispered. "He *died.*"

Silence. And then, Emily filled it. "It's not his secret anymore. Or mine, or yours." She tilted her head toward the stairs leading to the upper floors of the house, where she imagined their siblings were. "Someday, they'll know it, too."

"Sooner, rather than later," Alice said.

"Probably."

"Maybe not tonight, though."

Definitely not. "Greta doesn't need it tonight." A pause. "She really slapped Mom?"

"She really did." Alice whispered it, like she couldn't quite believe what she'd seen.

"God. Greta." Emily reached for the ice cream, almost soup now. "Did you know?"

"No." Alice shook her head, sadness falling over her face. "She'd never tell us. I wish she would have."

"I wish she'd made a break for it with Tony," Claudia interjected.

"Yes! Me, too!" Alice replied, slapping her palms to the table.

As if on cue, footsteps sounded on the stairs, precise and even. Everyone straightened.

Elisabeth appeared, lantern in hand, tiny votive barely hanging on. Her gaze tracked over them all, and Emily resisted the urge to hide the dirty spoon in front of her. She was pissed at her mother, wasn't she?

Except, she wasn't.

What was vulnerability on everyone else was cold anger on Elisabeth Storm, and Emily had spent a lifetime learning it. "Hi, Mom."

Elisabeth looked to Claudia, then Alice. "I'd like to speak to Emily, if you don't mind."

They did not move, and Emily loved them both a little more for that, especially when she nodded them off, and Claudia reached across the table to squeeze her hand while Alice leaned down to press an enormous kiss to her cheek. "I love you."

How long had it been since someone in this family had said those words?

Maybe things could change.

Probably not, but the work, Emily's work, would always be to hold hope.

Elisabeth slid into the seat across from Emily, her gaze settling on the candle there. Emily wondered what it must be like, keeping every thought, every response, positive or negative, hidden from the world.

Digging deep for her best meditative practice, Emily sat in stillness, listening to the rain, and waited for her mother to begin.

Realizing she wasn't going to be let off the hook, Elisabeth said, "I suppose you have questions."

Only a million of them. "Dad told me a lot of it."

Elisabeth's face went slack. "He had no right to—"

No. They weren't doing that. Emily held up her hands. "He had every right to tell me who my birth father was, Mom. What he didn't have the right to tell me was why. Or how. Those . . . they're your secrets."

"I don't want to discuss them."

Emily nodded. "And I won't ask." She wasn't ready to hear them. Not this week, not when she was raw with the loss of the man who'd been the only father she'd ever known, for better or worse.

"From the moment he found out about you," Elisabeth said, the words stilted and uncomfortable, "Franklin was your father."

She knew her mother well enough to accept that it was the closest thing she'd ever get to an apology, so Emily allowed herself a tiny win, a response that suggested the apology had been tendered. "Thank you."

Elisabeth's brow furrowed. "He left me with this mess. He was a part of every decision, you know. Keeping Greta close. Keeping Alice away. He was the architect of many of them."

It was only right for Elisabeth to defend herself, Emily thought. It was time for her to speak up. She nodded. "That must have been so difficult."

"You can't imagine how I regret things."

There had been a time when Emily, who had always lived out loud, not hiding anything—wouldn't have been able to imagine how it must feel to have to bear the weight of all those secrets. But she'd carried secrets of her own, now. And in that, she found sympathy. "There's still time to rectify those regrets, Mom. You could try."

Elisabeth flinched at the words. At the suggestion that she allow emotion to dilute her cool New England exterior. "Maybe."

Maybe wasn't *No.*

Maybe there would come a time when Elisabeth would do it. Maybe someday, she'd let them all see the things she kept so tightly locked away. Maybe someday, Emily would ask. But the truth was a strange, ephemeral thing, and they would all have to make peace with never knowing all of it. They would spend a lifetime coming to terms with that.

Across the table, the flickering light cast her mother's face into harsh, unforgiving shadows, and Emily thought about all the questions she would ask her father if he were here. One more minute. Less. One more question.

"That candle says *Peace,*" Elisabeth said, and there was a thread of something distant in her words. Something like humor. A glimpse of Lizzie.

Emily nodded. "It's a work in progress."

A little noise of agreement was Elisabeth's concession.

Maybe it didn't matter what the answers were. Because Emily knew she had been loved. Knew she still was loved. And maybe everything else was a secret that could be washed away by the storms outside.

Still, she couldn't help herself. "Mom, did you love him?"

Elisabeth looked up at that, drawn out of her thoughts, wherever they had taken her. The storm raged outside, louder than it had been, the wind screamed across the windows.

"I miss him."

It wasn't the answer. But maybe it was enough.

She reached out and touched Elisabeth's hand, the soft skin there like paper. Like sand. Full of footprints.

"Me, too."

It was too much for Elisabeth. She stood and left without a word, climbing the servants' stairs, lantern in hand. Emily imagined her washing her face by that lanternlight. Applying serums and creams and climbing into bed, waiting for sleep to take hold and put the whole day behind her. Forever.

Emily didn't move, instead setting the palms of her hands to the scarred wood of the table and watching the candle's flame flicker and dance as the storm raged outside. *Peace,* she thought, again and again, the word coming unraveled in her. Turning into sounds and letters.

Until it lost all meaning and lighting struck, bright and close, chased by a mighty crack, and a crash that shook the house.

CHAPTER

21

WHEN THE GIANT OAK crashed through the wall of windows in her father's office, Alice could think only one thing—*Jack*.

One moment, she'd been lingering in the hallway outside the kitchen with Claudia, not sure of what would happen between Elisabeth and Emily, wanting to stay close in case everything went off the rails. The next, things went off the rails in a completely different way, and she was running through the dark labyrinthine corridors to Franklin's office, heart in her throat.

She burst through the door, Jack's name on her lips. He was already turning from where he stood at the corner of her father's desk, his electric lantern outstretched, surveying the immense damage.

When she threw herself into his arms, he caught her with a soft "Hey."

"I knew you were in here . . ." she said, fast and panicked. "I heard the crash and I thought—"

"Hey," he repeated, his arms wrapped around her, one hand at the back of her head, stroking her hair. "I'm okay."

"All I could think was—"

He whispered her name to her temple. "It's okay, sweetheart. I'm with you."

The words shook something loose, bringing her back to reality. "I was worried." She opened her eyes and, over his shoulder, took in the damage. The tree, hundreds of years old, its canopy green and lush and wet with rain, was now spread across the lawn, through the stunning windows, and atop her father's desk, the desk chair disappeared from view. "Oh my god," she whispered, her heart beginning to pound again. "You could have been—"

"*Hey*." The word was firmer this time, pulling her attention back to him, the light from the electric lantern casting shadows over his face as he set it down, by their feet. Straightening, he framed her face, directing her gaze to his. He grabbed one of her hands and pressed it to his chest. "Feel. I'm here."

He was. As steady and strong as ever.

She kissed him to prove it, and it wasn't gentle or easy, it was harsh and rough, seeking proof that he was there and he was alive and the chaos that rained down upon this place and her family was nothing when faced with this man, who was somehow able to keep it all at bay.

He grunted his pleasure at the way she claimed him, her fingers sliding into his hair, pulling him closer, and he deepened the kiss, licking into her, lush and perfect and wicked enough to shake her out of her worry and into something much more powerful: *want*.

Before she could make good on that, he pulled away with a little disappointed groan and said, so close she could taste the words rather than hear them, "Not that I don't love that you came running to save me, but didn't we agree that I'm the one who is supposed to be protecting you?"

She pressed a kiss to his handsome mouth and smiled. "Didn't I tell you? I was a Girl Scout."

He grinned. "Really?"

She shook her head. "No. But I like the cookies."

"I like you," he said, with a delicious growl, pulling her closer and kissing her again, and it didn't matter that they were surrounded by half an oak tree and a wall of shattered glass. It only mattered that he was well, and Alice wasn't afraid to admit that she cared about something. Someone.

She pulled back from the kiss. "You weren't at the desk."

He shook his head. "I was in the vault." She looked to the book vault, the door still open, as he explained. "Your loathing aside, I thought maybe we shouldn't keep a Picasso on the floor."

"Ordinarily, I would say something extremely artistically sacrilegious about the cultural veneration of that man," she began, her hands sliding along the back of his neck, pulling him down for another kiss. "But right now, I'm pretty happy you got your views on art history from the patriarchy."

He laughed. "Maybe you could design a syllabus for me or something."

"Deal." She grinned. "You'll despise him by the time I'm done with you."

He pulled her close again, and she turned her face into the spot where his neck and shoulder met and took a deep breath.

One of his big hands stroked down her spine, firm and smooth, checking in on her. "Good?"

Was there an answer to that? Everything had fallen apart. "I don't know." She was telling the truth. "I mean, all the secrets are out, and that's good, right? But my mother—even after everything I expected from her . . . I never imagined this."

"Anger and grief get tangled," he said, the words a rumble against her. "Sometimes it can be impossible to separate the two. Or differentiate them."

"It doesn't forgive what she did. Then or now."

"It doesn't," he agreed. "You all get to decide the path from here."

He didn't try to explain it away or diagnose her mom or clean the slate, and Alice appreciated it even as his words underscored the work the family had ahead of them.

Franklin Storm, trailblazing genius, dead at seventy, leaving a power vacuum in the tech world. In the real world. And nowhere more significant than here, in his family. Who were they without him? How did they close the door on Before, and mark time in After?

Jack pressed a kiss to her temple, as though he could hear the thoughts. "You'll find a way. Whatever comes. And, whatever it is, Alice, I'm with you."

She met his gaze. "Do you promise?"

"I promise," he said, so sure and strong that she believed him, going up on her toes as he leaned down to meet her, rough and urgent, as though he could kiss the memory into her. "Do you promise you'll remember that?"

"I promise," she whispered.

Somehow, in this wild week, full of every conceivable feeling and a fair share of inconceivable messes, she'd found this man, steady and strong and safe. And though she wouldn't say it (there was no saying barely a week into knowing someone), she feared her feelings for Jack were as unavoidable as the tree that had crashed into this room minutes before.

Thankfully, before Alice embarrassed herself and told him so, her siblings arrived, storming into the room like Victorian throwbacks with their lanterns and candles.

"Yikes," Emily said.

"Mom is going to *flip*," Greta said, eyes wide on the tree.

"It will be good for her," Sam said.

"Jack! You're alive!" Claudia called from the doorway.

"I am," he confirmed. "Thank you for the concern."

"We gotta stick together," Claudia replied, and Alice couldn't help the little kick of warmth in her chest at that *we*.

"Do we like Jack now?" Sam asked, dryly. "That's my sister you're all over, man."

"I'm not going to apologize for it," Jack said, softly at her ear.

"Please don't."

His arm tightened around her waist. "Hello, Storms."

"God, look at this room—" Emily said, her gaze tracking over the wreckage. "Do you think Dad sent it? Like a sign?"

"A sign of what?" Greta asked. "Time to get new windows?"

"More like time to get off this fucking island," Sam said. "If someone had been at Emily's desk—"

He cut himself off as they all looked to him, the words sparking collective memory.

"I forgot about that," Emily said, the words coming like the rain, soft and misty.

"Emily's desk?" Jack asked.

Alice couldn't help her little smile. "That desk was made from the wreckage of an eighteenth-century pirate ship." All the kids snickered. "Dad swore it belonged to the owner of one of the longest-standing private casinos in London."

Jack's brows rose, already recognizing one of Franklin's over-the-top stories. "And how did Franklin get it?"

They'd heard the story a million times and knew every answer. Alice replied, "It belonged to her—the owner of the casino was a woman, allegedly."

"She passed it to her daughter, the first woman to own a major newspaper," Greta said. "It stayed at the paper through her reign and the reign of her daughter."

Emily took over. "Survived fire and war and politics and was moved from manor house to manor house for a while, before the family must have decided there was no need for such a massive piece of furniture."

"Dad bought it at auction the year Emily was born," Alice said, looking to her little sister. "He always said that a desk that had been owned by three powerful women was the perfect thing to commemorate the birth of his third daughter."

"He didn't care that I wasn't his," Emily said, happily.

Alice swallowed around the knot in her throat. "He definitely did not."

"He was a blowhard and an asshole," Sam said, "and I'm sorry to say, you *were* his."

"You are *ours*," Greta amended.

"That's what I said," Alice said. "There's no getting out. I should know."

Emily laughed through her emotion—the surest proof that she was a Storm. "And here I was, hoping for an exit."

"Take heart, we have our strengths," Alice said. "For example, I defy you to name a group that reacts more calmly to a tree crashing through a wall. Mom didn't even bother to get out of bed."

Another laugh, this the real thing. "I gave her a gummy."

Perfect.

"You talked to her? Again?" Sam asked.

"Yes, it's fine," Emily said, looking to Greta. "For me. For tonight."

Greta nodded. "I don't think it's fine for me."

They would walk their own paths.

"I'll call Charlie in the morning," Sam said, and everyone looked to him, suddenly shocked. "And I'll make sure it gets fixed."

"Samuel," Alice replied, voicing everyone's thoughts. "Are you . . . being responsible?"

Did he blush at that? "You know I'm a grown man with actual living children, don't you?"

"Yeah, but look at us, alive and well," Alice said. "How hard can it be to raise children?"

Sam shot her a look. "I have looked at us, Alice. That's why I'm concerned."

"Speaking of concerned . . ." Emily interjected, raising her Peace candle (defective, at this point) toward the fireplace. "Alice! Your painting!"

Jack was in motion before the words were out—of course, he was always watching and listening and ready, and he and Emily reached *In Progress*, face down on the now-wet carpet, simultaneously. He set his lantern down to lift the massive watercolor, but Emily stayed his movement with a hand to his elbow.

"Alice," Emily breathed. "Oh my god."

She stepped forward as Emily pulled something off the back of the painting. A manila envelope, the kind that artists often filled with provenance and too many patrons just left there, stuck to the art.

The envelope wasn't provenance, though. Emily turned it to face the room, angling it just enough that the lantern on the floor revealed the dark slash of ink across it. In their father's handwriting.

Alice.

He'd left her a letter after all.

"Oh my god," Emily repeated, something close to wonder in her tone. "He sent the tree. On purpose."

"Sure he did," Greta teased, but even she stepped closer, surprised by the find.

Alice looked to Jack. "Did you know?"

He shook his head, lowering the painting to his side but not letting it go. "No."

Alice traced her name in that familiar handwriting, slanting across the paper as though Franklin's thoughts were coming too fast and he was afraid he might not catch them if he didn't rush to get them down.

"Open it."

Alice—

By now you've probably heard it all—and you're probably pretty pissed. I never should have told you to leave. I should have told you to come the hell back. Another in a long line of things I should have told you.

I was proud of you, kid. Even when I was pissed at you. And I should have told you. I know I broke it. I hate that I left you to fix it by yourself.

Maybe you could use a fixer to help.

—Dad

Alice read it twice, unable to hear the rain on the broken glass or the wind in the leaves of the giant oak, as it was all drowned out by the sound of her blood rushing in her ears.

She looked up to discover her siblings, all curiosity. Her siblings who had spent the week—longer—buffeted by Franklin Storm. Emily, keeping a secret that should never have been hers to begin with; Greta, forced into choices she never should have made; Sam, bearing the impossible weight of their father's unreasonable expectations. She smiled, sad and aching, wondering what would come next for them. How they'd all survive now, without Franklin to control them.

But mostly, she wondered how she would survive now, knowing that what she had come to want over the course of the week had always been Franklin's endgame. Knowing she'd played right into her father's hands.

Her gaze settled on Jack, who didn't look comfortable anymore.

"You never told me what you get," she said. "For keeping me on the island."

There was a collective inhale in the room, every head swiveling to Jack, who did not answer.

She repeated herself. "He wanted me here. And you were supposed to keep me here. Not them." She waved a hand at her siblings. "Though they absolutely helped."

"Alice," he said. "You need to know I don't care—"

"He was afraid the inheritance wouldn't be enough," she interrupted. "You were supposed to keep me here. Until tomorrow."

"Until midnight tonight, yes," he answered, seeming to understand that the answer was an indictment. "But I didn't—"

"Don't." She stopped him. "You did the job. I'm here. Well done."

"Alice, I didn't keep you here."

"Don't sell yourself short, fixer," she said. "Come on. You were doing it from the start. Right from the moment you punched out a photographer at the train station. Before that, huh? You knew it was me. You knew I'd be there. You knew that I would be alone—you made sure of it. Griffin was gone. It was me on that train, looking for someone to protect me, because no one else ever had. Lucky you had those photographers on speed dial."

The words struck him like a blow. He recoiled. "The photographers weren't me. You think I would have risked that?"

"Fine," she said. "But the one-night stand? Without really pushing to tell me who you were? That was pretty helpful."

"Yes. It kept you off the island until I could be here with you."

"Until you could make sure I stayed." Betrayal was hot and bitter in her throat. "So you *did* intend to manipulate me into staying at the Quahog Quay."

"No. I wasn't planning to—" He stopped. Looked around the room to their audience. "For us to—"

"To sleep together," she said.

Shock and surprise sounded around the room.

"The first night!" Greta said.

"Before you even got here!" Emily.

"What an asshole," Sam said.

The chorus of replies pushed Jack and Alice into a strange, fleeting truce.

"Shut up," Alice said.

He lowered his voice and spoke directly to her. "I didn't expect that, Alice. And once it happened . . . none of that was . . . it was all real. Which was a real pain in my ass, I'll tell you what."

"Why?"

"Because I didn't expect to like you so much! I didn't expect to want you to like me so much!" He sounded incredibly annoyed, and she didn't hate it. "I had nothing to do with calling the press that night. You might consider the fact that your family isn't exactly unknown—that *you* were as much a story as anything that night."

"Yeah, I know," she said. "I live every day under the specter of my name; it's the most interesting thing about me."

Myriad noises sounded around the room, each representative of her siblings' disagreement. But they let Jack speak. "Don't say that. I fucking hate that. It's not true." He paused. "I had nothing to do with keeping you on the island after that night. That was all them." Another pause. "Not that I didn't enjoy the view when Sam took your clothes and locked them in the pantry."

She ignored her blush. "It wasn't Sam. It was Oliver."

"What?" Sam interjected, annoyed dad activated.

"He and Saoirse had overheard the terms of the game—and they thought that if I left and you didn't inherit . . . Sila might leave." Which had, in fact, happened.

"Shit." Annoyed dad became guilty parent fast. "I'm sorry. I didn't know. I would have stopped it."

"You locked me in the book vault to keep me here, Sam."

He had the grace to look sheepish. "Okay, fine. Maybe I wouldn't have stopped them. That was a pretty good prank." He cast about for someone to shift the blame onto (once an older brother, always an older brother). Found it. "For what it's worth, Emily isn't exactly innocent in all this. She's the one who told me you were leaving with Mike Haskins!"

Emily's mouth dropped open. "Um, to be fair, I *did* do that, but I didn't think you'd—"

"You knew exactly what I'd do!" Sam crowed. "You just didn't want your fingerprints on it."

"I think the important thing to recognize here," Jack said, "is that I did not do any of this. In fact, you might recall that I offered to help you get *off* the island before the boats went missing." When she started to speak, he held up a hand. "Which I also had nothing to do with."

She knew that. Alice could still feel his relief when he'd burst through the screen door, worried she was out in the storm on one of them.

"So . . ." Greta began, raising her hand like they were in school. "That one is on me." Everyone turned shocked eyes to her. "I'm sorry. I was just so *mad* that Mom had sent Tony—" Her throat closed on the rest of the words. "I thought, well now Alice *has* to stay or else it will all be for nothing."

This whole family was unhinged. "You know, Gabi thought you all might murder me."

"What?"

"I'm offended!"

"Why would we do that? That would only make everything *more* complicated," Sam added.

None of this let Jack off the hook, though. Alice rounded on him. "You still haven't told me what you get. For keeping me here." Her throat was closing, her mind was racing. "You told me you weren't in the game. That you weren't playing for anything. No carrot, right? No stick?"

"I didn't say I wasn't playing for anything," he said. "I said I wasn't playing for the inheritance."

Another riddle. "God, you are so completely like my father sometimes."

Sam lost his temper. "So is he in or is he—"

Alice raised a hand, cutting her brother off. This was her fight. One that was due with her father, but she had to have it here, now, with the man he'd selected as a second.

"So what do you get, Jack? When you're done seducing me?" *When you're done making me fall in love with you.* At least she didn't say that. How embarrassing.

"Hang on a minute. That wasn't part of it." He sounded furious. "That had nothing to do with it."

"Are you sure?"

Everything about him turned to stone. "Yes, Alice. I'm very fucking sure."

She wanted to believe him so much. It was hard to imagine that everything she'd felt in the days leading up to that moment had been hers alone. But if this was Franklin's plan all along, how could she be certain?

"Tell me, then."

He pushed a hand through his hair, frustrated. "A fairly substantial portion of Storm stock. Enough that I would never have to work again even if it didn't include the Class A stock, but if you remember, I was prepared to help you get off the island, so—"

Of course. "Class A stock," she repeated.

"What?"

"The deal was Class A stock."

"Partially?" His frustration was palpable. "The deal was that if I kept you here, through the week, through midnight, I would get Franklin's Class A stock. It's not part of the Storm family inheritance. Contractually, it has to go back into the pool or to someone who works at the company. And it's more valuable than—"

"I know what it is," she said, understanding dawning, chased by anger. And something else. Like triumph. She'd been right. "But Jack, you misunderstood."

His brow furrowed. "What does that mean?"

"I mean my father wasn't talking about the stock." She brandished the letter, in which Franklin had spelled out his plans. "He was talking about me. *I'm* Class A stock. That's what he used to call me. Class A. He played me." Jack was the other shoe, after all. "And he played you, too."

Franklin had known he was dying, known, too, that this was what he wanted—to tidy everything up. He wanted Jack in the family, controlling the show. And he knew that the only way to do it was to woo him in.

Jack and Alice were Franklin's endgame.

And she should have hated it. That this was Franklin's plan. That he'd won again. Endlessly controlling. Moving them all like pieces on the chessboard.

She turned to her siblings. "You said I was in control. Do you see it now? Do you see that he was messing with my life from the start, too? Not only for the week or for the summer. He's been messing with me for *years*. Since he kicked me out."

She was coming undone, tears streaming down her face in frustration and sadness and a particular kind of disappointment that came with finally, *finally* seeing your parents for who they were—human. "And I'll never get away from the last conversation I had with him, when he kicked me off the island. Because he's *dead*. And now, there are no more answers. There are only questions. A lifetime of unanswered ones." She looked at Jack. "Like how he convinced you that coming here was a good idea."

"He never convinced me that it was a good idea," Jack said, stepping toward her, stopping the moment she stepped back, toward her siblings, who were lined up behind her like an army, like they were all on her side for the first time in her life. He sliced a hand through the air. "I told him from the start that it was ridiculous. That he should tell you all the truth."

"Yeah, but you fucked me anyway, right?"

Everyone sucked in a breath.

"Alice," Emily whispered, as though she could stop her from making a mistake. Well. The joke was on Emily. Alice only ever made mistakes.

"It doesn't matter," Alice said, hating the way emotion finally, *finally* slid into Jack's gaze, like she'd actually hurt him with that. "I shouldn't blame you. You're part of it, too. Just another thing my father collected. You know what his truth was? He was so fucking *bored*. He was so bored with everything he'd built, he had to churn to build new stuff, to sell more, to be a bigger genius.

"He was so bored with the toys he amassed—the rocket ships and the hot-air balloons and the stupid cars—he had to crash one into the ground.

"He was too bored to care about how his kids might feel when he *died,* so he built us a game to play when it was over, forgetting that we wouldn't be bored. That we'd be *sad.*" She looked to her siblings, wide-eyed, nodding their agreement.

"He got everything he ever wanted and so he kept himself busy by collecting people," she said, finally, turning back to Jack. "And guess what . . . you're one of us. Like a bug under glass. He couldn't even set us free at the end. He had to leave us all here. Trapped. Manipulated into wanting exactly what he wanted for us."

Alice looked to Greta. "But you didn't want it."

Greta shook her head. "No, I didn't."

To Sam. "And you didn't get it."

"No."

To Emily. "And you *really* got screwed by all those secrets."

Another one of Emily's little laughs. "I sure did."

"Ask me."

Alice spun around to look at Jack, his face set like marble, so handsome it hurt to look at him. "What?"

"Go on, Alice. Ask me if I want the same thing he wanted for me."

She knew the answer. Knew that when he gave it to her, it was going to break her. Again. "No."

"I want it," he said, coming for her. "I want it, and you do, too. And the difference is, I don't care that your dad set it up. I'm grateful for it.

Because let him control it all if it means I get to do this whenever I want." He reached for her, and she didn't move, her traitorous body loving the way his hand slid into her hair, gripping, claiming her, tilting her up to him as he took another step forward, into her space, so close she could feel the heat of his frustration.

"I spent my whole life wanting this. Aching for exactly this—for this feeling. For the knowledge that I had someone on my side, and now you're here and you're fucking *great*. I want you. Not for the company or the stock or the money. Not out of some misplaced loyalty toward your dad. I want it for me, because I'm a selfish bastard, and I've wanted you since the moment I sat next to you on that train."

"Oh," Emily whispered. "He's good."

"I thought he was an asshole," Sam said.

"Both," Greta added.

Alice wasn't paying attention. She was too focused on him when he asked, "Do you want it, too?"

"Yes," she whispered.

"So what's the problem?"

"The problem is . . ." she said. "He wanted us to want it."

"Not to put too fine a point on it, Alice, but he's dead, so who the fuck cares?"

"Yes!" Claudia couldn't control her little outburst, and Emily shushed her.

"I want it, though," she said. "I want you. I want this. I want us." It was a wild thing to think, that word that felt weighted and important and terrifying because Alice hadn't ever really thought of herself as part of an *us*.

He reached for her. "I want us, too."

"Not because it's your job?" The question came out small and anxious, and she hated the way it exposed her.

Jack hated it for a different reason. He exhaled his disapproval. "No. Not because it's my job. Because you're going to be my life."

"Whoa," Claudia said.

"Oh, that's *game*," Emily added.

"It's not that impressive," Sam grumbled.

"It's impressive," Greta reported.

"Everyone?" Alice said, not looking away from Jack. "Please go away."

She didn't have to say anything more; the quartet left, taking their lanterns and candles with them, Emily stage-whispering and Claudia making supportive noises of agreement, and Sam grumbling, and Greta making the kind of noises older sisters made when they were trying to help out.

They weren't even gone when he reached for her, one hand curving around the back of her neck, pulling her close for the kiss she was aching for.

He kissed her like she was the only thing that mattered—in the room, on the island, in the world. And in that moment, in his arms, she believed it.

They didn't talk as he collected her painting and they left the room, dark and full of Franklin's tree and the island's rain, and climbed the stairs, up, up to the tower, where he pulled back the blankets and tucked her into bed with long kisses and no words.

She watched him as he crossed to the hearth, crouching to check the flue before he slowly and methodically built a fire there, coaxing it into flame before he returned to the bed, climbing in behind her, to run his hands over her body and whisper all the things he wanted to do to her, until she begged him to stop talking.

And then he used his mouth for other things.

Afterward, they lay there for a long time, staring at the dancing orange flames, listening to the storm outside, the thunder and lightning past, like the storm downstairs, leaving nothing but quiet rain, tapping against the glass, a lingering reminder of what had been. Everything would be chaos again in the morning—secrets didn't go back to being secrets by the light of day, but in that moment, he was there, like he promised.

After a long time, she said, "You built me a fire."

His grip on her tightened, pulling her close, as though if he held her tight enough, he could keep the storm at bay. The Storms at bay.

They lay like that for minutes, hours . . . until she lost track. Until she began to think it was true, that he might be able to do just that. And as she fell asleep in his arms, he whispered, "Alice, someday you're going to realize that unlike everyone else in your life, I keep my promises."

CHAPTER

22

ALICE WOKE TO BRIGHT morning sun.

Reaching for Jack on the other side of the bed, she wondered how long they could hide inside the tower before they had to face the wreckage (literal and figurative) of the night before. It was a tempting idea, taken off the table immediately when she discovered the crisp sheets empty and cool to the touch.

He'd left before she woke, no doubt at the crack of dawn, sneaking out of the house before anyone could discover them. He remained a decent guy—even in the wake of the revelations in Franklin's office, when he'd confessed to being a little bit of a scoundrel.

Just enough to make things interesting, if she was being honest.

Just enough to tell her that he wanted her, money be damned, family be damned, world be damned. Just enough to take her to bed and show her how much.

She stretched luxuriously, sitting up and running her fingers through her hair, shivering with pleasure at the memory, wishing he was there to show her again.

Before she could seek him out and convince him to do just that,

Alice's gaze fell to the windows of the tower—the cloudless sky, impossibly bright and cerulean, belying the massive storm that had uprooted trees, secrets, the family, and the island itself.

And Alice.

Maybe for the best.

She got up, digging in her suitcase for black yoga pants, a ribbed tank, and running shoes, pulling her hair up into a ponytail before catching a look at herself in the mirror and changing her mind, letting it fall loose around her shoulders—the only blessing of a week in air thick with the sea was a headful of beachy waves that would have cost hundreds at a salon in the city.

Downstairs, the power was back on, and she found a pot of coffee already made (someone was a hero), and she poured cream and sugar liberally (she deserved nice things) as she stared out the kitchen window at the place where her father's oak once stood and now lay flat across the lawn. It was hard to believe it had fallen, that tree that had seen so much more of this island and its secrets than any of them ever would.

A helicopter coming up the Bay pulled her from her thoughts, the whirr and growl of it louder and louder until it flew low past the house, whipping up the rain that hadn't burned off the grass yet—a great black harbinger of . . . something.

Whether it was good or bad, she couldn't say, but Alice could count as well as the next girl, and knew that anyone who arrived on the island today was likely to be part of Franklin's game. It had been a week since her father died and the game began, and Alice was still there, on the island, as requested. The rest of the family had completed their tasks, and the inheritance was activated, if the original rules were to be believed.

Not that Alice would believe anything about her father's game until she witnessed it come to pass. Stepping out onto the empty back porch, she made her way to the white seashell path that wound toward the helipad, curiosity getting the best of her. How would it all end?

Who would win?

Franklin, probably.

The island, definitely.

The door to the helicopter opened and Alice stopped at a distance, waiting. It was a comfortable moment for her—she'd done it a hundred times before. Her father made that hour-long trip from the roof of the Storm building on Park Avenue South, or the roof of the Storm apartment building on Park Avenue (proper) nightly in the summer. An hour door-to-door, the helicopter was a luxury he'd adopted the moment he could.

When they were little, Alice and Emily would watch from her bedroom window (a control tower fit for an air traffic princess) for the sleek black Leonardo to come up the Bay, then run to beat Franklin to the helipad. They'd wait where Alice stood now, all grown up, for Franklin to step out from under the still-spinning blades, and the muscle memory of all those nights of waiting brought her a wild thought. *What if he was inside?*

It would be a helluva game. And after she was through being furious with him, she'd be over the moon that he was back to give them another chance. A do-over.

But there were no do-overs, and Franklin wasn't in the helicopter. That said, this particular helicopter manifest did not disappoint.

She lifted her coffee cup in salute. "Hi, Tony."

"Alice." He raised a hand, but didn't move from his place beneath the slowing blades, as though he thought she might tell him he wasn't welcome.

Men were so silly. "A lot happened yesterday; we missed you."

"Yeah," he said, not looking away from her, the steadiest man she could imagine. Perfect for her sister. "I couldn't get back."

Excitement and happiness grew in her chest. "Want to come in and—"

The kitchen screen door banged open in the distance, slamming hard against the gray cedar shingles (they were getting a workout this week), and they both turned to look. Alice couldn't help the smile that broke at the view—Greta looking decidedly un-Greta-like, in running shorts and a *Storm Inside*™ tee, tearing across the grass toward them.

Not really toward Alice, though.

Toward Tony.

Big, silent, immovable Tony, who made a sound in his chest that

Alice identified immediately as relief. She stepped out of the way as Greta blew past her, throwing herself into Tony's arms. His enormous hands caught her, lifted her, held her like he'd been away forever—like he'd been to war.

And then they kissed like they'd *both* been to war.

Maybe they had been. Seventeen years of it.

"I'm sorry," Greta said in a panicked whisper. "I'm so sorry. I was afraid and I should never have—"

He cut her off with another kiss, and Alice turned away, not wanting to play awkward witness to whatever this was (she knew what it was but there was no reason to commit it to memory).

As she left, she heard Tony growl, "I should never have left without you. I should never have left you afraid."

Grinning wildly, Alice headed back toward the house with a singular goal. Finding Jack. She didn't have to go far, as he was looking for her, too. He came down the back steps of the house, dressed in a light blue linen button-down and cream-colored linen trousers. His aviators were on and she wasn't sure he saw her right away, until a wildly handsome smile whispered across his lips and the shiver was back again.

As they neared, she said, "You know I used to hate those sunglasses."

He reached up and whipped them off, frowning at them. "Why?"

"I hated how handsome you were in them. Very distracting when I was trying to dislike you."

One dark brow rose in acknowledgment. "In that case." He slid the glasses back on.

She made a show of considering him. "Exactly my point. You look like a hot bodyguard."

"I'll take it." He snaked an arm around her waist and pulled her to him for a kiss. "You weren't there when I went back to find you."

"You weren't there when I woke up."

"I had some things to do."

She didn't want to think about the game. Instead, she tilted her head toward the helipad, far enough away that Greta and Tony had an approximation of privacy, but close enough for Jack to clock what was going on. "Look who's back. I think those crazy kids are going to work it out, finally."

"Considering Tony is an incredibly rich man this morning, I think that's probably true."

"He is?" The words came out sharper and more inquisitive than she'd intended. Tony's finances weren't any of her business.

Jack nodded. "Your father left him one percent of his holding in the company."

Her brows rose, the only indication of her surprise, partly because she wasn't that surprised anymore, now that it was so obvious that Franklin was tidying things up before his death. Honoring Tony's years of service to Franklin and the company and the family was exactly the kind of thing her father would have thought to do—no game required.

It was the right thing to do; Tony had paid his dues in every possible way, giving up everything for Franklin . . . and for Greta. And now, he was a significant shareholder in one of the biggest companies in the world. Not that it would matter to Greta.

Alice looked to where Greta and Tony were deep in conversation. "After last night, Greta doesn't care a bit about the money. She'd live in a yurt with him if she had to."

"A yurt, huh?"

"Emily made me sleep in one once. We were supposed to set intentions during some full moon. Leo, maybe?" He nodded, like it mattered (what a man). "Anyway it rained all night and the yurt did not do a great job of keeping us dry or warm or happy." She paused. "Well, Emily was pretty happy, but that's because I'm beginning to think she's an alien of some sort."

"Next time, I'll come and keep you dry, warm, and happy."

She had no doubt of that. "Do you have intentions to set during the Leo moon?"

"Can my intention be to make love to you under the Leo moon?"

With a laugh she replied, "It's good to set the bar low."

"I don't know," he said, pulling her close. "In my experience, making love to you is astronomically good." She giggled (truly, a new day), and he pressed a kiss to the side of her neck, and she sighed her pleasure as he added, "Anyway. Tony and Greta won't have to sleep in a yurt. They get to have it all."

Hand in hand, they made their way in silence along the east side of the house, toward the oak, downed across the grass, and Alice lingered on that thought—the terrifying promise of having it all.

"You know, that was my dad's lifework," she said to Jack. "Having it all."

He looked down at her. "I see that. He was consumed with ambition. From the moment he set foot in your grandparents' garage."

"One thousand, one hundred and seven dollars and a dream," she said, parroting the words Franklin had said in every interview he'd ever given. "I've never met anyone with such a desire to win, and I spent my childhood around tech barons. He hated losing—cards, wagers, arguments."

"Negotiations."

"God, I bet he was brutal," she said. "And I don't deny that what he did with that ambition—he changed the world." It was a wild thought. "I don't think I've ever said that before. I don't think I've ever even really considered what it means to change the world. I mean, I grew up in a household—in a world—that was shaped by Franklin Storm. And I knew he'd done all that, but . . ."

She trailed off, and he was patient with her, waiting for her to find the rest of her words.

They had reached the tree at that point, and she set her hand to the enormous trunk, on its side, reaching nearly to her chest. Tracing over the rough bark, she said, "But it was hard to care about any of it when it felt like he'd done so little for us." He settled next to her, leaning back against the trunk, watching. Listening.

Making it easy for her to go on. "I'm angry with him," she confessed. "I miss him, of course, but I'm really, really angry with him. All that money. All that power. And he used it to buy friends and influence and thirty-foot yawls and helicopters and private islands . . . but he couldn't find his way to having enough grace to tell Greta she should be with the man she loved. Or enough understanding to see he'd been too hard on Sam. Or enough strength to tell us the truth about his future. Or enough courage to call me and tell me to come home."

A tear rolled down Alice's cheek, and he reached for her, pulling her between his thighs and whispering her name as he wiped her tear away. "Alice. Love."

She shook her head. "And now he's gone. And I can't come home."

"Maybe you can, though," he said. "Maybe that was the point of all this. Maybe you can find home again."

Home.

It felt like something she hadn't had in years. Not with her family, not with Griffin, not there, on the island. In the years since she'd fallen out of Franklin's favor, she'd lost the thread of home and what it was. Or maybe she'd never really had the thread to begin with. But now, after a week on the island, strangely, after the events of the night before, she could imagine it.

It was hazy and sweet, like the deep of summer, but she could imagine it. They made their way around the tree, past the broken windows, heading for the great lawn, rolling out lush and green to the sparkling sea.

They stood on the rise and took in the view—sky and sea and land, no evidence of what had come the day before. Of what it had done. The storm was past.

In nature, at least.

In the distance, a sleek, white boat approached with two people inside—one at the helm, the other looking severely out of place in a gray suit.

"I guess corporate has returned to a post–Labor Day wardrobe." She looked to Jack's linen trousers. "You're out of uniform, Mr. Dean."

"Maybe I don't want to be corporate anymore."

She caught her breath. "Really?"

"It's a thing I've been thinking about." He looked at her, and she would have done anything to see his eyes through his mirrored sunglasses.

Returning her attention to the boat, ever closer, she said, "So this is it. The last part of the game."

He nodded. "This is it."

"Do you know what happens now?"

"I don't." He took his sunglasses off, turning to face her, eyes serious. Honest. He reached for her hand. Squeezed it. "Wave to Larry."

She did as she was told, waving as Larry Manford, Storm Inc. board member and one of her father's oldest friends, stepped off the boat, ominous leather briefcase in hand. Tall, gray-haired, and absolutely handsome enough in his youth to have earned the descriptor *distinguished* now, Larry was the kind of person who made everyone feel at ease. Franklin had always deployed him in particularly difficult negotiations, a fact not lost on Alice or Jack.

"I told you there was another shoe," she said.

"I thought Class A stock was the other shoe."

She slid him a look. "That was a good shoe—"

"A great shoe," he corrected.

She flashed a little smile. "This is the other shoe. The not-great one."

"Maybe not."

She cut him a look as Larry began the climb up the slate steps from the docks. "Pretty Pollyanna for a fixer, Jack."

"I'm not a fixer anymore," Jack said.

"What?" She swung to face him, feeling panicked, like she wasn't getting enough oxygen. Like she was getting too much.

"I don't work at Storm anymore."

"Since when?"

He looked at his watch. "A little before midnight."

Before midnight. He hadn't finished the week. "You gave up the money, Jack . . . the stock was worth—"

"It doesn't matter," he said, watching Larry make his way up the slate steps. "That's not the stock I'm aiming for."

Her heart began to pound as he turned to face her, taking his sunglasses off to meet her eyes. "I don't ever want you to think I'm staying because of the money. I never want you to think I'm even remotely like that other guy."

He was perfect. He'd done the only thing he could do to prove he was in it for her. He'd given it all up. He didn't get the money for completing his task, and as he no longer worked for Storm, he couldn't claim the company's Class A stock.

But she would make very certain he always had her. "I don't think that. I would never think that."

"Good."

He was nothing like Griffin. He wasn't even in the same league as Griffin. That had been clear from the moment he'd sat down on the train. She looked out at the water, thinking of all the times she'd been in this exact place, wondering what came next.

Right now, though, she didn't wonder that. She knew.

Jack came next.

They came next.

She turned to face him, loving the way his arms came around her when she said, softly, "I used to think you were just like my dad."

"Me, too," he said.

"You're not," she said, thinking of her father's letter. "You're better."

"I don't know about that," he said, his voice going deep in his chest. In her ear. "I still want it all."

"What do you want?" she whispered.

He didn't look away. "A boat. The ocean. Someone to sail with me."

It was perfect. She pressed closer to him, suddenly nervous. Terrified that now he'd spoken it, he'd take it away. "Is that it?"

"Mmm," he said, the sound a low rumble in his throat as he lifted a hand, stroking his thumb over her cheek, pressing his forehead to hers. "Maybe she introduces me to her friends. Maybe she lets me watch her paint. Maybe she lets me love her."

"No maybe about it." Alice lifted herself up on her toes, breathless with the words. *Yes. Love me.* "It's a promise." She met his kiss, loving the way he tipped her back, and kissed her like they were by themselves, far from anyone who might take offense.

"Gross."

She broke the kiss with a smile as Jack leaned in to kiss her temple. "Good morning, Sam." Alice took in her brother's dirty T-shirt, jeans, and heavy rain boots that he had to have borrowed from somewhere. "Sam . . . have you been . . . working? Like, with your hands?"

"I figured someone should know what goes on here now that Dad is gone," he said. "I thought maybe I'd bring the kids back over fall break. Give them a chance to rake leaves or something."

"I would very much like to see that. Maybe Sila should come. She could use it."

He barked a little laugh. "Yeah. I don't think so. I think we'll try co-parenting for a bit."

The idea of co-anythinging with either Sam or Sila was terrifying, truly, but Alice wasn't interested in judging that day.

Instead, she said, "Well, I'm proud of you."

"You know"—he met her eyes—"I don't know that anyone in this family has ever said that to me."

She tilted her head. "Maybe we should start."

"Yeah, I don't know. It's kind of unsettling," he replied before turning to Larry, who'd reached the top of the steps. "Hey, Larry, couldn't get enough of us at the funeral?"

Larry didn't blink, but it wasn't a very good joke. "Hi, kids. Where are your sisters?"

Before any of them could answer, the roar of helicopter engines sounded. Everyone turned to look as the Leonardo Tony had flown in not thirty minutes earlier passed, loud and low enough to reveal Greta in the copilot seat, headset on, waving out the window like she was on the greatest vacation she'd ever taken, looking into the mouth of a volcano from a safe, luxurious distance.

She probably was, honestly. But good for her for getting out. If anyone deserved it, it was Greta.

Alice waved back, full of joy for her sister, who'd just gotten her happily-ever-after. Sam said what they were all thinking. "She actually did it. She actually left."

It was incredible. Liberation at its finest.

"Was that Greta?" came a shout from the distance. Emily and Claudia, crossing the lawn from the southern tip of the island. Emily with an enormous smile on her face. "Holy shit!" she shouted. "Did she just leave?"

"With Tony!" Alice shouted back.

"Holy shit!" Emily repeated, before she realized that Larry was there. "Sorry, Larry. That's just very cool!"

Larry raised a hand in quiet acknowledgment that it was, in fact, very cool.

"Are we late?" Emily asked. "We were meditating."

"You're not late," Larry said, leaning in to give her a kiss on the cheek. "Hi, Claudia."

"We're just waiting for Larry to tell us what we've won," Sam said.

Understanding dawned on the youngest Storm's face. "So, this is it? This is the inheritance meeting? Do we need Mom?"

They looked to the house, big and gothic, on the hill, and Alice imagined Elisabeth was there, in one of the upper windows, watching. Waiting for whatever was to come, suffering from no small amount of regret after the events of the night before.

"Not for this," Larry replied, clearing his throat. "I'll speak to her separately."

"Should you go inside?" Claudia asked, indicating the house.

"No," Alice said, firmly, surprising everyone. "I think we should do it out here. In the sun. It will be—I don't know—cleansing."

"Careful," Sam said. "You're starting to sound like Emily."

Alice ignored him. "*Also,* Larry looks like he might have a heart attack if we make him wait any longer to tell us the bad news."

A beat, and then Sam said, full of understanding, "Oh, shit."

Another throat clearing. "Kids—"

"Larry," Alice interrupted with a smile. "We've all been around our dad long enough that we know he had no intention of making this easy for anyone. So let us make your part a little easier."

"Exactly," Sam said. "Cut to the chase. What do we get?"

It wasn't quite the phrasing Alice would have used, but it got the job done.

"Well, kids. It's not quite so simple."

Silence met the reply, everything slowing down as they took in what Larry had said. And then, as they processed the strange, unexpected words, everyone spoke.

"There *is* money, isn't there?" Sam said.

"Sam. Chill." Emily asked, "Did something go wrong? Did we lose the game?"

"I'll tell you what went wrong. Greta is what went wrong," Sam said, frustration returning him to his zero state—blowhard. "She got Tony, and we all got screwed."

"Is that true?" Alice looked to Larry, then to Jack. "I thought the only rule for the inheritance was that if we completed our tasks, we inherited. Everyone did what he asked. Sam did his chores, our mother spoke her truths—"

"Did she ever," Emily interjected.

Alice waved a hand toward the helicopter, a tiny speck in the distance. "Greta broke it off with Tony—she only left with him this morning. A loophole, right?" She looked to Jack.

Jack nodded, returning to his role. "That was how I understood it, as well, Larry."

"Even *Alice* stayed," Emily said, like it was the biggest shock of all.

"It would be great if everyone stopped talking about me as if I'm the villain of the play," she said.

"Sorry," Emily said.

"Who cares?" Sam interrupted. "Are you saying there is no inheritance? Are you saying that asshole was just fucking with us this week?"

"There is an *inheritance*," Larry said. He opened his briefcase and extracted a thick document, which he passed to Emily.

Sam snatched it out of her hands and opened it as her father's friend pressed on. "The house and the island remain in trust for Elisabeth now, and in perpetuity for the family. Storm Island will be the home for Storms for generations to come."

That was good. The island mattered.

Alice stuttered over the thought and how settled she felt knowing this place was theirs, forever.

"As for funds, your father wished—"

"You are fucking kidding me." Sam thrust the document toward Emily and turned on his heel, walking a distance, shoving his hands in his hair.

"For you each to receive a predetermined amount."

"Oh my god." Emily looked up and met Alice's eyes. Passed her the papers. "See for yourself."

Alice read, her shock and surprise quickly overtaken with a level of self-satisfaction she would not soon forget. She turned to Jack with a triumphant smile. "I told you. Another shoe."

Franklin had left them each one thousand, one hundred, and seven dollars.

CHAPTER

23

"SNEAKING AWAY?"

Alice looked up as Sam lowered himself beside her on the end of the island's dock, where her feet dangled over the water below. She shook her head. "No. This time I was going to say goodbye."

"I think the last time, it was us who didn't say goodbye." They were quiet for a while, watching the boats on the blue water, bright and clean and beautiful, like postcards of Rhode Island. A cormorant flew low over the water. Sam leaned forward to meet her eyes. "I'm sorry about that."

"You are?"

Sam scowled at her surprise. "You don't have to be so shocked."

"I get it. I was a terrifying proposition." She tilted her head toward the house. "A cautionary tale. What happened if you crossed them."

"Yeah, but—" He returned his attention to the water. "We could have had a relationship without them. I could've come to Brooklyn. That's a lot of time we lost. And I . . ." He looked for the rest of the words. "I don't want to lose any more of it."

"Are you offering to come to Brooklyn?"

"Oof. You drive a hard bargain. What if I take you to dinner or something in Manhattan? Like, near the subway to Brooklyn."

She lay back on the dock and stared up at the blue sky. "I'll take you up on that now that you've got a thousand dollars burning a hole in your pocket."

He shook his head. "Seven hundred, thirty-eight."

Shielding her eyes from the sun, she looked back at him. "What's that?"

"That's how much is left, after I write Sila her check."

"Oh my god. One-third." She laughed. "I'm sorry, it's not funny. But it . . . kind of is?"

"You won't be laughing when I make you pay for dinner."

Spreading her arms wide in a magnanimous gesture, she said, "I will pay for dinner."

"Thank you. I accept."

"Unfortunately, you have to come to Brooklyn."

He groaned and Emily popped into Alice's field of vision, bright smile on her face. "When are we coming to Brooklyn?"

What a strange conversation. It had only been a week, and these people, who Alice had always thought were lost to history, had re-appeared and they were . . . here. Talking about dinners. Visits. Like family. Weird and messy, but family, nonetheless.

"You can come whenever you like," she said. "Everyone is wel-come."

"Hang on, Emily should buy dinner," Sam said, turning to face them as Emily dropped into lotus position near Alice's head.

"How'd I get stuck with the bill?" she asked.

"Well, you lost one father last week," Sam pointed out. "Very sad, et cetera, et cetera." Emily looked to Alice as Sam pressed on, "But you also *found* a father recently, one who just happens to *also* be a billion-aire. And one with no children, so if you think about it . . ."

Emily groaned. "Don't say *inheritance*."

Alice laughed. "I think he might be asking for a loan."

"Yeah, no," Emily said. "I barely know the man. And unfortunately for all of you, I'm Storm, through and through. Which is why I say this with all love, Samuel . . . you're going to need to get a job. A real one."

"I don't love that."

"No kidding," Alice said. She returned to staring at the sky. "Speaking of people who no longer have jobs . . . how do we think Greta and Tony are doing?"

"I think they are doing fucking great," Emily said. "Finally."

"I bet they are," Sam said, all innuendo, and the sisters groaned.

"You're going to have to stop acting like a teenager if you want to parent two of them, Sam. Has that occurred?"

"Vaguely," he replied as Alice sat up, and looked to her watch. "Three forty-five."

"Longing for the golden days of Sam not being able to speak during odd-numbered hours?" Emily joked.

"I will never not long for them," she replied. "Unfortunately, though, I *do* have a job. And I have to work tomorrow."

She said it like it was normal. Like they hadn't just spent the week in chaos and grief and emotion, like they hadn't just begun the tumultuous work of walking a new path without their father. Of mending whatever this was. And all three of them seemed to notice it.

"Did you already say bye to Mom?" Emily asked.

"I did." Elisabeth hadn't lingered on the farewell. "I'll call her tomorrow. After the first day of school." Alice turned a worried gaze on Emily. "What about you?"

A little shrug. "Claudia and I will stay for dinner and then . . ." She pointed across the Bay. "We're right there."

"You know you don't have to—"

"I know." Emily nodded. "But I live in hope that she'll—"

Alice reached for her. "That's why we love you." She hugged her sister and turned to her brother. "And you?"

He looked at his own watch. "I figured I'd use the helicopter one last time, before they start sending me a bill. It will be here in a few." He pointed in the direction of the helipad. "Do you want a ride?"

"No." She shook her head, pointing in the opposite direction, to the skiff that had been delivered from across the Bay earlier in the day. "We're taking the train."

He lifted his chin toward the boathouse. "He's waiting for you."

She followed Sam's gaze to find Jack in the distance, leaning against the weathered shingles with his bags at his feet, sleeves rolled up to show that sextant tattoo she now knew intimately.

Another impossible change the week had brought.

Jack noticed her watching and came off the wall, reaching down to collect his bags before he started toward them, slowly, as though he knew they needed more time.

They did. Time like this, without specters or secrets. Without the gothic manor house doing what gothic manor houses did. Dredging up the past. Haunting them.

Sam shoved his hands into his pockets, looking suddenly, strangely like a dad. "Text when you get home. So we know you got there safely."

She smiled at the words, the way he tried them on. "Let me know how it goes with the kids?"

"Yeah." He didn't sound sure it would go well. And truthfully, he'd deserve it. Of all of them, Sam had the most work ahead.

Emily lifted her phone. "We'll start a group thread. When we're off the island."

It felt important not to wait. To do it while they were there, on the island, the place that had brought them all together. That had raised them. That had seen them broken and, in the last week, had blown away the pieces. Left them with space to rebuild. If they wanted it.

Alice pulled her phone out of her pocket, smooth black obsidian and sapphire glass, that gleaming silver *S* on the back. The hurricane. She ran her thumb over it, tracing the letter, letting herself think about her father for a moment. How he had changed the world, big and small. How he had changed them. Before. And After.

She opened a new text.

"Emily," she said, adding the names to the address box. "Sam. Greta."
Opening the settings, she renamed the group.

Storms Inside.

And then, in the text box, she wrote the first thing that came. A fresh
start.

This is your sister.

ACKNOWLEDGMENTS

First things first: Thank you, Rhode Island, for raising me on salt air and clam cakes and chowder and beaches and stone walls and wild thyme and summer thunderstorms and those mysterious islands in the middle of Narragansett Bay that came with hundreds of years of history and lore. I'm so happy to have a chance to finally love you in print.

I owe much gratitude to the staff at the Brownell Library in Little Compton, Rhode Island, for making time for me and my questions about the history of the islands in the Bay. I encourage anyone interested in the "private island in Narragansett Bay" experience to check out the Rose Island lighthouse, which allows overnight visits. If you are, like me, just generally interested in private islands and the families that live on them, I cannot recommend Emily Sundberg's short film, *The End: A Gardiner's Island Story,* enough. Additional thanks are due to Brian Wallin, for his comprehensive explanation of the Newport and Wickford Railroad and Steamboat Company; to Terry Pepper, for his in-depth understanding of ancient island fog bells; and to Sharon Klein, for her patient explanation of blind trusts, and for not even blinking when I explained Franklin's unhinged game.

These Summer Storms is the product of many wonderful people encouraging me to write the story that I'd been holding at bay for years. I am endlessly indebted to Holly Root, a brilliant force, who did not hesitate when I told her I wanted to write a book about a dysfunctional family in an inheritance game and instead casually asked about it every time we spoke from that moment on. Through Holly, I've been incredibly lucky to work with Alyssa Maltese, Heather Baror-Shapiro, and Alice Lawson, a dream team for the ages.

Thank you seems too small a thing to say to my editor, Shauna Summers, whom I'd hoped to work with for so long. I'm so grateful for your ideas, your careful reads, your excitement, and for giving my Storms a home at Ballantine Books, where they've had such an incredibly warm welcome. Endless gratitude to the team there, including Kara Welsh, Jennifer Hershey, Kara Cesare, Kimberly Hovey, Jennifer Garza, Melissa Folds, Taylor Noel, Megan Whelan, Brianna Kusilek, Jennifer Rodriguez, Belina Huey, Kelly Chian, and Briony Everroad. A special thank you goes to Mae Martinez for all the ways she has made this book better.

I am so lucky to have a group of friends who are all infinitely smarter than me. I will never be able to thank Louisa Edwards enough for how she makes me better as a writer and as a person. Thank you, also, to Kate Clayborn, Jen Prokop, Erin Leafe, Sophie Jordan, Adriana Herrera, Diana Awad, Megan Frampton, and Nora Zelevansky, all of whom suffered endless phone conversations, text messages, and lunches as this book came to life. And of course, Kristin Dwyer, the absolute greatest cheerleader I could ask for—what would I do without your guidance and friendship?

It will not surprise you to know that when you write a book about a dysfunctional family, you spend a lot of time telling your actual family that the book is not about them. My sister and brother knew about the Storms from the very start and were passionate cheerleaders the whole way. My only regret is that my brother didn't get to see the finished product—he would have happily told the world Sam was based on him. We miss you terribly, Mark. Thanks, always, to my Mom for never telling me to turn out the light when I was reading after bedtime.

Love to V, for all the ways you believe in me and in this book—may you never have a family quite like this one; to Kahlo, for joining me on all my thinking walks; and to Eric, forever my person.

Finally, to longtime MacLean readers who joined me on this journey: thank you for staying and for believing. You'll never know how grateful I am to have you with me, still.

ABOUT THE AUTHOR

SARAH MACLEAN is the author of sixteen *New York Times* bestsellers that have been translated into more than twenty-five languages. She is the co-host of the weekly romance novel podcast, *Fated Mates,* and a leading voice in the romance genre. A product of Rhode Island summers and New England storms, Sarah now lives with her family in New York City.

ABOUT THE TYPE

This book was set in Garamond, a typeface originally designed by the Parisian type cutter Claude Garamond (c. 1500–61). This version of Garamond was modeled on a 1592 specimen sheet from the Egenolff-Berner foundry, which was produced from types assumed to have been brought to Frankfurt by the punch cutter Jacques Sabon (c. 1520–80).

Claude Garamond's distinguished romans and italics first appeared in *Opera Ciceronis* in 1543–44. The Garamond types are clear, open, and elegant.